Dmitri

Esterhaats

Other Works by Russell Hardin

Fiction

What We Go By

Perhaps It Was Never the Same

Non-fiction

Indeterminacy and Society

Trust and Trustworthiness

Liberalism, Constitutionalism and Democracy

One for All: The Logic of Group Conflict

Morality Within the Limits of Reason

Collective Action

Dmitri Esterhaats

A Novel By

Russell Hardin

San Antonio, Texas
2007

Dmitri Esterhaats © 2007 by Russell Hardin

Cover painting, "Stone North" © 1997 by Andrea Belag.
Courtesy of Mike Weiss Gallery, New York.

First Edition

ISBN-10: 0-916727-27-0
ISBN-13: 978-0-916727-27-7

Wings Press
627 E. Guenther
San Antonio, Texas 78210
Phone/fax: (210) 271-7805

On-line catalogue and ordering:
www.wingspress.com
All Wings Press titles are distributed to the trade by
Independent Publishers Group
www.ipgbook.com

Library of Congress Cataloging-in-Publication Data:

Hardin, Russell, 1940-
  Dmitri Esterhaats : a novel / Russell Hardin. -- 1st ed.
    p. cm.
  ISBN-13: 978-0-916727-27-7 (alk. paper)
  ISBN-10: 0-916727-27-0 (alk. paper)
  1. Pianists--Fiction. 2. Musicians--Fiction. 3. New York (N.Y.)--
Fiction. I. Title.

PS3558.A62322D65 2007
813'.6--dc22

2006100414

Contents

1	Horace Gmund	3
2	Sofia Milano	25
3	Colonel Weiss	53
4	Anton Staebli	77
5	Linda Ney	97
6	Jelly Ujfalussy	157
7	Marina Haimovich Esterhaats	181
8	Clara Esterhaats	201
9	Odyssey Deneuve	231
10	Linda Ney	253
11	Dmitri Esterhaats	291

Dmitri Esterhaats

Horace Gmund

Dmitri Esterhaats inherited a tall physique and long spatulate fingers from his father's Hungarian father, wide shoulders from his father's Russian mother, and a moody face and high forehead from his own mother, a Jew of Kiev. As an artifact of the combination, he was also given a capacity for wistfulness and loneliness. Among his earliest memories were women saying to his mother or his aunt how beautiful he was and reaching out to stroke him as though he were a pet. These women Dmitri remembered as always smiling at him.

As a child in Kiev Dmitri spent his days with his aunt while his mother and father either worked or attended meetings. His aunt was a pianist in a culture in which she had few options. Because she'd married a man who opposed her attendance at political meetings, piano was her one purpose and escape. While she kept Dmitri, she played, and Dmitri grew from lying in a basket on the bench beside her to sitting on the bench. By age three he was keeping time by tapping with his right index finger on the piano bench. Once, to tease him, his beautiful aunt changed the rhythm. Dmitri looked confused for a moment before he went on tapping in the new time. She turned to smile at him and he laughed.

"There is no doubt," she said, "*you* are the greatest laugher."

By age five Dmitri was playing socialist and Hebrew songs with a single finger. By six he wanted to do nothing but play piano, which had come to mean Mozart. But at seven, his parents took him from Kiev, from the beautiful aunt and her piano, from his days of laughter and smiling women. They ended in Amsterdam among a small community of Russians whose socialism had caused them to leave Russia either before the war or after. They would go back eventually, they promised, and therefore he and his brother Pavel went to Russian school.

In Amsterdam, Dmitri was able to play the piano only at odd moments during the week when there was no one in the lobby of their apartment house. His best chances for playing would have been during the hours he was required to spend in the Russian school. He was rescued for the piano at age nine when his parents were advised to remove him from the school and send him to private tutors. He'd embarrassed his teacher by correcting her quotation of a line from Tolstoy. She reprimanded him for his impudence, and, to prove his point, he responded by quoting the lines between which her quote was sandwiched. When she still was not convinced, he backed up several more lines and began quoting from there, quoting a full page verbatim before she brought him to a halt.

Dmitri's mother asked him to explain what happened.

"She didn't believe me."

"Didn't believe what?"

"That I knew what Tolstoy said, he said that Pakhom was too greedy and ran . . ."

"I'm sure she believed you, Mitya, she's been teaching that story for many years, she must know it very well."

"She said it wrong."

"Yes, but she knew enough to know you had it right."

"Then why did she scold me?"

"You embarrassed her, you called her authority into question. It's hard to keep enough control to teach a room full of nine-year-old boys if one of them questions her authority."

"She had no authority. She got it wrong."

His mother smiled and ran her fingers through his hair. "Such beautiful hair, Mitya, short enough that you don't have to braid it. I think I'll cut mine so I won't have to braid it."

"No, that would be wrong, Mama. If you won't cut it, I'll braid it for you."

She started to question his ability and his resolve, but she thought better of it. She loosened her hair and let it fall behind her. "You have to comb it out first. It won't be easy."

As he braided it into a long tail that she would curl onto her head, she said, "Maybe we can find a piano tutor, Mitya." He'd been talking almost continually with her, but now he turned silent. After a while she added, "But we'll have to get math and other tutors too, Mitya."

"Now what, Mama?"

"What?"

He showed her the end of her braid, which he had to hold to keep it from raveling.

"You have to tie it with this."

He took the band and fidgeted for a minute. "I only have two hands, Mama."

She laughed, his grip loosened, her braid began to ravel.

There was a surfeit of well-educated Russians willing to tutor emigre children at desperation wages. Dmitri's tutor was Ulyanov, a violinist, who spent half his time with Dmitri tutoring music and playing duets with him. Ulyanov taught Dmitri to sight read so that they could play from scores he was able to borrow for an afternoon at a time from other emigre musicians. Dmitri's technique and his span were inadequate to many of the pieces Ulyanov found, but his powers of memory were nearing their peak – after a couple of times through a piece, Dmitri would no longer bother to turn the pages of his score.

"You should spend more time practicing," Ulyanov said. "You are a pianist. You have perfect pitch, Mitya. Your hands are good, your memory is good. If your family were good and the times were good, soon you would be performing. If you had to be born, why couldn't you be born into a good family?"

"It wasn't possible in Kiev."

"Maybe it's for the better – if you'd been born into a wealthy family, you might become a lazy playboy like Rubinstein." Dmitri had to ask who was Rubinstein.

Ulyanov promised to make Dmitri a good pianist. But again Dmitri's parents moved, this time to New York, to Brooklyn. In its Dutch transliteration from the Cyrillic alphabet Dmitri's family name had become Esterhaats, and that was what it remained when he arrived in America at age ten. Unlike his parents, Dmitri quickly learned English, because they sent him this time to the native schools – they didn't wish him to go to a Hebrew language school and they no longer believed in their Russian future. As in Amsterdam, Dmitri ran afoul of the teachers in Brooklyn. The second year he chose not to remain in school to be taught by inferiors who could not remember the texts of what they read. His only worthy teacher was an old Polish pianist who seemed to know every note Mozart, Beethoven, and Schubert had written for piano, and who never bothered with sheet music. When the old Pole discovered someone who could remember the notes as well as himself, he gave young Dmitri all the lessons he wanted at token charges. The old Pole taught by first playing a piece and then letting Dmitri play it after him until he had it right. His only discipline while Dmitri played was occasionally to mutter the time, sometimes sweetly, sometimes scornfully, "One two three four," if Dmitri played too fast or slow. For two years Dmitri never saw a score.

To satisfy his parents' demands that he get an education, Dmitri spent an hour or so most afternoons of the week with a neighbor, a retired teacher and would-be writer. The neighbor loaned his books to Dmitri to read and then he quizzed Dmitri on his understanding of the history, poetry, or fiction of the books. Dmitri's English developed for a while with a slight Shakespearean datedness in mimicry of his teacher's affectation. That other Americans didn't quite speak that way merely attested to their intellectual inferiority in Dmitri's view. After being rebuffed in his efforts to correct others' usages, he reconciled himself to the doltish abuse of the language by those around him.

At thirteen Dmitri was coming home late in the evening after an aimless walk. From the entryway to his building he heard a piano whose pitch seemed uniformly off, and he followed the sound to a door behind which he heard the loud piano and occasional voices. It was music he'd never heard. When the piece ended, a scratchy loud voice began to speak of cigarettes only to fall silent halfway through a sentence. Thereafter, there were only the quiet voices. Dmitri spent his last waking minutes rehearsing in his mind the odd piece of music he'd heard, transposing all the notes down about half a tone. The following morning he went to the old Pole's apartment to volunteer his new piece for his teacher. He'd played less than a minute when the old Pole slammed his hands down on the keyboard and yelled, "Stop! I don't hear Liszt!"

Dmitri was startled, he'd been too immersed in his music to sense the fury coming, he'd awakened early in anticipation of playing it and hearing it right, he'd thought this would be his greatest moment. But his teacher was repeating his declaration, "I don't hear Liszt!"

Dmitri cried. It was not for the rebuke that he cried, the rebuke only revealed the limits of the old Pole's musical sensibilities. He cried because his playing had been interrupted, because he wasn't allowed to hear the rest of the piece. He asked once only, "Why?"

"I don't hear Liszt, I tell you."

Dmitri stopped crying and left.

For several weeks Dmitri was without a piano, too agitated to sit at home and read, so he walked the streets of Brooklyn. He crossed and recrossed the Brooklyn Bridge, stopping one day at its midpoint to stare at the graceful cable webbing. At first it looked to him like a gigantic suspended harp, but then it was transformed in his view into the strings inside the old Pole's grand piano, the only grand he'd ever played. He began to hear the finale of his Liszt, he heard it over and over, always saddened to have to begin at the broken middle. After a couple of hours he was too forlorn to listen to it again. Had he been a few years older, he might have jumped from the bridge, elegantly passing through the cables during his last seconds while hearing, no, playing Liszt on his grand piano over the East River. But he was only thirteen, hardly the age for romantic suicide, even for a lover of Liszt.

Dmitri didn't go home, but returned instead to Manhattan. He didn't bother to note where he was going, it was never necessary, the grid work of streets with natural landmarks would guide his homeward path later. After an hour or two, he stood before a book store wishing he had the money to buy a book. He had none. In a few minutes he reconciled himself to that minor loss and he turned to walk on. Inside the next window, however, was the one loss to which he could not be reconciled – there was a grand piano in the midst of a dozen uprights.

Dmitri stood at the window staring at the grand. What he felt was not the trivial hurt of the moment when the old Pole had stopped him from playing Liszt, it was a hurt too deep for childish tears, and yet independently of his emotion of the moment, his eyes wanted to cry. It had been pain enough to cry before the old Pole, he would not cry in public. After some minutes, his loss was tempered with anger which slowly built into determination. When the man inside the shop left his counter to go into a back room, Dmitri went in quickly and sat at the grand piano. As he began to play his Liszt, the man came out to scold him, but Dmitri refused to hear anything but powerful chords, quick rushes, delicate melodies. The man let him play and at last the tears he'd restrained broke loose. He closed his eyes to deny them as they washed his cheeks and dribbled off his chin at either side onto his shirt.

Dmitri held his head erect, resolved to know of nothing but Liszt as though there were no tears, there were no shopkeeper, there were no dozen uprights lining the walls, there were no Manhattan or Brooklyn, no Amsterdam or Kiev, no past, no present, no purpose but Liszt at his grand piano in the sky over the East River. As Dmitri played, his face grew hot because he'd never played the piece before and his fingers occasionally went awry. When he reached the end of the piece, he had no sense of what to do next, he hadn't planned for this moment. His tears stopped but his eyes did not open. He sat dumb. In this, the greatest moment of his life, he was humiliated. He decided to wait a minute until his breathing calmed and then to run from the shop. Before he could, the shopkeeper spoke.

"That was very well done, young man. Liszt is not my favorite, but you do it with restraint. Even Mozart might have liked it that way. Why don't you start at the beginning and play the whole suite?"

"I don't know it," Dmitri said, his eyes still closed. "That's all I heard."

"You heard? What do you mean?"

"I didn't hear the beginning, I only heard the end."

"How old are you?"

"Thirteen."

"You're big for thirteen. You're Russian Jewish?"

"How do you know?"

"My wife was Russian Jewish. No Russian Jew was as tall as you at thirteen. How old are you?"

"My . . ." he stopped the Russian word and found the English, "father is Russian and Hungarian. He was a socialist. I am thirteen. I will be fourteen in December."

"Mensheviki, huh? It's a bad mistake to be the losing group. Stay here." The shopkeeper went to the back wall to open one of the many large drawers to rummage through it. Dmitri became nervous thinking he should flee before the man gave him trouble. But he was not fast enough, the shopkeeper returned with a folder.

"What was that you played?"

"I don't know. Just Liszt."

"Look at this." He took a folio from the folder and handed it to Dmitri. "Is this it?"

Dmitri took the music and looked at it with his face squeezed together. It took him a few minutes to get used to reading music again, he hadn't read it since his lessons with Ulyanov in Amsterdam. Dmitri scanned the notes more slowly than he would have played them. Now and then as he recognized themes he nodded his head barely or opened his eyes slightly wider. He turned the pages and he began to nod his head regularly and more demonstratively before he reached the bar where he'd begun to play. "Ah!"

"You really had only heard, hadn't you?"

Dmitri missed the implication of the question, he would not have thought to lie, he had no answer.

"Play it from the beginning."

In the weeks since the Pole had stopped his hands, it had never occurred to Dmitri that he might eventually play the whole piece, the piece had become his private emblem of impossibility, it was beyond reality. He set the music in its rack, paused for a moment to steady his breathing, and began to play. While he played, the world around him disappeared, there remained only his hands, Liszt's music, and the grand piano. Nothing less than physical intervention would have distracted him.

Of course, he hadn't heard the music well enough through the door that night as he returned home from his walk. The actual was far greater than what he'd heard, even glancing over the score he realized that. It had more notes, it was more difficult, it was less shallow. Perhaps if he'd played it better, the old Pole would not have slammed his hand down on the keyboard but would have let him play, would have worked with him to perfect his technique with the difficult chords. Together they might have dedicated themselves to playing this music as it deserved to be played. When Dmitri reached the passage where he'd begun to hear, his chest grew tense. Then, as he played though the point of the old Pole's intrusion, Dmitri knew it was no good, the Pole would never accept Liszt, Dmitri would never return to his teacher. His chest relaxed, now he was immersed, he would seldom come up for breath over the next year. Although Dmitri would never develop his teacher's intense antipathy for Liszt's music, he would soon enough lose interest in it. But for the moment, it was the focus of his life.

When Dmitri finished playing he was surprised to hear a woman's voice say, "*Bravo, Maestro, bravo!* I wish I had time for an encore."

The woman was older, perhaps his mother's age or a bit more, she wore a hat with a net over part of her face, she wore a large necklace and several rings, and she had a long, narrow fur draped across her shoulders and around her upper arms to dangle free below her hips on either side. Dmitri had seen such women on the sidewalks of Manhattan, especially on Fifth Avenue, but he'd never heard one address him.

"He has a remarkable talent," the shopkeeper said.

The two of them talked for a minute and Dmitri didn't listen. He was wondering whether he should excuse himself, say thank you, and leave. But then the woman raised her voice to break his thoughts, she must have been trying to speak to him.

"Perhaps you would deliver it, young man?"

She'd bought sheet music as a gift and wished to have it delivered. She offered him a quarter plus subway fare. He had no idea what was involved, but the quarter was compelling. Had it somehow not been a person offering him the quarter, he would've accepted immediately. But it was too demeaning to reach out his hand to take money from the woman, that seemed too much like a beggar's receiving money. He said he would do the delivery, but not for money.

The woman began to insist, but the shopkeeper interrupted her. "If you come back here afterwards, you can play the Liszt again, or maybe some other Liszt that you'd like to try. You'll need the subway fare though."

When Dmitri asked directions after the woman left, the shopkeeper began to tell him but then interrupted himself. "You don't know the subway, do you?"

Dmitri became delivery boy to Horace Gmund, and in the hours between deliveries, while there were no customers in the shop, he was allowed to play at the grand piano. When the grand was sold, he played at an upright until a new grand came in. When an occasional customer wanted to buy music as a gift but wondered how it sounded, Gmund asked Dmitri to play it on the grand. Occasionally, Dmitri found the pieces too difficult, as for instance when a woman asked for Debussy.

"I've been hearing about Walter Gieseking's latest recordings," she said. "Do you have . . .? I can't remember the composer's name."

"Gieseking," Gmund said, "maybe he was playing Debussy?"

"Yes, that's right, Debussy. He's new?"

"He's been dead quite some time. End of the war, I think. But he's not well enough known. What were you hearing about? Maybe the *Images*?"

"Yes, I think that was it . . ."

"Book I? *Hommage à Rameau*?"

"I can't be sure."

Dmitri played it for her and found that he too could not be sure. But his playing was adequate for the woman to perceive that, although Debussy's music might be for Gieseking, it wasn't for her daughter.

"It doesn't sound like a sonata. Maybe I'd better get Mozart for her."

When Gmund asked why Dmitri didn't go to school, Dmitri said the teachers were not helpful, too often they knew less than he did. Gmund began to test him thereafter, asking him about literature and history. When Dmitri wasn't quick enough with his answers, Gmund would make him spend his delivery money on books from the used books next door to study what he didn't know. The hardest part was the math and science, which Gmund himself didn't understand, but for those he sent Dmitri over to the bookstore for an afternoon or two every week to learn from Mr. Spearman, who was clever with numbers and who enjoyed mathematical games, chess, and geometrical puzzles. Gmund and Spearman tried to get Dmitri to go to a different school, not too far from Gmund's shop, where they said the teachers were better and where Dmitri could learn music theory as well as geometry, history, and science. Eventually Dmitri relented and he began to spend his mornings in school, his afternoons making deliveries and sometimes playing Gmund's grand piano. But the cost of school was that much less time for the piano, and Dmitri grew dispirited with the waste of his time. One day he explained to Gmund that he wanted to quit school in order to have more time to play.

"It's December – you said you would be fourteen in December, Dmitri," Gmund said. "When in December?"

"Thursday."

"Oh – Thursday's too soon. Could you wait till Saturday?"

Without asking why, Dmitri said he could, and that evening he told his mother that she should not bake his cake or make his beloved *piroschki* Thursday but should wait until Saturday. At first she wanted to know why, but in the end, like Dmitri, she simply accepted that she should wait. On Friday, Gmund and Dmitri spent most of the day working on a used upright piano, cleaning it, replacing hammers, hinges, and ivories, and finally tuning it. At the late end of the afternoon, they waxed it and stained several scratches in the cabinet. Dmitri was enchanted at the ease with which they were able to transform an apparent derelict into a nearly new piano. When he started to leave for the night, Gmund asked him whether he could come back to the store tomorrow.

"It's my birthday, I told Mama I'd be home."

"Just for an hour in the morning – not longer. You'll be home before lunch."

Saturday morning, Dmitri helped Gmund and an old truck driver load the newly repaired piano onto a truck, and Dmitri rode with the driver to deliver the piano on his delayed birthday. He agreed to pay Gmund what he'd paid for the abused piano and replacement parts for it. For that price, he had a wonderful Steinway nearly as fine as the grand he played in Gmund's shop. If he paid half his delivery income, it would take nearly two years to retire his debt. Gmund's birthday gift to him was several damaged folios of Liszt's music. Spearman gave him a badly worn book of the scores of all of Beethoven's solo piano sonatas.

All day Saturday, Dmitri played Liszt, although he did not need many of Gmund's folios to know the notes. It was not until Sunday afternoon that he turned to Beethoven. Both days, it was only force that stopped him shortly before midnight and got him to go to bed. The book of Beethoven's sonata's was not intended to be used at the piano, the notes were too small to read, and the score of each piece was broken up into many sections with long passages of textual analysis between them, so that it was a nuisance to use. The textual analyses were in German, which Dmitri did not know, but which he could generally understand since much of it was cognate with Dutch and his beautiful Kiev aunt's Yiddish. But the text was irrelevant, it was the scores he needed. Rather than try to sight read at the piano, Dmitri would read through each sonata a couple of times to remember the notes, and he would play from memory.

In the spring Dmitri chanced to hear a radio broadcast of one of Beethoven's sonatas. The sound of the radio was poor, and the pianist slurred over many notes. Nevertheless it was clear enough that the pianist was playing the sonata better than Dmitri did. He returned home and got out the Beethoven book. He hadn't looked at it since December, and now, in checking over the score of Beethoven's *Sonata, Opus* 57, he discovered the text. The author of the book explained why different pianists played it differently, how styles had changed over the past century. The next day Dmitri challenged his music teacher at school to explain some of the author's German terms. The teacher spoke German, and he didn't at first realize that Dmitri didn't. He spoke very fast, becoming suddenly alive as Dmitri had never seen him before, his enthusiasm was so great that it was a long while before Dmitri could make him realize he was understanding little of what had been said. The teacher went to the piano to demonstrate some of what he was saying, then he asked Dmitri to try to replicate it, varying the tempo, first *allegro*, then *allegro ma non troppo*, playing Beethoven as Liszt would have and then as Schnabel played him. "Schnabel says Beethoven was careless in writing it all down, so the pianist has to supplement a little." In an hour, Dmitri's understanding of the piano was doubled. Everything he'd done up until then seemed childish, now he'd passed through a necessary rite. He began to play Liszt as Liszt would have, with hammer and tongs, and belatedly he understood why Gmund had said he played it with restraint that first time. It was another week before he realized he no longer preferred Liszt above all other composers.

Thereafter, the music teacher asked Dmitri to come to school early so that he could give him extra lessons in music theory and technique. He apologized to Dmitri that he wasn't himself an expert on piano, but maybe they could eventually find someone who was who could give him lessons.

Dmitri's days were now long. He rose early to get to school for private lessons, suffered through several hours of regular classes for the remainder of the morning, ate bread for lunch while he walked to Gmund's shop, delivered sheet music or practiced piano for the afternoon, then went back home and practiced until he was forced to go to bed. When summer came, both the private lessons and the school ended. Dmitri practiced twice as much but seemed to make no further progress. He studied new music in the shop and tried to overcome his block by playing only twentieth century composers. Perhaps because he'd never heard them, he was hampered by lack of technique for Schönberg and Prokofiev, and he even felt deficient for Debussy and Ravel. He began to wonder whether he wasn't very good after all.

In July, Gmund greeted him with a surprise when he returned from a delivery. The woman with the fur stole and the necklace and rings who'd heard his Liszt needed someone to play piano as background for an afternoon party she was giving, but her pianist was unable. Gmund had agreed on Dmitri's behalf that he would play and that he would be paid ten dollars. Dmitri's response was silence, and Gmund seemed to think he was just being modest in his usual manner.

"You'll do very well. She wants mostly Debussy, she'll buy you the sheet music for anything you play as long as it's half Debussy."

It didn't occur to Dmitri that he could say No. He simply accepted Gmund's arrangement as a *fait accompli*, and expected it to be his final humiliation, the end of his life as a would-be pianist. The nearest he came to demurring was to look at the floor and mumble, "I'm not good at Debussy."

"You'll practice. We can hold all the deliveries for one trip at the end of the day to give you more time."

For the next week Dmitri spent all his time in the shop trying to play Debussy. There was something he failed to understand in the Frenchman's music. The music was either too easy or too hard. He suspected it must be too hard while he played it as though it were too easy. The result was hardly worth hearing. Other than a certain consistency of sound, Dmitri could discover nothing to hold any of Debussy's pieces together. In one of his rare deviations from the score, Dmitri even went next door to Spearman's shop to try to find words about Debussy. The words he found composed long metaphors and gave him no meaning. "Impressionism is sensuality, it is the antithesis of development, of classical logic," one book said. "In *La mer*, the temporal element is stretched out so that time seems not like time but atmosphere or space, it seems to exist more spatially than temporally. We flow with the music, but it is not a flow through time from one point to another, it is a flow within time bringing us into harmony with the stiller depths of the sea in the evocative chords built on the dominant while swirling us through eddies on the surface, washing over us with wave after wave, all waves being in fact one. The instruments are heard as though they were immersed, their tones made richer, clearer even as they are muffled by the water." What Dmitri was missing in his understanding the writers hadn't grasped either. He grew despondent.

It was Dmitri's manner almost never to interrupt a piece but to play it straight through, errors or none, and then to go back to the passages he hadn't done well to repeat them until he had them in control. But now he was unable to get through any of the Debussy. The incidental failures along the way overwhelmed the general effect so that there was no point in carrying on with the whole until the parts were right. And the more he struggled with the parts, the less he was able to grasp the whole. He sensed his control slipping from him as though the piano were now trying to defeat him, to put him to public shame. If the woman had asked for Liszt, he could have surprised her with his dexterity, ease, and power. But she'd chosen to shame him with Debussy. For the first time he found himself even forgetting bits of the score. He would get so flustered with his working over a passage that he would have to check the score before going on.

"I will fail," he said to Gmund on his way out at the end of a day.

The following day Gmund arranged with a friend to find a teacher who would give Dmitri lessons on Debussy. It took two days before he found a woman who was said to be the best Debussy interpreter in Manhattan. She was *Mademoiselle* Meursault, she lived near Columbia University, and he would have to go to her apartment for lessons. She would charge a dollar an hour, so that the lessons would cost more than Dmitri would earn for his playing. The woman would not give lessons in the hot afternoons, but only in the morning, and she insisted that he show seriousness by agreeing to come for three hours every morning for a week. The longer Dmitri worked for Gmund, it seemed, the more he would go into debt to him.

Dmitri awoke early on Monday, he'd barely slept at all. It was hot and his room had no good cross ventilation. But worse than the heat of the night was the heat of his own irritation. He wanted to forget everything and go away, but he had no clue how to do that. He could fail to go to *Mademoiselle* Meursault's apartment, but that would mean also not going back to Gmund, to whom he still owed more than he cared to think. By now he'd grown to despise Debussy, whose music he never wished to play or hear again. He thought maybe the book in Spearman's shop understood it right, in which case it was worthless music. When he heard his father in the kitchen, he got up and went in to drink tea.

"Mitya, you stay up after everybody and get up before anybody. How do you live without sleep?"

"I slept."

His father put bread and cheese on the table and put on a kettle for tea. He put a plate before Dmitri.

"I'm not hungry."

"Are you thirsty after such a short night?"

"I will have tea."

Dmitri cut some bread and started to wrap it. Then he thought of what he would do with it. If he went to *Mademoiselle* Meursault's, he would not want to be carrying a piece of bread with him. If he didn't go to her apartment, he wouldn't need it. He put the piece back with the loaf.

In Dmitri's years of silence, his father had grown accustomed to watching without saying anything. Now he watched Dmitri. Dmitri caught his father's eye and started. His father shrugged his okay, he was not complaining, he was merely curious. Dmitri drank his tea and then left.

The sun was still low on the horizon, casting long shadows. It was much cooler outside than in Dmitri's room or even than in his family's apartment. It felt good to be walking, without connections, without burdens, without even a piece of bread in his hand. It also felt good to be undecided about where to go this morning. He'd decided not to decide about *Mademoiselle* Meursault, just to wait and see when the time came. Walking without goal or direction, he walked according to habit and soon found himself on the Brooklyn Bridge. Their beautiful shadows drew his attention up to the suspension cables and their lacework. Suddenly he found himself yearning for a piano to play Liszt. But, as was true on that day seemingly ages ago, he realized it was no good. He would have no piano to play Liszt. This time the loss was not imposed by the world, it was imposed by him. He could not go back, he never went back. Liszt was past.

Dmitri crossed the bridge and wandered over to Broadway, past shopkeepers already setting up their stalls for the morning. He walked at a moderate pace, not slowly as he sometimes did when he had no purpose, not fast as he usually did, and as he walked more and more people joined him in his seeming direction, urging him on by the example of their own haste, their own urgency to get somewhere. After a while he discovered that the pace had been exactly right to put him in front of a watch and clock shop around the corner from *Mademoiselle* Meursault's apartment a few minutes before nine. He stood at the corner feeling annoyed that he'd come this far, annoyed that he now had no necessity of failing to show for his Debussy lessons. He picked out the clock in the window that he thought must have the right time, then waited until it put him at her door at nine.

"Mister Esterhaats?"

"Yes."

"I am *Mademoiselle* Meursault. You are ready to begin?"

That was the full introduction. *Mademoiselle* Meursault was a rigid, unsmiling, beautiful woman. She spoke and moved with precision, she disciplined Dmitri's every movement, even his words with a metronome. She did not request or suggest, she commanded. At the end of two and a half hours she'd fractured Dmitri, whose resolve had never weakened in the face of anyone before, not even the autocratic, capricious old Pole. He froze at the piano refusing to play further, refusing to look at her or speak, too demolished even to leave.

Mademoiselle Meursault relaxed her voice. "*Mon pauvre, permettez moi*, please, move over, let me show you."

Dmitri moved over and was about to stand from the bench when she put her hand on his shoulder to stop him. She sat beside him, stopped the metronome, and set the music aside. She gently grasped his hand in hers for a moment and then lifted her hands over the keyboard. She sat as straight as ever, she used her body no more than Dmitri used his at the piano, but now she seemed relaxed and warm, and at the end of half an hour, Debussy was Dmitri's favorite composer.

When she finished playing, *Mademoiselle* Meursault stood, took Dmitri's hand and tugged him to stand up beside her. He was much taller, she had to look up to say, "You will not be able to do that tomorrow, it will take work. You will not even be able to do it that well next week, *Monsieur* Esterhaats. But someday, *mon cher*, you will do it better than that, I can promise you. I hope I will hear you." Her wonderful smile as she finished speaking recalled to him his beautiful aunt in Kiev. She served him coffee and a *liqueur*, and as quickly as he'd come to like Liszt and Debussy, he came to like her strong coffee and her orange *liqueur*.

Dmitri's second week with *Mademoiselle* Meursault began with a disaster. Her curtains were opened to the east in order to let in a breeze on a stiflingly hot day and Dmitri had some difficulty reading the sheet music against the glare. As the morning wore on, he realized he had a headache, which became increasingly severe, almost blinding with its pain. Dmitri struggled to remain civil and attentive to *Mademoiselle* Meursault's voice, but his concentration flagged. When she suggested they break for coffee and liqueur, Dmitri had no better sense than to drink with her, and his head began to pound violently. When he left, he was nauseated and dizzy. He walked idly without looking at anything, he crossed streets without looking for traffic, he thought it might be a relief to be hit and killed or even merely to be injured with pains to distract from the pain in his head. The oppressive heat filled his head and the bright sun hurt his eyes. After a while, he began to find his way into the shadows, where he walked away the afternoon and early evening before he finally went home long after dark.

The following day, Dmitri reached *Mademoiselle* Meursault's apartment early and he paced outside until his chosen clock in the clock store said it was time. That morning he was ready for everything and Debussy fell before him, he was master of the most radiant, shimmering passages, and Dmitri began to see the possibility of a future. He continued for three weeks down to the day before he was to perform for Mrs. Wolfe, the woman with the fur stole. *Mademoiselle* Meursault reduced her fee to half for the second week, and to half again for the third. On the last day she said, "You will play wonderfully for Mrs. Wolfe tomorrow."

Dmitri was startled, he wouldn't have thought he'd told her about the party, it must have been the *liqueur* and her ease with conversation one day after the lesson. He was normally too private, too discreet to have told her. Or maybe Gmund had let it be known.

"Thank you."

"I'm sorry, I should never compliment you, *mon cher* Esterhaats, you always stop talking."

She refilled their coffee cups. "You now love Debussy. You hated him when you came here, I think."

"Yes. I couldn't understand him."

"To understand him, you must first hear him. You heard him for the first time when I played for you, did you not?"

Dmitri smiled. It felt like the smile of wisdom, as though he were *Mademoiselle* Meursault's age, the age of his mother and his aunt in Kiev, the age of those women who made life good. He reached out to put lumps of sugar in their coffees.

"Now you will help others understand. Understanding will multiply."

As Dmitri left, *Mademoiselle* Meursault said, "In Russia or France we would have to kiss each other goodbye. New York is less elegant. But we two have the right to do as we would in Russia or France, do we not, *mon cher* Esterhaats?"

Dmitri was required to wear formal dress for his performance, and he rented a suit from a shop not far from Gmund's. He washed himself in Gmund's back room, then dressed in his magnificent suit. He was unable to make the tie work and he had to get help from Gmund. Then he took the subway to the Upper East Side to pace the sidewalk outside Mrs. Wolfe's building until it was time for his arrival. When he went up punctually at two, she told him he was the only person there other than herself and the servants. He was to start playing before the guests arrived and, unless someone stayed unduly late, he was to continue until after the last guest left. He was to play Debussy at least every other piece, or entirely if he chose. He could also improvise – Mr. Gmund had told her of his talents – but only if he was sure his improvisation was literally an improvement. "But I'm sure you won't embarrass me, Master Esterhaats."

Dmitri had been playing a couple of hours when he heard Mrs. Wolfe addressing someone behind him. "I told you I'd find someone in New York who could play Debussy as well as you, Colette. Now you see it's true. Mr. Esterhaats is one of the finest young pianists in New York, perhaps in all America – in fact, if he's one of the finest in New York, then he must be one of the finest in America. Maybe you haven't heard of him – if not, you should have. He must be the equal of any younger pianist in France."

"No, you are right, *Madame* Elaine, Esterhaats is a name one has not yet heard in the world of piano. I am surprised at how good he is. I would have thought it impossible. He is superb. *C'est un pianist très très cher.* You cannot know how proud I am to hear him here."

Dmitri at his piano closed his eyes and bit his lip, letting his hands and his mind detach themselves to handle their task of the moment. He recognized Colette's voice as that of *Mademoiselle* Meursault. He heard no more of the conversation behind him, but put all his concentration into playing. The only words he could hear were Mrs. Wolfe's, "I'm sure you will not embarrass me," and *Mademoiselle* Meursault's "You will not be able to do that tomorrow . . ." Mrs. Wolfe hadn't thought of the implausibility of Dmitri's being naturally better than Colette Meursault at Debussy. She'd merely commanded him to be, as she commanded others to fulfill her desires.

The party around Dmitri disappeared, and he began to discover structure in the prelude he was playing that he hadn't noticed before. After beginning the piece as Debussy had written it, he seemed now to be inventing the rest of it as he played. For the first time in his four week immersion in Debussy, Dmitri was in control. Playing that music with such control made him feel, as he'd never felt in all his life, graceful and elegant, in the manner of his aunt in Kiev or of *Mademoiselle* Meursault, relaxed and at home in his world.

Much later, he was not sure how much time had passed, Dmitri ended another piece and paused a moment to decide on his next piece. *Mademoiselle* Meursault spoke behind him. "Do not turn around now to spoil your success, *Monsieur* Esterhaats. I told you someday you will play it better than I could. You have learned very fast, *très très vite*, I think you have even learned during this afternoon. I am glad I was able to hear you do it. Now, I think there is nothing more you can learn from me. No – do not turn around. Play Bach for me, please. *Adieu Monsieur*."

Dmitri began to play Bach. His posture sagged as he heard *Mademoiselle* Meursault thanking the butler for holding the door open for her to leave. In half an hour, Mrs. Wolfe interrupted his playing by tapping on his shoulder. "That's enough, *Maestro*. The butler has an envelope for you, you should go before it's too late."

The butler's envelope contained not ten but twenty dollars. Dmitri hadn't embarrassed Mrs. Wolfe, or at least she didn't know he had. But he had embarrassed himself, because in the moment of his success he'd been too weak to turn around and address *Mademoiselle* Meursault to admit his debt to her. He'd let her cover for him even to the point of being ungracious to her. He'd let Mrs. Wolfe feel victory over her. In his memory of her tenderness toward him at the end of his first day's lesson, he was sure she wouldn't have treated him so ungraciously if their positions had been reversed. It was many months before he could play Debussy without a sense of embarrassment for his weakness at the party, a weakness compounded by his failure even to call on *Mademoiselle* Meursault again, as though he were merely acting on her injunction, "I think there is nothing more you can learn from me." He could learn much from her, even if nothing more in piano technique.

Dmitri thought he'd be over forty dollars in debt for his performance, but instead it was a little over thirty. During the following month he was asked by two of Mrs. Wolfe's guests to play at their parties, and by the time school started in the fall, he'd paid off the remaining cost of his lessons and even part of the debt on his piano.

Dmitri's fifteenth birthday had none of the pleasure of his fourteenth, and the year which followed it was the most dismal of his life. He lost weight and spent half his time with minor illnesses because he did nothing but play his piano or go for walks when he was neither in school nor in Gmund's shop. Frequently, instead of taking the subway home to Brooklyn in the afternoon, he walked across the Brooklyn Bridge. When he heard orchestral or chamber works on the radio or at occasional free concerts, he would discipline his memory by transcribing in his head for piano. He heard Beethoven's *Ninth Symphony* on the radio, and he transcribed the *Ode to Joy*. If he could have taken his piano out onto the bridge to play the ode there, he would surely have ended it by plunging directly into the water in the ecstasy of the finale. He'd only regret not being able to take his piano along. In lieu of the plunge, thinking out scores while he walked became a purpose to get him through the day. For an entire year he hardly spoke, the most he needed to say to his mother was a nod of the head or a wave of the hand. In school he began to fail, he who could have quoted Shakespeare's *Macbeth* almost in toto failed a test on *Macbeth*. He who knew the kings and queens of England and all their intrigues as only delirious English school children know them failed in English history. Given that he failed history and literature, it was foregone he would fail geometry, but to everyone's surprise he did not.

Halfway through the fall before his sixteenth birthday, Dmitri began to miss school more often than he attended. There was no plan, no thought to the missing, it simply happened that when he finished breakfast and left the apartment he frequently failed to reach the school. Some days he grew too despondent along the way to continue past the Brooklyn Bridge. If the city had had the sense to make the schools nearer his home better, he would have seemed to be a better student. Many days Dmitri was merely bored and, after he crossed the bridge, he wandered down to the Battery or up to Central Park. There was less interest in sitting through his classes than in walking a new street, where at least the visual details would differ. The stonework, the ironwork, the placement and variation of windows, the roofs and chimneys of the houses, and the excessiveness of the skyscrapers and public buildings were technically interesting in a way that biology and history were not. To discover that much of the stonework of the houses was not stonework at all but molded sheet metal or stucco veneer gave Dmitri greater pleasure than to be told that ontogeny recapitulates phylogeny or that chlorine is a halogen.

Once the routine of his mornings was broken, the foundation of the routine of Dmitri's afternoons began to crumble in his mind. He lingered downtown too long to be able to make it to Gmund's without being conspicuously late and, though his lateness would not have bothered Gmund, he chose to miss the entire afternoon rather than face the moment of entering the shop – conspicuousness in *absentia* was better than conspicuousness in person. It came as a discovery to him that he was glad not to be in Gmund's shop, that he no longer found solace in playing Horace Gmund's grand piano while waiting between sporadic requests for his services as delivery boy. Though he was oblivious of his steps and of the details around him, he enjoyed this, only the second afternoon he'd failed to go to work in his year and a half with Gmund. When he returned home in the evening, his principal memory of the afternoon, other than enjoyment, was that it rained almost steadily.

The last of Dmitri's daily routines collapsed when shortly thereafter he stayed home and played his piano from six in the morning until his father yelled him into silence shortly before midnight. When Gmund asked him on one of his old routine days what he wanted, the best he could answer was, "Not to be Dmitri Esterhaats."

The following week, Gmund told Dmitri he'd finished paying for his piano.

Dmitri didn't answer. He accepted the fact as equal to other facts, neither to be denied nor enjoyed, and a week passed before he thought enough about this fact to realize it couldn't possibly be true. That too was neither to be denied nor enjoyed, and Dmitri didn't raise the issue of his factually unfulfilled debt to Gmund. It was possible Gmund was letting him choose to stop working for him if that was what he wanted. He wondered about that while making a delivery of sheet music to Mrs. Wolfe, the customer for whom at least half his delivery work was done.

While going up in the elevator to her penthouse, Dmitri decided he would indeed quit, perhaps already at the end of that day. He made the decision while staring without seeing at his reflection in the cut glass mirror of the elevator wall before him. He still had the childish habit of mouthing the words of the elaborate dialogues in which he thought out his activities and troubles.

"Plato wrote dialogues because he was just transferring his thoughts directly," Mr. Spearman said. "It's the most natural way to think."

It was also natural to form the words which one thought, Dmitri answered in the dialogue in his head about the dialogue in his head. As the elevator slowed toward the height of its climb, Dmitri began to see what he was staring at in the mirror. It was the elevator operator staring at him staring back while mouthing the silent dialogue.

Mrs. Wolfe asked Dmitri in to play her new music for her.

"I have to get back."

"Not even for a few minutes? Perhaps next week then."

Dmitri was unable to lie even as part of inconsequential small talk, but answering that he might not be with Gmund next week would begin a tedious conversation. Between two such unappealing choices, he stood unmoving and silent. Even that was lie enough to bring his face to blush.

"Are you sure?" Mrs. Wolfe said again. She was unaccustomed to denial as much as she was ignorant of self-denial.

As though to redeem his lie of silence, Dmitri relented. It was an unthinking reflex that cost him as much tedium as an explanation of why not next week and as much pain as an outright lie, because the music was Kodály's *Marosszék Dances*, whose melodic peasant dance rhythms on the page were sufficient to drive Dmitri into the streets for a long, morose walk without the necessity of his actually playing them. He disciplined his mind into another world long enough to play one dance, and then he excused himself against Mrs. Wolfe's further imploring. Only at the bottom of the elevator's slow descent did he realize he'd denied a request from her for the first time in his year and a half of servitude. It was the brightest moment of the long dull fall.

When he reached the street, Dmitri walked west toward the park. A horsecart vendor whom he often encountered on his deliveries to Mrs. Wolfe was wearing an extra topcoat over the ragged one he usually wore. The horse was in its failing years, its respiratory ailments jolted it with occasional sneezes. Dmitri, who wore no topcoat even on colder days such as lay ahead soon, tilted his head back so the skin of his throat stretched taut while that of the back of his neck rumpled into his collars. Realizing what he'd done, he smiled for the second time in many days, the first time having been a few minutes before at the bottom of Mrs. Wolfe's elevator. This second smile was for his mimicry of the horse, which stretched its own neck out to clear its throat for a cough, shaking its remnant of a mane while its nose pointed almost vertically upward.

On first encountering the vendor on a foul day a year earlier, Dmitri thought the man was out of touch with the world because he showed no concern for the agonies of his horse and he didn't notice Dmitri's presence as he approached the old horse and even patted its neck. But he'd since seen the vendor noticing other people in the streets, people who looked as though they might have money in their pockets. The vendor came more nearly from Dmitri's world than from the world of his customers, but the world of his customers governed his responses. In Dmitri's mind, the vendor's responses were equated with his sympathies, and Dmitri gave the man as little sympathy as the man gave him attention as he passed. Now it seemed the man was not so unlike Dmitri in his attentions, so heavily lavished on Mrs. Wolfe, and Dmitri was beginning to have some sympathy for him.

The horse lifted its head until its outstretched neck was horizontal. Wads of drool fell from its mouth, and Dmitri winced when it coughed its least audible cough. The horse tilted its head as though to rest it against an imaginary pillow in the air and closed its eyes. Dmitri withdrew his hand from the pat he'd intended to give the horse's neck, and he closed his own eyes momentarily as he walked on.

Along with the dozens of older men there, Dmitri spent an hour in Central Park loitering, more than walking through it on his return to Gmund's shop. He knew if he quit working for Gmund, he'd spend half his days in similar activity, walking in order to pass the time rather than to reach a destination, rummaging a foot through the leaves along the path to give himself a semblance of purpose rather than trying to find anything there. On his productive days he would spend sixteen hours at his not-fully-paid-for piano; on his other days he'd spend almost as many hours meandering through the city. It wouldn't really be so different from his life now while working for Gmund most afternoons, merely that it would be freer and oddly that it might seem more orderly since all of his days would have coherence they now often lacked because the full range of activity for each day would be set by his morning choice of whether to go out or stay in after breakfast. And there was so little money from the job that he'd hardly been able to pay the expenses it caused him to incur.

Dmitri kicked over several leaves to look at their patterns on the ground. He saw such minute details so clearly and sought them out with such diligence, yet he'd failed to notice the larger pattern to his own desultory life over the past few months until Gmund gently pointed it out to him by releasing him from his indenture over the piano and, by implication, over all the favors Gmund had done him. While he stood looking down at his leaves, Dmitri was jostled aside by an older man who was rummaging carefully through the leaves and bits of trash beside the path. The man trampled through Dmitri's leaves, and Dmitri, not bothering to look at the man, turned to renew his walk south to Gmund's shop. By the time he arrived there, he'd quit his job.

"I understand," Gmund said. "I wish there were something I could do. Promise me one thing, Dmitri, promise me you'll go for an audition." Gmund went to the back room to get Dmitri's pay, and he came out with a newspaper. On the page there were several announcements of auditions. Gmund studied them and selected one. "They want someone who can play to accompany a soprano, someone who's flexible and able to improvise. Half of what you play now is a transcription from orchestral music, you would do very well. If you promise you'll go for the audition, I'll give you a big enough bonus to buy a suit." He cut out the ad and handed it to Dmitri.

"Okay," he said, to speed to the end of the conversation.

As he was about to leave, Gmund said, "One thing, Dmitri. Please let me know whether the audition succeeds."

Dmitri nodded yes without looking at Gmund while shaking his hand. As he was leaving, he thought it should have been an emotional moment. A year earlier it would've been. He'd looked away from Gmund's eyes not to hide emotion but only to avoid the syndrome of emotional response, a syndrome out of his past which threatened a reaction from his past self to events which his present self would sooner merely get behind him. Gmund's nervous request was stated as though it were an afterthought – "One thing, Dmitri, I'd like to hear from you now and then. . . ." – but Dmitri suspected Gmund had planned for many days how best to say it. Dmitri had spent less time deciding to quit his job and leave Gmund behind.

Dmitri walked home very slowly, lingering on the bridge until the sun set behind Manhattan and New Jersey, and then walking in the dark through the streets of Brooklyn. He didn't wish to get home so early as to provoke discussion. He gave little thought to Gmund along the way until he recalled he'd have to go back into the city tomorrow for his audition. Then, in the privacy of his walk along Brooklyn streets, his face turned hot in the cold air. Gmund had given him money he hadn't earned, had tacitly canceled his debt for the piano, and Dmitri hadn't even thanked him, hadn't even acknowledged Gmund's generosity toward him. Dmitri would suffer private embarrassment for several months thereafter whenever he chanced to think of Gmund because he'd been ungracious toward him as he'd been toward *Mademoiselle* Meursault. The worst of it was that the trivium of his embarrassment would prevent his being gracious enough in the future to call on Gmund to tell him about the audition, even if it succeeded.

Sofia Milano

Dmitri went for the audition. It was almost too complicated for him in his maudlin state. He first had to be scheduled and then to return at the appointed time two days later, and it was only chance that brought him back on time. He forgot about the audition until he happened to walk past a radio playing classical music. By taking the subway he was barely able to get to the room near the Metropolitan Opera where the auditions were being heard. An irascible man ordered him to take the piano and play the music opened there. In his diffidence, Dmitri didn't bother to turn back the cover to see whose music it was. He simply began to play. The music was new to him, lyrical and full, easier than Liszt, much easier than Debussy, it could be sight read without doubting his interpretation. He guessed it was mid-nineteenth century, there seemed to be borrowings from Haydn and Beethoven.

After he played a couple of minutes, the man interrupted him. "Okay, hold it right there. Go back to the beginning and try it again, only knock out several beats in the first line and work them into the second. Pretend you're playing for a singer who's too fast at the beginning but who gets too slow, she changes the number of syllables in the words. Go ahead."

Dmitri thought the man was telling him he hadn't done well and was now making fun of him. He was irritated, but he played it the way the man said. Before the end of the second line, the man yelled, "Make the chords heavier, loud, loud!" He obliged, and again the man said to stop. Then he yelled to someone else and Dmitri thought he was being dismissed. But when he stood, the man yelled at him, "Hey! Where you going? Sit down. Hey George, damn it, I said where's the record?" He took away Dmitri's music. Dmitri still didn't know who was the composer.

Another man, who must have been George, came through a door and started a record player. The irascible man now turned back to Dmitri. "Okay, I want you to listen to this woman sing and then I want you to start playing as soon as you think you can improvise along with her. Have you got that? Do you know what improvise means?"

"I know," Dmitri said. It took control to say so little.

George started the record, and Dmitri immediately recognized the voice version of what he'd been playing, but he now understood why the man wanted him to alter the flow. He began to play, and he was allowed to continue far beyond the few lines he'd sight read. The longer he played, the more he forgot his purpose and the more he began to enjoy the voice on the record and the delicate effort of accompanying it. His enchantment was disrupted eventually by the man's yelling at George to turn off the record.

"What's your name?" the man asked.

"Dmitri Esterhaats."

"Esterhaats? Esterhaats. I never heard that name before. Hey, it's good. Dmitri Esterhaats. That sounds right. Not bad. Sofia Milano, accompanied by Dmitri Esterhaats. It grows on you. How old are you, Dmitri?"

Dmitri lied by a month. "Sixteen."

"SIXTEEN! God damn! Can't you lie a little, kid, damn, don't go around telling people you're sixteen. I can't hire a sixteen year-old kid to go on tour. I can't tell Sofia Milano she's gotta sing while a sixteen year-old plays her piano. Look at you – you must be six feet tall, more. Now why do you have to go and tell me you're sixteen. If I could find anyone else who didn't already know *La Signorina*, I wouldn't even talk to a teenager. Tell me you're nineteen. Or twenty – twenty, that's the number. Come on, Dmitri, say it, say I'm twenty years old, Mr. Schein. Come on, say it."

"Am I hired?"

"If you say you're twenty, you might be. I can't do the final hiring until you meet Miss Milano and play with her for a while to see if she can take you. Hell, mainly to see if you can stand up to her, she can be a holy bitch. Are you twenty, kid?"

"If I were not twenty, I would have told you, Mr. Schein."

A few days later Dmitri sat at Schein's piano awaiting the arrival of Sofia Milano. The folio of music he'd played was still there, it was Verdi. Dmitri was pleased to be starting with a new composer, even though he didn't seem especially challenging. As their wait for Miss Milano dragged on, Schein became kinder, more solicitous. He had George go out to get coffee and sandwiches for them.

"This is a funny business. Sure you wanta get into it?"

Dmitri hadn't thought of it as a business. "I play the piano. It's the only thing I do."

"I've heard a lot of pianists. You're pretty damn good for your age – I think we discovered that was twenty, huh?"

Sofia Milano arrived without apology. She was a big woman, she was not so much fat as made larger than other women, she was nearly as tall as Dmitri and much wider and deeper. Her Roman nose focused her strong face to make it soft or harsh by turns to reflect her mood. Her face alone would have been sufficient to manipulate a deaf man, her voice added to it could intimidate, overpower, demolish, or it could endear, caress, elevate. She was simultaneously skeptical and effusive when Dmitri was presented to her. After a few minutes of banter with Schein and George, she decided to get to work. She began to challenge Dmitri as only *Mademoiselle* Meursault had done. At her words his back straightened, he sat at the grand piano, waiting mute for her to tell him where to begin. She did nothing of the sort but merely began to sing.

The record had done her grievous injustice. Sofia's live voice stopped Dmitri, he'd heard nothing so beautifully new since the day *Mademoiselle* Meursault first played Debussy for him. But Sofia's voice was a new category of beauty and wonder – he couldn't think to intrude on it with his lowly piano. He sat, eyes closed, his face turned straight ahead, immersed in the sound of her voice. It took him a long while to realize that the words she sang had ceased to be Italian to become English. It took him longer still to realize she was singing to him, asking him why he was mute, why he was wasting her time, was he so dumb? She ended on a return to Italian sounds, "Dmitri, DMITRI! DMI-I-I-I-I-I-I-I-I-TRI, Dmitri-i-i-i-i, *povero* Dmitri? *STUPIDO.*" The "*stupido*" was sung to a devastating chord at the depths of her lowest register.

For the remainder of his two hour test session with her, Dmitri was given sheet music, so that the only test was whether he could adjust the notes on the page to the notes in his ears. Just at a moment when he was convinced he'd failed to meet her standards, she turned to gesture at Ben Schein.

"*Beniamino, tu sai,*" she said, and then she abruptly put her fur coat on and left without a further glance at Dmitri. "*Arrivederci tutti.*"

"This is Miss Milano's address. She wants you to show up ready for a full day of work beginning seven a.m. tomorrow. Got that?"

"Got that."

"Good luck, Dmitri."

Dmitri started to repeat the words Good luck as a question, but he swallowed the thought.

"You'll need it working with *La Signorina*, Dmitri. If you two are working well together at the end of the week, you'll be booked in Philadelphia for a concert in three weeks. Tell your mama now so she doesn't say no when the time comes. You're going to work like hell for the next three weeks."

"I'm not afraid of work."

"Dmitri, you don't know what work means. That's the first thing Sofia will teach you."

Dmitri nodded and turned to leave.

"Hey, another thing, Dmitri. In this business you don't get paid for preparation time. You get paid for performance. Performance before a paying public. There's nothing in it for you unless you and Miss Milano succeed as a team. Got that?"

"Got that."

"Try to start with a good night's sleep, kid."

The whole conversation was obviously directed at a young teenager and, if he'd really been twenty, Dmitri suspected Schein would be calling him Esterhaats.

Dmitri nearly overslept. He took the subway without eating breakfast, taking two slices of his mother's bread with him, and all along the way he kept telling the subway to move faster. One bad connection and he'd have been very late. As it was, he was a few minutes after seven before he reached the lobby of Sofia's hotel. The doorman asked his name. "Oh yes," he said. You're supposed to go up without being announced. Take that elevator."

When Dmitri rang, no one answered, and he wondered whether he had the wrong door. He looked around for a while to make sure, then he rang again. Convinced he was at the wrong door but not sure what to do about it, thinking he was so late he'd irreparably angered *La Signorina*, he pushed the buzzer repeatedly. As he was about to walk away, he heard an Italian *aria*, and in another moment, Sofia opened the door.

"You! Dmitri. You have awakened me. Come in, we will have breakfast."

A bellboy brought a lavish breakfast of foods he had never had. "That is called *'pain perdu'*," Sofia said. "It means 'lost bread' in French. It is what the French do with bread that is stale. It is good that French bread is stale so fast."

After breakfast they talked, or Sofia usually talked while Dmitri listened. For several hours there was no work, no rehearsing. During the morning, bellboys came and left, bringing fresh coffee and taking away dirty dishes. In the end they brought lunch.

"Did you see the look he gave you?" Sofia asked. Dmitri did not have time to answer before she continued. "He is asking himself why you are still fully dressed and I wear only this," she slipped her hand under one of the many layers of her gauzy nightgown and whisked it into the air to let it float back into place. "Bellboys and night clerks have the filthiest minds in the world."

After lunch she said, "We will practice. If you must have it, I will try to find the music for you. Must you have it?"

She did not give him time to answer but began to sing a new *aria*. After a few bars she stopped. "Can you do that on my piano, Dmitri?"

He went to the piano, sat for a minute as he rehearsed the notes, and then played her *aria*, even continuing at the end several bars beyond where she'd stopped singing.

"*Perfetto*, Dmitri. You have improved on Puccini, the angels must be jealous."

She jumped from the couch, the layers of her gown flowing in conflicting eddies around her, and walked over to stand beside Dmitri. She didn't speak again for several hours. She sang and Dmitri struggled to stay with her. When she stopped singing now and then, he knew he was supposed to repeat the previous passage to get it right, and then she would start off again. He suspected that everything they did was Puccini, although he'd never heard Puccini before. To have a new composer was almost as exhilarating as to hear *bel canto* for the first time from a voice six or ten feet away.

"It is six o'clock," Sofia said. "You are tired. You have worked hard, Dmitri. I rested sometimes while you played, you did not rest. We will have dinner. You may rest on the couch while I bathe."

Dmitri was awakened by Sofia, who stood before him in a glorious dress with her hair piled on top of her head in elegantly ordered disarray. "Dmitri, you are lazy," she laughed.

At this moment, Dmitri felt lazy. He couldn't remember ever taking a nap before. "I've never taken a nap," he said. "That proves I am not lazy, just tired, that was a strain."

"No, no, no, Dmitri, that is even greater proof you are lazy. That was not so much work to make anyone tired enough to nap."

They went down to the restaurant in the building, a residential hotel. When Dmitri fretted with the menu and ordered something that must've been wrong, she countermanded him and told the waiter what he wanted. One of the things he wanted was his share of a bottle of wine. He'd tasted wine in small quantities before, but it was a different wine. He felt his tongue escaping his control as the meal progressed, and he suspected that Sofia was laughing not at what he said so much as at the way he said it. It was very late when the meal ended and Sofia dismissed him to return tomorrow again at seven.

"Tomorrow is Saturday," she said. "Are you religious?"

"No, we are socialists."

"Of course. All artists are socialists. Except those in Italy who are fascists. If the fascists were not there, I would be."

Sofia's treatment of him became harsher by the day and Dmitri began to think the week's trial would end in rejection. The breakfasts continued to be splendid, but the lunches and dinners grew sparer each day. On the Friday which began his second week with her, there was no breakfast before they began to work, and Dmitri grew dizzy as they moved into the third *aria* of the morning.

"It is no good!" Sofia yelled in the middle of an *aria*. "Dmitri Esterhaats, you are better than that. If you are not better than that, you are useless, because I am certainly better than that. Why are you wasting my time?"

Dmitri treated the question as rhetorical. He stared straight ahead as though there were something of interest on the underside of the open lid of her piano. But the question was not rhetorical, she repeated it, again, and again. She walked away to a chest far across the large room, fumbled in one of the drawers and returned to fling several folios of music at him. He was unable to catch them before they fluttered randomly to the floor.

She laughed at him. "Dmitri is even clumsy."

His face flushed bright red, it was a physiological response he could not control. It penalized him more than it did most people, at age fifty he would still blush too easily. He selected one of the pieces. Momentarily he recalled his first morning with *Mademoiselle* Meursault. His back straightened. Suddenly he knew the right gesture. He stood to pick up the other folios and, when he had them all in hand, he straightened to his full height to face down at *Signorina* Milano. He set the extra folios aside, sat on the bench, and began to play the *aria* spread open on the rack before him. He played it with insistence and when Sofia sang with him she was leading him part of the time and part of the time he was leading her. When the time came to turn the page, he did not turn it but continued from memory of their having worked on the *aria* before and by extrapolation from the first two pages.

In the afternoon, Sofia recommended that Dmitri study the music so that he might know how the composer had written it and not only how she sang it. "Then you will know when you are creating and when you are only repeating what is well known."

That evening, again they had a sumptuous dinner. They finished their bottle of wine before they finished their meal and Sofia started to order another bottle. When the waiter arrived, she corrected herself. "No, we have changed our mind, we will have no more. And we will not have dessert tonight. We will work some more."

During Sofia's bath before dinner, Dmitri had studied scores of the Verdi *arias* she'd got out for him that morning. Now, after dinner, when he sat at the piano, he didn't wait for her to choose the *aria* but began on his own. She was quick to follow the lead and she let him make the choices for a couple of hours. For the first time they were now in concert, partly because at last they'd worked themselves together and partly because at last they'd turned to Verdi. When Sofia sang *Aida*, Dmitri played with his eyes closed, and at the end of her *aria* he sat in silence, awed by what they had done.

After several minutes of silence, Sofia spoke. "We will not do better than that tonight, but let us not do worse. We stop."

It was long past midnight when Dmitri returned home, and the next morning he was back. Saturday morning they spent talking and drinking coffee. Saturday afternoon they tried Verdi again, but it was a fretful, unproductive three hours before Sofia walked away from the piano and sat in a sulky mood on the couch. It was several days before they returned to the heights of their midnight *Aida*. When they did, Sofia retired to her couch, again in a sulky mood.

Dmitri joined her there. It had been an accidental success, it happened because Dmitri went to the piano to try an *aria* whose score he'd been reading while waiting for breakfast to arrive. It had been the right moment, but now the moment had passed and breakfast was being announced at the door. They ate in silence, neither of them seeming to enjoy the food, though both had spoken of hunger only a few minutes earlier.

They spent the morning talking rather than rehearsing, and at lunchtime Sofia said, "The afternoon will not be good, Dmitri. We could find a better way to use it. You will go home and then you will come back here. We will dine together. Not in the same restaurant – we have exhausted the chef's talents. I will take you to an Italian restaurant to show you *la cucina italiana* you have never eaten. I don't like to practice according to a timetable like a train. I like to practice when I like to. If you're not here when I like to but you are here when I don't like – you understand, Dmitri? You will tell your mother you are not coming home tonight."

Sofia selected all their dishes, and she began the meal by selecting two bottles of wine. They'd never drunk more than one before. It was Thursday night, so the restaurant was not full. There was a violinist walking around the tables, singing sad Italian songs. When it was no longer possible for him to avoid their table, he walked over and bowed with his violin extended in one hand off to the side and the bow in his other hand. He spoke Italian, and all that Dmitri understood of his words was, "*Per la Signorina Milano, bellissima cantante, per favore . . .*" He played an *aria* of *Aida*, but he did not sing.

When he finished, Sofia spoke to him in Italian to say something about Dmitri Esterhaats, *pianista proprio bello*. The violinist insisted that Dmitri be allowed to play the piano, and now, apparently sensing that Dmitri Esterhaats didn't understand Italian, he asked him in English.

He demurred but Sofia volunteered for him. "Play it twice," she said.

Dmitri played the grand *aria*. As it came to an end, he led into it again with finesse and he heard Sofia's voice rise behind him. The piano was not in perfect tune, but it was good enough to let them come into concert as they'd done that morning before breakfast. When they finished, the violinist, the waiters, the guests at half a dozen tables applauded, whistled, and yelled *Brava, Bravo, Bravi!* It was the first applause Dmitri had ever received, and he thought it must be intended not for him but for Sofia, until he turned around to see that Sofia was standing, facing him, and applauding with the others. Then he noticed that all were facing not Sofia but him. In his private thoughts he was modest enough to know it was all Sofia's trick, when she turned the applause to him the others would have been ungracious not to follow her lead, just as he as her *pianista proprio* would've been ungracious not to follow her lead when she chose to sing the *aria* with her own flourishes. Now he knew she'd definitely decided he would accompany her on her tour.

The elegance of the cuisine which followed was lost on him, his thoughts and sensations could not focus on food. Over the last glass of wine, she toasted him, "To my young Dmitri Esterhaats, *pianista proprio bell*o. Today I have decided you will accompany me to Philadelphia, Washington, Chicago, San Francisco, and all those terrible places in between."

"Yes."

"You will play beautifully. I will sing beautifully. It will be my greatest tour."

After dinner they did not seriously practice but merely toyed with Puccini for a while before Sofia consigned Dmitri to her couch for the night. When he awoke in the morning, she brought him a housecoat to wear over his pajamas, and she collected all his clothes, including the suit for which Horace Gmund paid with his bonus, and put them in a box. They had a long breakfast, which was interrupted momentarily by George, who came to take away the box of Dmitri's clothes. They were still drinking coffee in late morning when George returned with another man, who set about fitting a suit to Dmitri. He was made to try on several pair of shoes and to keep the pair that fit best. He was presented with cartons of underwear, of socks, and a large carton of shirts. After lunch he was presented with a pair of striped pants and a satin jacket for wearing in Sofia's apartment. Dmitri found his hands wandering into his cuffs to feel the satin cloth of the jacket.

"Now you look like the pianist you are," Sofia said.

They had exactly one week before Philadelphia and Sofia declared they were not ready. They would have to work twice as hard from now on, and when they were not working, Dmitri would have to study the scores, Rossini, Puccini, and Verdi. For the following week, their breakfasts were adequate without being elegant or time consuming. Lunches and dinners were served in the room. They napped in the afternoons, and worked late into the nights. There were hours when they spoke not a word. Thursday morning Dmitri was sent home to tell his mother he would be on tour for a couple of months. That evening he and Sofia arrived in Philadelphia with Beniamino to stay at a hotel near city hall not far from where Sofia was scheduled to sing Friday night. All day Friday Sofia grew more nervous and irascible. Over dinner she seemed to have to restrain herself to keep from scolding Dmitri.

When they were in place behind the curtain hearing the audience shuffling around, Sofia said, "Dmitri, you are *pianista proprio mio*, do not fail me tonight." She kissed him and then held him away from her at arm's length. "I will sound only as good as you sound, that is the tragedy of a soprano, Dmitri, she cannot control her success – you must sound as good as I do, Dmitri, please."

When the curtain rose and they walked out, Dmitri was startled to hear the applause, he hadn't anticipated it. It had a great effect, it made his and Sofia's presence on the stage seem self-contained. When silence returned, Dmitri's was the first sound as their performance began, and thereafter their concert grew as they progressed from Rossini to Puccini to Verdi to end with *Aida*. They would give many better performances, but they would also give many worse. The applause at the end produced two encores. Sofia selected the first and then she invited Dmitri to select the second. His was the better choice and the audience would not end its ovation afterwards until finally Dmitri and Sofia failed to return for a fifth bow. It was Sofia's applause, as it had been in the restaurant, but Dmitri was delighted to share in it. They performed again Saturday night and then Sunday afternoon in a suburb, and then they had four nights to rest in Philadelphia before going to Washington.

Sunday evening before dinner Sofia asked Dmitri to rub her shoulders with his strong, spatulate pianist's fingers. The rubbing ended with her pulling him into her bed where, to her confused delight and roaring humor, she found there was more to teach him than merely how to accompany her on the piano. Over the next several weeks she taught him many things. She taught him how to use his fingers for purposes other than to play a piano, she taught him to use them to draw music from her directly, heavy chords from the depths and ascending scales to the heights of her passion, to transcend the use of fingers, to indulge her by indulging himself. In their hotel room in the city where they were performing that night, they would begin the afternoon practicing her *arias*, and to one listening through the wall it would have seemed they'd begun with nineteenth century masterpieces and progressed without a clear break into premieres of current experimental works as their rehearsal ended in lovemaking with them standing against the piano, seated on the stool or bench, or sprawled on the floor, sucking, stroking, pumping, Sofia giving vocal accompaniment, Dmitri occasionally reaching for the keyboard with a free hand to counterpoint her sensations or to caress her further with improvisations from all the masters. Every consummation was a further challenge, every scale ascended was another promised.

They napped before dinner and then, well rested, they had a very light dinner in a fine restaurant where their flirtation would be kept under control so that they reached the height of their sensuality at the moment when they walked on stage for their performance. There were *arias* in which Dmitri was convinced he could bring her with his piano, passages in which he suspected some improvisations would insure her climax, while others would compel her frustration. In these passages Sofia's face would turn as red as it did in making love, almost as red as when he played her with his tongue. He chose never to confirm his suspicions, because Sofia in sexual frustration would wreck the remainder of her performance and she would hate him for the public disgrace.

After their first performance together, Sofia never again showed the nervousness she showed that day before they went on stage. When Dmitri realized that fact one afternoon a month or so later while Sofia slept on the bed beside him, he finally realized at once that her nervousness was for him, that he would fail in public as he hadn't failed in private. The test in the

Italian restaurant hadn't been rigorous enough to be sure of his composure. But once she knew he didn't shy before an audience that first night, she never doubted him again, and thereafter the day before a performance in the evening was always one of her lightest, happiest days. The afternoon before a performance she would indulge him in any whim and would love him for it. All her caprices of invective were reserved for other days, and he grew to love performing the more because it made her so delightful in anticipation.

To balance the beauty of the performing days, the other days were often sultry, occasionally acrimonious. Their ill humors seldom lasted more than an hour. They could often be broken by sexual assault, at other times merely by musical invention. If it was Sofia who sulked, Dmitri would read a new score, and then he would turn to the piano and begin to play as though he were practicing for himself alone. He'd make an error or miss the tempo or he'd simply lack sufficient animation, and at that point Sofia would correct him by Ahhhh-ing through the passage until he had it right, and then they would be rehearsing it again and again. When she altered the flow, he moved with her. When they worked on the *aria* ten times and then in the eleventh she improvised by lengthening a trill or inserting an extra scale, he was startled at the beauty, the impact on the whole of the slight change in the part, and in that moment of new found beauty he would know the rancor was past.

Soon Sofia would open to him and tell him things he'd never expect to hear from anyone. Once, speaking of the fragility of things, she said, "I will not tell you how old I am, *Dmitriano*. But I might be double your age."

Dmitri suspected she might be more than triple his real age, if only they knew. She'd been through a long career on the opera stage before doing occasional concert tours. She was surely older than his mother, older than *Mademoiselle* Meursault, much older than his beautiful aunt in Kiev from when he sat beside her at her piano a decade ago. She did not have the grace of *Mademoiselle* Meursault or of his aunt, but she had the energy of his mother and she was more explosive than all the other women together. She didn't merely challenge him in his piano playing, she challenged him in his core, she wrenched parts of him into view that had never been seen before, parts he'd never have known face to face without her. She was grand and petty, loving and dismissive, generous and mean. Most of the time she was grand, loving, and generous, so that the low moments gave contrast to heighten the good moments. Among the greatest lessons she taught him was that anger and hurt were not terminal states, he didn't have to walk out on every old Pole who rebuked him for his urges, never to return.

But Dmitri couldn't equal Sofia's gift for quickly living past the bad moments.

Sofia said, "You are not old enough yet, *caro mio*."

"No, I am not Italian enough."

She laughed. "Maybe it's better not to be Italian, *Dmitriano*. You don't get angry as much."

"Italians have more chances to learn to get over their anger."

"Even if the anger is always just, as mine is with you, *carino*."

Dmitri caught her grin. He would've flipped her the backside of his hand, but he was certainly not Italian enough to do that without feeling false.

Alas, if he didn't get annoyed as often as Sofia did, his *piques* lasted longer. It took more both to irritate him and to soothe him once irritated. They were rehearsing on a Monday morning in San Francisco and Dmitri's tempo was lagging.

"*Stupido caro*, Ah-ah-ah-ah-ah-ah-ah-ah," Sofia ascended an octave at high speed. "Do it like that."

But her "stupid dear" annoyed him, and he ascended slower, not faster.

Sofia roared at him. "Sometimes you are adolescent, *Dmitriano*. I should not sleep with you like a lover – I should scold you like a mother." She reached over and swatted the back of his head as Italian mothers swat their miscreant children. She raised her arms, "*Ahi!*," then let them fall to slap her hips, her many-layered robe jerking, floating to accent the whole gesture. She walked away to the telephone and ordered coffee and pastry. In apparent answer to a question she yelled into the phone, "For two, for one, I don't care," and then she slammed it down. "If you are lucky, *Dmitrino*, there will be two cups."

Dmitrino the diminutive was lucky, and they sat for an hour drinking coffee, Sofia doing most of the talking. The more she talked, the warmer she became, and in an hour she was caressing him. As the months had passed and one tour was followed by another, they'd become a small world unto them-selves – *il mondo piccolo di due*, Sofia called them. As she caressed him now, "*Mondo piccolo*," she said. "The city changes, the audience changes, *Dmitriano*, we are constant."

An hour before, she'd been angry. "We change too."

"You mean I'm capricious, *è vero?*" she shot back. "*La vera italiana capri-ciosa*." She flipped the back of her hand.

He did not answer.

"You would be better if you changed too, *Dmitriano*. It's boring to stay the same all the time. Or perhaps you wish to remain an accompanist."

When she said *my* accompanist, it sounded like a declaration of love, but when she said *an* accompanist, it was a derogation of his character.

Sofia waited a minute or two for him to answer. When he did not, she gave him her vilest gesture, a mock spit with the tip of her tongue between her lips before the minute explosion of air. "Nothing. A kumquat who plays piano." She took off her slippers and threw them at his piano, then she stood and turned her back to him. "Open me," she said.

He unbuttoned the top of her robe, and she let it fall as she walked away, stopping at the bedroom door to pick it up by bending over to show him the wide expanse of her buttocks. The last was a gesture which Dmitri often found funny, and it usually led him into bed behind her, but now it left him sitting. In a few minutes he heard the bath running. While she bathed, Sofia commonly mocked baritone and tenor parts, singing them an octave or more higher than they were intended. Now she sang *Figaro*, only the male parts, Figaro's most joyously. She sang, "*Se vuol ballare.*" Dmitri knew the opera only from Sofia's singing and her telling him the background for her *arias*. He knew that the Count was after Figaro's Susanna and he supposed Figaro must sing *Se vuol ballare* behind the count's back: If you want to dance, my dear little Count, I'll play the guitar. Sofia was singing the role of a servant, challenging her employer, the role of an accompanist, reversing her role with Dmitri. She sang her *aria* with a taunt to rival any servant's.

Dmitri sat at the piano trying to distract himself by thinking out a complex fugue on a Verdi theme. He'd worked it out and was ready to play it when Sofia walked past him to pick up the telephone to the hotel desk. She was fully dressed as Dmitri seldom saw her during daylight except when they were traveling. "This is Miss Milano," she half sang into the telephone. "I will be down in a minute. Please have a taxi for me." She left without speaking to Dmitri, merely swirling the bottom of her coat at him as she put it around her. She walked out singing, "*Fi-ga-ro, Figaro, Fi-i-garo . . . Figaro coglione.*"

In contemplating what she'd done, Dmitri slowly realized he'd lost the fugue in his head. Eventually he was bothered more by that odd failing than by Sofia's *pique*. Over the next half hour he reconstructed the fugue and then for nearly two hours he played it before he finally broke off for lunch.

When Sofia returned, she brought several cartons of her new purchases, including a coat for Dmitri and one for herself. Though Dmitri was not yet entirely friendly, she made him try on his coat and walk around to show it off for her.

"The next time I get mad at you, I will buy you a scarf and gloves to match the coat." She smiled at him but he was not responsive. "And the next time, maybe a hat. Or would a mask be better?"

She went into the bedroom to put away her other purchases and in a few minutes she asked Dmitri to bring her the new coats. When he came in, she was lying nude in the middle of the bed. She might have been a model to Rubens in his earlier, somewhat leaner years, though the pinkness of her flesh was tinged with olive, the narrowness of her waist came as a surprise between the full hips and the large breasts rolling off the sides of her chest, and the whole was overlaid at the moment with Mondrianesque stripes where the elastic bands of her underwear had left their marks. On her broad underbelly lay a generous slice of a Russian coffee cake which Sofia knew Dmitri especially liked.

"San Francisco is like New York," she said, waving her hand as though to point out the body on display lest he miss seeing it, "there are Russian bakeries, *Dmitrovo* – maybe its sweetness will infect you."

"Do you think it's enough?"

"Maybe I should have bought the whole cake. And maybe a jar of honey? You can begin with this."

Dmitri sat beside her and ate the cake. She refused his offer of a bite.

When he finished, she said, "You have left crumbs on my belly."

He leaned over her to lick away the crumbs, ending by licking out the long stripe which crossed her belly from hip to hip beneath her navel. Sofia grasped his head to keep it against her belly and to push it gently lower. From being merely compliant, he now became actively involved. She Ahhh-ed with the movement of his tongue, ascending in scale as the rubbing neared her to climax, descending as his tongue faltered, ascending again, then ending at last in a long drawn out descending Ohhhhhhhhh. They spent a long late afternoon and evening in bed before taking a taxi to a Russian restaurant for dinner.

"You call them *pelmeny*, I call them *ravioli*," Sofia said as they ate.

"They're different."

"Not really, *caro*."

"You should never argue with a Russian."

"Yes, I have noticed. But if I do, I can get some coffee cake again."

"It would be too obvious the next time."

She smiled at him while noisily chewing another of her *pelmeny*. "*Dmitriano* is becoming sly. So I see – it's not true that you never change, Dmitri. But sometimes you *are* adolescent. *E brutto*. Every man is an adolescent with women until he makes love." She lifted her wine glass to him. "But he always stays a little bit adolescent with the first one. I am your first." She checked the wine bottle to see that there was no more. "I have made love to twenty men? Thirty? So I am not adolescent, I am capricious. That might sound no better to you, *caro*, but it's easier to live with."

Desserts were served and Sofia passed hers to Dmitri, who ate both. "You still *eat* like an adolescent, *Dmitriano*. If I ate like you, I would be a soprano Zeppelin."

"With a kumquat pianist."

As they left the restaurant, she said, "I was lucky – my first time was an older man. Someday you will know you were lucky too to start with an older woman. I hope you will have kind thoughts of *La Signorina* then, *carissimo*."

They rested in San Francisco for two weeks and Schein joined them for a few days to work out programs for future performances he'd scheduled for them. With each program, Dmitri suggested they try something they hadn't done before.

When all was settled and Schein was gone, Sofia said, "Braid my hair, *Dmitriano*. I will kiss you for it." While they were between tours she often chose to wear her hair in a single, fat braid in order not to be bothered with it for a few days. "It's the only thing I learned in Austria," she said when she did it in New York after their first tour. Dmitri took over from her, undoing what she'd done in order to do it better. "You have talent, *Dmitriano*. Does your mother braid her hair?"

"Sometimes. In winter."

"But not this winter?"

"She can do it herself."

Now in San Francisco Dmitri combed out Sofia's hair into three thick strands. She'd told him her hair was a brown blend of her mother's black southern Italian and her father's blond northern Italian hair, just as her manner was a blend of northern finesse and southern temper.

"We didn't schedule anything different," Dmitri said.

Sofia was exasperated. "How could we, *Dmitriano*? We've done everything there is by Puccini and Verdi, everything by Rossini, Donizetti, Bellini, even the little ones, Mascagni, Leoncavallo."

"There are others."

"Others!" She flipped the back of her hand at the others.

Dmitri contemplated his defeat for a long while in silence as he finished the braid. Then he went to the piano. "I know something of Verdi we haven't done," he said, somewhat spitefully. He played his Verdi fugue.

After long confusion, Sofia half-knew. "It's *Aida*. What have you done, Dmitri *caro*?"

In answer, Dmitri unpacked his fugue, playing first the few measures from *Aida* which comprised the basic theme and then slowly developing the theme into his fugue. At the end he said, "It's like braiding your hair."

"If I were not one but three, I would sing it," she said, "or *we* would sing it."

Later, as they lay in bed about to sleep, she said, "You are very smart, Dmitri." It was one of the few times she ever used his name without an Italian suffix or an adjective of endearment. "My music is not smart enough for you – someday you will insist on playing smarter music."

"Your music is beautiful."

"Beautiful, yes. It's not the same – I am beautiful, you are smart. Do you not know the difference, *piccolo mio*?"

Dmitri's silence was assent.

"*Caro*," she said.

"We could try Mozart," he suggested.

Sofia's silence was denial.

Dmitri recommended Mozart because she frequently mocked *Figaro* in her bath and because he now enjoyed playing Mozart when he had moments to himself with the piano. As a result of playing for Sofia, he found it impossible to play without improvisation; at last he'd returned to Mozart's keyboard music, his first love as a child when he played his aunt's piano in Kiev, because the effect of improvisation on Mozart was transcendent. Mozart assumed enough of a gift of creativity in his pianists to require them to add their individual originality to his. Pianists with knowledge of developments which followed Mozart could easily abuse their right to improvisation by importing romantic or other strains to wreck Mozart's coherence. But pianists who found their greatest freedom within the bounds of disciplined coherence could enjoy their liberties with Mozart while serving him well – Dmitri was with Mozart, as with Sofia, a good servant who enjoyed his liberties.

When Sofia returned to their hotel suite from one of her shopping expeditions in Chicago on a non-performance day of rest, she overheard Dmitri's Mozart. When she came in she asked why he stopped.

"You came in."

"You were playing Mozart. You do it well. Don't stop."

He resumed the sonata and, when he finished, Sofia began to sing in Latin. Dmitri knew it was Mozart, although he didn't know what, and he created the piece to accompany her.

"I have been using Mozart as a joke," Sofia said when they finished, "singing *Figaro*."

She called Beniamino and asked him to send them scores of Mozart's soprano *arias*. For two months thereafter, Sofia sang at least one *aria* from Mozart at every performance. It was many years since she'd done Mozart, she said, because it was played so badly by her accompanists and her orchestras. "They embellish too much. I should be the one to embellish. They try so hard to be pretty that they are weak."

Dmitri understood now, nearly a year after she'd said it, how truthfully she meant it when she said, "I will sound only as good as you sound, that is the tragedy of a soprano, Dmitri, it is not up to her . . ."

With Mozart on the program, their rehearsals became more energetic even while they found greater energy for bed and for walking the streets of their various cities. "You have great influence, *Dmitriano*. I have walked more with you than I walked in ten years. And I sing Mozart again."

Sofia took such great pleasure in Mozart with a pianist who left the embellishments to her that she began to tease Mozart the way she teased Dmitri, ending an occasional series of encores by mocking *Figaro* as she did in her bath, adding and deleting lines to make the story more obviously *risqué*, at least to those who understood the Italian. She left audiences in Boston and Washington laughing too hard to yell their final *bravos* before she and Dmitri escaped. Audiences in New York, forewarned, stomped their feet in unison to a chant of *Fi-ga-ro-Fi-ga-ro* to let her know what encore they wanted. While singing an encore *aria* intended for Figaro himself, Sofia danced around Dmitri, gesticulating at him, swatting the back of his head, and finally hugging him to sing almost into his ear at no little peril to his eardrum.

At her best with Mozart, Sofia took off or put on years to fit her role of the moment, she flirted or schemed, she was joyous or angry, spontaneous or determined. Sometimes Dmitri almost started at his piano to see her transformation. He fell in love with her in a dozen guises, which all evaporated at the final notes. Mozart's Austria was somewhere between Sofia's Italy and Dmitri's Russia and it seemed to be the ideal meeting ground for them. But their meeting there was always temporary, it was at more than arm's length, and at its most intense it was always before an audience. Dmitri would be moved to love by Donna Anna, Zerlina, Fiordiligi, or Susanna – and then she was gone. Sofia could do them all because she was herself so various in character and mood. But she could sustain none of them.

"I cannot even – what was your word, *piccolino caro?* – I cannot even sustain myself," she said.

She lay on her back and he sat on the bed beside her after a performance. He was struck by the incongruity of a woman who was surely fifty portraying a naive, exuberant peasant girl. And especially *this* woman. Sofia was too grand in her excesses, too knowing in her experiences – it was not possible and yet she'd brought Dmitri to infatuation with her *naiveté* and youthful exuberance on the stage that evening.

"Zerlina," he said with a smile and a shake of his head.

"You cannot believe that," Sofia answered as she reached up to pull his head down to bury his face between her breasts. In that moment, Dmitri no longer believed it.

As the performances multiplied, Dmitri's infatuations fell off, he could not fall for every Zerlina or Fiordiligi who was destined to evaporate before his eyes. Mozart didn't live long enough to sustain Dmitri's urge for novelty. Dmitri sensed his former boredom returning – they needed something new. He was saved temporarily by the end of the tour and a break in New York during which he could play his music. The available range for him was so much vaster than for a soprano that he never risked the sense of unending repetition while he played solo piano works. When they began a new tour the programs soon ran thin for Dmitri: Puccini, Bellini, Verdi, Mozart, Puccini. At the end of a month they were in New Orleans waiting to perform two days hence. After rehearsing a Mozart *aria* they argued, not violently, over programming, and they went to bed to try, to no avail, to change the mood.

"The trouble with Mozart," Sofia said, "do you know, Dmitri? He seems to be too easy, it is possible to learn the technique and to miss the music, as lovers do. You have all the technique and still you find the music, when you play Mozart."

Dmitri was instantly angry. "It takes two to find the music in bed."

The frequent resolution of such moments was for Sofia to leave the hotel to go shopping by herself and for Dmitri to play music which was composed for the keyboard rather than for small orchestra and voice. This time, as he occasionally did, Dmitri left the hotel. He planned at first to go for a long walk through the French Quarter and along the river, and because she taunted him with her depreciative *"Amantonzolo mio, vuoi essere ridicolo?"* – Botched lover, do you want to be ridiculous? – he expected to be gone a long while.

Before he reached the river a beautiful tall woman beckoned to him from a wrought iron archway. He approached her wondering what she wanted, but in a moment he understood. He fumbled in his pockets to see whether he had money, as anyone wearing such a suit must have. He was not paid much for his accompaniment, five dollars a performance two or three times a week plus all his expenses on the tour and all his clothes, clothes which made him look well paid. At first he'd given the matter no thought, but now he figured out that he should be paid more. It didn't matter except that it was a point of pride to be paid better. He'd sent home a couple of hundred dollars even at five dollars a performance. At the moment, however, all that mattered was that he had money in his pocket. He accepted the whore's entreaties, and for two hours he tried to have technique so fine as to be self-obliterating, as *Mademoiselle* Meursault said was needed for Debussy, so that all that would be detected was the sensuality of his lovemaking. At the end of his two hours, when he put down his money and left, he knew it had been too deliberate to transcend method, but at least he'd had a woman other than Sofia to whom he could compare *La Signorina* so that he might now be more nearly her equal in bed.

As he walked back to the hotel, clothed again in his elegant suit and tie, he suddenly laughed. Her last words to him before he left the hotel were to ask whether he wanted to be ridiculous. If he'd answered, he'd have said No. But now he was. He paused to look at a wrought iron balcony, only to realize as he stared that there was another whore behind the window beckoning down to him. He smiled at her and shook his head. I'm too ridiculous, he thought. He'd never before in all his life noticed a whore, yet today in his present mood he saw them everywhere.

Friday evening they were to perform, and Friday afternoon they rehearsed their way into making love on the couch after three days of austerity. Later, before she drifted off to sleep for her nap, Sofia said, "You are getting better, *Dmitriano*. Did I not notice before? Or did my rebuke help?"

"The answer might be both."

"Or neither?"

"Or neither."

"I hate Russian logic, *caro*."

Saturday morning, Beniamino brought a newspaper clipping to Sofia, as he did whenever the critics were kind to her, as they usually were. In reading the reviews of their performances over the past many months, Dmitri had learned that the critics who wished to praise Sofia very highly nevertheless had to look for a flaw in the evening in order to show their balance and to prove their credibility. Occasionally he was cited as the flaw. The first time, he was chagrined to read how badly he'd done. But after a day's pensive reconsideration of the evening he realized the things the critic accused him of were the things he did to the music to emphasize those aspects of Sofia's treatment of it which the critic praised so highly. It occurred to Dmitri that the critic was both right and wrong – right in what he noticed, wrong in how he interpreted it. Dmitri was impressed with both facts and he wouldn't forget them. Thereafter, he would dismiss as ignorant those critics who were not right in at least the first sense of noticing the right things. Better critics were at least puzzled by the odd things they noticed. The best critics took their greatest pleasure in just those things which made Dmitri's performance Dmitri Esterhaats's.

The critic of the *Times-Picayune* said their performance of Friday night was exceptional – Sofia Milano's visit was one of the high points of a relatively good season, and she'd at last found an accompanist who suited her. The flaw was that, although the critic had heard her sing Wagner in her younger years when she needed to have something to distinguish her from other Italian sopranos, she no longer chose to sing Wagner. Therefore she diminished her own achievement by shying from greater demands. She was one of the few sopranos alive with the ability to rank as one of the best *bel canto* sopranos and simultaneously one of the best Wagnerian heroines. From a few of the critic's technical and interpretive remarks, Dmitri was convinced he was intelligent and worth listening to.

Dmitri asked Sofia why she chose not to sing Wagner.

"Wagner," she answered. "Oh . . . I am too tired for Wagner. Do you know Wagner, Dmitri *caro*?"

He did not know Wagner.

"Let me think awhile and I will show you," she said.

Sofia stood and walked about the room holding her left hand hard against her temple as she looked at the floor where her feet paced. Soon her right hand began to dance in the air, her left hand relaxed away from her temple, and she began to hum and murmur German words alternately.

"In Italy," she said, "Wagner is sung in Italian. In America he must be sung in German. I learned all the German, I speak German better than English, but when I came here, they did not want me for Wagner. For Wagner they chose Germans and Americans. To sing Wagner I had to go to Austria or Switzerland. It was a joke. Listen."

She sang from *Lohengrin*, and Dmitri jumped to the piano to play with her. In Dmitri's scale of values, with his voracious demand for novelty, the *aria* gained almost as much from his never having heard it before as it did from its intrinsic beauty. He demanded more Wagner, they sent a telegram to Schein to get scores for them, and they spent the day with novelty, Dmitri trying to create the notes at the piano from Sofia's singing. The sole fortune of the familiarity of their programs for that night and Sunday afternoon was that they needed no further rehearsals, so they were freed to play with Wagner.

A week later Sofia began to sing Wagner for encores. The performances were flawed, they were not as adept as they would become, but they were alive with the spontaneity of discovery. Beniamino arranged to have more scores of Wagner's soprano *arias* waiting for them when they arrived in St. Louis, and the four days and nights of rest before their three performances in St. Louis and vicinity were as beautiful and erotic as their first days of lovemaking and performance because together they were recreating Sofia Milano's Wagner. Wagner never earned more than one number in any performance, but he moved up from encore to central billing just before intermission or just after return from intermission. There was more of Wagner than of Mozart, enough to sustain spontaneity for several months.

"Do you love Elsa as much as you loved Zerlina, *Dimitriano?*"

Dmitri laughed. "Only a Wagner hero could love Elsa."

"You are wrong. Not even Lohengrin loved her. You don't understand Wagner. We will have to go to one of his operas. When we don't have anything to do the whole next day. We will need that day to recover."

When eventually they began to bicker over programming again, Dmitri sought another composer and found Richard Strauss. Sofia was too young when she sang in German to sing the Countess on stage. Therefore she now assented to Strauss. Strauss demanded the hardest work they'd ever enjoyed together, although this time the greater burden was Sofia's because she was more distant from this music than Dmitri was.

"This is smart music for opera, *Dmitriano,*" she said when she had difficulty. "I made you work too hard at the beginning, now you get revenge. Is it sweet, *carino?*"

Strauss took them around the country once before they ran out of him back on the east coast. In Boston, Dmitri suggested Sofia turn to songs, to *Lieder*. In New York he hunted for scores. He started first to go to Horace Gmund's shop, but then he didn't wish to get involved in the discussion which would ensue. He went elsewhere and searched through scores of *Lieder* and song cycles. Those which seemed to pose the greatest challenge were by Mahler. While she was shopping, Dmitri studied his Mahler and, when she returned, he sat down without announcement and played for her.

She was graceful enough to await the finale before she spoke. "What is that?"

In his enthusiasm, Dmitri didn't take sufficient note of her scornful tone. "The Boy's Magic Horn."

"Mahler?"

"Yes, Sofia *carissima*."

"Gustav Mahler."

Dmitri began to sense it was wrong from the way Sofia used "Gustav" as a curse of "Mahler."

Their New York performances were not well received, one of the critics went so far as to say Sofia's accompaniment was a trifle better than she was. The timing was bad. In New York, Sofia's concerts were to be recorded. For the record, she scheduled her standard repertoire – no Strauss or Wagner or even Mozart. It was the great Italians. Dmitri assented to the recording because he was paid an extra fifty dollars as royalties in advance to assign the earnings from the records to Sofia. He might still have objected to the whole enterprise, which he found intrusive and ugly, but he overheard Sofia insisting to Beniamino Schein that Dmitri should play for her, he was the best she'd ever had at following her where she chose to go. But when the concert came, Dmitri was refusing to follow where she chose to stay.

Afterwards, Sofia was anxious to know how long it would be before she could hear the records. Dmitri wasn't sure he even wanted to hear them. He'd heard Sofia from a distance of two or three paces for more than a hundred performances and countless rehearsals. If the record sounded as bad as the first Liszt he'd ever heard, he wanted no part of it. At least with the Liszt there was the beauty of discovering something new. There was nothing new to be discovered in Sofia's record. Worse than that, there was only a relatively bad performance, far from the best Sofia regularly did. Dmitri was embarrassed that he'd helped to make the recording a worse one than they could've done. He didn't need the further embarrassment of having to listen to the recording.

Monday afternoon in Philadelphia, after talking about the recording without getting any apparent interest from Dmitri, Sofia asked, "You did not visit your mother in New York, did you, Dmitri?"

Dmitri didn't answer, but for Sofia that was enough to tell her the truth.

"I thought you went to see her. But you went to buy those silly songs.

One of those songs, do you understand the words? It is about a mother who is afraid she will lose her son."

"No," Dmitri said, "*he's* afraid."

"It's not so different."

When Dmitri recommended they try one of the songs, they quarreled. Somehow, Dmitri's failure to visit his mother became entangled for him in this quarrel over singing Mahler. He became too morose for the quick tease to bring him around and he doted on the possibility that all the great composers had failed him, they'd produced nothing more for him and Sofia to do together.

Sofia became exasperated. "Great Mother Russia has caught you again, Dmitri, she won't even let you laugh. Smile, Dmitri *caro*, smile."

Dmitri did not smile.

Friday as they rehearsed for the evening's concert, the first of the week, Sofia's limited patience ran out. "You play badly, Dmitri," she yelled in the middle of an *aria*. "You have your petty little mind on Mahler when you should be thinking only of Puccini. *Sei stupido, caro? Sei un piccolo stupido? Non faciamo* Mahler, *non mai, Dmitriano, faciamo Puccini, il grande Puccini, capisce?*"

His understanding of Sofia's Italian was now virtually perfect. He could put many of her phrases to Puccini or Verdi. If he heard this with music, it would be with horns and a hundred screeching violins, it would not be possible to accompany it on the piano. She was calling him stupid, a stupid little one, she was telling him they would never do Mahler, they were doing the grand Puccini, did he understand that?

Their rehearsal didn't end in lovemaking. For more than a week they'd argued about Mahler, but Mahler was not the point, the point was to find something new, something that challenged. When Sofia went to bed for her nap, Dmitri lay on the couch, where he only half dozed. After her bath, Sofia came to him and caressed him, asking him to forgive her fury of the afternoon, kissing him, stroking him, hugging him with a strength sufficient to suffocate him. Over dinner with Beniamino she tried to tease him. "Beniamino, do you know what *Dmitriano* wants? He wants me to sing Mahler. Mahler. Can you imagine Sofia Milano singing Mahler? I am from Milano, where is *La Scala*. *La Scala* is the scale, the staircase. That's how I sing – up the stairs, fast, Ah-ah-ah-ah-ah-ah-ah-ah! I don't moan like Mahler, Uhhhhhhhhh-ummmmmmm."

Dmitri could not be soothed by teasing unless he was at fault, if at his most honest perception of things he thought he was clearly in the right, he found her teases insulting. "We have taken Strauss into the twentieth century and then we have turned back. There is nothing more to be provoked from Mozart or Puccini. We are stale, we are *pain perdu*, we should be turned into something new and better. But we refuse."

"*Dmitriano* wants to be dipped in egg and fried, Beniamino. And he does not know history. Even I knew *il grande* Puccini. Puccini was writing after Mahler was dead. I did not meet Mahler, I don't regret that."

The syndrome of the quarrel had taken over now. Their retorts would escalate to Sofia's ultimate torment. After several more exchanges over the soothing voice of Beniamino, she finally said it. "You are nothing but accompaniment, Mister Esterhaats. You are not paid to choose the program, you are paid to play what I choose. It is me they pay to hear, not you and your silly Mahler."

"I don't care about Mahler or Puccini or Mozart. I care about playing the piano."

When their meaner quarrels ended the night before a performance, he had time to overcome his anger, but tonight barely an hour remained before curtain time. They fell silent. When Beniamino tried to cajole them into harmony, Sofia shut him up with a flip of the back of her hand and a curt "*Ahi!*"

They took a taxi the short distance to the Academy of Music, the three of them – pair-wise – avoiding eye contact. Once in position on stage, Dmitri and Sofia managed their initial necessary communication still without eye contact, as if by intermediary. In the first *aria* they both performed near their peaks in a mutual challenge standardized in numerous angry rehearsal sessions. During the second *aria*, Dmitri played beyond Sofia, improvising independently of her, more coherently than she would, therefore making it seem as though she'd misremembered three bars. It had happened before when he'd become so involved in the sounds of his piano that he'd stopped being attentive to her voice, that was the cost of doing nothing new to sustain interest. But this time it was becoming deliberate. If she wouldn't accept the challenge of new music, he would challenge her with the old.

During the intermission, he remained on stage behind the curtain while Sofia went to her dressing room. His thoughts lingered on her words, "You are nothing but accompaniment." He was not hearing the intended insult, which could have been delivered with other words, he was hearing only the exact words themselves. He *was* nothing but accompaniment.

Sofia began the second half of the concert with an *aria* from Mozart, the Mozart whom he'd got her to sing again and whom she'd taught Dmitri to love again through improvisation and the wonder of her voice. Dmitri now teased her, irritated her, mocked her, he improvised in little ways to break her concentration, a bar or two, a chord at a time. She'd become dependent on his piano, when they'd first worked together he couldn't have misled her because she would've ignored his music and depended on hers, but now she'd come so heavily to depend on the rightness of his sense for her and for her *arias* that she faltered with his manipulations as he played here and there a bit faster or slower, ascending two notes too high very quickly only to descend two notes too low very slowly. Only then did she glare at him as though at last she'd caught on – it was their first direct communication since the restaurant. But even if she understood, she was now helpless and, knowing that, she deteriorated through several numbers. For her final *aria* she'd scheduled her triumph, she would sing *Aida* because it pleased her most to read critics who said Sofia Milano was the greatest Aida of the day. Because critics and audiences in Philadelphia tended to be her most favorable, she gave them her best achievements. As it happened, of all Sofia's *bel canto* composers, Verdi was Dmitri's favorite because, like Mozart, he permitted improvisation, indeed penalized method, in his subordination of musical line to character.

While Sofia sang her *Aida*, Dmitri recreated his Verdi. The audience became uneasy as pain began to color Sofia's voice. Dmitri could hear the raspy buzz of occasional whispers – he didn't need to discern the words to guess the sentiments: "She's getting old." And when Dmitri overreached her in ascending a scale, he didn't have to look up at her face to know tears were cutting through the powder on her cheeks. But he did look up and she glanced at him to plead her hurt, to beg his sympathy. His glance in return was not his usual smile, nor was it sympathy. Her voice began to crack and his volume rose, and in the finale he demolished her.

There was no encore, there was not even a call for an encore. A few dispirited *bravos*, lethargic applause, people exiting to beat the rush even before the curtain touched down, a single curtain call, a perfunctory rise in the volume of applause, then silence but for the shuffling of feet.

Sofia cried through the night, sleeping briefly in the early morning, then waking to cry through the day. Once or twice she momentarily held Dmitri tightly to her, but mostly she faced away from him. Never once did she look into his eyes, never once did either of them speak. Dmitri ordered breakfast up for her and he went down to eat in the dining room. He found the morning paper and read the *Bulletin's* critique of Sofia's "unexpectedly weak voice" and her "remarkable young pianist who provoked the best from Miss Milano." By lunchtime the *impresario* had clearly failed to come around with his usual cheerful report on the critical reception of Sofia's performance. He finally came in the evening, but Sofia, still crying in bed, wouldn't speak with him, and she didn't join them for dinner. It was only at the last minute that Beniamino realized that Sofia, who'd never failed before, would not perform tonight. It was then too late to prevent the hall from filling with patrons who'd come in from the Mainline or who'd come from dinner parties for the gala evening.

At curtain time the impresario announced that *La Signorina* Milano was ill, she'd had trouble with her throat the past week. Therefore, he wished to invite all patrons to consider staying to listen to a young pianist who was widely coming to be considered the finest young pianist in America – that was the way Dmitri was written up in all of Sofia's programs. When Dmitri blushed on first reading it, Schein apologized by saying, "Art is an exaggeration, Dmitri, don't take it personally." Dmitri knew the exaggeration came from hucksterism, not from art, but he let it pass. To soothe tonight's audience for *La Signorina*, Schein offered full refunds for anyone who wished even if they stayed to hear first. He then introduced Dmitri Esterhaats.

Dmitri had to play pieces he'd played recently enough to be sure he had them under control. It was not the concert he'd have played if he'd planned longer than an hour for it. In some respects, however, it was one of the best concerts he would play because he had little choice but to introduce life through spontaneity rather than through perfected, invisible method. It was also the last time he'd play before a full hall for many years, and therefore it was the most well-rounded ovation he'd receive for a decade. Although the audience was largely trapped, the ovation which they gave Dmitri at the end of the concert was genuine enough, and for his encore he had the right sense to play a passage from *Aida*, a piece this audience could be expected to appreciate, so that he shared his final applause with Verdi. By the time he began his Verdi encore he'd got over his anger at Sofia's insulting tease and he wished she might be standing there to sing with him, although he knew he'd played his choice of music without rehearsal better than he could've played hers after a week of preparation. While he played the final measures of Aida's *aria*, he thought of Sofia lying in their hotel room where she probably still cried. If Dmitri could've seen her in that moment, he would've apologized and made love to her. The vision of them together again was broken as the theme of the *finale*, without his having planned it, developed into his Verdi fugue, which Sofia declared herself too few to sing.

The success of Dmitri's solo performance was measured less by his applause than by the fact that few of the patrons chose to return their tickets for refunds afterwards. When Schein reported that to him, Dmitri said, "I should be paid more than five dollars."

"Okay, I agree with that. Twenty-five."

"Three hundred."

"Dmitri!"

"Three hundred."

"Fifty."

"Three hundred."

"Dmitri, you don't understand, you gotta bargain, that means you gotta give a little. If you come down, I'll come up. Otherwise we'll never meet."

"Two hundred and fifty."

"That's a bit grudging, don't you think? But, okay, it's a start. One hundred."

"Two-fifty."

"Dmitri! Christ, two."

"You have done well for two hundred, Beniamino." It was the first time Dmitri called him by first name.

"Why don't you call me Benjamin, or Ben. Beniamino is just for Italian *divas*. When Sofia says it, it's either a compliment, a request, a flirtation, or a curse. You don't mean any of those."

"I will call you Ben."

Ben took out a check book and wrote him a check. "For two hundred I don't guess I need to pay your transportation back to New York, do I?" He shook his head in sadness as he handed Dmitri the check. "I don't know what happened, and I wish it hadn't. You two were great together. You were the best Sofia ever had, no one else ever caught her sense so well. But hell, Dmitri, you've been at this too long and you're still younger than I want to say to anybody. It's better you went back to New York and worked alone so you can be challenged by the music. Go up to Juilliard or get a good teacher for a year or two. Maybe you'll come back and see me when you're ready to go out alone. What the hell, here, I've got a ticket to New York, I wasn't going on to Baltimore with you guys, but I don't need it yet, I should stay with Sofia a while. You can have it – one last trip on me."

Not wanting to stay overnight with Sofia again, Dmitri decided to take a late night train back. He packed while Sofia slept undisturbed by his presence and then he went down to wait in front of the hotel for a taxi. It had begun to snow and Dmitri walked out from under the hotel canopy to feel the snow falling against his face. His thoughts were jumbled. Last night he finally had become a *piccolo stupido*, yet tonight he'd had his greatest moment since Mrs. Wolfe's party. As on that occasion, the grand was tangled with the petty, and he couldn't separate them enough to enjoy the one or berate himself for the other. His cheeks flushed hot enough to melt the snow and he closed his eyes as though to stop the flow.

After a long while, a taxi rounded the corner and Dmitri was soon at the station, where he saw by the station clock that he had two minutes to get his train. To hurry that fast with Sofia would be impossible, but by himself it might be possible. Dragging his trunk with one hand and holding out Ben Schein's ticket in the other he barely made it aboard. As the train pulled out and his breathing slowed toward normal, Dmitri no longer had the necessity of trivia to distract his mind. He thought sadly of the day when Sofia would receive her recording, of the pain she might feel from recalling his bad part in her life, of her helplessness before the past that put him on the record with her. To stop his fall into despondency, he kept other thoughts away by working through his Verdi fugue anew, modifying it, playing it to himself over and over, occasionally fingering chords on his knee, hearing Sofia sing three parts in unison, bringing them together. She was so various in his mind there were more than enough of her to do it.

Colonel Weiss

Dmitri found an apartment off the Bowery and rented a grand. He found teachers who specialized in different composers and he used up a teacher every month or two. He found a teacher who called himself an anatomist of the piano who told Dmitri he was clumsy and inefficient in his use of his skeleton and muscles. He didn't care what Dmitri played but cared only how he used his body when he played it. The percussive playing of some of Dmitri's composers required exercise to strengthen his muscles, the lyrical playing of others required different, nearly contrary exercises. In a week the anatomist destroyed Dmitri's control over the keyboard, so that Dmitri, who occasionally got jobs as accompanist to singers, violinists, and cellists of modest renown, could no longer successfully audition, so that he even lost a trivial audition to play Schubert for a *Lieder* singer.

It took him half a year to regain his earlier mastery but then he'd gone beyond it. When he stopped thinking about bone position and muscle flexing, he knew he'd made them his natural response and he went on to another teacher who specialized in music rather than technique. He now played Arthur Schönberg, Sergei Prokofiev, and Béla Bartók, not least because they were difficult enough to make him work. When he learned Bartók had come to New York, he wished he would somehow accidentally meet him, maybe at an audition or at a performance. In his modesty he couldn't think Bartók might be pleased to have an admiring young pianist call on him, even a pianist with a partially Hungarian name. He tracked down rumors about Bartók among teachers and other musicians, and he occasionally went up to the Bronx to walk by Bartók's apartment building. He imagined himself seeing Bartók and being seen by him without either speaking but with recognition that they had sensibilities in common. When he heard a rumor that Bartók was ill, perhaps dying, he alternately found it impossible to play Bartók and impossible to play anything else. Dmitri found a teacher who was a Hungarian who spoke no English, with whom he communicated through the teacher's botched German and his Dutch.

But words were of little consequence to working together, the important thing was the teacher's access to Bartók manuscripts and his knowledge of how to play the master.

War had followed the emigres to America, but Dmitri was too old for the first rounds of the draft. Only after about a year of war, when all the younger men had been taken, was it finally Dmitri's turn. On his last day before induction in Brooklyn, he took the subway to Manhattan to say good-bye to his Hungarian teacher and maybe to play under his tutelage one last time. But when he reached the stop where he should leave the train, he sat still and continued on to the Bronx, to Bartók's apartment. He walked the streets around it for an hour before he turned south. He took a bus to the top of Manhattan and then he wandered for several hours, bearing generally south until he reached the Brooklyn Bridge at sunset. He watched the light through the cables until the sun was down and then he glanced back at Manhattan in its eerie darkness in the wartime blackout. The thought that he was now like Manhattan, facing wartime blackout of his piano, made him smile and laugh. Here where he'd often felt maudlin as a young teenager he now felt almost nothing. The world around him had taken on purpose for the time being, leaving him void and empty, without purpose.

At six the next morning Dmitri reported for service. After physicals and various shots the men were led into a large room where they were sworn in before a few of them were selected out to report to particular bases or to be rejected, leaving the others to be trucked to New Jersey. The sergeant called out, "Bauman," and Dmitri was surprised to see a familiar face, a pianist whom he'd met at the Schubert audition. The sergeant then stumbled over another name and it was a minute before Dmitri figured out that it was Esterhaats. He and Bauman were given railway passes and instructed to report immediately to a base in Alabama. They took the subway together to Penn Station.

"What do you suppose this is all about?" Bauman asked.

"A division of pianists to fight the Nazis?"

"The Nazis must be quaking. Somehow, though, I doubt we're going to see another piano before this thing's over."

Before they finished basic training, Dmitri was summoned along with Bauman and half a dozen other new arrivals to report for an audition before the base commander, Colonel Weiss, and his wife. Bauman and Esterhaats were selected and the others returned to basic training. Bauman and Esterhaats were made household servants in the home of Colonel Weiss. They reported to Private Rashevsky, who treated them with disdain bordering on hostility. They were given three hours to practice at the Colonel's grand piano every day. When, on the second day of their service, Dmitri heard the grand being played very well while he and Bauman were working in the kitchen, he understood. Rashevsky was a pianist too and they were in a contest for talent, a contest whose losers probably went to war.

"Is that the Colonel?" Bauman asked.

"Rashevsky."

"How many pianists does one house need?"

"It doesn't need three."

"That's why Rashevsky seems to hate us. Swine."

"He's no swine. He's okay."

"He's okay?"

"Sure. He just wants to play the piano. He's like us. Would you rather play the piano or go to war?"

"Play the piano or go to war?"

"Yes. We must be in a contest to see who gets chosen to play piano for the Colonel."

"So that bastard wants to beat us and you say he's okay? Esterhaats, you're crazy."

"Maybe soon you'll want to beat me. Will that make you not okay?"

"That would make me selfish and brutal. Is that okay?"

Dmitri shrugged. "It won't be your fault. Were you selfish and brutal when we auditioned together and you were chosen to play Schubert for that *Lieder* singer?"

"Esterhaats, that was a contest we could both win and no one was sent to war for losing. I won that audition and you won the other one we were in. That was a reasonable world."

"Not everyone won. Hundreds lost forever. How many didn't even qualify to get into this kitchen?"

While he was cleaning the large living room, Dmitri looked through the music scores to discover what was the Colonel's and his wife's predilection. He discerned no pattern. When it was his turn to practice in the afternoon he noticed the sonata Rashevsky had been playing earlier. Evidently Rashevsky needed the score in order to play it, even though it was Beethoven and his style with the piece sounded familiar and tutored. But this must be the music the Colonel wished to hear. Dmitri didn't need the score, but he idly picked it up. He noticed that it was badly worn, in the margins there were pencil marks which were smeared from long ago. On the last page, in a small hand, was delicately printed Timothy Weiss, 1899, New York. Colonel

Weiss must have been a school boy in 1899. It was not Beethoven he wanted to hear now as a mature commander of a wartime training base in a corner of Alabama.

Dmitri went through a nearby stack of scores to find the ones which showed least wear. There were several new scores printed in the past few years, Ravel, Debussy, Prokofiev, Shostakovich. Near the bottom of the pile were several pieces by Bartók. Dmitri removed the *Sonata*. Because a corner of a pair of its pages had been turned inward at the moment of cutting the pages, the score had come from the printer with its middle section unopenable, and it had remained unopened since. As with all the scores, it was marked Timothy Weiss and dated. Under the date, 1935, was written London. Sometime between 1899 and 1935 Timothy Weiss ceased to be a player of music and became a collector. From rummaging through his scores, Dmitri suspected the Colonel knew very well what he was collecting. There were no duplications but some composers, especially Beethoven and Debussy, were complete so far as Dmitri knew them. The Bartók *Sonata* was probably only one of many of his collected scores which the Colonel had never heard. Dmitri played the *Sonata*.

At the end of the following week, Esterhaats and Bauman were told they would be asked to play as background to small dinner parties which the Colonel was giving, Bauman on Friday, Esterhaats on Saturday. At the time when he was studying with the anatomist of the piano, when Dmitri desperately needed money, Bauman won an audition by playing Schubert *Lieder* far better than Dmitri could with his confused, anti-lyrical muscles of the time. On Friday night, Bauman played his lyrical Schubert with Schumann and Chopin as fillers. Dmitri waited table.

Throughout the meal there was constant conversation. The officers argued over the course of the war, over Roosevelt's leadership, over General Marshall's military judgment, over the true extent of the success of the German army in Russia. Deference to rank turned all conversation toward the colonel, whose attentions never faltered.

"I love that piece," a major said over after-dinner brandy, "what is it?"

Colonel Weiss turned to Dmitri, "Can you tell us what that is, Private?"

Dmitri had no doubt the Colonel knew. The colonel should've had no doubt Dmitri knew. "Chopin, Sir, *Sonata in B flat minor*."

"There it is," the colonel said to the major, who seemed to accept his claim only after it was seconded by the colonel.

Dmitri didn't have to check the scores to know that all of Bauman's selections were from scores in Colonel Weiss's collection which showed greatest use. Dmitri wished only to perform for himself, he didn't want to be in competition with Bauman or Rashevsky, both of whom he liked. Still, he couldn't discipline himself to play for himself, to play only Bartók or Prokofiev as he would do if free to choose his own program without consequences. In competition he had to pursue variety to display the fullness of his talent. Mrs. Weiss asked him what his program was to be. Without thinking, he immediately said he would open with Schubert's *Sonata #17*, which had been the centerpiece of Bauman's performance, and would follow with Ravel and Debussy before concluding with Bartók's *Sonata*. Mrs. Weiss's eyes widened.

"I wish you well, Esterhaats. You have courage. To choose such a program . . ."

"Courage?"

"The colonel will be very interested in most of your program. He may judge you harshly unless . . ." She interrupted herself. "I wish you well. I'll tell him what you'll be playing."

Dmitri hadn't actually made a final decision, but now it was made anyway. In a minute he was embarrassed to realize he'd probably included the Schubert because Bauman bested him in the Schubert audition, not because it was something he himself wanted to play, but because he wanted to show he could do it at least as well as Bauman, for whom Schubert was the crowning achievement. He didn't wish to be competing with Bauman in the colonel's odd game, but he couldn't suppress his competitive response to his earlier encounter.

As he performed that evening, Dmitri was less bothered by the background conversation than he'd thought he'd be. He remembered when his aunt had taken him to a *café* in which there was a string quartet playing. He'd been astounded that the other people in the *café* actually talked and ate while such music was filling the air. "Beauty is in the eye of the beholder," his aunt said afterwards.

Dmitri shook his head. "No. That music was beautiful."

By now he was willing to grant that maybe things were not beautiful independently of the sensibilities of beholders, but he still had difficulty with noisy beholders. As he began the Bartók sonata at the end of dinner, although he was unable to see the guests seated at the table behind him, he realized they were not talking, the room was silent but for Bartók. From the scraping of chairs and clearing of throats a few minutes later, Dmitri suspected the guests didn't enjoy the percussive treatment of the piano and the lack of lyric sections to rest their lazy ears. But it wasn't their tastes which interested him, it was the colonel's tastes as implied by the lack of conversation. Clearly the colonel didn't want extraneous noise to distract from his hearing Bartók.

Without noticing the absurdity of the notion, Dmitri supposed that the abject silence was a demand for an encore. At the end of the sonata, Dmitri improvised a few bars of Bach to maintain his control over the sounds in the room while nevertheless allowing his listeners to relax briefly. When he thought enough time had passed, he drew himself up demonstratively, as Sofia had taught him to do, to show that he was about to begin anew despite his own momentary silence. He played something for which the colonel did not seem to have the score, something he himself had learned from the notes of his Hungarian teacher over the past few months. He chose several pieces from the massive *Mikrokosmos*, displaying his ease with bitonality, tone clusters, and chords built in fourths, all striving toward strenuous lyricism. As a manipulatively gracious afterthought of the kind he'd often proposed to Sofia for her encores, he ended with one of the *Dances in Bulgarian Rhythm* from the end of the *Mikrokosmos* to soothe the hurt in the ears of the colonel's guests.

As he ended, there was applause from many hands and a single *bravo* from the colonel. Dmitri stood, turned toward the table, saluted, saying "Colonel Weiss," bowed almost imperceptibly, and walked out to the kitchen. All but the bow were according to instructions given by Mrs. Weiss.

Bauman shook his hand. "Not my cup of tea, Esterhaats, but you made it sound as good as anyone could."

Dmitri blushed slightly at the continuing embarrassment of his playing the Schubert sonata. "You must like Debussy and Schubert."

"You made Schubert race a bit for my taste, but your technique has really improved since we auditioned. I was surprised you chose that. That took a lot of nerve."

Dmitri winced at the double *entendre*, wondering whether it was intended.

On Monday morning, after returning from weekend leave, Rashevsky left the colonel's household, and Dmitri feared Bauman wouldn't be long in leaving.

"My dear Esterhaats," Mrs. Weiss said as she took his hand in hers, "you were very good. It didn't take as much courage as I thought. Just talent. I hope you'll be glad to stay in our house for a long while."

"Is Bauman leaving too?"

"I . . . I don't know. That isn't my decision, Esterhaats. I don't know that any decision has been reached about anybody but Private Rashevsky."

"It must have been very hard for Rashevsky to do it alone. No one could survive here without help." He marveled at his own double *entendre*.

"Do you like Bauman, Esterhaats?"

"Yes, he and I work very well together."

"Yes, you do, I can see that, Esterhaats."

Dmitri was moved into the room off the Weiss house where Rashevsky had been living. He would live there for most of three years. Bauman continued to come up to the house from the barracks and he was made the back-up pianist against the possibility that Dmitri might be on leave or ill.

"I mentioned to the colonel that you don't have enough time to practice, the chores around the house get in your way, so it would be useful to keep Bauman. He thought that was a very good idea. Don't you think so too, my dear Esterhaats?"

Dmitri smiled as he seldom did. "Thank you, Mrs. Weiss."

Every few weeks the colonel received new sheet music by mail from New York or Zurich. When he turned the scores over to Dmitri, invariably they bore his legend in the form, T. Weiss, 1943, Zurich. To Dmitri's knowledge the colonel seldom left Alabama in the three years. And he never touched his grand piano, Dmitri was its master. The years in Alabama were like a second career in Gmund's shop only with more free time to play the piano. Weiss had at least as many twentieth century piano scores as Gmund did. And Weiss hardly ever intruded on Dmitri except occasionally when he came into the house while Dmitri was in the midst of a piece and asked him please to begin it again so the colonel could hear the full work. The orderly perfectionist's touch displayed in his collection of music ruled his ear as well. It was Dmitri's long habit not to interrupt a piece even if he made errors, but rather to play it through and then to rehearse the parts he did badly before playing the whole through again. To have to interrupt in the middle in order to satisfy another's whim irritated him as nothing else in the years he spent with the colonel. Nevertheless, he interrupted as ordered in Weiss's cautious terms, "Could you start that from the beginning, Esterhaats? It's jarring as a fragment."

After a few months Dmitri and Bauman had passes for the same weekend while Colonel and Mrs. Weiss were away. Bauman suggested they go into town together. Dmitri was pleased. He never quite knew what to do with weekends free of the base. It was too far to go home and there was nothing to do in town except go to a movie, usually a western double feature.

"Do you prefer white or Negro," Bauman said as soon as they'd parted from others on the truck into town.

Dmitri sought patterns when he didn't understand immediately, but the first pattern he saw was his keyboard with black and white keys. When he saw a black man in the back of a truck moving along the street, he got the right pattern. "Does it make any difference?"

"Yeah, it makes a difference. I couldn't begin to explain it, though. The way we're walking now is white."

"Okay."

"What do you usually do when you come into town, Esterhaats?"

"Nothing. Walk around. Sometimes go to a movie."

"Where do you spend the night?"

"I slept in the theater once. Once I went back to base."

"You walked back? That must be ten or fifteen miles."

"There was no hurry."

"You're gonna find a better place to sleep tonight, Esterhaats. Have you ever . . . you know?"

Dmitri grinned at him.

"Okay, okay, sorry, it's just . . . well, who knows about you, Esterhaats. Hey, back in New York I'd call you Dmitri and you'd call me Al."

Dmitri's memory was challenged. "Al?"

"Well, back in New York you might've called me Adolph. But Adolph isn't a great name to have right now. Hey, look, that's Sally. She's one of my favorites, she's very *simpatico*. I bet she's your type. Do you need an introduction, Dmitri?"

Dmitri laughed. He wondered why Bauman felt such a need to take care of him.

"Okay, good luck, Dmitri."

Dmitri spent Friday night with Sally. She was the first woman his own age he'd ever really known. In many other ways as well, she was the most unusual woman he'd ever met. She was a part of her local world as no one he'd ever known was. His parents, his aunt, Sofia Milano, even Horace Gmund were not really at home in their worlds, they constructed their own worlds, they were at ease only when their own worlds worked. Sally fit, she didn't need to make a world of her own. She fit so well it seemed odd she was a prostitute, as though she were a misfit. She had a natural understanding of her world, understanding that came so easily she couldn't have put it into words. She talked with Dmitri through the night, slept with him through the morning, then told him he had to pay more or leave. She said it straightforwardly, as though their long hours of sex and conversation implied nothing.

"Time's up, Soldier. You have to go so I have time to clean up this place. Or you can save me the bother by paying for another night if you want."

He paid to stay through Saturday night.

Sally smiled. "You've already heard all my new jokes. When I run out of jokes all I have left is the story of my life. Are you sure you wanna hear that?"

"Where were you born?"

"On a crummy little farm just outside town. Daddy went bust. Most of the little farms around here went bust. I don't even know where he and Momma are now. They went up to Tennessee about a year ago. My brothers all joined the army when they could. Maybe you've met my sister," she laughed. "She's called Tulip. She says Momma didn't know it when she gave her that name, but it's just right. She's pretty and soft looking on the outside ,all ready for pickin' but tough and a teensy bit twisted on the inside. She looks like me but she's real different, she's a lot smarter. I'm just ordinary, she says her smartness makes her a lot madder, she sometimes throws soldiers out. She's hard to be around but I like her, she's the best friend I've got. The only friend I guess. Do you have any friends, Dmitri?"

"Bauman, maybe. You must know him."

"I don't know any last names. I don't like men having their last names right on their jackets or shirts, I won't look at those, I won't learn anything but first names, I can put those with faces instead of shirt pockets."

"Al."

"That really narrows it down," She laughed. "There must be ten Als in the last year. Not many Dmitris, though."

When Dmitri left Sally Sunday afternoon, he tried to figure out why he enjoyed his time with her so much. He decided to walk back rather than be dragged into the banter in the back of the truck with the other draftees. Sally had often talked for an hour or so while Dmitri listened. If his mother had seen his face while Sally talked, she'd have said he was smiling; those who knew him less well couldn't have been sure.

Eventually Sally would say, "I don't know about you, Dmitri, you don't talk much do you?"

Dmitri would begin to play with her and they were soon making love. Sally was not very talented in bed. Having become a professional at sex, Dmitri suspected, she was not so different from an ordinary native. And not only in sex. She sang children's songs, "Mareseatoats and doeseatoats and littlelambseativy, a kiddleeativytoo, wouldn'tyou?," recited children's riddles, and told jokes which only someone whose early years had been spent as a child in America could understand. Dmitri would ask for the explanation of a joke, and then he'd know the joke was funny in a way too different from catching the joke to make him laugh. Sally was the most American person Dmitri'd ever known. As he walked and thought about his weekend with her, there were moments when he thought the richness of all she knew that he couldn't know overshadowed his knowledge of the piano and its music. Maybe, he thought, if he saw her more often, her novelty, which held up so well over a weekend, might soon wear out.

After several monthly visits to Sally, a couple of months passed before the next. When Dmitri found her, she smiled. "I was afraid you got shipped out and I was made the fool."

"Why were you made the fool?"

"I got a surprise for you, Dmitri. If you're comin' with me today, that is, or some other time if you'd rather."

She had an old piano in her rooms, a badly used upright. Dmitri ran up the scale to hear most of the keys out of tune or dead. He remembered what he'd learned from his days with Gmund, and in spare moments while talking with Sally he repaired almost all the non-working keys. Then he tuned the piano.

"How can you do that? I thought you need a tunin' fork or somethin' for that?"

"I have a good enough ear to do it without forks. But it would be a lot easier if I had the right kind of wrenches."

When he had it ready, he said, "Sing your favorite song."

She sang and he asked what the song was called.

"'You Are My Sunshine,' you mean you don't know that? Ever'body knows that. I'd bet ever' American knows that."

Dmitri shrugged. "It's nice. I'll try to play it."

"Mind, it really is my favorite song, I wasn't tryin' to say anything to put you on the spot."

Dmitri played it through once and then asked Sally to sing it while he played it again.

"You are a barroom pianist, Dmitri. You can play anything you hear, you just make it up, and if I sing it wrong, you make it up right. I never seen anybody that good."

Dmitri was floored by her compliment. He smiled and pulled her down onto the bench with him. "It probably seems hard, but it isn't. If a song works, there must be good musical reasons, which means anybody who's half a musician ought to be able to recreate it."

"That must mean I'm not even a tenth of a musician."

Dmitri wrote his mother to ask her to arrange to send repair parts and a few tools for Sally's piano, and soon he had it in good working order. Once Sally asked him to play what he liked best, and he did a percussive Prokofiev sonata that pounded the piano out of tune.

"I'm real impressed, Dmitri," Sally said, "I don't know if I like it but I think I do, cause I know you like it, I could see that just watchin' you."

What she liked best of all his music was some of Debussy, for some of which he was able to find at least the French words in Colonel Weiss's sheet music. He taught her to pronounce the French as he supposed it should be pronounced, and she learned several songs in a Russified, Anglicized French with a southern lilt, a combination that may have been more fitting for the music than any of the pure originals were.

The largest of the shipments of music during the time Dmitri played for the colonel was a large envelope of mostly Stravinsky. He had not found pleasure in playing Stravinsky, and he frowned when the music was handed to him.

"This man is a genius," the colonel said. "Can you handle him, Esterhaats?"

Dmitri seldom spoke to the colonel, even to say "Yes Sir," grated with dissonance rather than assent. He didn't answer the colonel now but merely took the music to flip through the pages with open indifference.

Over the next week or so Dmitri began most days with Stravinsky only to switch soon to someone else. In his first struggles with Debussy he'd thought it was he and not Debussy who was at fault, but now he was sure the composer at least shared responsibility for his displeasure in playing. When the colonel asked whether he found Stravinsky interesting, Dmitri's deliberate failure to answer momentarily brought harshness to the colonel's voice.

"Esterhaats, don't you . . ." he slowly became calmer. "Is he too much for you?"

Dmitri didn't restrain his sneering reply. "Stravinsky?"

A few days later, Weiss brought in a sheaf of articles on Stravinsky and several records of his music. "I wish I'd been at that first *Rite of Spring*. It must have been wonderful. People rioting against genius – it's what you'd expect."

Dmitri didn't know the story.

"It's right here, you'll want to read it, Esterhaats. And here, these might help." The colonel put on a record, but to his annoyance he'd chosen wrong and the music was orchestral. "Damn, Esterhaats," he said, "I don't have time to listen to this and to the piano. But now this has started. We'll hear this, and then you can listen to the piano later."

The music was the *Rite of Spring* and for the first time Dmitri found pleasure in Stravinsky, for the first time he saw value in a record player. The colonel now paid careful attention to the records as he turned and changed them through the piece. Dmitri almost laughed at the last turning when he realized how he and the colonel had sat almost enraptured while the music played and then had been jolted into robotic attention to the mechanics of the record player during the changes. Somehow they both seemed to maintain their line of attention to the music.

After the colonel left, Dmitri didn't play the recording of Stravinsky's piano music but instead repeated the *Rite of Spring*. Already in its second playing, the piece lost its spontaneity from the mechanical perfection in its repetition of the beauties and likely flaws of the orchestra. Dmitri would not want to hear that recording again. Dmitri spent the next few days transcribing and improvising from it rather than taking up the piano compositions. But there was something lacking in his effort, he didn't have adequate music theory to handle Stravinsky's composing methods. Finally he gave up and turned back to the piano compositions. He soon realized his trouble with them was they were not as good as Stravinsky. Instead of methodically working through the pieces roughly in order of their composition, he now searched through them to find any which looked as though they'd be more interesting than most. After a couple of hours, he selected *Trois Mouvements de Petrouchka* and set all the other pieces aside. As he found pleasure in the piece so he found it easy to play.

At the end of the afternoon, the colonel handed Dmitri a program of pieces to be played the following night at dinner. Dmitri had learned to estimate the importance of the dinners for which he performed by the extent to which the colonel decided the program. Casual dinners for officers on the base were left entirely to Dmitri's discretion. Tomorrow night's dinner was decided entirely by Colonel Weiss. The program included three of

Stravinsky's pieces – *Trois Mouvements* was not one of them.

"These aren't good, Sir," Dmitri said. "The *Petrouchka* ballet would be better."

"Esterhaats, you don't understand Stravinsky, do you? Can't you play the *Sérénade*, Esterhaats?"

Dmitri didn't answer.

The following morning, Mrs. Weiss gave Dmitri a different program, a mixture of his Bartók and romantics. Private Esterhaats was relieved of the duty to play Stravinsky and he wondered what other duties might follow.

Three weeks later Dmitri was told he would supervise the auditions of four new draftee pianists. While he listened to them, Dmitri wondered how malignant the colonel's pique could be – only one could even half-seriously be compared to Dmitri Esterhaats but in full seriousness there could be no doubt of Dmitri's superiority. The colonel selected the half-serious pianist, Lufkin, to work in the household for a few weeks and sent the other three back to the barracks to finish basic training.

"Private Lufkin will be working with you, Esterhaats," Mrs. Weiss said that evening before dinner. "Could you make sure he knows what to do?"

Only in that moment did Dmitri finally see the large pattern of the world he'd created by balking at Stravinsky. "Bauman, what . . ."

"I'm sorry, Esterhaats. He'll no longer be an orderly. He's finishing basic training." She reached up her hand to stroke Dmitri's cheek.

Dmitri felt like a child. Mrs. Weiss's gesture was like that of his mother when he was a child and, if his foggy memory was right, of his aunt in Kiev. They stroked his cheek or combed their fingers through his hair to sympathize with some hurt or loss or to express their own loss. This time he'd brought on loss by his own stubborn actions. Could it really have pained him to play the colonel's Stravinsky program? Bauman was the nearest he'd ever come to having a friend, and now he'd sent Bauman to war.

For several days Dmitri had difficulty thinking of anything he wanted to play during his assigned hours of practice. He found himself playing Bauman's music, then Sofia's, then his aunt's Mozart. Nothing drove the thoughts from his head. He recalled his ungraciousness to others, to *Mademoiselle* Meursault, to Horace Gmund, to his mother, and his cruelty to Sofia Milano. All out of the weakness of character that led him to such carelessness as to send Al Bauman to war. Dmitri needed discipline to control his thoughts but he had none, he had only remorse. At the end of a week he found Bach, who drove the thoughts from his head and brought him calm.

Two weeks later, Dmitri had a weekend pass. He didn't want to go into town for two nights but he wanted even less to stay in the Weiss's home. He planned to avoid Sally, to go instead to others who might not expect conversation. But in the moment when he approached her house, what he wanted most was a piano. He went in with Sally when she caught his eye.

Sally let Dmitri play for two or three hours without conversation. When he then paused without speaking as though he were trying to think of what to play next, she stood behind him and put her arms around his head and pulled it to her.

"Are they finally going to . . ." she started, ". . . are they going to ship you out, Dmitri?"

Dmitri was so startled he almost laughed. "No. Not yet anyway. My friend…"

"Al?"

"Yes, you remember his name."

"Al Bauman."

"Even his last name?"

"He came last Sunday. He got real flustered when he saw the piano. He said he shouldn't be here. He played the piano for a little while, then he left."

"That might be the last time he plays a piano for a long time. I sent him to war."

"You sent him? How could you send him? To them you're nothin' but a private."

Dmitri told the story. He spoke for a long time, answering questions, backing up to fill in details, debating with himself about their relevance to the result.

"You know what I think?" Sally said. "I think you don't understand the way Colonel Weiss thinks, maybe you couldn't ever understand, but maybe that's good, cause it might be a lot worse to be the kind of a person who could understand him, you know what I mean?"

Dmitri smiled. "Maybe."

Sally continued to justify Dmitri to himself for a while before seducing him. "You know, I don't want to change the subject, but that's more than I ever heard you talk before. Now why is that? You talk a lot better than I do, Dmitri, you had to learn English and you know it better 'n me, but here I do almost all the talkin'. That don't make sense – there, see, I did it again. I try not to talk like that around you. I'm gittin' better." She laughed. "Only you wouldn't know how much better, cause you don't hear when you're not around, do you?"

At the end of Sunday afternoon, Sally said, "I been thinkin' one thing, Dmitri, I just wonder, would it really hurt you a bit to play what that colonel wants to hear? You can say it's none of my business and I won't say another word."

"I won't say it's none of your business."

"But you won't say another word, either, will you? Well, I just hope they don't ship you out, I don't know who'd play my piano and I really been wantin' to hear this new guy, Stravinsky, I just like hearin' new things so much and way out here you can't hardly find anybody to play new things. Like Stravinsky."

Dmitri laughed, Sally laughed harder, they fell into bed again. Dmitri missed the truck and had to walk back to base. As he sweated his uniform through on his brisk walk through the sultry evening he realized it wouldn't really hurt him a bit to play a little Stravinsky.

That week Dmitri spent his allotted time at the grand piano mastering Stravinsky, especially the *Sérénade en La*, inventing a nearly impossible fugue to transpose its ending into the beginning of *Trois Mouvements*. He wondered if he would be given another chance to perform at the colonel's whim.

Later in the week, the colonel encountered Lufkin in Dmitri's presence. "Mrs. Weiss is having a dinner Friday night, Lufkin. Do you think you could work up some pieces to play for background? Say two, two and a half hours. Mrs. Weiss will discuss the time with you. She'll be talking to you too, Esterhaats."

Mrs. Weiss explained to Dmitri how he was to serve the dinner. "You won't have any trouble with it, my Esterhaats. You might find Stravinsky more pleasant than serving."

Lufkin's performance was too dull for his own good, though he couldn't know. He played Beethoven, Liszt, and Chopin. He sounded competent but not alive – Weiss's guests might judge Lufkin superior to Esterhaats, but Dmitri and the colonel knew better. Afterwards a month passed and then Lufkin was asked to perform again. And again Dmitri served the table. When it was time for dessert, Mrs. Weiss joined Dmitri in the kitchen to help arrange the servings. She gave him a sad frown. "My Esterhaats, why aren't *you* playing?"

Dmitri shrugged.

"Is it just because you don't like Stravinsky? Don't you know the colonel has never heard Stravinsky except from some records he bought a few weeks ago? He might even agree with your taste if he ever gets a chance to hear Stravinsky. Wouldn't you just give him a chance?" She put out her hand to stroke the side of his face. "Couldn't you try one more time? I enjoy seeing you so much. Next Friday is very important to him. You daren't say I told you. He's going to be promoted to Brigadier General. There'll be several generals coming down here for dinner. Only generals."

Mrs. Weiss placed all but one of the desserts on a large tray. Dmitri picked up the other dessert and added it to the tray. Mrs. Weiss picked it back up and set it on the table.

"Couldn't you try, my Esterhaats? If you promise you'll try – I seem to have an extra dessert. Here . . ." She poured liqueur over all the desserts, pouring a little extra over his and over one other. "Be sure the colonel gets this one. And that my Esterhaats gets this one."

Monday afternoon when he saw the colonel approaching the house while he practiced, Dmitri quickly broke into *Trois Mouvements de Petrouchka* roughly at the middle and continued playing from there. The colonel came into the room and listened without speaking for a minute. Dmitri regretted being unable to see the colonel's face and hence unable to guess at his thoughts. But it was the first time in many weeks that Colonel Weiss had cared to take even a minute to listen to him. The occasion was marred only by the colonel's failure to ask him to begin the piece anew. The next morning Dmitri was asked to play for the colonel and his wife, who were dining alone that evening. He was given no program.

The dinner was carried out with the full formality of the other dinners, merely that for the first time there were no guests. It was a full-dress audition, brought about more by Lufkin's failure and Mrs. Weiss's tact, no doubt, than by anything Dmitri might've done. Dmitri sat down to begin playing promptly at eight, and after a few bars the Weisses entered the room and sat at opposite ends of the unexpanded table. Before starting to play, Dmitri lit the candles on the dinner table, turned off the main lights, and turned on the small lamp which lit the keyboard. As he played, he could hear Lufkin coming and going through the swinging doors to the kitchen, fumbling to serve food, and inhaling nervously before pouring wine, his heels clicking slightly each time he bent over the colonel or his wife to serve them. As the meal progressed, the Weisses talked quietly but Dmitri, immersed in his music, did not bother to overhear them, nor would he have cared to hear them even if he hadn't been playing.

Dmitri played several short pieces, including one by Stravinsky. He then capped his performance with *Sérénade en La*, at the end of which he passed via his short fugue into *Trois Mouvements de Petrouchka*. By that juxtaposition he hoped to score his point against Stravinsky without having to argue it in words. At the end of the performance, as Mrs. Weiss had instructed him to do at his first such dinner, Dmitri stood and faced the table to salute and say, "Colonel Weiss," before bowing slightly.

"Thank you, Esterhaats, maybe we need an encore with brandy. Your favorite short Bartók would be good."

The next afternoon the colonel came to ask, "What was that last? That was *Petrouchka*? We'll have to hear that again sometime, Esterhaats. By the way, could you perhaps play this program Friday night? We're having dinner for some visitors. I won't be here tomorrow to give you the program. I'll be flying back from Washington for dinner. Mrs. Weiss might not get back in time to instruct you – just begin at eight as usual. I trust you'll have no trouble, Esterhaats."

Stravinsky was not in the program, Bartók and Prokofiev were. Dmitri suspected Lufkin's last duty in the household would be to serve the dinner. On that account, at least, he was wrong, Lufkin would leave already that evening.

Mrs. Weiss walked through as Dmitri stood from the piano. "My Esterhaats," she said, "don't let me disturb you, you play so beautifully." She came over to stroke his face again, she was much shorter than he, she had to reach up. "The colonel nearly refused to let you play even last night." She retracted her hand and frowned at him. "It would have been too bad. You don't have to yield very much to get a lot sometimes. That's something men never seem to learn."

On Friday there were no candles for the dinner, the generals hadn't brought their wives. When Dmitri finished his prescribed program, he stood and turned to face the table, saying, "General Weiss." He could see pleased surprise in Weiss's changing facial expression.

"Thank you, Esterhaats, I told the generals you'd make it worth their while to fly down here. It's still a bit early, perhaps we need a couple of encores. Play something the generals would like."

In Dmitri's three years in Alabama, that was Weiss's warmest verbal compliment, ceding to him the choice of music for an important audience. Dmitri returned the compliment by playing something the new general would like rather than something the old generals would like. He played Prokofiev's *Toccata* followed by *Five Sarcasms.*

"What was that last, Esterhaats?" the new general asked.

"Prokofiev, Sir, *Five Sarcasms.*"

"I'd sooner say *Five Bedlams*," an old general said.

"A god-awful way to end dinner," another added.

"You didn't like it?" Weiss asked with a sly twist.

"God damn, man, who could?"

The next morning Dmitri found taped to his door a four-day pass. He'd never had so long off before. It was just about enough time to go home, kiss his mother, and come back. He counted his money, put a few things in his bag, and went into town. He had to walk past Sally's street on the way to the rail station. He was so engrossed in thinking through the possibilities that he followed his habitual path and was soon with Sally. After an hour of his diffidence, she said, "You're thinkin' about somethin', I know. What is it, Dmitri? Or do you just want me to be quiet?"

He didn't answer immediately and, out of her own unconquerable habits, she continued to talk. "The colonel didn't like your Stravinsky. You're gonna git shipped out."

Dmitri laughed.

"Good lord, he can laugh! I woulda' forgot that."

"He's not a colonel anymore, he's a general. And he liked my Stravinsky so much he wanted me to play something else for his promotion dinner."

"When was that, Dmitri?"

"Last night."

"Last night?" She sounded incredulous. "Why? I mean, why in the world, Dmitri, are you sittin' here sulkin'? You should be jumpin' up and down and hoppin' into bed."

She came over to sit on his lap and soon enough he was hoppin' into bed.

"I got a new joke," Sally said later.

Suddenly it struck Dmitri with the clarity of the sunlight coming through the crack between Sally's curtains that she always had new jokes because she heard them from her new customers. That was something he had to know from the beginning, but it registered only now. Usually when she offered a new joke, he smiled, even grinned at her to await the punch line, and he was more pleased with those jokes he couldn't understand because they required an Americanism he didn't have than with those he could understand. Instead of smiling at her this time, he must have been looking a bit annoyed with his new-found comprehension.

"You don't look very humorous, fella. Maybe I oughta save it, I never saw anybody so unpleased about gittin' what he most wanted, maybe you oughta play somethin'. What did you play last night? Did you have an encore?"

"*Five Sarcasms.*" He laughed. "One of the generals said it sounded more like *Five Bedlams.*"

"Must be by that Russian you like. Prokofiev."

"That's right! Shall I play it for you?"

"Sure. Only you might have to tune the piano after. And you will have to, cause I wanna hear somethin' nice too."

Dmitri kissed her forehead, played Prokofiev, tuned the piano, and then played some very nice Mozart and a couple of Debussy songs for Sally to sing.

Dmitri spent his four days with Sally and never went to the station. He rationalized his pleasure late that night after Sally fell asleep. If he'd tried to go to New York, he'd very likely have spent his time on trains and in train stations, agonizing with delays, traveling away from Alabama for two days and then traveling back for the next two, never getting to New York. He would ask for a full week's pass to have time for a real visit. Then he began to wonder what were his rights. Was it even possible to get such a pass? Whom would he ask? Bauman would either have known or would have known how to find out. But Dmitri had shipped Bauman off to war.

"Now maybe you're ready for my new joke," Sally said after Dmitri laughed at something the next afternoon. "You ready? Here it is. Why did the chicken cross the road?" She laughed.

Dmitri shrugged his ignorance.

"Dmitri! You know that, you have to. He crossed the road – why? Remember? – to git to the other side."

That was Mr. Spearman's kind of joke, a twist back to the obvious that was a surprise. Dmitri was pleased with it, that it had made him look silly.

"You don't make any sense, Dmitri. I told you that one cause I thought it was funny, anyone would think it was a new joke. Ever'one knows that joke."

Dmitri was so much at ease talking with Sally that he almost said what he wondered: Who'd told her such an obvious joke? But he caught himself with the realization he'd had only yesterday that it was one of her other customers. This customer was one she evidently thought stupid beyond redemption for thinking he had a new joke. Dmitri grinned at her. "Do you think I'm stupid beyond redemption?"

"I know you're not stupid, Dmitri, I just don't know what you are. The guy who told me that joke is the one who's stupid."

Dmitri was at least a bit stupid, he realized. He could openly have asked her source without embarrassment, just as she volunteered it without embarrassment. After more than a year of occasional weekend visits, he was still being surprised by her openness. He found it easy to accept her as she was without quarrel or complaint, without any urge to remake her to fit him or any urge to banish parts of her from his life.

At Sally's request, Dmitri explained the differences between several composers.

"When you say it like that, Dmitri, it all sounds real good and I'm convinced I know what it all means, but then you play it and I can't tell anymore. How'd you learn all that?"

"I've had a lot of teachers."

"A lot?"

He should have said, but did not, "You're one of my teachers." He knew how the conversation would've continued. "Don't say somethin' like that that ain't true, Dmitri." "I've learned a lot from you." "What? Name one thing." There the conversation in his mind ended because he couldn't find the right word. It was something like tolerance or acceptance, but before he could get it straight, he was distracted by her talking and he lost the moment.

Dmitri remembered from counting his money for New York that he didn't have enough for four days with Sally. He gave her what he had on Tuesday, saying he was sorry he didn't have enough for another night.

"How long is your pass, Soldier?"

"Until tomorrow."

"This night's on the house, no one's gonna come knockin' on a Tuesday night. You know I like havin' you here. I might git tired a little sooner than you, maybe," she laughed, "you guys are trained to fight in the trenches until ever'body else has the sense to give up. If we're gonna be fightin' in the trenches tonight, I just hope I don't have to git up early tomorrow to git you back on time."

Sally didn't have to get up before the early afternoon sun reached her face. She turned to Dmitri, who was already awake. "You got another hour or two, Soldier. Or would you rather have breakfast? Dmitri wanted nothing more than to lie there in comfort with her. After a while she got up to make breakfast, which they ate while sitting across from each other at her spindly table.

"This seems awful natural, Dmitri, I've known you longer than anybody but my sister Tulip, all the other soldiers come and go but you've been here for it seems like years, somebody must be lookin' after you to make sure you don't git shipped out. Even if you don't git shipped out the war's still gonna end and then you'll go. It's gonna be real lonely around here when you leave, and you will leave, I know you will."

He was silent.

"You're not gonna say anything. Why is it men always do that when they think their answer is bad? Big men. Big cowards. Maybe it's not a bad answer, it's just the truth. Well, I guess if the war ends *all* the soldiers will leave and I won't have any reason to stay here either, will I? I guess ever'thing has to end, even the good things." She laughed. "You might think I was sayin' the war is a good thing. Well, maybe it is, some parts of it."

"Yes."

"Well howdy do, he can talk, I was gittin' worried."

In a few months, sweaty, sultry months, Sally was proved right. On one of the hottest, stickiest days of his life, a few weeks after a local newscaster announced that the United States had dropped the atomic bomb on Hiroshima, he filed a request to take his freedom. General Weiss couldn't stop him and perhaps he wouldn't have stopped even if he could've.

"I have your request, Esterhaats. I'm told it takes a couple of weeks to get it done. I guess . . . they'll be mustering everybody out pretty soon, maybe even take back the last couple of years' promotions. Well, Mrs. Weiss says this will be a quiet place, maybe it won't even be needed. Anyway, I'm just glad you didn't become another Paul Wittgenstein."

Dmitri's face must have revealed his ignorance.

"You don't know about him? He was a pianist, from Austria. He lost his arm in the first war. He paid some composers to write piano pieces for the left hand. Then he didn't really like their music, he was more classical in his tastes than modern. Well . . . I was a pianist, Esterhaats. My father sent me to a military school. Music is different in a military school. You were born in Russia. You know Tolstoy. Tolstoy approves of history, he likes it when nations are pulled into movements, when history uses whoever happens to be available. If you'd stayed in Russia, you could've been used by history, too, Esterhaats, pulled up into the movement of a whole generation or two. Or if you were German, you could be Nazi or anti-Nazi, those would be the only choices. If you really wanted to, you could even be used by history here. Poor Wittgenstein got used, he didn't have a . . . well. . . ."

Dmitri added the final word in his mind: protector. He wanted to say out loud, Maybe Wittgenstein had only one protector when he needed two. Instead, he merely nodded his sympathy for Wittgenstein.

"Do you know what happened to Rashevsky?"

"No, sir."

"He was supposed to fight in Italy. His landing boat capsized and he drowned, drowned in the Tyrrhenian off Anzio with Lieutenant Blake and half his squad. Goddamned waste. He didn't really have the stuff as a pianist, but that's no reason for such waste."

The general stiffened, Dmitri knew to salute, the general returned the salute and left the room.

Weiss had told Dmitri more in a few minutes than in the previous three years. Dmitri had thought of him only as a self-centered, mean-spirited man redeemed slightly by his love of modern music. For a few minutes now he thought of Weiss as a generous man stuck in the wrong time and place and he wondered whether he would find both the opportunity and the stature to thank him. A quick glance over his past suggested if he found the opportunity he wouldn't take it.

Dmitri continued to perform at dinners almost every night until his release came, but the General didn't speak to him again, so that Dmitri didn't get to test his stature.

The day before his departure, Mrs. Weiss said, "We'll miss you around here, my Esterhaats. I almost wish the war had never ended." She stroked his face. "My Esterhaats."

Dmitri thanked her, his second protector, for her kindness and asked her to thank the general as well.

Mrs. Weiss started to respond but then she closed her mouth and took his hand in hers to clasp it for a long while as they both stood silent.

Dmitri was given a railway pass to New York. He went into town to buy other clothes before setting off. It was a weekday but he thought he'd look for Sally. He dawdled over the clothes, which were not to his taste, but he despised the choices available less than he despised his uniform, which he left, piece by piece, as he found civilian replacements. He went by the train station to check the schedule. There was too little time for a genuine visit to Sally before the next train to Atlanta. He debated whether it was better to rush over to her to say a fleeting goodbye or better just to let her be free of him. While he debated the case he lost his chance for even a fleeting good-bye. As he traveled overnight up the east coast from Atlanta, he wondered why he'd been in such a hurry. He could have spent that night with Sally. A few months earlier he'd passed a trip home to spend four days with Sally, now he was so hurried to get home, where he had no purpose, that he'd omitted a two-block walk to Sally's.

"I know you're not stupid, Dmitri," he heard Sally saying again, "I just don't know what you are."

Anton Staebli

4

After a couple of weeks at home, Dmitri looked for an apartment in Manhattan. Returning soldiers competed for too few places and Dmitri eventually reduced his sights to a return to the Bowery. He was reluctant to stay at home, where his piano playing through the day must grate on others' nerves, especially his brother's. Because he was several years older than Dmitri, Pavel hadn't been drafted until after Dmitri. But he had no protector and he was just in time to fight his way across a series of Pacific islands, where he contracted a fever that put him in a hospital in the Philippines the day the atomic bomb destroyed Hiroshima. The fever got worse and Pavel was sent home where it might be more comforting to die. He slept fifteen hours a day, but he seemed to awake in renewed fever whenever Dmitri played his best music, especially Bartók and Prokofiev, and he seemed to sleep only with Chopin. Bartók and Prokofiev literally turned Pavel green, which added variety to his fever's usual splotchy purple and yellow. But Dmitri would've been the first to say the green was no improvement.

"Mitya," his father said as Dmitri started to play one Saturday afternoon when he thought Pavel was still awake after lunch, "at last we have peace and you try to bring back war."

In that moment Dmitri could not face playing Chopin. He closed his eyes and leaned over his piano. "Sorry, Papa. I'll go for a walk."

He walked to the Bowery and began the search again. Outside one building he saw several policemen, and then out came a stretcher. Dmitri went to the crowd outside the building and asked who was the owner or manager.

"What, you want a room, Soldier?"

People called every male his age Soldier. "Yes."

"It's not clean. You have to clean it yourself. We don't do janitor service."

Dmitri had a cold-water walk-up, but it was a room, and for what he saved on the rent he thought he could afford to rent a grand piano. He walked back home, walking idly in his pleasure, finally feeling the freedom he hadn't yet felt after escaping the army. It was a glorious October day, the end of a season of growth in the world about him, but the delayed beginning of his own season. When he neared his family's apartment, he quickened his step. He was afraid he'd kept dinner waiting and he was also excited to tell them he'd found an apartment at last. He generally ran up stairs, he seldom ran on level ground, but stairs irritated him to a run. But now he realized he was walking up the stairs, walking very slowly. A minute earlier he wanted to tell his family about the apartment but now, when he imagined telling his mother, he lost all his enthusiasm.

The first musical news Dmitri learned after moving was that Bartók had died. Dmitri went to check posters for auditions and met his Hungarian teacher from just before he went to the army. He forgot about auditioning, he neglected finances, he lost control of his daily routines. For a month he played nothing but Bartók. When he couldn't play the music without thinking about the man, he went for walks to break his thoughts, and the walks, as though by the will of his feet, led him onto subways or buses to the Bronx, where he continued walking near Bartók's apartment, where he couldn't escape thinking about the man. Eventually he would return to his grand and play until he was ready for sleep at whatever hour.

When at last he chose to play someone other than Bartók, Dmitri turned to his one acceptable piece of Stravinsky. It was more than a year since he'd played it for then still Colonel Weiss before his promotion, and he hadn't played it since. To his great astonishment he now couldn't entirely remember the score. For the first time he would have to buy a score, something he'd never thought of doing. When he went to a music shop to buy *Trois Mouvements de Petrouchka*, he browsed for a while through the Schönberg, looking for something to memorize. He soon gave up. As a teenager he'd been able to remember entire scores in an hour or two simply by studying them and, with a little invention, he could remember them from a single hearing. Now his youthful powers were fading. He wouldn't forget scores learned earlier, but hereafter he would find it much harder to memorize new works. He'd have to play them several times first and, even then, if he didn't play them occasionally over the next few months, the notes, the chords, even the tempos would begin to slip, sometimes whole patterns would collapse in his head.

Dmitri debated whether to buy Schönberg's *Five Piano Pieces* as well as the Stravinsky. If he didn't, he'd have nothing with which to challenge himself. If he did, he'd soon have a habit which would exhaust his money supply. He decided to buy the music and to look for work. He began to go to every plausible audition. The first one he won earned him the depressing right to accompany a German tenor through two evenings of Schubert *lieder*. But, to his astonishment, he was not depressed by Schubert's songs. When the tenor, Anton Staebli, asked him to join him in drinking champagne at the end of the second evening, Dmitri, too slow to think as usual, blundered into accepting. When the first bottle was finished, Staebli wanted to order another.

"No, Esterhaats, you know, I really don't like this stuff anyway. I think I'll have a beer. You want a beer?"

"Sure."

"You sure you're sure? That's a bad idea, you know."

Dmitri did not respond.

"Wein auf Bier, das rat ich Dir; Bier auf Wein, das lass sein."

Dmitri's Dutch let him understand that wine after beer was well-advised but beer after wine should be left alone.

Dmitri grinned.

Staebli guffawed. "You don't give a damn for commonsense!" They ordered beers, or, rather, Staebli did.

"Funny we should meet here, huh? A German who used to be the enemy and a Russian who's going to be the enemy. You play a great piano, Dmitri. A natural for Schubert."

Dmitri nearly choked on his beer. "I'm not so good with Schubert."

"I like it your way for a change, you pick up the pace a bit, makes me work for it and think about how to do it."

"You don't have a regular pianist?"

Staebli laughed. "I'm not that regular a singer. We were at war with Germany, remember? Who do you think wanted to have a German sing German *lieder*? You got drafted, didn't you, Esterhaats?"

"Yes. And you?"

Another guffaw. "Look at me. I'm so fat nobody would put me in a trench. Every few months or so they called me up and then they sent me back home and told me to lose weight. They must think people are stupid – the only good thing fat ever did for me besides give me bigger lungs for singing was to keep me out of the war. Imagine what my life was like. Too fat for the army and the only thing I know to do is sing German *lieder* while we're at war with Germany. For the last few years before the war, I sang all the time, then the war and I've hardly ever sung."

"Did you ever meet a pianist named Bauman?"

"Adolph! Yeah, I met him. He even played for me a couple of times. My pianist suddenly went back to Germany just before a concert, so there was an instant audition. Those were hard times. Bauman was okay but there wasn't anybody really good. The next best of those guys played Schubert as though it were Bartók. The rest of them were even worse."

Dmitri grinned. "Maybe I was the Bartók. I auditioned once with Bauman, who beat me. It was to accompany a lieder singer, Schubert and Wolf."

Staebli guffawed. "Esterhaats! I should've remembered a name like that. Hey, you've improved a lot."

"I wonder if Bauman got through the war."

"Yeah, a few weeks ago I bumped into him in Grand Central Station. And when *I* bump into you you stop to notice. He said he got through half the war in Alabama before he was sent to England for the invasion. But they made him a staff person, he could type as fast as he could play. Fewer keys, he said. Said he was going to Yale soon, said he couldn't stand the city anymore when he came back. Didn't think he was good enough to be a concert pianist. Said he met somebody up close who was too much better than he could ever be. Was that you, Esterhaats?"

Dmitri didn't answer.

"Funny thing, Bauman did a lot better than the guy he replaced as my pianist. That guy went back to Germany and was missing in action at Leningrad along with one of my cousins. Probably froze to death and got plowed under."

Over another beer, Staebli became even more open, as though he had to tell his story. "My grandfather was Swiss, that's how I got this name Staebli that makes me sound like a damn yodeler. But I was born in Darmstadt in Germany, then we came here when I was twelve. It was a good thing too – there's hardly any Darmstadt left. It was a bad thing too – there's hardly any demand for German singers here. I do some choral work and in a couple of months I get to sing again. Maybe we could work together again. It depends on you."

"I would like that."

"You shouldn't be too sure. I told you where I was born . . ."

"In Darmstadt."

"But you didn't go on from there to tell me where you were born. Russia? Budapest?"

"In Kiev."

"Esterhaats sounds more like Hungarian than anything else, but you look Jewish."

"My mother is Jewish. My father is Hungarian and Russian."

"In a couple of months I'm singing for the Heidelberger Klub. It's their first meeting since before the war."

Staebli's tone was portentous and Dmitri felt he was missing something.

"That doesn't bother you, Esterhaats? Playing for Germans?"

"Are they Nazis?"

"No. Most of them are probably lifetime Americans. For them Germany is *The Student Prince.*"

Dmitri shrugged.

"You really don't have any racial prejudice against Germans?"

Dmitri didn't have an instant answer because he'd given the matter no thought before. "I am a Hungarian Russian Jew in America. I would be a fool to have racial prejudice against anybody."

Staebli laughed hard, a booming Nietzschean laugh that fully engaged his powerful diaphragm and big lungs. "Let's drink Brüderschaft! Hey, Maxie, two fresh steins!"

With their fresh steins they linked their arms together as they drank.

"I'm Anton," Staebli said.

"I'm Dmitri."

Anton emptied his stein, but Dmitri managed only half. Anton laughed again when he saw Dmitri nearly choking. "*Also,* Dmitri, let me help you finish it."

Dmitri went to other auditions and he found success, thanks to Colonel Weiss's rigid training. He played Stravinsky to accompany a dancer. He was leery of the role, but after being selected in the audition he agreed to try a couple of days with the ballerina, Julia Smythe. They were making love at the end of the second day and Dmitri would not have known how to back out at that point. Julia told him how delighted she was with him, with his hands, his body, his piano playing. He didn't say so, but he was delighted with her as well, with her energy, her grace, her good nature, and her powerful legs. He soon loved Julia's body as he'd loved Sofia's voice. During the time between their first love-making and the beginning of their short tour, Dmitri was as nearly happy as he'd ever been, as happy perhaps as in his first couple of months in Horace Gmund's shop. If their tour had been delayed a year to give them more time to practice, he wouldn't have complained.

But it was not delayed. After three performances Dmitri was aware that Julia was treating him differently, she no longer seemed pleased with him. It made little sense, she was not capricious like Sofia and his behavior hadn't changed. At their next performance a few nights later in Buffalo, after his solo in the first half of their program, Dmitri began to understand when he saw Julia standing off stage behind the curtain. As his applause began, she closed her eyes as though in pain. He'd never noticed their applause, but from now on he did. His solos received greater applause than her dances.

Dmitri tried to make it otherwise. He tried playing trite pieces, but then his applause escalated. If he'd known any really bad music, he'd have played it for Julia. Finally, he turned to the harshest sounding of his own music for his solos, and the audiences began to prefer Julia. But it was too late. In Rochester, the morning after the last performance of their scattered tour, they received a telegram that roused them from their morning lethargy: NO FURTHER ENGAGEMENTS STOP SORRY STOP SASHA DEMSETZ.

"I didn't make it," Julia said.

Dmitri wanted to share the fault. "*We* didn't make it – not yet, anyway."

"No, we didn't."

Dmitri realized Julia had changed the subject. After they got up and dressed and had their bags packed for departure, she hugged him gently. She stretched up onto her toes to hold her head beside his where there could be no eye contact.

"You're very good, Dmitri. I thought I would even love you. I wish . . ."

Dmitri thought she was going to cry. Instead, she kissed him, shrugged her shoulders at him in the most reserved of her intimate disclosures, and left him there.

Dmitri returned to New York. He called Sasha about possible auditions and learned that he need no longer audition. Many agents and managers wanted him. It seemed idiotic. He was losing his memory, he was losing women faster than ever, he'd just failed on a short tour, he might be in total decline. And now they wanted him.

Dmitri gave a matinee performance at Columbia in a contemporary music series. At the end, he was treated to a series of loud bravos whose timbre he recognized. Anton Staebli's tenor eventually pulled other voices along into his chorus, and Dmitri had one of his greatest seeming successes. Staebli then dragged him back downtown to a Seventh Avenue bar not far from Carnegie Hall.

"Hey, I want you to meet someone," Anton said. "This is Jelly Ujfalussy. Jelly . . ."

Jelly Ujfalussy spoke to Dmitri before Anton could say his name. "If you make jokes with my name I will never speak to you again. That would be too bad for you – you might never hear such voice again."

"You're a singer?" Dmitri asked.

She looked at him as though with contempt for his stupidity. "No. I not sing, I talk."

She turned her voice to the benefit of others and said nothing more to Dmitri, who thought he'd seemed as dopey to her as he had to Sally when she asked him why the chicken crossed the road. In fact, although she was outrageously beautiful – easily the most beautiful human he'd ever seen – and apparently grossly self assured, Jelly seemed like a Hungarian Sally with venom. Like Sally, she was a talker. The voice he risked never hearing again was a contradictory combination. It was lilting and resonant while being quick and clipped. Its range seemed far greater than Sofia's, both at the top and the bottom, and her accent was the oddest one he'd heard, while her diction and grammatical constructions were precise and careful. If she'd had no accent, the precision and care would still reveal she wasn't a native speaker. Dmitri grinned at the thought of telling some of Sally's jokes to Jelly, to all this crowd. Then he, Dmitri Esterhaats of all people, would have to explain them.

Staebli turned his attentions elsewhere when Jelly Ujfalussy began talking with her beautiful voice and unique accent. When Ujfalussy turned away, Dmitri was alone in this small crowd of oddly dressed people. He was in black tie after his performance, Staebli was in a jacket and tie, Jelly was wearing a shoulderless evening gown, all in black; a few others were well dressed, but most were in sweaters or casual dresses. Anton said they were all performers or followers of performers. Jelly seemed too young to be a successful performer, perhaps she *was* only a talker.

The crowd made Dmitri tired. He was usually high after performing, but his spirits were flagging now. Others in the crowd took opportunity to speak with him, always very briefly, often while passing from their cluster of round bar-tables on the way to get another beer or drink. Dmitri began to study them all, trying to guess their nationalities. A few were clearly Americans, but most seemed to be European, from both sides of the war. He was certain Jelly was Hungarian, although he wasn't sure why he thought that, her name shouldn't belong to any language. Her odd accent was beautiful to him, as was her spectacular face, which, along with her shoulders, was too milky white for good health. While watching her, he noticed that she and he were the only ones with nothing to drink.

In a lull in her conversations, he intruded. "Would you like a beer or something?"

"In this stupid country I am not old enough, even for beer."

That would never have occurred to him. "How old do you have to be to drink beer?"

"I'm seventeen."

Now Dmitri had to struggle to make conversation. "When did you come here?"

"Last year."

"Your English is very good, you must've studied."

"I have gift for language, I told you – I am talker. I learn English here. Before that I was in Switzerland two years, there I learned French. Before that I spoke many languages, especially Hungarian, German, Russian. But all the Hungarians I knew are gone, I am the only one left. And no one would want to speak to the Germans and Russians I knew."

He thought it time to introduce himself. "I'm Dmitri . . ."

"Esterhaats. I know. I heard you play. I have often heard you play. Whenever I can find a way to get in free. I told the doorman at the back that I am your cousin – it is not so wrong, we are both Hungarian. I think he did not believe me, because if I am your cousin then you should get me a pass. I am lucky, I am so beautiful I can almost always get in. But I do not always get a good seat. If you would arrange passes for me, I would always be there, I would like sometime to sit in the front row or in the farthest box on the right side where I could see your face as you play, I love to watch the faces of performers. You are good at Bartók. I love Bartók, there is not enough Bartók. When I came here, I wanted to meet him. Even the Hungarians I do not know are all dead."

He had no idea how to do it, but said, "I'll arrange passes."

"Thank you, Dmitri Esterhazy, I will not make fun of your name either."

Dmitri did arrange a pass for Jelly Ujfalussy at his next performance, a pass to sit in the first row two-thirds of the way across where she could see his face. That was odd, he thought, he'd have wanted to sit at the middle or toward the other end where he could see the pianist's hands.

The night after the performance, Dmitri went home for dinner, where he mentioned that he'd played.

"Oh," his mother said, with evident disappointment. "Please tell me next time, Dmitri, so I can buy a ticket."

Dmitri blushed.

"Or maybe that wouldn't be good?" she said.

"No. I will get you a ticket. You will certainly not have to buy one, Mama." The annoyance in his tone and phrasing was for himself, not for her.

For the rest of the evening, he failed in all conversations because he was constantly distracted by the perversity that Jelly, a frivolous, momentary acquaintance, a teenager, was going to get his mother into one of his concerts, the mother who'd heard him play more than anyone else had or probably ever would. It was so natural to think of her hearing him that he'd never thought to arrange for her to hear him in public.

"What did you play, darling Mitya?" she asked him.

He told her the program and she asked to hear part of it.

"Pavel is much better, maybe he would like to listen too?"

"I would like to hear, Mitya, if it doesn't turn me green again."

Dmitri was hesitant until Pavel laughed to relieve his concern. He went to his old piano, fearing it would be out of tune. He rippled the keys from bottom to top. It was in tune. He sat before it and his head began to clear, his failure to get his mother into a concert, his absence from her home except for occasional visits for dinner, his poor presence when he was there, all dissipated as his teenage agonies had dissipated when he sat here. Because he didn't want to lose Pavel, Dmitri decided to change the order of the program, beginning with Mozart and leading up to the percussive pieces, using Mozart as a soft introduction rather than as a consolation. He didn't follow such principles in organizing public concerts, and therefore he gave little thought to doing it this way now. But, as soon as he began, he sensed it was wrong, it wouldn't work – perhaps it would work for Pavel, but not for himself. Mozart transported Dmitri back to the piano in Kiev, where he sat beside his aunt as he played it for the first time, for the first of many times. Debussy then brought him forward by a decade, into his teens, to the bench of *Mademoiselle* Meursault and all the rest of that time. He could play these pieces in performance without such memories, but this was the very home of memory, here everything had a past, a past that flooded out the present.

Dmitri didn't wish to go further.

"I will come back to play the others sometime."

Dmitri stumbled through the rest of the year giving occasional concerts, usually accompanying someone, singers, violinists, cellists, flutists. With the vastness of his remembered repertoire, he had a reputation as a reliable last-minute fill-in for others who were ill or who failed to show. As a fill-in, a second choice, he demanded, and got, what he thought were reasonable fees. For his scheduled performances he got less than it took to live. Anyone less frugal than he was would soon have to quit.

Anton Staebli and Jelly Ujfalussy were his main expense. They came to almost every performance in the city and then dragged him off to one of their bars afterwards.

Anton lifted a toast to Dmitri. "To be born in Kiev and to choose to be a pianist, it is a two-fold blunder if your name is not Horowitz, Dmitri Esterhaats. They're all too dumb to recognize what they've got here."

Dmitri had finally learned to smile tolerantly when he was excessively praised by people in the musical world. Agents did that, Ben Schein had praised Sofia so far beyond the point of truth that his praises seemed to Dmitri like a flirtatious joke. But Sofia sometimes treated them as real and true. Sasha Demsetz now praised Dmitri beyond embarrassment, especially when he had to tell him he had no performance to book him into.

"Dmitri," Sasha said, "you're one of the greatest I ever heard. If everybody thought of you the way I do, they'd book you into Carnegie Hall. Hell, they'd book you every other week. It's a terrible time, Dmitri, it's terrible when such talent goes unrecognized. What can I say?"

"Sasha says," Anton said, "you're a genius but nobody recognizes it because it takes a genius to recognize one."

"It's good *Sasha* recognizes one."

Anton guffawed. "Too bad there aren't more geniuses in the world."

"If God wanted the world full of geniuses," Jelly said, "there would be a lot more Hungarians."

Pavel now worked in Wall Street. He left a message under Dmitri's door, telling him to come to dinner Sunday night or to phone him in his office or otherwise let his mother know if he couldn't come. Dmitri was not performing, he hadn't performed in a few weeks, so there was nothing to keep him from dinner other than forgetfulness. It was a problem even to remember which day it was, they were all the same. For most of the day Dmitri worried about forgetting, about getting involved in his music and playing right through the evening into the early morning as he often did. Finally, the distraction of worrying about forgetting intruded too heavily in his music and he left his apartment to take a long walk that would end at home.

The dinner was set much more elegantly than usual, as though this were more than a family meal. But there were only the four of them.

"Did Mama tell you?" Pavel asked Dmitri. "I'm getting married."

Dmitri smiled, then rose to kiss Pavel. Funny, Pavel, who was some- times teasingly called Pavel Pavlovich as though they were in Russia, who, because he was several years older when they came to New York, still spoke with a Russian accent, that Russian Pavel was hesitant to hug or kiss his younger brother.

"Congratulations! This justifies a celebration!" Dmitri glanced at the lovely dinner setting. "I will meet her soon, I hope." He wondered why she wasn't there.

Now that Dmitri finally understood the elegance of the dinner, he felt so much a part of this small family that he found it easy to talk, and soon he realized he was probably dominating the conversation.

"I'm talking too much," he said, borrowing a line from Jelly, except that Jelly always kept talking after saying it.

"Mitya, I have never heard you talk too much," his mother laughed.

"Play maybe, not talk," his father said with a perhaps grudging laugh.

"Not so long ago deathly ill, now to be married. That is wonderful, Pavel!"

Dmitri felt embarrassed at having drawn attention from Pavel, whose occasion it was. Again and again that happened as the evening continued. It now seemed to Dmitri that from his earliest memories he'd got attention when Pavel should have, probably because he was six years younger, a fact that never changed and that therefore put him at perpetual advantage in the family. It wasn't fair. Finally, with that thought to distract him, he began to lose touch with the conversation. They sat while his mother cleared the dishes after ordering him and Pavel to stay seated. Dmitri began to wish he'd had a concert that night and hadn't been able to come. He was then jolted out of that thought when his mother brought out his favorite cake. Pavel didn't like that cake and might not even eat any. Dmitri himself had outgrown it but didn't have the heart to say so to his mother. His mother gave Pavel a bottle of champagne to open and then she cut the cake.

"Pavel?" she asked.

"A very thin piece, just for Dmitri," he said.

His face must still have betrayed his consternation at Pavel's odd answer as his mother turned to ask Dmitri if he wanted a piece.

She looked alarmed when she saw him, but then she smiled as though to convey her understanding. "It's your birthday, Dmitri. You are thirty. You are not a young man now. You are a man."

It was as if someone had paid him an undeserved compliment, he could not immediately return her smile, he felt ridiculous.

His father stood to lead a toast, then Pavel led a toast, then his mother said, "To my darling man."

That phrase sounded so ridiculous that Dmitri finally smiled. But his mother called him Dmitri, not the diminutive Mitya. She declared him a man, a man of the new world. He didn't wish to contradict her in this moment, but he was not a man of the new world. He was also clearly not a man of the old world. He was a man of no world.

The cake didn't help the champagne, but the champagne helped the cake, so that even as he drank like a man, Dmitri felt like a boy.

"How is it to be a concert pianist?" his mother asked.

Instantly Dmitri became morose. "No pianist ever waited until he was thirty to start, Mama." Having forgotten all about his age, he hadn't thought of that before.

"I read these, Dmitri." She emptied a large envelop full of newspaper clippings, from the *Times*, the *Herald Tribune*, from papers he'd never seen, even from papers outside New York. "They say you're a fine pianist." She handed them to him. Julia Smythe and Sofia Milano would have wanted to read them immediately. Dmitri didn't want to read them ever.

"I got a piano tuner Friday, Dmitri darling. Play for me."

Dmitri played Chopin, Liszt, Beethoven, Mozart, the pieces his mother had grown to love in his two year ritual at his piano from Horace Gmund.

"And Debussy, one Debussy," she said when he finished and started to rise from the bench.

He played it as though his mother were herself and *Mademoiselle* Meursault together, he played it wishing it would not end.

As he finished, with his eyes closed, his mother sat beside him on the bench. Unlike Pavel, she was still Russian through and through. She kissed him and held herself tight against him. "What can you do, Dmitri? If these reviewers all know you're good. Can you go back to Mr. Schein, Dmitri?"

"I don't know, Mama. I will try. Tomorrow I will try."

Benjamin Schein had a large folder full of clippings of reviews of Dmitri's performances. He, too, had read them all.

"I been thinking about you, Dmitri. You're gonna be it someday, I told you that – how long ago? at least ten years now, isn't it? You might be it already except for records – records are killing us, Dmitri. People want whole orchestras if they're going out for the evening. Pianists they can get on records. Schnabel, Rubinstein, Horowitz, Gieseking. So they think, Who needs to go to a lot of trouble to hear some guy whose name they never heard. Even if Esterhaats is supposed to be good, how much could he improve on Schnabel?"

But Ben took Dmitri's address and told him not to give up – in a few months maybe there would be a good ensemble.

Two weeks later Dmitri was asked to come to see another impresario, Giorgio Gaspari.

"Ben Schein told me you're good. You're reliable on tour, you work hard, you can do all the hard twentieth century stuff. You played for Sofia Milano on her last tour?"

The slight lifting of his eyebrows was Dmitri's assent. He started to ask, Was that her last tour, but he didn't.

"What did you think of Sofia Milano?"

"She had a beautiful voice."

Gaspari looked attentive as though he expected Dmitri to say more. Dmitri said nothing. "What happened to her?"

"I don't know. I haven't heard from her. I don't usually read newspapers."

"No, that's not what I . . ." Gaspari inhaled demonstratively. "You haven't heard anything? She went back to Italy almost immediately after the war. She wanted to teach."

"That was always what she wanted to do. But she wouldn't go while the fascists were there."

"I heard stories you were very close to her."

Dmitri frowned.

"Was that wrong?"

"Many people thought that. It was only natural, we were traveling together. But I was just her accompaniment. When she said it, people wanted not to believe it."

"You're right, she sure as hell had a beautiful voice."

"Yes, her Aida."

Gaspari said he had a possible opening for Dmitri. A good trio was probably going to need to replace its pianist sometime in the spring because the pianist was thinking of emigrating to Israel. "You won't get another chance like tha."

Dmitri suspected that to go with the trio would mean he had to play what the senior members chose, and it definitely meant he wouldn't be playing the strongest keyboard music.

"In a trio I would disappear," he said.

"Would it be so different from what you've got?"

Dmitri became irritated. Gaspari was going to be of no help.

"Hey, look, Esterhaats, Dmitri, I understand. I've got a violinist, she tells me every week to get her something, a two week tour, one real performance in New York, anything. But not a trio or a quartet. She wants to play her violin. She asks me if I don't think she's good enough. I tell her, Hey Linda, you're the best violinist in New York under forty, if I wanted to listen to a violin I'd want it to be yours. That's what I'm telling you, Dmitri, she's the best and I can't get her booked. And now you want to get booked too. So what am I going to do, Dmitri, I can't book one, how'm I going to book you both?"

Dmitri went to Gaspari's window and looked out. "Book us together," he said.

"Hey!" Gaspari walked around without talking for a minute as though debating with himself what to say. "Look, Dmitri, how can I tell you? You've got a reputation, you wreck women. I could book you with Linda next month. It was the first thing I thought of, but I couldn't do it, Dmitri, you'd get into her pants in a week and she'd be washed up in – how long did it take Sofia Milano? Three years? And that dancer, I don't even know the story on that one, she was with Sasha Demsetz, how long was it? I don't know what to say, Dmitri, maybe I believe you when you say you had nothing going for Milano, I don't know."

Dmitri turned to leave.

"Wait a minute, Dmitri, hey. Make me believe you, tell me what happened. If you give me a good line and I believe you, I'll get you in Town Hall next month, maybe six weeks. What happened, Dmitri? Make me believe."

"I don't know what my reputation is. But it was not that. Sofia was on her last tour, I was on my first. She wanted to do what she knew best, I wanted to experiment. I couldn't play *Aida* for three years. That was our conflict. If your violinist wishes to play the same twelve pieces every week, I don't want to play with her." He turned again to leave.

"Hey, Dmitri, wait a goddamned minute, come on. Linda's as good as Sofia and as young as you and she hates getting stuck in a rut, that's the way she says it. And she's a better violinist than Julia Smythe is a ballerina."

Dmitri was silenced.

"Call me Giorgio, Dmitri. Come on, say it for me, Giorgio. Huh?"

"Giorgio."

"How broke are you, Dmitri?"

Dmitri remained silent.

"All right, tell you what. I'm going to fix you up for Saturday afternoon. It's nothing great, but it'll pay you a little to get by. I had another pianist for it, but you're better and you need it worse maybe. Come back this afternoon to see my man about Saturday and see me next Monday to find out whether we can work out something with Linda."

Dmitri's wry smile as he shook hands with Giorgio was not a smile of thanks but of recognition that Giorgio needed the Saturday engagement to test him more than Dmitri needed it for whatever money it might bring.

Dmitri played on Saturday afternoon to accompany a tenor, Peter Schrank, whom Dmitri had met on occasion at Anton Staebli's favorite bars. Schrank was to sing German *lieder* on call from the audience, who were a dozen well-heeled young celebrants at the engagement of one of themselves to a German he'd met at the end of the war. Dmitri felt like a traitor to Anton in playing for another tenor. Worse still, the slavishness of his role revolted him, but he'd been paid in advance and now he played as instructed. The audience's interest in the entertainment was sustained by the challenge of finding *lieder* to stump either the tenor or the pianist. Twice they caught the tenor ignorant of some of the words, but never did they catch Dmitri. The selections became odder and odder and the tenor missed two in a row, to which he had to hum most of the way. He was a quick witted, jovial man who sensed what the sport was, to show that these amateurs were nevertheless superior even to these supposed professionals.

"You can't beat this fellow," Schrank said. "He's got a reputation for knowing them all."

He then walked away from the piano to get himself a glass of the party's punch, as though to show his own superiority in their chosen game of partying. If it were a real contest, Dmitri had little doubt that Schrank would win that one.

"Let's make it more interesting," one of the guests said. "A dollar says you can't play Prokofiev's *Marche*."

It was a trivial challenge and Dmitri almost indulged his revulsion by walking out. Instead, he indulged a different weakness and played the *Marche*.

"You got your dollar," the challenger said. "Who'll take on Dmitri for double my challenge?"

Dmitri was irritated at the man's familiar tone, a tone reserved for children or servants. He stopped hearing much of what was said other than the challenge titles. Someone doubled and Dmitri played the piece. The sport continued for thirteen consecutive challenges. It was a trivial task – none of the guests seemed to be even half seriously interested in music. Dmitri suspected he could've played everything they'd collectively ever heard without severely testing his own reservoir. They couldn't know they were up against Sally's barroom pianist. Thanks to Sally, he could even play many of the popular songs they knew, although he wouldn't let them know that.

At Bill's call for a fourteenth challenge, someone said, "Hey, do you bastards have any idea how much we're in for?"

None of the bastards had any idea. One of them quickly figured it out: 1, 2, 4, 8, 16, 32, 64, 128, 256, 512, 1024, 2048, 4096. "$4096," he said.

Disbelief required that others refigure the amount. "No, Frank, I get only $288," someone said.

"Damn it," Frank said, "I'm an accountant, the one thing I can do is numbers, especially when they spell money. It's $4092 exactly. That's what we owe the son of a bitch."

"That's a pretty good joke," Bill said.

"You did not mean it as a joke," Dmitri answered.

"Hey, Dmitri, be serious. We didn't have any idea we were playing away that kind of money. Come on, here's ten dollars, call it a day."

"I've been playing more than three hours. I made ten dollars in less than an hour."

"So what do you want? Thirty dollars for three lousy hours?"

"You will default."

"Twenty dollars, Dmitri, that's all. Take it and go."

"Twenty dollars would not pay the ushers at my performances. You are graceless boors." Dmitri's words surprised himself. He had no idea how much ushers were paid and he'd never told anyone off so straightforwardly. His main pleasure in that moment was not that he'd bested them, in besting them he'd been responding to their whims, playing pieces selected for their oddity rather than their quality. His main pleasure was that, as they all stood facing him, it was clear that he was taller than they were, they were looking up at him or down at the floor, they were embarrassed. Even Bill with his tough tone was red in the face more from embarrassment at being a fool than from anger.

"Someday you will be business leaders," he said. "That is how you will do it then too, defaulting whenever you can get away with it. Keep your twenty dollars. You may need it."

As they left, Schrank stretched his range to boom out Figaro's "*Che vuol ballare*," straining his voice downward, telling the manipulative count, if you want to play, I can play at this game too. Dmitri only wished he could accompany on the piano while walking out. Sofia often nearly wrecked her voice to taunt Dmitri with that *aria*. As he listened to Schrank now, he was filled with all the warmth he had for Sofia and for Anton, somehow blended. Schrank stopped singing when they were halfway down the block.

Dmitri wasn't ready for the moment to pass. "No, don't quit."

Schrank did the whole *aria* and while he sang Dmitri followed where he led.

When Schrank finished the *aria*, Dmitri reached out to shake his hand in farewell.

"I promised Anton I bring you to the bar."

Dmitri didn't want to go, but for Schrank, for whom he felt such warmth, he would do it. "You shouldn't break promises, I guess."

"Hey, Dmitri, Peter, we nearly gave up and got drunk without you," Anton said.

Schrank told the story of the afternoon's exploits with great gusto as though he were still invested with the character of Figaro. When either he or Anton laughed, the other laughed too, and their booming laughter shook Dmitri's chest.

Anton wanted to know more. He badgered Dmitri to tell his own version of the story.

"I thought it would be too much for them to pay, they didn't know what they were doing. I was going to wait until after one more song and then call their bet. I didn't want to stay any longer. But they figured it out before I had the chance."

"How did you know, Dmitri?" Jelly asked. "You're not *that* kind of Hungarian."

Anton was not sure whether he should be insulted. "What kind is that?"

"The ones who do the mathematics and physics to make atomic bomb, who do what you could never understand."

"And for that you think we need more Hungarians?"

Jelly ignored that question. "How did you know?"

Dmitri, who hadn't enjoyed math in school, had enjoyed the puzzles of Spearman in the bookstore next door to Gmund, and best of all the puzzles he enjoyed the mythical history of the invention of chess. The inventor of the game was supposed to have been asked by the *Maharaja* what reward he'd like to have for his ingenuity. The clever inventor modestly asked for one grain of wheat on the first square of the chess board, two grains on the second square, four on the fourth, and so on for the sixty-four squares of the board. Like Dmitri's boorish celebrants, the *Maharaja* thought nothing of so simple a wish and even pitied the inventor for setting his sights so low. He ordered in a sack of wheat to count out the reward. That first sack took care of many squares. The next sack took care of only one more, and the next did only half a square. It didn't take many more sacks to make clear the magnitude of the inventor's request.

"In fact," Spearman said, "it would be more wheat than there is grown in the whole world."

That long afternoon was one of the few times in Dmitri's childhood after coming to America that he could remember laughing. He hadn't really believed the tale until he and Spearman spent the rest of the afternoon and half the evening figuring out the number, and every time an impossibly big number – a million, a billion – was exceeded, Dmitri laughed harder than before until Spearman teased him, saying, "If your laugh escalates with the numbers, you'll explode before we get through all this."

They then figured out how long it would take Dmitri to play as many notes as the chess inventor was owed grains of wheat and how long the keyboard would be if each note he played were different. If played one note per second continuously twenty-four hours a day without pause, it would've taken half a million million years on a keyboard a hundred million million miles long. At those calculations, Dmitri nearly wet his pants. When he got home very late for dinner afterwards, his parents were helpless to scold him because he told his story with such exuberant insistence they had no choice but to laugh with him. Now, fifteen years later, he remembered Spearman's lesson and used it well as he played. He soon realized Bill and his friends would be unwilling to meet their own challenge, and thereafter he played to savor the moment of reckoning.

Today, in the retelling, Dmitri didn't laugh as he had years ago, but he laughed more than he had since then, not so much at his story, as at the laughter it provoked from those around him. In addition to the booming tenor laughs, he especially enjoyed Jelly's high-speed giggling laugh that triggered him to laugh with her.

"*Mein Gott*, Dmitri, you are a classic," Anton roared. "So you knew how much it was going to cost them."

Dmitri was too honest. "No. I just thought it was more than anybody thought it was."

"That is a contradiction," Jelly said. "How could you think it was more than you thought it was?"

In that moment, Dmitri agreed with Jelly that God should have peopled the world with more Hungarians.

"So what did the inventor get?"

"Spearman said the *Maharaja* had power to overcome his embarrassment at having to default. He had the inventor's head cut off."

Anton guffawed one last time. "You're lucky this is modern New York, Dmitri. You knew where you were taking your risks, didn't you?"

On Monday morning Dmitri stood before Giorgio Gaspari.

"You made asses out of those guys, didn't you, Dmitri? You are a competitive son of a bitch, you know. So that's what happened to Sofia Milano. You told it straight, didn't you?"

He suspected he'd passed the test, but didn't answer.

"All right. If it's competition like that you want, Linda can handle it. I don't know how good you are. Ben says you're damned good. You'd better be, cause Linda's damned good. Check with my man first thing in the morning about the schedule. You can try rehearsing together in a quiet room upstairs that has a grand. You'll probably start tomorrow morning, but I've got to talk to Linda first to make sure."

Dmitri heard Giorgio's sighing whistle as he left. He still doesn't trust me, Dmitri thought.

Linda Ney

When, halfway through Tuesday morning, Dmitri realized Linda Ney was studying him as sternly and dismissively as he was studying her, he almost laughed. Jelly Ujfalussy should've been there to comment. At his smile – perhaps it was a smirk – Ney became irritated.

"Are we playing?" she asked.

"Yes," he said, and then he smiled again when he realized he'd heard her question as, Are we playing with each other? "We need something harder," he said.

Ney wouldn't play anything until she'd learned it well enough to do it without the score. But neither of them had ever played many violin and keyboard duos and they didn't know the extensive repertoire. Ney knew violin concertos with orchestra from the baroque to Brahms and Dvorak, but Dmitri did not know the orchestral reductions for them. Today they were stuck playing what both already knew or what Ney knew that Gaspari had sheet music for. It was a clumsy test of their combined skills.

"What do you suggest?" Ney asked.

"Bartók or Prokofiev?"

Ney frowned.

"Bach?"

She instantly came to life. She rattled off titles until Dmitri interrupted and told her the titles of the available scores. With Bach they played until Dmitri's stomach was audibly groaning from lack of food, the groans especially provoked by the violin's lower register, Bach's moaning passages, until his stomach surrendered and fell silent. Dmitri wondered whether Ney needed food.

"I'm starving," she said. "Don't you ever quit?"

Dmitri laughed slightly. They'd been contesting with each other to see who'd give up first. "I'm long past starving," he said. "There's a deli a bit up Seventh Avenue . . ."

Linda frowned. "Near that musicians' bar? I don't want to get near that place."

"You don't like musicians?"

"Musicians who talk about music, yes. Those people are musicians who talk about musicians. Half of them aren't even musicians, they're silly followers."

They went to another deli, one Ney chose.

Ney had beer, Dmitri didn't really like beer, for him it was a social drink, and this was not a social occasion. But when Ney finished her first, she ordered another for herself and one for Dmitri as well, not noticing he hadn't been drinking beer. When the beers came, she took hers by the handle and looked hard at Dmitri.

"Look, this might not work. We have completely different tastes."

"Not only in music," Dmitri said, eying his unwelcome beer.

Ney almost smiled but she quickly recovered. "I was talking. As I said, it might not work. But we can enjoy it for a couple of weeks no matter what. You pick ten duos you'd like us to work on, I'll pick ten, I'll ask Giorgio to get the scores for us. I'll play what you want so long as I know you'll play what I want. And even if it doesn't work out in the end, we can still be civil. I'm Linda. May I call you Dmitri?"

Dmitri nodded his head slightly, it was more a bow than a nod of yes. He took up his beer and clinked his glass against hers. She downed half her glass, he took a sip. "Linda."

"Dmitri." She almost smiled.

Dmitri began to look at her now. She was moderately tall with gracefully long black hair. Her face was sharp and he thought her eyes must be darker still than his own. While they'd played, when he didn't have to pay attention to the score, he'd watched only her hands, which seemed firmly, masterfully in control. He loved to watch violinists' hands at work, he could become entranced, could nearly lose his place in the music, as the visual music trumped the aural. Now Linda's hands were painfully nervous, she needed both hands on her glass mug to keep her beer under control. Her sandwich fell apart from her shaking it and fumbling with it, then she picked at it until it was all gone, until there was no crumb left on her plate. She frequently ran a finger under her long black hair to lift it behind her ear, and just as frequently ran all her fingers through her hair as though to comb it to lift it out from behind her ear. She seemed to need to pause before speaking to work up her energy or her determination to carry through. Then she talked much faster than Dmitri and used more words, as though nothing stood in her way.

Over the next few days, Dmitri learned that her constantly nervous hands became immediately calm when she lifted her bow and began the first stroke of her violin. Mistakes in playing made her angry, but then her anger concentrated her attention the more. Not only did she refuse to play a piece before mastering the score, she was uneasy even about rehearsing with Dmitri before she thought she had it under control. When she didn't yet have something right, her resolve was sterner than *Mademoiselle* Meursault's or the old Pole's. If Dmitri grasped his part before Linda grasped hers, her face became an imitation of Medea in her madness. Her body could be as reserved as Julia Smythe's, her face as unreserved as Sofia Milano's. Alas, however, she stood as she would if they were on stage in a performance, near the piano but facing away from it, away from Dmitri, as though to look at the audience, so that Dmitri saw more of her tall figure and her energetic right arm and hand at the end of her bow than of her facial expressions.

Dmitri's chief doubt for the first three days was Linda's dreadfully earnest manner. She visibly suppressed any urge to smile. He feared she wouldn't recognize a joke if she heard one, she would gut the few pleasures of daily living, and Dmitri might go crazy in her presence. When she announced that it was lunch time on Wednesday, he wanted to do something outrageous, anything, the more outrageous the better, perhaps he'd eat his food with no hands. Or if he were a gymnast, he could stand on his head while eating. Or he could dip his sandwich in beer, bite by bite. He was struggling with further ideas when he stood awkwardly and a penny fell from his pocket to bounce off the bench onto the floor.

Linda instantly giggled. "You laid a penny."

Dmitri stared at her in startled disbelief, he laughed, harder and harder, he laughed from relief as much as from her wit, now Linda laughed anew and he suspected she was laughing at him, possibly also in relief, they'd been withholding humor, smiles, and laughter as they'd withheld hunger their first day together. We must be idiots, Dmitri thought. He had no idea what Linda thought. He knew only that she laughed, her giggle now mixed with guffaw. In the end, he felt sheepish because she'd been less reticent than he had, she'd broken through their silliness over admitting to hunger and she had broken through their cowardice in introducing humor while he had failed on both accounts.

The scores Linda told Giorgio to get for them were stamped on the back, in very small letters at the bottom, "Horace Gmund" with the address and telephone number. When he saw that, Dmitri paused, staring at one sheet as though to try to read what it said. He should've gone to Horace Gmund's to buy sheet music, even to rent his grand. But he hadn't, he'd always gone elsewhere, he didn't want to get into discussion, there was too much left unsaid that stood in the way of saying new things, the past barred the path to the present. He was glad at least these scores came from Gmund's shop, he wished to tell Giorgio to go buy thousands, to buy everything in the shop, and to stop by the bookstore next door and buy half its stock as well.

Their first two days with the scores, they played Brahms, which Dmitri could sight read, to give Linda time to learn one of his chosen pieces. Friday and Saturday they worked on Bartók as well, and Linda's face several times turned red with her anger at her failure.

"I don't understand this . . . this . . . this *thing*."

She sounded as though she were speaking through lips disciplined to control her enormous anger. For her Dmitri did something he'd never done for anyone but Sally in Alabama, he tried to explain why it was the way it was, how it worked, how to master it. While he spoke, Linda looked down at her violin and bow, which dangled at the ends of her arms in her forlorn, loose grip. She looked like a sheepish child, gritting her teeth to take a scolding.

"Okay," Linda said through clenched teeth, "I'll try one more time. Today."

That time was better but Linda knew as well as Dmitri that she hadn't yet got it. She closed her eyes while clenching the bow in one hand and the throat of the violin in the other, causing Dmitri to wonder whether they would break. "I thought I had it. That's why I thought I was ready to rehearse yesterday. I don't have it. I'll have to work on it tonight and tomorrow before we come back Monday. I'm sorry."

"Would you like a beer or something?"

Linda put down her violin and bow, pressed her hand against the back of her neck, and rubbed it while rotating her head for a while. Dmitri suspected she was trying to decide what answer to give him more than she was trying to relax.

"Okay," she said.

They went again to her deli. They talked very little while Linda downed her first beer and began her second. Throughout, she managed to find it necessary to keep her eyes on her beer, thereby avoiding Dmitri's gaze. Halfway through her second beer, Linda began to get her hands under control, and then she looked up at Dmitri, her gaze firm and sure.

"We ought to be able to make it work. You probably don't want my music and I don't want yours, but we need each other. I don't think we'll know whether it's going to work until we try a couple of performances. We should keep it equal, your music and mine. I also want to do some solo pieces, I'm sure you do too. We should keep that equal too, my solo one night, yours the next, or both in one program. Look, that was hell today. I know it. Giorgio wants us ready in five weeks, he says we have to tell him Monday morning or he'll have to get someone else. I think we should do at least ten hours a day."

"We did ten hours today."

She put her hands to her face, dragging them slowly down until they were under her chin. "Ten hours of humiliation."

Dmitri smiled, very big, too big.

"You bastard! Are you making fun of me?"

He wasn't sure what to answer, he wasn't even sure there was an answer.

"You're doubly a bastard," Linda said after a long wait to let him stew. She was almost laughing. "You're sitting there trying to think what to say because you're afraid I'm an irrational . . . an irrational . . . what? . . . an irrational bitch, that's what. That's what you're thinking, aren't you?"

Now he was slow to answer because she'd smiled for the first time that day and because he was stopped by the transformation of her face and her character.

"You and your Bartók irritate me so much I . . . Well, by Monday morning, you have to decide whether you're going to work with an irrational bitch. You might just be too damned reasonable for that."

He started to say that, on the contrary, he'd done that before, but he hesitated to bring up Sofia Milano just now. In any case, he didn't have the chance. Linda quickly downed the rest of her beer, put some money on the table, stood, and said, "Eight o'clock Monday. Bring a lunch. Eight to eight. Twelve hours. You and Bartók had better be ready to work on Monday."

Bring a lunch. Yet again, she'd broken through their silly formality to suggest what he wanted to do as soon as she proposed it, he couldn't long afford their daily lunches, but it hadn't occurred to him to stop them. Naturally she'd proposed it not for financial reasons but for reasons of greater time for their work. Dmitri sat and watched her as she walked in her resolute way through the deli, out the door, and down the street and away. He had no idea where she went from here. She did not once look back. Single minded resolve seemed to be her characteristic mode.

Sunday Dmitri walked up Manhattan. In the late afternoon as he was going back south, he decided to pass Anton Staebli's Seventh Avenue bar, where he found several of the usual group, the group Linda evidently scorned.

"I heard you're playing with Linda Ney," Anton said after a bit of idle conversation.

Jelly looked up with surprise.

Dmitri smiled. It was true that they usually talked about musicians rather than about music, that musicians provoked greater interest. "Yes, Anton, we're rehearsing together. If it works out, we'll perform. Do you know Ney?"

"Yeah, I sang with her once. Schubert. She's not your type, Dmitri, she never gets beyond last century."

"Be careful, Dmitri" Jelly said, "she will cut off your balls." Jelly never smiled except when she laughed her infectious, *staccato* giggle, and her face now was stern as she spoke. But the lilt in her voice was smiling, almost laughing.

"This man survived Sofia Milano," Anton said.

"Oh?" Jelly said to Dmitri.

"That's a story for another day."

"A day in the past, I would bet," Jelly said. "It does not matter. I have not met Sofia Milano, but I know she is a nicer person than Linda Ney. I can prove it with certainty from only meeting Linda."

"Hungarian logic," Anton guffawed.

Dmitri smiled at Jelly. "Linda might not be that bad."

"If you want to crawl back after she finishes with you, we will try to make you welcome, Dmitri."

Linda and Dmitri worked twelve hours a day, six days a week, and Linda mastered Bartók in time to play him in Town Hall. She also took up Debussy, whom she mastered almost immediately.

"Are you sure you want to do the Debussy?" Dmitri asked.

"I have learned the score. I'm ready."

Dmitri hesitated, then decided to say it. "Debussy might take a lot longer than Bartók."

"That's ridiculous."

They tried it, and Dmitri was startled at Linda's natural ease. He'd bled to master Debussy, he'd taken weeks, most of the time discouraged as he'd never otherwise been about his talent, or seeming lack of it. Linda treated Debussy as an extension of her beloved Mozart, Schubert, and Brahms and she played it as a natural on her first attempt. It was inconceivable to Dmitri. Sadly, though, there was little Debussy for them to play together.

They had a program, half Linda's, half Dmitri's. Their last week was no longer trying to find themselves together, it was rehearsing what they'd already found, rehearsing the new duo Ney-Esterhaats. Giorgio came to hear them Friday afternoon, then sent his man out to come back with a bottle of champagne.

"This is the greatest pairing I ever made," Giorgio said as he lifted a glass. "You'd never have paired yourselves."

Linda blushed and Dmitri wondered what she was thinking.

"If you have any doubts, just remember," Giorgio said, "I'd never put anyone in Town Hall if I thought they'd embarrass me. I need Town Hall more than I need most performers. You guys will be great. But let me give you one bit of advice, no more, just one. Play half the time to make the average person in the audience happy and you can do whatever you want the rest of the time. I've heard what you've been practicing and I know your program for tomorrow. Tomorrow's okay the way you have it. Do it that way all the time. A little Bach and Schubert go a long way when it's time to applaud. If you guys just have the sense to give the audience one they like for every one you play for yourselves, you're gonna make it. This duo is worth more than the sum of its parts – and the parts are damned good. And if you think I don't really mean that, let me tell you, I never started anyone in Town Hall before, that's how sure I am of you guys."

Dmitri knew, and suspected Linda knew as well, that Giorgio needed them for Town Hall to cover for a string of cancellations from a group that disbanded on short notice.

Saturday they worked only half the day, went their separate ways, and came back together that evening a half hour before curtain time. Linda, who was always buttoned to the chin and the wrists for their practice sessions, was wearing an evening dress like the three Jelly Ujfalussy always wore, without shoulders or sleeves. For the first time, it struck Dmitri that Linda was beautiful. But she was more nervous than ever, she could hardly speak, her mouth was intensely active though silent, her hands were shaking as he'd never seen them, she alternately clasped them together and let them hang at her sides. When she once reached out her bow hand, Dmitri thought she was offering it to him and he took it between his hands. From the gesture of her left hand then he realized she'd merely intended to shake her hand in the air to calm it, and he started to release his grip. But she now put her left hand on his. Her hands grew calm as they stood in their foolish pose for several minutes until it was time for them to prepare to enter. Linda fetched her violin and as they headed for the stage she said, "Thank you." In the glare of the stage light, she looked more deathly white than Jelly Ujfalussy. When at last she began to play, her hands became calm and the rich olive color slowly returned to her exposed skin.

The hall was at most half full, but they'd been prepared for worse and, if Jelly's Hungarian logic was valid, the half who came proved to be the better half. In their practice sessions, Linda usually set the tempos and led their playing, except when it was Bartók. But now she let Dmitri take the lead. It was not until the second half of the program that she finally played as well as she did daily for most of their twelve hours together. To Dmitri's great surprise the turn came as they played Bartók. Then they ended with a Bach fugue for violin and *continuo* in which the Ney-Esterhaats duo finally came into its own. Linda soared in her solo role while Dmitri provided the lush background to lift her higher, and the audience was given reason to forget most of what had gone before.

In their Bach fugue, the duo became genuinely more than the sum of its parts, as Giorgio said with self-congratulation. It would continue to be worth more than the sum of its parts for more than five years.

Afterwards, Linda asked Dmitri to put out his hand.

"You aren't at all nervous. I don't understand that."

"What's to understand?"

"Why aren't you nervous when you face an audience?"

Dmitri'd never thought about it. He shrugged. "I don't really care about the audience."

That wasn't completely true, he realized, he cared about his mother in his audience, especially when she was an audience of one, about Colette Meursault when he discovered she was in his audience, and about Aunt Clara in Kiev. He'd even cared about Sally in Alabama and Sofia Milano. Now he cared about Linda Ney. But he could hardly care about an anonymous audience of uncounted size with indistinguishable faces.

A few weeks later, Linda and Dmitri arrived in Chicago to perform two nights, one at the University of Chicago and one downtown. They'd seen Giorgio's man in Detroit a few days earlier and heard their expenses were barely being covered by their ticket receipts. On the train to Chicago, Linda fretted continually over their impending failure if they couldn't generate larger audiences.

"We could cut expenses," Dmitri suggested. "Skip breakfast, lunch, and dinner."

"Don't tease me."

Why not? Dmitri wondered and, wondering that, he smiled only to realize the smile was inappropriate for Linda in that moment.

Now the desk clerk who was checking them into their Chicago hotel said, "I'm sorry, this must be wrong. You want a double room, don't you?"

Dmitri started to say no, two singles were right, but Linda spoke more quickly. "They always do that, just because we're Ney and Esterhaats. The least expensive suite would be good, we certainly don't want separate rooms."

In the room, she said, "It's cheaper. We can take turns sleeping on the couch. I'll flip you for the first night." She took a coin from her purse and prepared to flip it. She had difficulty steadying her hand. "It's cold in here. I'm shivering."

"That's okay, I'll sleep on the couch both nights."

"No. We do everything fair, fifty-fifty, or not at all."

She half threw and half flipped the coin, which hit the ceiling and then the floor before it rolled under the couch.

Dmitri laughed. "Whoever finds it sleeps on the couch tonight." He slept on the couch that night.

In big cities on the road, they were put in hotels near an agency office that let them use a rehearsal room for their practice sessions. In smaller cities, they often had no practice facilities unless their hotel had a salon with a piano, which Dmitri often had to tune. They therefore came to know the smaller cities well as they walked their streets for want of anything better to do, and they learned little about the larger cities. Today it was too late for rehearsal, so they went for a walk. Dmitri knew Chicago from his travels with Sofia Milano and, yet, as usual, Linda took the lead. She knew a route she wanted to walk, a route that took them past the most famous buildings and over to the fountain near Lake Michigan. They walked for several blocks, with Linda identifying buildings along the way, before Dmitri realized she always said, "That must be . . ." before identifying each building.

"You haven't ever been to Chicago?"

"No," she said.

For their second concert in Chicago, before a university audience, Dmitri had the solo piece immediately after intermission. He played Bartók's *Piano Sonata*. He received a loud ovation and, as he swiveled on the stool to turn backwards around to face the audience, he caught sight of Linda standing offstage cheering. After bowing, he walked off to tell her she shouldn't do that, her hands were too valuable.

"You clap for me."

"Then I will stop clapping too."

"Okay. But that was very good. I still don't really love him, but I can see why you might."

There was ambiguity in that judgment, but there wasn't time to pursue her meaning. They had to go back out to do Linda's Brahms. When time came for a second encore, Linda insisted Dmitri do another Bartók solo piece. He capitulated to her wish and played three pieces from the *Mikrokosmos*. With her manipulative wisdom, they received the best reception they'd yet enjoyed. Their applause that evening wasn't distributed according to her fifty-fifty rule but he had no doubt that soon she'd have an evening's preferred role.

Afterwards, in their hotel suite, as they sat on the couch that would soon be Dmitri's bed again after being Linda's the night before, they drank wine to calm the shaking of Linda's hands, which would shake for five years before and after performances and occasionally at other times while critics would praise her extraordinary control over her bow.

"That was the best I've ever heard you play," Linda said. "That's what you like best, isn't it?"

"Bartók? Yes."

"No. Solo piano. When you're all alone up there." Dmitri didn't answer and she continued. "You're lucky. I never get to do what I want to do."

Dmitri was startled. "What do you want to do?"

"Violin concertos. You know, with the orchestra playing accompaniment and me playing solo. You really want to be alone up there. I want a hundred people sitting behind me. And a conductor."

"What would you play?"

"I would play anything that was beautiful and difficult."

Dmitri suspected that excluded Bartók, and no doubt Prokofiev too, who were likely merely difficult.

Linda thought for a moment as she slowly sipped from her glass. "I would start with Pietro Locatelli."

Monday morning while Linda wanted to struggle without witness with a new solo, Dmitri went to a music shop and found no Locatelli.

"He's fiendishly demanding," the salesman said, "you've gotta be a concert violinist to play him. We never have any demand for him. I could try to track something down for you."

For the shorter term of that day, Dmitri was directed to the city library where he found *L'Arte del Violino* in an old India ink copy. Clearly that was Linda, the art of the violin incarnate. Even the lush paper and glossy hand-lettered ink fit her, she should have a gown made up from these scores. As he read through the scores, Dmitri could see why Linda loved this music, it was, like her, a combination of the frenetic and the controlled, it had range and energy coupled with drive and tension from beginning to end, it was a trial, it was at once beautiful and difficult, as she said she wanted her music to be. When not being played, it should be hung on the wall to display its visual beauty. He regretted his loss of easy memory for learning scores. The sales-man had suggested Dmitri take a pad of music paper and a proper pen with him, and it now took him several hours to reduce and copy half the orchestral score for *Concerto number Twelve*. He would have to return later in the week to finish it.

Tuesday morning when they went to the small rehearsal room a couple of blocks from their hotel, while Linda tuned her violin, Dmitri waited at the piano. When Linda finally rested the violin on her shoulder and shook her head loosely backwards to make her hair fall down her back, before she could say as she invariably did, "Where shall we begin?," Dmitri sounded the opening *continuo* bars of Locatelli's concerto. Linda, who normally played facing slightly away from him, turned to look back at him. The dark brown and black pupils of her eyes were surrounded by white. She recovered imme-diately to use her bow to conduct him up until the last moment before the strains of her violin rose out of the background. In her next pause, she unbut-toned the top of her blouse to free her neck before lifting her bow again to conduct him through his own part. Dmitri smiled at her and she returned his smile, he'd never seen her genuinely happy before. When Dmitri's score ran out, Linda's continued and he did his best to accompany her where the orchestra had a part. At the finale, she came to him, hugged him around the shoulders as he sat, and kissed the top of his head.

"I'm only a *small* orchestra," he said.

"You were the *tutti*, I was the solo. That makes you many more than me. You were wonderful." In a minute she picked up his score. "You did this? It even looks beautiful on the page."

Dmitri reduced and copied three of the dozen concertos before they left Chicago and Linda arranged to have her scores of Locatelli sent to them in St. Louis. In New Orleans, after ten days of rehearsal, they scheduled Linda's Locatelli to follow the intermission. During the break, her hands shook as hard as they had the night of their first performance, and Dmitri held them for her through most of the break. He had asked the stage manager to move the piano slightly farther back to put Linda alone at center stage, and when they walked onto the stage to open the second half of the concert, Dmitri had to tell Linda not to stand where she was near his piano but farther forward and at the center. She was so nervous she didn't understand his instruction and he had to put his arm behind her and gently force her three steps forward where she could stand entirely clear of the piano.

When he played his *tutti*, Dmitri played with the love he'd once lavished on Bartók, with the love he'd given Liszt in his youth. During the final long solo passages at the end of the concerto he took the liberty of turning to watch Linda play. Despite his odd angle on her, she was in this moment the most beautiful thing he'd ever seen. He wanted the impossible, to hold her as she played. She wore a long purple gown, her shoulders and arms bare, her long black hair flailing her back and shoulders, her head moving with her bow, her bent arm radiant in the spotlight, she was the very picture of the music she made.

When he turned back to his piano to rejoin her for the twenty second finale, his ears were distracted by the silence in the hall and their anticipation of the cacophony to follow. He seldom paid attention to the applause, so that now when he wanted to compare the level, he couldn't, he could merely judge that the duration of Linda's ovation was extraordinary. Against her hand waving to him to join her at center stage, he stood his ground in the wing until she dragged him back on stage with her after first walking off. As he had had to drag her away from him at the beginning, so now she had to drag him along with her for the finale. Again, Dmitri wanted the impossible, he wanted it to be her moment alone and he wanted to be with her during it. For their first encore, Dmitri insisted Linda solo.

"What can I play?" she asked.

"Giorgio would tell you to take advantage of the audience – play a movement of Bach, an *allegro* movement, the more *allegro* the better."

Linda took full advantage of the audience.

The critic of the *Times-Picayune* would call it the "best fiddling in New Orleans within memory."

Over wine in their hotel room afterwards, Linda said, "You're a wonderful *tutti*, Dmitri." She laughed at her own alliteration.

"The only thing missing was the conductor," he said.

"You didn't pay attention to my bow?"

While they drank through most of their bottle, Linda smiled beyond control. Finally, she gained control and her smile faded slowly. Dmitri lost his own smile in his sadness that this wonderful moment was past. He started to say something, but then, as he too often did, he inhaled rather than speaking. In an instant he grew wistful for the mood of the past many days, days of spontaneity and energy as though together they had invented Locatelli and then lived through all his pleasures. There was nothing Dmitri could think to say to bring that mood back, to note that it had passed would be to make it irretrievable – Linda's moods could not be overtly managed.

When her face had become completely serious, Linda's hands began to shake again. She put her glass down and a burgundy ring soaked into the program on which she set it. Dmitri watched the wine on the base of the glass flow over the edge into the paper, spreading the ring both under the glass and beyond it, until the remaining wine dried on the glass down to the edge, as though it were evaporating with the mood.

"Maybe we could both sleep in the bed tonight," she said.

Linda's spectacular audacity prefaced with her tentative maybe. No one had ever caught Dmitri more by surprise, not even the old Pole's slamming his hands down on the keyboard to stop his playing Liszt came as a greater shock. Dmitri had to restrain any reaction lest he react foolishly. He wasn't certain what Linda meant, wasn't even certain what she'd said as he now thought about it with his mind racing, but he wasn't prepared to push for greater clarity – it wasn't clarity he wanted now but beauty. The moment was so far beyond reality that he had no sense how to handle it, it was magic and, he feared, it must be fragile and with his large hands, trained for banging out Prokofiev, for turning the piano into a kettle drum, dared not reach out for it.

It was to have been Linda's night for the couch, which he'd had the night before after their arrival in New Orleans. It wasn't long enough for him, it wouldn't be long enough for her either, and it was the lumpiest they'd had with its uncomfortable buttons, its coarse upholstery, and the ridiculous double curve of its back.

"It's not a very comfortable couch," Dmitri said.

Linda looked up at him. She shook her head very slowly, he thought she must be viewing him with contempt, he'd been foolish after all. His mouth turned too dry to let him speak further even though he felt as though he were being roasted so long as the silence continued.

She smiled, just slightly. "Dmitri *tutti*. I never know what to think of you. I especially don't know what you're thinking."

"Sometimes it's safe to bet I'm not thinking."

Now she smiled. "I believe that. It's stupid, Dmitri, but I believe it." She stood and turned her back to him. "Would you undo my dress?" Then, as though in an afterthought, she added, "Please." For her, thoughtfulness seemed often to take deliberate thought.

Dmitri's days and nights of practice with Sofia Milano and Sally came back more quickly than he expected.

"If this works out," ever-practical Linda said, "at least I'll have someone to hook and button these dumb things. Otherwise I'm going to bend my arms someday so they'll never straighten again." She held her arms crooked behind her back as though holding a bow and stroking a violin. "It wouldn't work, would it?"

In more ways than one, he'd never seen her as he saw her tonight. After she went to sleep, he lay, his head propped up on his hand, watching her face in the odd light coming through the inadequate blinds of their hotel window on St. Charles off the French Quarter. She was a wonderful creature of reticence and control suddenly leavened with audacity, as when she put them in the same room in Chicago and the same bed in New Orleans. He knew he felt things he didn't understand. He loved both her audacity and her control even though he suspected the control was mostly invoked to block her own audacity. Perhaps if she gave her audacity free rein, it would overwhelm her life. Already tonight as he'd watched her play, when watching her almost caused him to miss his cue at the piano, he suspected he was loving her, perhaps he was loving her already in Chicago when she proposed they take a suite with one of them sleeping on the couch, or when he first played her Locatelli for her, perhaps already in New York during their most difficult moments or when he held her hands to calm them before their first performance. In any case, whenever it had begun, he was certain he loved her now. It was only odd, he thought, that she finally brought him close to her after he'd ceased to be her duo partner for a while to become her *tutti* accompaniment, her orchestra in miniature. Dmitri watched Linda, at ease while asleep as she never was while awake, he watched, loving her more by the hour, until dawn, when he leaned over to kiss her forehead, and then apparently he fell asleep.

He awakened when she brought breakfast into the room.

"I ordered room service, I never did that before, I wanted to do it for . . ." she caught herself.

When they'd mostly finished breakfast and Dmitri was still finding more coffee in the pot, Linda said, "Get up, we're taking a bath, and then we're going for a walk."

Dmitri smiled at her commands. And then he got up to join her in the tub, on the walk, wherever she might order.

A week later, Linda and Dmitri learned that their room service breakfast in bed was the slight difference between making and losing money in New Orleans. For all the beauty of their tour it could not go on. Ben Schein was right, "Records are killing us." Ney and Esterhaats never filled a concert hall in a year and a half. When they spent the dead summer months in New York, Giorgio suggested they go to Europe for a year.

"I could get you some foundation money to cover some of the expenses and you'd make more there than you do here with lower expenses besides. When you came back, you'd be billed as triumphant."

Dmitri didn't care what they did so long as they continued together. Having their income cover their full expenses was enough for him. But Linda was dissatisfied with their seeming failure.

"What would you do with money?" Dmitri asked.

"It's not money. Money would be nice, but it's not what matters. I want invitations to play with great symphonies, you do too, Dmitri, we're not getting anywhere like this."

They went for a long walk to debate their future. It was hot and glaring and they had missed lunch but for pretzels from a corner stand. But they were so intensely engrossed in their discussions that Dmitri failed to notice his hunger and realized too late that they spent most of their time with the glare of the afternoon sun in his eyes as he turned his head to the right to talk with Linda as they wandered south down the island. He was not alert to the sensations of his own body and he noticed that his head was about to explode only when Linda suggested they stop for a beer and his stomach rolled at the thought. His stomach had better sense than his head.

Linda had seen him once before with a severe headache and now she recognized the symptoms. "You have a headache?" she asked, almost in a whisper. She had noticed it at least as soon as he had.

Dmitri wanted to laugh at her sweet solicitousness, but he could not laugh without great pain. "Yes."

Linda, who was alert to wasteful expenses at every turn, flagged a taxi and took Dmitri to his apartment. She closed all the shades and rubbed Dmitri's neck and shoulders for a while. Then she stood and gently held his face in her hands. "I'm going out, but I'll come back in an hour or two. Let me have a key so I don't have to knock."

In two hours she returned with a large suitcase and her violin case. From her purse she produced two tablets for Dmitri to swallow with water. "About an hour now," she said. After an hour she gave him another of the tablets. By then she had unpacked her suitcase and had generally straightened up his apartment. "Would you like to lie down for a while, Dmitri? If you do, I should change the sheets, but I couldn't find any others."

Dmitri smiled and went to a closet, reached up to its top shelf, and produced fresh sheets. He helped to change the bed.

"You must be feeling better."

"Those are magic pills. What are they?"

"They're codeine. They're very hard to get. Those were the last ones my mother had. You have migraine."

"Migraine?"

Linda explained it to him.

"Why do you know about it?"

"My brother had migraine. My mother also has it, but not as bad or as often. She says they almost stopped after she was fifty." Linda pulled Dmitri down to sit on the bed and she sat behind him to rub his neck. "You know, I was afraid to give you the codeine. It's really powerful, you're only supposed to have one tablet every six hours. But that doesn't do anything for migraine. Mama takes two, then one and one after an hour each. She's afraid she's addicted, that maybe she gets migraines in order to take codeine. But she's even more afraid of going through a migraine, for several years she just had to live with them, she's afraid if she had to do that again someday she'd kill herself to get rid of the headache. You're lucky, Dmitri, you don't get them often enough to get addicted."

That was only true since he'd been with Linda, Dmitri thought. Before that they had come much more frequently.

After a while, Linda proposed they take a bath.

At the mere thought, Dmitri was instantly transported back to their bath in New Orleans with all its wonderful sensations. But one of the most memorable of its sensations was the scalding pain he felt when he first sat in the tub. Linda had laughed at him for turning bright red from head to toe, but brightest of all from mid-torso to toe. He'd insisted she was trying to sterilize him, and then he'd turned as red in the face as elsewhere at his unintended double entendre. "There's no hot water here," he said.

"I was afraid of that. I saw there was only one faucet in the sink. And you don't have big pots to boil enough water for a deep bath. We'll have to settle for a shallow bath. A shallow bath in the winter is a hateful thing, but on a hot summer night it's not so bad."

After their shallow bath Dmitri was still not hungry and he went to his piano. "What would you like to hear?"

"It's too late for that, isn't it?"

"Yes, but nobody cares. This is the corner room and the bedroom is on that side and the kitchen on that side, it's the top floor, and the guy below specifically told me to play anytime, he likes it, especially if I occasionally play a bit of jazz or rag. He loaned me all of Scott Joplin and Jelly Roll Morton. The people across the street might care, but one of them plays cello at all hours while sitting right at the open window and one of them is a soprano who sings only after midnight. She likes Verdi. I know every Verdi soprano accompaniment in piano reduction, so sometimes I accompany her, she leans out her window and yells *Bravo* at the end of our numbers, she and the cellist finally met one night about two or three in the morning when they leaned out to yell *bravo*. When she goes home she brings me food from her mother, she says her mother is a wonderful cook but a terrible mother and she never eats the food, the nicest thing she can do for herself, her mother, and me is give me the food, that makes everybody feel better."

"Mozart is good for recovering from migraine, I'll join you if you play Mozart."

At the end of the sonata, she lifted Dmitri's treble hand from the keyboard and led him to bed. The next morning, she went out to get something for breakfast and she returned with food and three lobster pots for their future baths. Without discussion she had moved in with him in his primitive apartment. He suspected she'd never lived in such grim conditions, but Dmitri was delighted, he only wondered why he hadn't proposed it as soon as they'd returned to New York from their tour. In truth he'd supposed she'd never consent to live in such a place, and he now wondered whether she would have moved in on a mere invitation. He'd never had so welcome a headache. Linda was her mother's codeine to him, he would happily have migraines more frequently to keep her in his life.

Linda and Dmitri went to Europe. They took with them a suitcase of contemporary American compositions and they followed Giorgio's principle: a Brahms for a Carter, a Bach for an Ives, a Beethoven for a Copland. Immediately they were playing larger audiences in smaller halls occasionally to fill the house. Their European agent knew where they should play Debussy and where Prokofiev, and once when he met them in Dijon he recommended they go to Germany if they wanted to make the most money.

"No," Linda said.

Dmitri said nothing. It was largely a matter of indifference to him who his audience were, and the offer of more money had little meaning since there was nothing on which he chose to spend money beyond what they already made.

It was a beastly day in July, the sky was perfectly clear except for a haze rising from the town, and the sun had freedom to glare down at them. Its glare had driven a rooster and a chicken into the hallway of their hotel soon after dawn to awaken them hours earlier than Linda would've wanted, and in the morning heat and rising noise level outside they found it impossible to get back to sleep. Because they couldn't rehearse in the church where they were to perform, their agent arranged a small rehearsal room near the center of the city. The room was in an old building at a big intersection, it had no ventilation, it seemed hotter than out of doors, and it was disturbed by the noise of heavy traffic with overloaded and underpowered old trucks and worn out cars. The upright piano was bad, it was out of tune, its action was slow, and one of its pedals was missing. Dmitri tuned it while Linda stood with her violin oddly ready, as though she were impatient to begin. She hated being hot, so Dmitri thought she must be getting frazzled by the heat. When finally she got to use her violin, their efforts to rehearse went badly. Linda's violin kept sliding from under her chin and Dmitri offered her his handkerchief to help keep the violin dry and in place. She frowned at the idea, but after another half hour she capitulated and took the handkerchief. Then she seemed constantly irritated by the presence of the handkerchief. At midday she was ready to quit in frustration. None of these problems might have mattered, Dmitri thought, they could simply take the day off for leisurely strolling through the city and sitting in the cool cathedrals and maybe rehearse a bit in the evening. It mattered only because Linda had a plan for the day and she couldn't be at ease if she didn't carry it out. He therefore suggested they go back to their hotel, where she could rehearse her own music, a Bach solo violin sonata for their Friday program.

In her apparent irritation, Linda walked fast rather than slowly, hardly slowing her pace to eat bread and cheese on the run, and they became soaking wet, with their hair matted to their heads, and Linda's long hair clinging to her face whenever passing traffic created a breeze to blow it. Linda was averse to conversation, as though Dmitri and not the weather were her complaint. That seemed odd, she could usually keep her angers in order and well directed, she even tried to engage him on her side in her angers at the greater world.

Rehearsal conditions didn't improve in their hotel, which was outside the city, in a building that had somehow survived two wars with its angled walls and uneven floors. The hotel was set in a farm with its chickens, dogs, pigs, and a few geese and its own stand of house vegetables for the peasant cuisine it served. They had to decide whether to keep the window open, their room had either noise or no ventilation. They were both dripping wet. Linda wiped herself with what she called the dishtowel that French hotels often provided. With the window closed she was almost immediately wet again. Linda was irritated at the noise, but she couldn't stand the heat, so she reopened the window. Dmitri would've preferred to go outside, to walk down to the river or just to sit under a tree, but Linda had become dependent on his presence during her solo rehearsals, and he stayed.

Outside, the chickens were especially noisy this afternoon, the rooster had lost any sense of time and was crowing randomly, a dog was barking past endurance, and the couple who ran the hotel and the chamber maid were talking or even yelling, either outside or down their hallway. There seemed to be mild pandemonium, growing more intense with the afternoon heat.

Soon, before Linda had enough of the sonata right to play it clear through, she stopped and dropped her violin and bow to her sides. She looked angry, as though she wished she could throw them without harming them. Dmitri stood to get her towel to let her dry off again.

With his movement she spoke, "You would do that, wouldn't you?"

Dmitri had no idea what "that" was, but he recognized her angry tone as the beginning of a bad scene. Once he'd recalled her mention of a strange museum in Boston and mistakenly suggested they not rehearse one afternoon and go to the museum instead.

Linda flared, "You would do that, wouldn't you?"

He was slow, but he soon understood she was upbraiding him for his frivolous willingness to skip rehearsing for the afternoon for a mere museum.

He answered, truthfully, that he wouldn't go to the museum for himself, but he thought she'd enjoy it since she'd sounded . . .

But she interrupted him and they neither went to the museum nor rehearsed. Their concerts in Boston were much worse than their audiences might've perceived for the accidental reason that they scheduled relatively dissonant and not widely known music. That was music she needed to rehearse if she was to handle it well. Halfway through the first of the concerts, Dmitri began to smile at the thought that he especially enjoyed this music, while Linda found it grating. Then he was dismayed by his seeming pleasure in Linda's pain, he didn't want vengeance, he'd sooner have her be at ease with him again, he only smiled at the thought that she'd brought on their hostility in just this moment when she most needed rehearsal and closeness to get her through the music. At that thought he began to feel guilty, to sense he really had been wrong to suggest the museum. He was at ease with the music, she was not, it was not fair of him to impose a museum on her or even to treat her need for rehearsal so cavalierly.

Recalling these thoughts from their Boston concert, Dmitri inadvertently said, "I'm sorry."

Then he recalled that today he didn't know what he had to be sorry for.

"*What* would I do?" he asked. As he did, he began to wonder what the next twenty-four hours might be like as Linda suffered through whatever pain and anger she felt. In the heat of the day, the chickens and geese were noisy and a dog chased one of the chickens into the hotel through a side door. The chicken ran down the hall outside their room, cackling and shrieking as it passed, while the dog came and went, barking, yapping, taunting the chicken, perhaps trying to chase it back outside.

"You would go to Germany. For money. Bastard."

After their first row in Boston, they established a manageable syndrome of a day or two. The only course now was to let her accuse him for a while, yell a bit, pout several minutes, resort to quieter accusations, pout momentarily again before crying dry tears, and end by turning her back on him for the night. The most difficult part would be to negotiate her to dinner. He would wait a couple of hours before beginning.

A sudden, welcome gust of air blew dust in their window, dust stirred up by activity outside. Now outside their window the hotelier and at least two women were yelling, other chickens had evidently got out of the pen. "*Fermez, fermez!*" the hotelier yelled. *Fermez* was a word Dmitri knew because some form of it was posted on doors that should be kept closed. He almost smiled at his paltry French, but a smile would've been grossly misplaced just now, he might be detached from the emotion of the moment, but he must stay available to it.

Linda changed the syndrome. "You don't even respect me, Dmitri. You're sitting there thinking, Oh no, not again. Sometimes I hate you, you're so smug."

Dmitri was startled that he could be so transparent.

Linda waited a minute while a rooster ran down the hall, crowing now and then.

"You never answer. I could yell for a year. Answer me, damn it! How did you get to be so smug? I never saw a smug ox before, Dmitri. Dumb Dmitri *tutti*, ox at the piano. If you don't answer me, Dmitri, I'll scratch your face, use your tongue, speak, don't be such a smug dumb-ox. That damned rooster has more to say than you do. All you can do is use your hands at the piano, and use your . . . your . . . in bed. Damn it, Dmitri, use your tongue!" She grew before him, she slapped him hard, harder, hardest, she knocked him off his balance and swung again as the rooster crowed past their door, skidding on its claws on the hard wooden floor, followed by the cackling hen and the barking dog.

"*Aprez, aprez maintenant, ils arrivent . . . Non! non, pas encore. Merde, merde, mon Dieu, quelle merde.*"

The hotelier's wife screamed, "*Ahi! Dans les legumes, Ah! Non, non, mauvais chien!*"

Dmitri finally stopped thinking, stopped trying to understand, stopped standing beside his life and watching it. He grabbed Linda's arm before she could slap him again. When she raised her other arm, he grabbed it too. She shoved and they toppled to the floor. He was bigger and stronger, he had only to stop thinking to gain control. They were both bathed in sweat and now the dust of the floor turned to mud on their arms. They rolled, Dmitri's grips slipped on Linda's sweaty arms. Then he rose above her, pinning her to the floor.

"I will break your neck," Linda said.

Dmitri was startled. It was a preposterous threat, she didn't have the strength, he wanted to laugh but didn't, that would've been ridicule, it didn't fit the moment, they were beneath ridicule. He stretched his neck out and let go of her hands to let her try it. She writhed free for a split second to get greater reach and she slapped him with a muddy hand. She slapped him so hard he nearly lost his balance as he sat on her. Maybe she did have the strength to break his neck. He'd been stupid to start thinking again, he grabbed her arms and pinned her back against the floor.

"*O merde!*" the hotelier yelled.

"*Merde*," Linda said, "*merde*, Dmitri."

"*Encore, ils vent. Aprez la grille, aprez, aprez, immediatement, vite!*"

"Open the god damned gate," Linda translated, "immediately, damn it, get them back in. I hate you, you bastard."

Dmitri realized she'd gone beyond mere translation.

He finally found a grip he could hold, he held Linda's upper arms where her short sleeves reached, until her blouse ripped and his grip began to slip off as she writhed free of the blouse to try to slap him again. Her blouse gave way completely and he grabbed her wrists again, holding firm despite the lubrication of the mud. She made a final lunge to escape his grip, leaving her skirt between his knees on the floor, but he kept her wrists in his grip as he fell on top of her. They now formed a misshapen T on the floor between their bed and the dresser in the crowded room, with its walls canting at odd angles, without perpendiculars or parallels, in dizzying perspectives above and around them.

"*Enfin, enfin, enfin! Fermez la grille! O merde, quelle journée. Colette, l'autre coq s'il vous plait!*"

Linda stopped struggling. "Finally," she said, and Dmitri wondered what she meant. But then she continued to translate as she often did for his sake. "Finally, finally. Close the gate. Oh shit, what a day. Colette, the other cock, please. They're making fun of us, Dmitri."

Colette, the chamber maid, trudged through the hall outside their room on the hunt for the other rooster.

Dmitri relaxed his grip on Linda's wrists. She twisted her head around to turn them into an ampersand instead of a T so that she could kiss him. "Stupid Dmitri *tutti*," she said.

After a long while, they got up, leaving half their clothes as dusty, sweaty rubbish on the floor. Linda pulled Dmitri's belt out of his torn trousers, shoved him onto the bed, lifted the belt as though to threaten him with it, and then threw it across the room as she pushed him down to lie beside him. They were in no hurry, Linda's plans for the day were long shattered and forgotten, they had only dinner before them that evening, and maybe a walk in Dijon or down to the river. At last Dmitri used his tongue.

Soon they lay basting in their own sauce, *au jus naturel* as Linda called it, because the hotel had a rubber sheet under the cotton sheet to protect the mattress. In the late afternoon heat, they sweated their love for each other while, half a day out of time, a French rooster crowed kikiriki over and over.

"Illiterate rooster," Linda said. "I'm making love to the goose while the cock crows. *Merde alors.*"

After a long while she said, "Now what do we do?"

Dmitri didn't know what the answer was, not least because he didn't know what the question was.

"*Mon dieu*, still the man doesn't answer, what am I to do with him? Look at you. Look at me. We look ridiculous. And what do we have for that? We have a stupid pitcher of water and two dish towels, that's what we have, and a bidet basin on its rickety stand, if you tried to sit on it, it'd collapse and dump you on the floor. How can the French be the world's greatest lovers without being utterly filthy people?"

When they'd checked into the hotel, they were shown their crowded room and they were shown the outdoor toilet and a room at the end of their hall with a sink. Then the chamber maid, who spoke admirable English for a French woman who'd never been more than fifty miles from Dijon, said, "The bath is upstairs. But it costs more than the room and sometimes the water she's cold. The public baths they're better and cheaper." She went to the window. "There," she pointed at a building perhaps half a mile up the road toward town. "They're open Friday and Saturday. That's when most people takes their baths."

"It's neither Friday nor Saturday," Dmitri said.

"And that pitcher is not enough. You have to get dressed and go ask for the key to the bath. I can sneak in so we have to pay for only one."

"What if the water's cold?"

"Might be good for us, don't you think? A cold bath two hours ago might've saved us a lot of trouble."

As Dmitri left to fetch the bath key, Linda yelled after him, "Hey, Dmitri, don't forget to get soap. Cold water without soap wouldn't help much with this muck."

He got soap but he forgot towels, and they had to sneak back to their room naked and dripping wet. The only one who saw them was a renegade hen still wandering their hallway. The hen shrieked and clucked at them in their nakedness as they dribbled along their path of wet footprints. Dmitri dried Linda with one dish towel and then she applied the other to him.

"Hey," she laughed. "This thing is soaking wet and you're still dripping. Look at you! All those hairs store up water. You'll have to evaporate dry. You look incredibly silly. Like a rat that's abandoned a sinking boat."

In that moment, as she stood staring and laughing at him, he couldn't have been more pleased to look so silly. When her laughter got out of control, she put her hands to her face to cover her eyes, which trickled tears down her face, she was laughing so hard.

"Your wrist!" Dmitri said with alarm.

"What?" she laughed.

"Your wrist. Look, it's swollen."

Now Linda became alarmed as she compared her two wrists. The right one had about twice the girth of the left. Dmitri reached out to her and then she noticed his left wrist was swollen. Immediately, he realized that it hurt, that it was terribly uncomfortable. Linda laughed for a minute at the odd asymmetry between them before she turned serious again.

"It hurts," she said. "What should I do with it?"

"Soak the towel from the pitcher and then wrap it around your wrist. You want to make the swelling go down. We need colder water. We have to find a doctor to see if it's seriously injured. It's your bow hand."

"We have to see if yours is seriously injured too. It's your bass clef."

Linda came to Dmitri to hug him and share his wet. "I slapped you so hard, I hurt my wrist. I guess it doesn't pay to be so mean, even to a goose." She giggled. "But it was fun."

They found a doctor in Dijon, who arched his brow for a moment, then reached to take Dmitri's left hand and Linda's right, pulled them across their bodies and put them hand in hand. "*Oui, je sais*," he said.

"Yes, he knows," Linda laughed.

They left with their wrists firmly bandaged and with advice to let them rest from further struggles for at least three weeks.

"We have to cancel everything," Dmitri said, somewhat tentatively, fearing Linda would be upset at interrupting their tour.

She smiled. "*We* have to go to Paris."

They found their agent to tell him of their misfortune and then they walked back to their hotel in the dusty late afternoon, with the setting sun glinting from enameled tile roofs and noisy cars and small trucks drowning out half their conversation.

"At least we're equal," Linda said, as she crossed to Dmitri's other side and took his good hand in hers, "your left, my right. If I walk on your right side, we can still hold hands."

"Still" was the wrong word, they'd never had the habit of holding hands.

Before they went to bed that sultry night, they removed the rubber sheet from the bed. "Our bath has to last us to Paris," Linda said.

At four in the morning, when the illiterate rooster crowed, Linda raised her head, cleared her thoughts for half a second, and muttered, "I hope they eat him for dinner." Then she went back to sleep while Dmitri, now fully awake, lay watching her. At eight o'clock they were on the train to Paris.

Paris was their honeymoon, they were forced to forgo work, they had only each other, they could walk and they could make love. They spent the August doldrums there while most of the French were elsewhere. It was unusually pleasant for August. Most days they walked all day, but on two rainy days they chose to stay in bed most of the day. Linda said it was possible to see everything in Paris by foot. She said it as a dare but Dmitri, who'd walked hundreds of times from Brooklyn to mid-Manhattan and farther, took her estimation as a promise, and they saw all of Paris by foot. It soon became clear they were not walking to see Paris, they were merely walking in Paris. They visited the Eiffel Tower only because it blocked one of their paths, the cathedral of *Montmartre* because it topped the tallest hill in Paris, and *Notre Dame* because the *Ile de la Cité* was their most frequent crossing point from left to right bank. Many shops, bars, and restaurants were closed but more than enough were open. Some shops with heavy tourist trade, antique and specialty shops, were open, and Linda and Dmitri, vagabonds without fixed domicile, found themselves looking at antiques in lieu of other things, looking at whatever there might be for Linda, the compulsive shopper even when she had no money.

For four weeks, Linda's hands seldom shook, although once it seemed Dmitri's did. They bought pastries in a shop on *rue Grenoble*. Dmitri's was a thousand leaves of pastry with cream between and dusted on top with powdered sugar. As they walked away from the shop, Dmitri took a bite of the alternately crisp pastry and creamy filling and a gust of wind dusted him from shoulder to shoe with powdered sugar the full length of his dark suit.

Linda laughed. "*La patisserie* Dmitri." His name rhymed too readily with words of Latin paternity.

In a scene that brought the attention of other pedestrians, Linda brushed Dmitri off with her hands while he stood, arms wide, holding a pastry to either side in his hands, and while both of them laughed, especially Linda. Part of the sugar found its way into the fibers of his wool suit, so that Dmitri bore his stripe for two days until they walked past a small men's clothing store and Linda took him in to be fitted for a new suit. From that day she slowly rebuilt his wardrobe with the aid of shops in Paris and along the stops of their tours. He'd grown up too poor to develop the habit of shopping for clothes and he still couldn't do it well. In reciprocation, she let him help her rebuild her own by listening to his advice on how she looked, and she began to buy blouses and sweaters that didn't button firmly up her neck or out to her wrists. As she became freer, she looked freer, she smiled more often, she teased him more, she spontaneously agreed to do things that didn't fit into her apparent but unannounced plan for the day, she would soon even do things spontaneously in lieu of rehearsals.

Dmitri dated these changes from Paris and their first freedom from the demands of rehearsal and performance. He suspected she dated them from their fight in Dijon, which she called "our own *moutarde de Dijon*, our Dijon mustard, special blend."

"That was our low point," Dmitri said.

She smiled. "I thought it was our high point." She slapped him gently with her bandaged hand, the one not held in his. "And just look what it got us." She waved her bandaged hand at all Paris.

They passed a musical instrument shop and went in. Linda could spend hours looking at and testing violins and bows. She went from one item to the next for a while and then she suddenly stopped. "A Kittel," she said.

It was in a case, whatever it was, along with several violins and bows, and she couldn't see it well enough. She asked the saleswoman if it would be possible to take it out of the case.

"Are you a violinist?" the woman asked with disdain.

Dmitri bridled at the surly tone, but Linda was accommodating. "Yes, I am a professional, my tour has been interrupted by an injury." She showed her bandaged wrist.

The woman was almost willing to suspend disbelief. She opened the case and asked which one.

"The Kittel."

The woman became a bit more open with someone who evidently recognized a Kittel on sight, and she took out the bow and laid in on the counter. There was no price marked. Linda asked how much, and the woman answered. Linda looked at Dmitri and evidently guessed he was struggling with the conversion. She laughed at him. "She said it's too much. Several hundred dollars. Someday I'm going to have one. But I can't afford it yet."

Dmitri began to fumble in his pockets to check how much money he had.

"No, Dmitri darling. You don't have it. It's hundreds of dollars, it's more than my violin, you can count your money ten times, you can even multiply it, and it won't be enough. We will have our days, but not yet."

They were having their days right now, Dmitri thought, having thousands of dollars would not be a great improvement.

The woman was now sympathetic. She took out a violin and offered it to Linda to try the bow.

"I'm sorry, I'm afraid I can't afford it. I haven't seen one in a long time and I didn't know they were so expensive."

The woman waved her hands. "Just play. I will not try to sell it to you."

She relented and played a Bach *chaconne* and then handed the violin and bow back to the woman, who now smiled.

"You need such a bow, you deserve such a bow. I hope you have one soon."

Occasionally as they walked Linda would suddenly turn pensive and say, "No, let's go that way," or she'd simply turn suddenly, as though expecting Dmitri to follow. The first couple of times, Dmitri tried to bring her back into conversation, but then he learned to let them, to let her, walk on in silence for a while. Once they were walking along a very long block when she wanted to change directions, and they had to reverse their path. As they regained the previous intersection, Dmitri caught Linda and hugged her gently.

"I'm sorry," she said.

"Would you like coffee?"

"Brandy."

Dmitri had lost track of the day and at first he thought it must still be morning. But it was afternoon. They went into the bar on the corner and sat at a small table at the window, with mirrors behind and before them. Edith Piaf was singing as she wiped wine glasses behind the counter, she was oblivious of the world, she was in her own private agony of love and loss. Linda ordered brandy for herself and Irish coffee for Dmitri. He started to say he didn't want Irish coffee or anything else with alcohol, he didn't even really want coffee.

"Sorry, would you rather have *Pernod*?" she asked.

"No," he said, insufficiently.

Linda's hands grew calm as she held her brandy snifter, warming its brandy, which she sipped slowly, and she and Dmitri were silent until the brandy was nearly gone.

"If it weren't impossible that she'd be working in such a job, I'd swear that was Edith Piaf," Linda said. She began quietly to sing along, Edith Piaf of the bar turned to glower at her, Linda stopped singing, and Piaf continued her song alone, in keeping with its forlorn words.

Linda laughed slightly, leaned against Dmitri as though to get warmer, and smiled at him in the mirror across their table. "How far is the hotel?" she asked.

"Maybe twenty minutes."

"Not close enough. Let's walk fast."

They walked slowly but they were sped up when they had to run to catch Linda's hat when it was blown from her head and along the bridge from *Place de la Concorde*. They went back out for dinner and a walk and they happened onto a late Mass at *Notre Dame*. Neither of them knew what the occasion might be.

"It's not *Roshashana*, you can bet," Linda said.

The worshipers seemed mostly to be teenage girls wearing robes of varied colors, a large group together in one color, then another color, subdued oranges, yellows, and violets on white or gray. At the entrance, the girls of a color formed ranks and went in in order. Linda grasped Dmitri's hand tighter and pulled him with her into the cathedral, where they found places near the center of the hall. Inside there was already row after row of teenage boys in various colors of robes in bold groupings at the front and along the sides. Linda and Dmitri stood and watched the slow assembling for the Mass and listened to the muted shuffling sounds seldom broken by voices.

"There are times when the French are the most orderly people in the world," Linda dared to whisper.

Slow, stately movement continued for perhaps half an hour, ending with priests walking along the aisles to either side to take their places at the front behind the altar. When all was in order and after a few preliminaries that Dmitri didn't understand, the enormous assembled choir prepared to sing from all parts of the cathedral.

"Vivaldi's *Gloria and Credo*," Linda said, at the first note. Dmitri had no idea how she knew, perhaps she'd understood something that was said.

With almost everyone in the cathedral singing, Linda joined in. At first when Dmitri heard her voice beside him, he thought his hearing had suddenly cleared to give to each of the sounds of the Latin phrases the distinction which was its due. Engulfed in such beauty, he was slow to deduce it could be Linda's voice he heard because he'd never heard her sing more than the little bit of Edith Piaf that afternoon and he'd never given any thought to her as a singer. During the solo passages, Linda was silent with the other hundreds of singers, but with the clarity and strength of her voice so near him, she turned the choral passages into solo with *tutti arias* for Dmitri despite the enormous power of a thousand voices around him. She couldn't know that in this moment she finally achieved what she most wanted: to perform as solo to massive accompaniment under the hand of a masterful conductor in the greatest of concert halls. The only shortcomings were in her instrument, it was not her violin, and in her audience, it was an audience of one. But, for an hour in *Notre Dame*, she had her accompaniment both as numerous and as talented as she wanted with an innovation in Vivaldi's form that Locatelli would have appreciated, with the addition of her own *sancto spiritu* to Vivaldi's. When the Mass ended, Dmitri wanted to applaud, to yell *bravo*, to throw flowers, to turn and hug her. *Notre Dame* was not the place.

They sat on a bench looking over the Seine, where Linda in her new, airier clothes, shivered a bit and leaned against Dmitri. He was talking about her wonderful voice.

"My mother taught me voice and my brother taught me violin," she said. "I wanted to do both. But there's only one life. Sometimes not even one."

Dmitri hugged her more tightly to him. "I wish I could hear you sing more."

"Maybe we should go to more Masses."

But when they happened into other Masses in France, where the choruses were smaller and usually down in front behind the altar, Linda kept her silence as the French worshipers around them did. Only in several Masses in Italy did she sing, as many Italians around her did. One of Dmitri's few regrets in their European years was that they didn't spend more time in Italy and less everywhere else. *Gloria in excelsis deo* came to mean to Dmitri to be at Mass with Linda singing solo beside him.

During their fourth week in Paris they began to exercise their wrists. Not to play, but only to follow a regimen of strengthening the unused muscles. They exercised together, with Linda taunting Dmitri when he forgot to keep his wrist in motion as they walked, and laughing at him when he unconsciously craned and twisted his neck in mimicry of his wrist as he exercised.

"I'm the one who needs neck exercises," she said, "I have to have a tight neck to keep my fiddle in place."

At the end of the week, after they were packed and were about to go down to get a taxi to the train station, Linda hugged Dmitri for a long while, then pulled his head down to kiss him hard.

"I almost hate to leave," she said. "I think we should just stay here. But we have to go on, don't we?"

Then, when the hotelier, attentive to their wrists, came in to take their bags down, Linda turned and immediately started down the stairs. She did not look back. Sometimes Dmitri wondered if she ever would.

Before resuming their tour of cathedral towns, they went to Autun to rehearse for more than a week in preparation, to build their hands back into form. Their agent arranged a tiny house on the square facing the medieval cathedral for them. They played and went to Masses, and when, back in their house, Linda sang after Mass to Dmitri's accompaniment on his piano, the priest invited them to participate in a Mass, no matter that their participation would not go beyond the music. When they were ready to leave Autun to go back on tour, the priest had them first perform for an afternoon without charge. Their audience grew as they played beneath the downward glances of the medieval creatures of the tiny cathedral, the faces of greed and charity, Joseph and countless devils, of others neither Linda nor Dmitri could've identified, carved by Gislebertus. Dmitri especially liked woeful greed, caught in the act by charity, but then Dmitri suffered only the avarice of wanting his life to continue indefinitely as it was now, to continue far beyond its allotted course.

In the intimacy of the cathedral, they played six hours, letting the audience choose half the composers, Dmitri soloing with Debussy and Prokofiev for a Catholic who said he was a Communist, and Linda soloing with Locatelli to Dmitri's *tutti* and with Bach by herself. The priest left for a moment after a couple of hours and returned with a cello and a bundle of scores, and the performance ended with trios as sunset filled the room with orange light before throwing them into the dark.

The priest took them to dinner, which was mostly wine. He was bubbling with energy, he was full of opinions, *ex cathedra*. Linda leaned over to whisper to Dmitri, "He's practicing to be Pope."

In another minute Linda and the priest disagreed about something, and the priest, too accustomed to talking dogma in the service of tradition in his daily rounds, did not pay enough attention to what Linda said. He said Schubert was a source of great mystery to him. He loved the music but he deplored its lack of structure.

Dmitri recalled his own showdown with Linda over Schubert. They were struggling with a piece. He shrugged as though he were annoyed with it. Linda looked sternly at him and doubled his annoyance. She softened.

"You have to explode into it, Dmitri, don't you feel it?"

"Schubert is too sloppy, he never really knows what he wants to do from one melody to the next." As he exhaled his resignation, he noticed Linda's eyes. "You're going to correct me."

"Correct you? I'm going to *destroy* you."

They broke for lunch, they bought a *baguette* and a bit of cheese and went to sit in a park so that she might destroy him more expansively in the open air.

"Destruction is not without its charms," Dmitri said as they returned to the practice room.

"Then I failed. I will do better next time."

He had no doubt that she would, but the next time had not yet come.

Back at their instruments, Linda said, "Now remember, Dmitri, the quiet part has to be followed by a banging, crashing, throbbing part. You have to explode into it." She startled him by shaking him hard by the shoulders. "But *you* have to do that, Dmitri. Work with poor Franz. The notes can't do it by themselves. Let him transform you and you will transform him. Dmitri, you do it with Bartók and Prokofiev and Shostakovich – do it with Schubert." Her constant "Dmitri" was intended to belittle even while she was trying to strengthen his resolve. Clearly she had a natural advantage in understanding the contradictions in Schubert.

Now the priest said there was no structure in Schubert's composition. Dmitri expected Linda to shake the poor cleric by his shoulders, to shake sense and structure into him.

Linda quietly, almost sweetly said, "No, no, there is wonderful structure. Just note one little piece of it. Schubert had Dmitri playing *piano piano* very gently," her hands spread gently before her, "and then instantly transformed him into a dynamo," her hands turned to fists that drove into the air above them, "charged with speed in a *forte forte* part. That was electric, that was Schubert. And did you notice? When he made the transition, Dmitri grew, he straightened his back, filled his chest, galvanized his arms and fingers, then he exploded with enough music to flood your cathedral. Putting the two parts together transformed both. That is structure, brilliant structure, beautiful structure. Schubert is a great architect."

Dmitri thought Linda had portrayed her own character, with her *piano piano* control pierced on occasion by *forte forte* audacity. But the dogmatic priest couldn't hear her argument any more than he'd heard structure in Schubert and he repeated his sense of mystery that it could possibly work as well as it did. Linda seized the discussion and put her views forcefully, increasingly loudly, but, most of all, insistently.

The priest looked as though he might not handle her rebuke well. "What do *you* think?" he said to Dmitri.

Before listening to Linda many times on this subject, Dmitri would have agreed with the priest's views of Schubert, but Linda had taught him grudgingly to love Schubert. He sometimes still thought that the structure she found was hers rather than Schubert's. Certainly the structure Dmitri played was hers. "She may have expressed her point volubly," he said, "but it's compelling. Clearly, she has reason on her side."

Linda turned to the priest and, reversing the architectonic of Schubert after her *forte* blast, said, *sotto voce*, "*Celle-ci, la Raison, c'est* Dmitri." They began to laugh and Dmitri struggled to interpret the poorly heard French. In the end he knew she'd said, roughly, "Reason – that would be Dmitri." He was always reason, she said, reason beyond reason.

He laughed, blushed, and basked at once. Linda's wonderful laughing face held him, her laugh was an impossibly elegant blend of giggle and guffaw, it was contagious, it could wipe away hours of serious talk. As he laughed with her, love flooded over him as though it were an epileptic seizure, flowing from his head downward to his fingers and toes. It was better than the wine, it was better even than Bach and Bartók, it was the most wonderful sensation of his life. He wished it were as contagious as Linda's laugh. The mystery of the moment was that Linda's sudden twist in the mood finally moved the priest to hear and maybe even to accept her view of Schubert.

A few minutes before she fell asleep that night, Linda said, "Life can be really nice, can't it, Dmitri darling?"

At that thought, Dmitri could not sleep for a long while. It sounded too retrospective, as though she were saying, But now let's move on and forget that.

Over breakfast, Linda's hands returned to their normal routine, they were shaking almost too hard for her to drink her coffee.

They took the train to Auxerre, Bourges, and Beauvais, and in a widening spiral about Paris they reached Brussels, Luxembourg, Strasbourg, Geneva, Orange, and lyrical town clusters along the way before going to Italy. They came back through France to the Loire and more cathedral towns. They reached Chartres with enough time to spend an afternoon in the cathedral and to shop for lace. Because it was raining they started with the inside of the cathedral. They were found there by their Paris agent, who was desperate to locate them. He spoke with Linda in French, but Dmitri could now follow well enough that Linda skipped the translation.

"We need you for a concert in Paris."

Linda smiled. "Anytime."

"Saturday night."

"No, we can't do that, we play here Friday. I hate to travel the day of a concert. I need the day to calm down and rehearse. I can't play in different cities on successive nights."

"That is regrettable, but I understand. They will be sad. They thought you were the best people for the concert. It's for Ginette Neveu and her brother."

"Ginette and Jean-Paul? Schedule it later and we'll be glad to do it. Will they be in it?"

"She . . . no. It is in her honor. You haven't heard?"

"What?"

"She and her brother died yesterday. They were flying to America to give a tour. Their plane went down."

Linda closed her eyes and shook her head many times. "No," she said.

"I am sorry, *Mademoiselle*, you knew her?"

"I met her. She was very good. I'd like to be that good. We'll do it, I don't know how but we will."

"We can go first thing the next morning," Dmitri said.

Linda grimaced. "What if the train was late then, we'd be nervous wrecks."

Linda would be a nervous wreck. But a nervous Linda was a nervous duo. "It isn't far, is it?" Dmitri asked. "Maybe we could go at night after our concert here. You can't ever get to sleep after a concert anyway."

"If there's still a train," Linda said. She was always finding difficulties, especially difficulties in the way of things she wanted to do.

"I will send a car to bring you," the agent said. "I will arrange everything."

"Okay."

"You can choose the program, but they would like to have Ginette Neveu's special numbers. Ravel's *Tzigane*, Debussy's *Sonata for Violin and Piano*, Suk."

"I can't do the Ravel."

"We'll rehearse," Dmitri tried to encourage her.

"I *never* do it," she said, half plaintively, half angrily.

Dmitri recalled her refusing to do it. "You don't like it?"

"I could never do it as well as Ginette."

"Would you want to try for her sake?"

"Dmitri, damn it, don't do that." She put her hand up to rub her face. "Okay, damn you, I'll try. But if I can't do it, we have to change the program at the end. That's the only way, okay?"

They made up a program and the agent left, promising to return personally to escort them to Paris.

"Ginette was only thirty," Linda said after a long silence that he'd decided not to break. "I'm almost thirty. When she was about fifteen she beat David Oistrakh for the Wieniawski competition, she played Ravel. Oistrakh was already in his twenties. I heard her do Ravel just before the war, she was fantastic. Now her records are all there is. Dmitri, no one is good enough to do the memorial for her."

Dmitri thought Linda was good enough, he thought she was good enough for anything. He worked harder for the week they practiced *Tzigane* than anyone should work in Chartres. He never got to see the lace with Linda, he'd wanted to buy her some, and they never saw the outside of the cathedral, they went immediately from the inside to their rehearsal room to make arrangements to play late into the evening. Their memorial concert was a highlight of their lives together until then. Neveu hadn't received as great recognition in France as abroad, and now they got some of the recognition she deserved at her expense. They even got bookings Neveu had never got. They became known, they came to enjoy their receptions, they stayed in Europe for three years.

On their third and last trip to Italy, Linda and Dmitri began to talk about going back home. When they reached Basel, it was decided. They were drinking wine in their hotel bar to calm Linda's hands after performing.

"We will go back triumphant, Dmitri *tutti!*" she said with the flourish of a calmed hand in the Italian style to wave out the figure who stood behind his name.

Their waitress was standing beside her. "*Was sich liebt, das neckt sich,*" the waitress said, with a smile of warm indulgence and tenderness.

Dmitri's Dutch was inadequate to her Swiss German, he didn't understand, his smile to the waitress was slightly silly.

Linda, who refused to go to Germany and who'd used only English, French, improvised Italian and Dutch, and a bit of sung Latin in Dmitri's presence, said, "It's a German proverb, or maybe it's Goethe. In German it's always one or the other. It says: Who love each other tease each other." As she translated it for him, she drew her finger down the ridge of his nose and then tapped the end of it.

It seemed to Dmitri the most revealing thing Linda had ever said. She said it teasingly, with evident pleasure in the moment, with pleasure in him. To tease him while explaining the meaning of teasing, that was typical Linda. But that was only half the revelation.

"How do you know German?" he asked.

"I was born in Berlin."

The Linda who spoke with alacrity, who hurled challenges and details at his ears to provoke him and to inform him, who told him life histories and repertoires of great violinists, who explained the richness of the Masses she sang, who talked long hours into the night after a performance though they had to rise early to go on to the next town, the Linda whose voice was as resonant to Dmitri as her violin, the Linda of a hundred talkative moods fell silent.

For an hour Dmitri pulled out a few details. It was a task as difficult as his first encounter with Debussy, it lacked grace, it led to frustration, and it left him feeling the less for his effort. Linda's family had gone from Berlin to Paris, but Hitler eventually followed them there. They got out to Switzerland and then to New York. Linda's father was a violinist, her mother a singer. They taught school. To all of Dmitri's questions Linda's answers were Yes, No, or short, simple sentences with the barest answering content. Only once did she become at all expansive in telling the story.

"Our name was Neimann," she said, "but that looked bad for the American immigration people, so the man changed it to Ney, I don't know why that was supposed to be better. My mother's brother had his Polish name changed to McKendrick. He didn't speak English very well, he tried to explain that it was Slonimski. The guy kept saying McKendrick. Slonimski. McKendrick. Slonimski. My uncle couldn't understand how anyone could misunderstand so willfully. Finally, the guy slammed his form down and said, 'Buddy, it's McKendrick or you get back on the boat. We got no more quota for Slonimskis.' My uncle looks and sounds like a Polish Jew and he'll resent that name until he dies but he won't go to court to change it back." It was a story that should have been told uproariously, but Linda told it so quietly that Dmitri could barely hear parts of it.

In the end Dmitri had an outline of how she'd come to be the Linda he'd met in a rehearsal room at Giorgio Gaspari's agency, that Linda without a past as though she were Diana from the head of Zeus. So little did they know of each other: everything since their first meeting, nothing before it. At the end of the interrogation Linda sat looking not at him while holding her wine glass with both hands to keep from spilling its wine as she drank.

Dmitri led Linda up to their room. With their success on the tour, they'd begun to spend more on their rooms, and whenever possible they'd asked their agents to line up rooms with pianos so they could practice there. In their room, Linda said, "Play for me, Dmitri."

As she said it, she picked up her violin, and he knew what she meant. He played her music, Locatelli and Bach, he was the background *continuo* to her solo. In her solo passages he turned to watch her play with her eyes closed, and during one of them it occurred to him as he watched her and she saw nothing of him that she knew as little of his past as he'd known of hers before tonight. She'd never ask him to tell her and, except for two more details, she would not soon tell him more of her past, nothing more than the empty facts of place and age with all the dissonant variety of feelings and relationships these might imply if he chose to deduce them. It was only fair that he knew no more, Dmitri thought – as the world knew them, they were people without pasts.

At the end of Linda's concerto Dmitri waited for her to select another piece. After a moment of silence, there was a delicate knock at their door. Dmitri opened the door to the hotel manager.

"*Es tut mir leid, etwas zu sagen. Es ist aber spät.*"

Dmitri understood that the manager was telling him with great gentleness that it was late. He wanted to protect Linda against the need to invoke again her German past, but he spoke no German and he was reticent to answer with Dutch. He nodded his apology, saying clumsily, "*Entschuldigen.*"

Linda intervened in German of such liquid tenderness as to surprise Dmitri, she was as creative with German as with Schubert, she made it flowing and beautiful, she made it sound right. "Please excuse us – we were feeling so good after having some of your good wine. We forgot ourselves. I hope we haven't disturbed anyone. We're very sorry."

The manager nodded in a slight bow. "In fact, it was beautiful. I only wish I could just stand here and listen. I was at your concert earlier. You were extraordinarily beautiful. I'm thankful to you, that you came to Basel to play."

A few minutes later a maid delivered a bottle of wine, with its cork already pulled, and two stem glasses. They drank and, in their tipsiness, barely found their way into bed. Dmitri put his arm around Linda and she turned to look at him.

"Es ist aber spät," she said, Alas, it's late. She put her hand to his head and stroked his forehead with her thumb. As late as it was, as tipsy as they were, they soon made love, and she clung to him long after she was asleep.

When they left in the morning, their hotel bill for the long weekend was one Swiss franc. The manager was not there to hear any argument, they could not force their money on anyone, they couldn't even discover what they really owed. Linda finally gave up arguing with the woman at the desk and took a card from the hotel.

"I will send them a gift from Paris," she said in their taxi. She was committed to fairness above almost all else.

As they were about to board their train to France, they were bumped by half a dozen girls fighting their way off the train. One of the girls scolded another, *"Du Sarah."*

When they were seated in their compartment and their train was underway, Linda interrupted something Dmitri was saying. She was oblivious even of the fact that he'd been speaking, she was in another world, sending only a short message from it to the present. She spoke while looking out the window, evidently watching things as they passed, never glancing at Dmitri. "I'd like to love Switzerland. It was the Swiss Germans who got us to America. The worst curses in German are *Du Schwein* and *Du Sau*. I don't know why hog and sow should be such curses, but that's German. The next worst is *Du Sarah*. It sounds like a child's euphemism for sow. But that isn't what makes Sarah such a dreadful curse. It's the epitome of all names for Jewish women. My mother's name is Sarah."

Linda and Dmitri had three weeks of engagements between Basel and Paris, where their current schedule was to end after two weeks' free time and a final concert in Paris. Paris would therefore be their farewell to Europe. While there, Dmitri planned to ask Linda to marry him, it was the scene of the most blissful part of their life together, a proposal could not go wrong there. Anton Staebli had once asked a woman to marry him near the top of a mountain in Switzerland and she had agreed, but she reneged when they came back down from the giddy altitude to lowly Darmstadt when their holiday ended. Dmitri thought Paris should work better, they might even marry then and there before they escaped the giddy atmosphere of the city.

They arrived in Paris too late in the afternoon to do more than check into their hotel and go for a walk and dinner. They walked past Invalides and on into the smaller residential streets toward the Eiffel Tower. Suddenly Linda stopped. She took Dmitri's hand for a moment, then let it go again. Her hands were shaking. She put one hand to her face to press her eyes closed for a moment. Dmitri vaguely remembered they'd detoured around this area during one of their many walks while they were in Paris convalescing from their sprained wrists.

"Okay," Linda said as she took her hand away from her face. She turned back to walk into the forbidden street. She looked around skittishly at the buildings. Finally she crossed the street without looking at the traffic that threatened her. She stood outside a building for a while and then went in. It was a hotel. She asked the *concierge* if there were rooms.

"*Oui, Madame. Pour tous les deux?*"

Dmitri, whose French under Linda's tutelage had become passable, started to intervene, to say they did not want a room here for the two of them, but then he changed his mind.

"Yes," Linda said.

They were shown a room, in which Linda stood looking about for a while. She ended by going to the window and staring down onto the street and across at the buildings on the other side of it. In a terribly nervous voice, unique in Dmitri's experience of her, she asked how much the room was, then reacted with surprise at the high price, saying she was sorry, that was too much for their budget. It was in fact about half or less what they would be paying in their hotel.

Dmitri had been mystified at Linda's odd behavior during their convalescence here. But now he thought he might understand at least in rough terms, although he couldn't know, he could only surmise. Linda had spent several years in Paris between escaping Hitler in Berlin and escaping him again here. This very building must've had a part in her life sometime in her late teens or early twenties. The building must've been greatly altered since then and she now visited it to restore it to its place in her mind.

Every day thereafter, against her normal rules for lengthy rehearsal, Linda insisted they go for midday walks. She always led the way, talking little, usually only to ask him whether he wanted an apple, a pastry, or a coffee, or to say the name of a street for which Dmitri guessed she must be looking. In her face he imagined he could decipher the memories she was invoking but not sharing. As in the Mass at *Notre Dame*, he was her audience of one in her solo to the accompaniment of her Parisian past. Although Linda didn't drink much beyond wine in the evenings, especially after performances, she wanted to end each of her explorations with brandy or an *aperitif* in some secluded *café* where she could sit in silence until she warmed herself back to the present.

The final pilgrimage they made was to the street on which she'd suddenly turned around to walk back the way they'd come. They got up early that morning and began to rehearse. Nothing went right for Linda, she lost her place, once after a mistake she even corrected herself by starting on the same chord in another piece. It was a spectacular transition, it transformed the day and Linda in Dmitri's mind, it seemed like an impossibility, a gross disconnection in her memory. She apologized, saying that was the piece she really wanted to do anyway. Dmitri started to say it was not on their program for Sunday, it didn't need rehearsal. But then he joined in attempting the fugue from the beginning. At one point she stopped and let her bow arm and bow hang straight down while she still stood with her violin resting on her shoulder with her head slumped forward.

All morning Dmitri tried talking with her but she clearly didn't wish to talk. Now he suspected her mind was elsewhere and it would not come to rest until she'd also been there.

"Would you like to go for a walk, Linda?"

She led the way with tentative requests, "Could we go this way?"

Of course they could, they would go whichever way she wished, Dmitri was glad enough to be her accompaniment. When they reached the street of her destination, Dmitri remembered their earlier visit when they'd been walking without destination until she'd suddenly turned to retrace their path, her destination anywhere but farther up this street. This morning, with a clear destination, Linda had been walking very slowly all the way to here. Now, as they entered the street, she wanted to walk even more slowly. She looked around only in quick bursts of intense scanning, otherwise she walked without looking, with only a vacant stare. Eventually she stopped and turned to face across the street. Tears streamed down her face. Dmitri had only ever seen her tears flow from laughter.

She'd told him almost nothing, what he knew was merely that she was Jewish and her mother was Sarah, her name was Neimann until America made it Ney, her mother had taught her voice and her brother taught her violin because her father was too busy, she'd given up singing for the violin, she'd gone from Berlin to Paris – while he was hiding from the war in Alabama, she was hiding from the Nazis in Paris. He seemed to know her as well as she wanted to be known, he knew a few brute facts without frills, he expected to hear nothing more.

"My brother was visiting someone in that building over there when the

Gestapo came," Linda said, and then she was silent, her eyes closed against the steady flow of tears.

"What happened?"

"He's dead." She didn't choose to elaborate.

After a few minutes Linda spoke again, too quietly for Dmitri to be sure he heard right. "I play the violin for him."

She let Dmitri hold her but she made no move. She was shaking from top to bottom as though she were bitterly cold. He talked to her and rubbed her back. And in that moment when she likely heard nothing he said, he said he loved her.

"Would you like to go in?" he asked after a long while.

"No." It was the only one of her remembered buildings she didn't wish to look into.

They stood without moving, near a tree with its iron grating surrounding it. Pedestrians passed them with a quick look or none at all, except for a few school kids in gray uniforms, who stopped a minute to watch them. Dogs came to pee on the iron grating and the tree and their owners tugged their leashes to move away from this odd scene.

After a very long time, when the shadows of the buildings across the street reached them, Dmitri released his hug and turned to walk back with Linda. She didn't move. He took her hand, but then she followed at arm's length as though she were being dragged. He went back to her, hugged her for a minute, and then walked beside her with his arm firmly around her waist. He gave her most of her slow forward momentum for the length of the street and still thereafter until they reached the Seine. Once across the river, she began to walk more of her own accord, but only so long as he kept his arm around her. She ate and drank nothing for the evening, she said not a word, she sat on the edge of their bed for several hours until she turned to lie on it. Dmitri had to coax her to undress and go to the bathroom before he put her under the covers, where she lay still whether sleeping or not. She ate none of the continental breakfast that came to their room in the morning when civilized people in hotels in France must arise to eat or face the contempt of the chamber maid. She spent the day in bed, answering nothing to Dmitri's entreaties and suggestions, letting Dmitri explain to the chamber maid that their room could wait for cleaning.

Still the next day Linda was morose and distant. She got up to go to the bathroom, raising Dmitri's hopes she would return more nearly to normal. But afterwards she wrapped her robe about her, and went back to bed. On the third day, Dmitri became afraid for Linda, he did not know what to do, he suspected she must be growing weak from hunger, and he had no devices for breaking into her mournful agony.

"I could tell them to cancel the concert," Dmitri said. He did not in fact care a damn about the concert, he was only appealing to her compulsive view of their obligations to try to bring her back to life. Then, without thinking and certainly without knowing why he said it, he added, "But I thought you'd want it to be our concert for your brother and I don't want to interfere with what you want for him, Linda."

Linda stirred slightly. In a few minutes she sat up on the bed, letting the covers fall away from her. She put her hand to her mouth and blocked whatever sounds she was making by holding her fist tightly against her barely open lips. Soon she got up and went to the window, where she stood for a long time – whether looking out or with her eyes closed, Dmitri didn't know.

Dmitri pulled a table toward her with her morning *croissants* and *café au lait* still waiting for her. She shook her head. "Play the Bach fugue, you know, the . . ."

Dmitri knew. He sat at the piano and began. Linda let her entry pass and she finally entered several bars late. Dmitri had to slow his tempo a bit to accommodate her until, in her solo passage, she gained strength and speed. Her back straightened, her head rose slightly as she tilted backwards, and she played now with power she seldom displayed. When they finished, he started again and this time she played it better than he'd ever heard her do it.

Linda didn't speak all morning. At the end of the piece, she merely turned to motion to Dmitri with her bow. He couldn't have interpreted the meaning of the bow's slight turning, but he knew Linda's meaning. She wanted him to play the piece again.

In the early afternoon, Dmitri phoned the desk and asked to have a lunch brought to their room. The *concierge* was evidently reluctant, and Dmitri, in his odd French, had to explain the urgency of getting food to "*ma femme*" – "my wife," he thought immediately in translation, his French was not up to the relevant distinctions – who was not well. Several times he had to say, in answer to her assertions that the hotel didn't do room service, "Yes, I understand, but I will pay."

Over lunch, Linda finally spoke. "We have to change the program, Dmitri. I'm sorry."

"Take out Bartók and Prokofiev?"

"Would you choose a Mozart and a Bach instead, Dmitri? Anything you want by them I'll do."

It was unfair to the audience, who might be coming specifically to hear the modern music. But Dmitri suspected they would benefit enough from the intensity of Linda's playing to make up for any loss. To end the program, he chose Linda's fugue, which he now suspected had been her brother's fugue, and thereby let their audience have the most spectacular performance of Bach they were likely ever to hear. While Linda bathed and returned to the life of order, Dmitri went off to arrange to have an insert for their program to announce the changes and to include the dedication Linda wrote for him: In memoriam, Jerusalem Neimann, 1911-1941.

Linda was torn between wearing her most conservative clothes and wearing her most dramatic. But her choice was finally decided by her self-starvation for most of the past ten days or more. She was too gaunt to keep her strapless gowns in place. She asked Dmitri to try to squeeze them more tightly together in back, but then she looked odd in the mirror. The problem of dressing might have presented an insurmountable crisis except that Linda, always afraid to be late, always dressed well ahead of time. It took Dmitri, with his compelling visual memory of her in all her moods and clothes, to resolve the problem and to get her into a gown with straps and a light half jacket that she normally only wore when their concert would be in frigid quarters. That gown was black, as suited the occasion, so Linda accepted Dmitri's advice.

In the end, after Linda's difficult efforts to dress, they ran slightly late to their concert. Then, in an odd error, they made a wrong turn while walking down from the *Boulevard St. Germaine* to the church. Dmitri would never have made such a mistake on his own, but tonight he was attentive to Linda and not to the streets, while he suspected she was not taking her usual lead but was letting him get them to the church. As they finally reached the church, they turned around to the side of the church to avoid the main entrance, and there they saw two elderly couples, conspicuously English, struggling against the uneven sidewalk to get there as soon as possible.

"You're okay," Linda said, "these things never start on time."

Dmitri was startled by her speaking. She was compulsively punctual about performances, she was never late in all his memories of her, and she was often irritated by the lateness of others. Now on this most important of all her concerts, she was being humorous about being late. Most remarkably, she was being humorous for the first time in many days, and in this peculiar moment.

One of the women answered, "But this is France, not England or America."

The man holding her arm added, "The bloody frogs know how to do culture, that's one thing they start on time."

"I can promise you, you won't be late," Linda said with a reassuring smile.

Somehow, although they had no reason to recognize her authority in these matters, they seemed reassured, and now they even took their time.

As it became clear Linda and Dmitri were not going in the main doors, the woman who'd first spoken said, "You're going to miss a very special event."

Linda then lost her ease and found no further banter.

"Thank you," she said, no doubt to the brief mystification of the couple.

Dmitri suspected the couple had their views of the punctuality of the French and the tardiness of the Anglo-Saxon world confirmed when they saw Linda and Dmitri come before them as the responsible parties for that evening's tardiness.

Because she stood near him on the small dais and because he knew her well from fuller days, Dmitri was in pain to see Linda so gaunt, but near the end of the concert he realized she might now be more beautiful than he'd ever seen her. He was not comfortable with the thought, her beauty in that moment was a distant, formal, iconic beauty, intangible, making her seem untouchable and unreachable. Although she would've blanched at the cross-cultural associations, she looked more saintly than human, she looked as though she belonged outside the world, outside Dmitri's world.

"I was never going to go back there, Dmitri," Linda said as they stood off-stage in the priest's entryway waiting to return for another bow, "but that would've been wrong. Thank you for getting me through it."

"They might deserve an encore. But it isn't necessary."

"I will do it."

As she went on stage, Dmitri suddenly thought it was wrong to get an ovation at a memorial concert and doubly wrong to encore. How could he have been so slow-witted as to send her out there to do it? Linda was trusting him to lead her through the evening and now he'd misled her. She at least had the wit to play a slow movement of Bach to quiet the crowd. For years to come, he would be embarrassed at the thought he'd sent her out for an encore at Jerusalem's memorial.

They left for New York the next day and Linda, in complete exhaustion, slept almost all the way except when they were on the ground in Gander, where she wanted to get out and walk in the cold mist. Dmitri sat beside her as she slept, keeping her covered, letting her rest her head on his arm. At times when he glanced at her he was overpowered by the images of their final days in Paris, of her pilgrimage to the past and her great crisis. The final image was of her standing on a stage in a small church playing her Bach fugue for Jerusalem Neimann. Their French successes had begun and ended with memorial concerts for people from Linda's past, with concerts in which he was merely the accompanist to Linda's elegies.

As Linda slept beside him on the airplane over the Atlantic, Dmitri recalled that he'd planned to ask her to marry him in Paris while they had so much time together again without a harsh schedule. He was never as good as Linda at planning and executing deliberate actions, but this time when he would surely have done it well, his plans had been disrupted by the intrusions of her past. What was more relevant to the needs of the moment was that Dmitri began to understand Linda's control and the audacity that contended with her control. Linda carried out audacious moves with astonishing ease as though they were casual matters, her control vanished for her in those moments, but then it came back to govern almost everything she did until the next unlikely break. He hadn't tried to understand her urge for control of herself and others, he'd just taken it as one of the constraints with which he had to live, but now he thought he was beginning to understand the origins of the need for control. When she imposed her control of herself on him, she treated her own constraints as the constraints of the world, which meant they should be observed by others, by him, as much as the laws of physics should be observed not only by her but also by him. He'd supposed that her breaking through her control in occasional moments of audacity was caprice in the world she'd lived through or, just perhaps, caprice in her character. But now he thought her dispiriting control was her response to the caprice of the world, to the caprices she had suffered. Her audacity was her own willful character occasionally breaking through her orderly effort to deal with the caprice of the world. Or perhaps he still did not understand, perhaps he needed Jelly Ujfalussy's Hungarian logic to get the matter straight.

Linda moaned as she struggled to turn, and Dmitri carefully replaced the blanket over her shoulders. He gently used his fingers to comb her hair back from her face. He strained but could not lean over far enough to kiss her head while keeping it supported as she slept. He wished he had the character to wake her and ask her to marry him in this neutral territory in the sky between their wonderful past life in Europe and their future life back home. Better still, the plane should turn back. It was Paris he needed, the Paris of sprained wrists.

But there was never to be another Paris.

Linda and Dmitri returned to less success in filling halls but to greater success in making money.

"The halls are usually bigger here," Dmitri explained.

"So are the cities," Linda retorted.

Every time they talked with Giorgio, she said they needed an orchestra.

Giorgio pleaded with her to be patient. "I'm trying, God knows I'm trying, it's not easy. You'll have to get known here for a while and then we'll get orchestras. But even then, you know, don't expect instant miracles, in this business the miracles take a while, they have to be scheduled, and the scheduling is usually way in the future. When an engagement comes, it'll be for next year or the year after, not for tomorrow. Right now we've gotta get you performing, especially in New York, maybe Chicago, we want exposure. Even that's hard, hi-fi and TV are killing us, we're getting squeezed dry between Horowitz and Lucy. A couple of records might help us get you the bookings."

Dmitri wouldn't do records. He wasn't even especially interested in an orchestra. He told Linda he'd happily play Brahms for the rest of life to be with her, to be her *continuo* through all his days, so she wouldn't need an orchestra. She took her cue from his character in such difficult moments: She didn't answer. Days later it occurred to Dmitri she might have stayed silent because to speak the truth would've meant to tell him she didn't believe him, not that he was a liar, but that he was too muddled by the moment to know himself in the future when, although she didn't know the history to put to him, he would become as impatient with her as with Sofia Milano. Dmitri couldn't be sure enough of himself to say he'd never chafe under a regimen of sameness without great new challenges. But he did know he'd learned from Sally the capacity of accepting, of accepting Linda as she was, and loving her as she was. Accepting wasn't something he'd known, or even conceived, with Sofia. Now he thought he finally had the character to do it, but Linda's plans were elsewhere, she might not be available for acceptance. There's only one life, she'd said of her choice between violin and voice, you can't have both.

Perhaps Linda needed novelty, too, only not novelty in her composers. "Giorgio has a violist and a cellist for us to do piano quartets," Dmitri said.

"What would we play? Sonata for three pigeons and a duck?"

"You don't care for piano quartets?"

"There are worse combinations – alto, tenor, and base clarinets with calliope, maybe."

Dmitri sensed that, in truth, she didn't care for any combination, she wanted solos or solos with orchestra, anything in between was a compromise, and playing duos with him was the limit of her willingness to compromise. She saw the options as a hierarchy that ranged downward from the peak of solo with orchestra, through pure solo, then duo, to the dismal squalor of small numbers. Dmitri had a non-numerical principle, or perhaps none at all, he preferred duo with Linda to solo, he did not mind squalor, and he did not especially like solo with orchestra. There was room for compromise, but his worst was her best and he feared she must eventually get her best.

They were to perform in Philadelphia and they came several days early to enjoy a short break there and to be more relaxed in their rehearsal schedule. They had not traveled in such leisure since returning from Europe. On the second afternoon, Linda was fretful over their concert schedule. She wanted to go to Giorgio's Philadelphia office to check whether there were possibilities that hadn't come to the New York office and to check their finances. Dmitri hated both those tasks and Linda didn't ask him to go along. She suggested he go for a walk instead or work on his solo pieces.

Dmitri let her go alone and he went for a walk. After an hour of aimless wandering, he passed a large music store. He went in to look at the instruments on display. To him they were objects of overpowering beauty, he could watch them at work or just sitting on display and be filled with pleasure at their sight. His pleasure in them was not like Linda's, she wanted to possess them, he merely wanted to behold them. He'd always liked violins and bows, but now they seemed to him transcendently the most beautiful manmade objects in the world. They had gained beauty from Linda, just as she gained beauty from her violin. Now this particular store gained from its association in his mind with the shop in Paris where Linda had jealously looked at the Kittel bow.

A salesman came to help him and Dmitri said he was just looking. Then, without planning, he asked whether they had a Kittel bow.

"We do," the salesman said. "It's very odd you should ask. They never stay very long. Every one is usually reserved before we ever get it in, some wealthy man usually buys it for a child or a wife who plays at church or family gatherings. Pretty soon there won't be any available for real musicians."

Suddenly the salesman blushed. "Who . . ., who would this be for?"

Dmitri decided not to say.

The man brought out the bow in contrite, stuffy silence. The Kittel was even finer than the one in Paris. It also had a finer price.

"I don't have that much with me, but I can get it, maybe by tomorrow."

The salesman was reluctant. "How much *would* you have with you?"

"I don't know, let me see." Dmitri took a wallet from his jacket pocket and removed all its bills. Then he dug into his jacket and trouser pockets and he pulled out more bills, all of which he piled on the counter as the salesman watched with growing alarm. Dmitri counted $167 plus some *francs* that he put back in his pocket. Except for money he might have in pockets in other clothes, this was his entire bank account. "I should keep a little bit for taxis and dinner," he said, and he left $150 sitting on the counter.

"That is a sufficient down payment to hold the bow, I'm sure," the salesman said. "If you could give me a local address and your name, I'll have to get the manager's approval to write this up." He handed him a pen and a pad of sale memos.

Dmitri wrote his name and their hotel address.

The man picked up the pad without looking, then gathered up the money, crumpled and apparently unclean as it was, and said, "One moment." Then before getting very far, he turned back and asked, "Esterhaats?"

"Yes."

"Ney-Esterhaats?"

"Yes."

"This bow would be for Linda Ney?"

"Yes."

"One moment please." He came back to the counter to pick up the bow as he left this time.

Dmitri was startled by the gesture and he wondered whether Dmitri Esterhaats was to be seen as less trustworthy than someone with no name at all. He was reminded of Jelly Ujfalussy's quip that, knowing Linda Ney but not Sofia Milano, she could conclusively prove that Milano was the nicer person. By now he could conclusively prove Jelly wrong, at least to his own satisfaction.

The salesman returned and presented a bill for the remaining sum to Dmitri. "If you would please sign here. You'll notice we've discounted it twenty percent and we will service it at any time Miss Ney has problems with it. We don't usually give out merchandise that isn't paid or guaranteed. But for Dmitri Esterhaats and Linda Ney we make an exception. The bow is being checked. If you'll wait a few minutes, we'll make sure it's in perfect condition and then wrap it for you. I've sent the boy around the corner to get a rose to tie to the package for Miss Ney. I hope she can use it tomorrow evening. I would love to hear it."

"Thank you," Dmitri said, "I hope she will." His smile for the salesman was tarnished by his doubt, he was afraid Linda wouldn't accept the bow, she might object to the gift as unfair because she couldn't reciprocate.

"No, Dmitri, you can't, it's not fair," Linda said when she opened the package. She struggled to keep from crying, the struggle to keep from getting angry may have helped, she soon won both tests.

"You can't do this, I won't accept it."

"Try it at least. Please. For me."

The shaking of Linda's hand was magnified down the length of the bow, whose end cut a dangerous swath before her. Dmitri smiled at the vision, Linda's stern face broke and laughed.

"I will try it, but I won't keep it. It wouldn't be fair."

"I promised the man you would use it tomorrow night, he's bringing the whole staff to hear it, they've sold many but they think they've never heard one." Where had he got all of that? he wondered. Somehow it wasn't quite like a lie, he'd never lied to Linda other than to keep silence.

"How much is the rent for one night?"

He spread his hands and grinned to display ignorance.

"How much was it?"

"I don't remember."

Linda didn't press him. In truth, he did remember the original price, but he hadn't bothered to look at the discounted price he'd signed for.

"You're terrible with numbers," Linda said, "especially numbers of dollars. And *francs* and all the others too."

She picked up her violin. Then she laughed again.

"It's really not fair, Dmitri. You knew I couldn't not try it if I got it in my hand. It's just not fair," she said as she lifted the violin to her chin, trapping it against her shoulder. "I'm not going to use it. Four or five bars only, that's it."

She drew the bow down in the firm opening stroke of a Bach sonata for solo violin and with that stroke she closed her eyes not to open them for the rest of the piece. Dmitri was bathed in music and in the glory of Linda's beauty as she played. He knew she couldn't stop until she finished the piece and he knew she would then not be able to surrender the bow. He only didn't know how she would handle the gross unfairness of his gift.

"You know it is Russian," Linda said. He didn't know. "I think it was made in St. Petersburg last century, it must have played many violins since then. Nicolaus Kittel. I'm not going to keep it, Dmitri," she added in her last words before going to sleep that night. She was given to making her biggest commitments peremptorily as not merely the last word of a discussion but the last of the day. It was a powerful device which he could wreck easily enough by forcing her to stay awake and talk. But he could never bring himself to intrude in her sleep, not even to propose marriage to her over the Atlantic.

After the Philadelphia performance there was a huge bouquet of roses for Linda with a card from the bow salesman. The card read:

> Dear Miss Ney,
>   You play beautifully. The bow is fortunate to be in the hand of so fine a fiddler and we are proud to have been able to put it there. Nicolaus Kittel would be pleased to know it is yours. I hope you will cherish it and I know you will use it well. Whenever you are in Philadelphia – may that be often – please bring it by for checking and stringing.

"It still isn't fair," Linda said.

Dmitri took her "still" as her grudging acceptance of the bow and from Linda's reticence over accepting his gift, Dmitri inferred other things, too, many things. Or maybe he only confirmed those things, because he'd worried about her accepting the gift even before he made it. Whatever, he thought, I don't even know what I think.

Giorgio said it again, without prior prompting from Linda, they had to record if they were going to become well known. Dmitri frowned. He was not so quick to say No as Linda had been to the suggestion they go to Germany for their careers, but that was more a difference in the alacrity of his speech than in the strength of his view. Linda agreed with Giorgio and pressed Dmitri.

"I don't like records," Dmitri said.

"Why, Dmitri?" Linda asked gently.

"They ruin the music. I listened to two of Beethoven's sonatas, they were supposed to be the greatest ever recorded. The second or third time, they were dead. I played them with greater creativity when I was fifteen. If I'm recorded, I'll be dead after the third or fourth time too."

Giorgio and Linda argued with him for a while. Dmitri became adamant. It seemed odious to have a particular rendition of a piece be selected for endless replaying with never a hope of improvisation, not even the least flourish or change of tempo, it was to be condemned to one of the worst of Dante's repetitious hells. And with it all, the recording wouldn't even be good enough to capture that one rendition well.

"Would you rather be condemned to have no rendition available?" Linda asked sternly.

"Dmitri, your ear is too good," Giorgio said. "But think for a minute, think of those who'll buy the record. They don't all have ears like yours. They'll think your record's wonderful. They'll be right too, it will be wonderful. Most people's ears are only approximate, a good ear can be a curse. So what if you don't want to listen to it. Who'd want to listen to recordings of his own playing? That's not what it's for, Dmitri, it's for *them*. Come on, Dmitri, give it to them. Remember Caruso. He had a great ear, he heard everything better than anyone. But he had the sense to make records. Now those were some lousy recordings if you want perfect reproduction. But that's all the Caruso we've got and it's damned well a lot better than none."

"I haven't heard Caruso. But I've heard records."

Giorgio gave him a look of astonishment. "You've heard records?"

Dmitri misunderstood the reason for Giorgio's astonishment. "Yes. The *Rite of Spring* and two of Beethoven's sonatas." Dmitri thought he might have heard other recordings. There was also one Verdi *aria* sung by Sofia Milano for his audition at sixteen, but he did not wish to mention Sofia Milano. The first Liszt he'd heard – it must've been over the radio, maybe it was from a recording. That was adequate for discovering new music, it was not adequate for listening to music once heard correctly.

"Two sonatas and the *Rite of Spring*? That's what you've heard on record?"

"Yes."

"That's all? Christ, Dmitri, where've you been? Who was the playing the Beethoven?"

"Schnabel."

"When was that? That was recorded in the 'thirties?"

"I don't know. I heard the Beethoven soon after the war, Stravinsky I heard during the war."

"Christ, those were 78s, Dmitri, 78 revolutions per minute. At that speed they could only fit a few minutes on a side, three minutes, maybe four at the most. What we've got now is 33 1/3 r.p.m. records, they can put twenty minutes or more on a side, enough room for a whole piece or movement, for one of Linda's Bach sonatas complete. And the sound's a lot better too. You wouldn't be fooled, but lots of people are just as happy with records. That's why records are killing us, Dmitri. The only thing records can't hurt today is opera, one Wagner can take maybe fifteen sides with changes in the middle of numbers, who wants that? But piano or violin or duos? That's another story, that's your story right now."

Dmitri looked bored, he shook his head now and then as the others spoke, now he closed with his *obiter dictum*: "To record is to create a past."

"Dmitri, we're not creating the past, what do you mean? That's silly. If we record, we're creating the present, the way we are right now. And if it helps us get symphony bookings we're creating the future."

Linda, whose fingers were precise beyond imagining, was treating his words too cavalierly for comment. That move irritated him, it was a device for conquest, not for convincing argument.

"Look, you guys," Giorgio said, "it's up to you, maybe you can work it out some other time. It's not urgent."

Linda didn't want to wait for another time. "Dmitri darling," she began again, dropping the rampaging conqueror style, but letting him have fair warning he would have difficulty defending his position, "we don't want to record just to have records. We have to record if we want conductors to recognize us and invite us to play with their orchestras. And you may not want a past. But I have to have one or I'm dead, Dmitri. Ginette Neveu has only records left, like Caruso, otherwise she's gone without a trace. And then Jerusalem . . .," she stopped talking, as though her accusation were already forceful enough without adding the grievous weight of Jerusalem Neimann, who had not even records left, who was gone without a trace outside Linda's memory.

Dmitri didn't want invitations to play with orchestras, that was Linda's want. But if she so desperately wanted a past, he was willing to help her construct it, even if it meant helping her relegate him to it.

"Let's talk about it again tomorrow," he said.

By then, Dmitri relented, and they soon made a record. Linda's fairness forced them to combine Brahms on one side with Bartók on the other. Dmitri's hatred of the whole process was confirmed by the way in which they had to play short snatches of their music over and over to satisfy the engineers. When he and Sofia had recorded, it was in concert, and the engineers did their best to capture what they did.

"Are they such good musicians they can judge what we do better than we can?" Dmitri demanded of Giorgio, who had the sense to be present at the sessions to help manage Dmitri's reactions.

"They're electronics men. They're working on making the equipment get it right. It's touchy business."

"What good are little pieces of music?"

"Well, hell, Dmitri, you know. They patch it all together in the end."

Dmitri was appalled. "They patch it? We don't get a recording of what we play straight through?" Dmitri didn't think there could've been any patching of Sofia's recording.

"Come on, Dmitri. Most of it might be from straight through, that depends. But they'll have to patch it here and there."

Dmitri gave Giorgio a blank stare. He went through with everything else that was demanded by the engineers and the producer, but he did it only for Linda and, even for her, he wondered why she wanted such a record of their life and music.

"There've been weirder records," Giorgio said when it was over.

"When do we get it?" Linda asked.

"That takes a while. Maybe half a year, maybe a year. I'll push them."

Dmitri wondered if it would arrive in time for him to hear it with Linda. He wasn't sure he wanted to hear it at all, but he certainly didn't want to hear it without her.

It wasn't even soon enough for Linda's purpose. Shortly after their last recording session, Giorgio's man called to ask them to visit Giorgio as soon as possible. They went to see him immediately.

"Okay guys, I've got a possibility. It's only a possibility, so don't get too hopeful. Ormandy needs a fill-in in Philadelphia. Sviatoslav Richter postponed his American tour. Now here's the wrinkle. Richter was booked twice for Philadelphia. Ormandy wants a substitute pianist for Brahms and he'd take a violinist for the other night to do Schumann or Dvorak. There's not a lot of time. He heard about your Philadelphia concert and he thinks you might be what he needs. But we got a problem. His man called to ask for records. I told him there aren't any records."

Linda looked angrily at Dmitri.

"Wait a minute, wait a minute. It might be better anyway. He could audition you tomorrow afternoon if you can be in Philadelphia from one to three, that's one hour each. If not, he'll just have symphonies without soloists. Ormandy is the most punctual man in music, a minute late and you're out. Look, now. Auditions can be risky, but so can records. You guys are photogenic, you *look* like great music, he sees you he's going to like you even more than just hearing you. Looks matter to Ormandy, he has the best looking orchestra in the world, they are beautiful, I can tell you, I love to watch them, their ties are straight, their bows are all together, they are beautiful, and in my business you don't go around watching someone you don't have any chance of handling. But Ormandy also likes perfection and you have to be perfect in audition. That's the risk."

"Linda should play both nights," Dmitri said.

"Look, Dmitri. That's not the offer. We're not the ones making offers, it's all in Ormandy's hands. It's a package. The one part that's certain is a pianist has to play Brahms. If you won't do Brahms, the deal falls through for sure."

Dmitri shook his head. "Okay."

"You don't have to," Linda said. "We'll probably get other chances."

Dmitri was surprised at her apparent equanimity. He didn't believe it. As he thought about it, he finally heard her "probably" as if she'd yelled it for emphasis. "Philadelphia's always been good for me," he said. Then, after quick further thinking, he added, "In some ways at least."

"You won't regret it, Dmitri," Giorgio said with a generous smile, "it could change your life."

That was why Dmitri thought he would regret it.

"Okay? So it's settled. I'll call back to let them know you'll be there, and punctually."

Implausibly, it was Dmitri who asked a practical question. "When do we have to leave to be there in time?"

"There's probably a train about ten – that'd get you there in plenty of time for one o'clock. If you had to, you could walk from the train station, it's only about fifteen short blocks, not Manhattan blocks, a nice walk down Walnut."

Dmitri started to say he knew those blocks well.

"What if the train is late?" Linda asked.

"Go at eight if you want to be sure."

"Let's go this afternoon."

"I can't, not until tomorrow," Dmitri said.

"Dmitri, please," Linda pleaded.

Her voice was more plaintive than he'd ever heard it. But he couldn't go tonight, he'd promised to be home for dinner. He looked up to explain. Linda looked frayed and upset, her hands were shaking. He knew that on her scale of fairness, she felt wrong to ask anything of him since she now might expect to return nothing. Hers was such a trivial worry, it shouldn't upset anyone, but now it was upsetting him in turn to see her so unhappy at even the slight risk of losing her opportunity, her opportunity to play without him. It was ironic. He didn't especially care for playing Brahms with the Philadelphia Symphony while Linda craved nothing more, yet Ormandy probably wanted him as the nearest equivalent to Richter he could get on short notice and would accept Linda as part of the deal. Ormandy was wrong, he should've wanted Linda for both nights. She'd been practicing all her orchestral solos with Dmitri as her *tutti* orchestra in reduction, while he'd never played an orchestral solo because he'd never had another pianist to take the orchestra accompaniment. This was her world, not his. She'd said he didn't have to do it if he didn't want to, they'd probably get other opportunities. But apparently, if he did audition for it, he had to make sure he was damned early.

"Okay," Dmitri said. He wanted to lay his hand on her cheek to reassure her, he wanted to do anything for her, he wanted to pick her up and carry her to Philadelphia on his back if need be.

Giorgio sat silent through their exchange, watching them closely. He now evidently noticed Dmitri looking at the phone. "There's a telephone in the room next door where you can be in private, Dmitri," he said.

As he left to telephone Pavel to ask him to apologize about dinner, Dmitri heard Giorgio beginning to speak to Linda. "I told Ormandy's man your hands are often very nervous before things but they're absolutely solid when you play. If he wants to hear Dmitri first, try not to be seen too much before you . . ."

"Forgive me, Dmitri," Linda said as they went down the stairs and out to go pack, "I had no right to make you change the dinner. You don't owe me anything."

"It isn't a matter of owing. We don't have debts."

Linda didn't respond.

Dmitri played Brahms's *First Piano Concerto* in Philadelphia. He might have played it better for some tastes if he'd still had his teenage love of Brahms or if it had been more difficult. He played as well as he did only because he'd never played it before, which made it seem difficult enough to be a challenge, and because he was playing it for Linda. Ormandy asked him to play the piece for his audition and Dmitri did it from sight reading of the score. Before they started, Ormandy instructed his orchestra, "This is not a rehearsal, it is a performance, there will be no stopping to correct failures." Dmitri found his accent beautifully pleasing, even soothing, he sounded like a conductor as much as he looked like one. Dmitri felt slightly silly in his black tie and tails while the orchestra were dressed in daily, often sloppy, attire, but Ormandy's demeanor and posture salvaged the moment.

When it was Linda's turn, Dmitri worried that Ormandy would instruct her what to play and might choose something on which Dmitri had not been working with her. She would fail if she had to sight read. But Ormandy asked her what she wanted to play. The night before she had said she thought she might do best with something other than what Dmitri did. Now she chose Dvorak and Ormandy seemed genuinely pleased. Richter was to have done Brahms and Rachmaninoff. As she played, Ormandy never once glanced at her except to signal her to come in or to conduct her tempo. But Dmitri noticed two men who seemed intent on watching her and who frequently whispered to each other as she played. Dmitri grinned at the thought they were checking whether she was a good visual fit. Linda must be one of the best visual fits they'd ever seen.

They had auditioned the pieces they were to perform, but in five years they had not known the intensity and sometime harshness of rehearsing with an orchestra under the baton of a strict disciplinarian, a tyrant for the cause of beauty. They'd wielded their own batons, Linda had even used her bow cutting through the air to redirect Dmitri. Now she could be abruptly ordered to stop while Ormandy or an associate conductor criticized her and the orchestra. Linda survived the ordeal only through many evenings of woeful reconstruction of herself with Dmitri's help. But every morning, she exploded from their bed and started anew, she fit her own description of Schubert's music. Dmitri played Dvorak to accompany her more than he played Brahms, but that was closer to his preferred way to prepare for a performance.

Linda was ecstatic after Dmitri's solo as they drank champagne she'd ordered for them to celebrate. "It was beautiful," she said. "All the violins, their bows going up and down in unison. They're not satisfied if it only sounds like Brahms, it has to look like Brahms. That was your greatest moment, Dmitri, and I was part of your audience."

Dmitri didn't contradict her to say it wasn't his greatest moment at the piano, but two days later he enjoyed what he knew was definitely her greatest moment with a violin. When the critics didn't praise her more highly than they did him in the clippings Giorgio wanted them to read, he thought they'd been unfair. When he said so, it caused half a quarrel because she insisted his performance had been beautiful. The quarrel was cut to half when Linda said, "You're being ridiculous, Dmitri, I'm not even going to discuss it with you. That was the best exchange we ever made – your Brahms for my Dvorak with a whole orchestra at our backs."

That the orchestra hadn't been at his back as it had at hers was not the least of her misperceptions.

Linda came to understand and to correct her Philadelphia misperceptions. Several times Dmitri tried to convince her they would be better off if they kept their duo schedule while also seeking solo appearances with orchestras. He proposed again and again that they get married, until he stopped proposing for fear he was harming the prospects. But Linda had been infected in Philadelphia and she asked Giorgio not to schedule them for further duo performances, to withdraw them from more distant engagements where he could, and to try to arrange solos for them with symphonies and chamber orchestras. Their last firmly scheduled duo concert was in New York before they were scheduled to have a break for the summer doldrums. But they still had a month's concerts before the New York finale. In spare moments, Dmitri helped Linda practice concertos by playing the orchestral reductions of Brahms, Beethoven, and Mozart concertos. One afternoon, while he was playing alone as she rested between solo parts, he recalled the pain he'd given Sofia when she'd been reluctant to expand her *repertoire* to accommodate his urge for growth. Still today, in thinking about that time nearly twenty years ago, he was embarrassed at his treatment of her.

"Dmitri, you're red in the face!" Linda said with sudden alarm. "Are you okay?"

"I'm well," he said.

In New York they lived in a residential hotel whose walls and ceilings were not ideally insulated to contain the sounds of their music. Much of the time, it didn't matter because no one else was around and some of the apartments were not occupied. But on the day of their last rehearsal before their final duo performance, it did matter. They'd worked through everything after getting up very late and then they'd gone to dinner and returned too early to go to bed. Dmitri tried conversation over dinner without great success and now he was reluctant to make further false attempts. He sat at the piano and ran up the keys to check its tune. It was an idle thing to do, something he did often because he so often played different pianos and needed to check them, and he did it with varied patterns, twice up three, down two, and then the same pattern over and over again, or hand over hand in rippling patterns of sixteenth through whole notes that sounded like a variant of Debussy. He did it extraordinarily fast, as though it were a show-off piece by Scarlatti or Chopin he was playing. Linda often told him she wondered how he kept all the keys under such perfect control.

"I still think that's miraculous," she said now.

He smiled at her. He'd long thought the greater miracle was finding the right unmarked spots on four strings at once while sometimes bowing with ferocity. Linda returned his smile and Dmitri tried to think what to play to bring her to life. As usual, she had the quicker wit. She suddenly jumped up from the couch.

"Mozart! Play Mozart," she said.

She went to a large suitcase she'd left behind when they'd gone to Europe. She fumbled through it and found the right sheet music.

"This, Dmitri, can you do this?"

Linda didn't take up her violin, she wouldn't need it. She stood beside Dmitri to sing *Exsultate, Jubilate*, conducting Dmitri as she went. Dmitri didn't need to understand Latin to sense that she was singing of jubilant exultation. Linda was the embodiment of jubilant exultation, she was magnificent, she was beautiful, she pranced about the room, singing to him, smiling her joy at him *exsultate jubilate*, kissing his ear in a vocal pause. In the midst of such beauty, as the very object of it, Dmitri hesitated to grasp it for fear it would dissolve in his hand. He merely watched, playing to sustain the beauty through the long song, knowing it was a small fragment of their life, a momentary excess, his Linda for this brief passage of joy, a fragmentary passage doomed to end too soon with a return to the normal, to the disciplined Linda whose life was being shared with him now but not forever. As she reached *Alleluja*, he sensed the moment fading and as her voice rose to nearly shouting her *Allelujas*, someone pounded on the ceiling beneath them and Linda laughed to break the song many *Allelujas* short. The moment was past.

As though to memorialize the moment, as her laughter abruptly stopped, she hauled Dmitri from his stool and hugged him long and hard. Too long, too hard. "Dmitri," she said.

Later in bed, they did not make love but only talked.

"Sometimes I wished I'd get pregnant," she said. "I tried, I never used anything, it was like a gamble, except I wasn't ever sure which was the winning payoff and which was the losing one. Mother says she tried very hard all the time and it only worked twice. I think I maybe missed the winning payoff. Things would've been different then. I'm sorry, Dmitri."

He rubbed her back while trying to find adequate words. Again he was not fast enough.

"You know, Dmitri, you taught me to love Bartók. I really thought that was going to be impossible – I guess I underestimated my teacher. But you didn't get Bartók to write enough for me to play with you."

Their last concert was one of their oddest. It was wistful, as though it were a farewell to Bach, Beethoven, Debussy, and Bartók all at once. Linda insisted Dmitri take the first encore and then when there was enough applause to make another seem justified, she took it. She stepped to center stage. Though she had to hold her violin and bow together in both hands to keep her hands calm, she spoke in a firm, loud voice, saying, "This is for Dmitri Esterhaats." Dmitri admired her steely resolve, he even loved her for it, though he knew it was in service now to push him out of her life. Linda played part of Bartók's *Violin Sonata*. Dmitri had never heard her play the piece before and he wondered when she'd rehearsed it. He suspected he'd never know. But he knew she'd begun her life apart even while they were still together, learning this difficult solo without him, without his even knowing, learning it specifically for her farewell from him. He felt, as he listened to her Bartók sonata, that it was a memorial to him, that Linda had deliberately scheduled her memorial early enough to let him hear her performance of it.

Their final exchange was of freedoms. Appropriately, Linda was free to go first. After her bags and boxes were taken down, she came back in to Dmitri.

"I would love you, Dmitri, I would love you more than anyone. But that's not what I'm for. Do you understand?"

For this once, at least, his silence was not reticence, he was not meant to answer; it was supposed he understood because it was supposed he might've said the same if he were given to speaking as readily as Linda was.

She kissed him. She stepped back slightly from him and stroked his face with her bow hand. The hand was shaking very hard, as though she were about to begin a great new performance. Dmitri started to reach for the hand to calm it, but he interrupted his motion and did not.

"I know," she said, "I can't depend on you anymore." She paused a long while. "*Au revoir*, Dmitri *tutti*."

Still she stood there, as though not knowing how to bring the piece to a proper resolution, as though their life together was an unfinished composition by Schubert. Dmitri had no interest in bringing it to any end, and he did not help her now.

"*Du . . . Lebewohl.*"

Dmitri's eyes widened, not at the farewell, but at those particular words, Linda's first German words ever used for him, "*Du . . . Lebewohl.*" He knew they roughly meant, You . . ., live well. But he had no idea what was the meaning of her saying them to him just now. It seemed fitting that he could not understand her farewell, that their life together should end with a misunderstanding.

Soon Linda found a way to tie the strands of their life together to bring it to a final resolution. Her eyes flooded as on that dreadful street in Paris. But this time she had the strength to turn and go immediately. For the last time in their five years together, she did not look back.

6

Jelly Ujfalussy

The next months were a difficult time. To discipline his thoughts, Dmitri took up works he'd never or seldom played. For the remainder of the spring and summer he avoided Bartók – to play solo Bartók was to sense Linda standing offstage. If he'd had solo Locatelli in his *repertoire*, he might not have played it for years. When at last he relented to Giorgio's entreaties to accept bookings, he had the ease of getting engagements he'd badly wanted after leaving Sofia and for all those years before meeting Linda. He even got requests for orchestral performances, which he began to accept for the distant future, but never to exceed one in any month. His income doubled, redoubled, and redoubled again and yet again, as in his challenge with the celebrants the weekend before he met Linda. All of that in the space of six months when he hardly played, when his abilities were certainly not greater than while he was with Linda. He began to understand part of the reason his fees grew so quickly: He was hard to get. He wasn't hard to get because he was too heavily booked, he was hard because he didn't wish to play. Contrary to all of Giorgio's claims that what he and Linda needed most was exposure, he was succeeding best without exposure.

Dmitri soon moved into a large apartment on Fifth Avenue across from Central Park. Most of its interior walls had been removed to give the effect of a small rectangular concert hall. That hyper-modernist renovation of the apartment made it undesirable for others, who feared the costs and burdens of re-renovating it, and therefore made it available to Dmitri. He'd never have designed the ideal apartment for himself, he wouldn't have been able to think through the relevant issues or even to be sure what they were. But he was sure when he saw it that this was as nearly perfect for him as he could find or imagine. At one end he placed a Steinway, his Steinway, his first grand. At the other was a magnificent replica of an eighteenth century harpsichord, found for him by Giorgio from a small church that was closing.

It was the first in a collection of harpsichords, tuned to different keys, that would slowly fill in the outer edges of the room.

To buy his Steinway, he asked Giorgio to arrange to get it from the shop of Horace Gmund.

"Gmund? That's the shop we used to use for everything we ever needed. It's gone, Dmitri. I think there's a skyscraper there now. A couple of years ago maybe, maybe three, while you were in Europe."

Dmitri's face must have displayed his great disappointment and sense of loss.

"I'm sorry, Dmitri. I think Gmund retired and moved to Florida or somewhere when they canceled his lease to tear down the building."

"And there was a bookstore next door."

"I don't know a bookstore. But the whole block is gone, it's a big building, Bauhaus or something, lots of glass, must be full of lawyers or bankers or insurance men."

Dmitri nodded and asked Giorgio merely to arrange the Steinway however he thought best, just that Dmitri wanted it immediately.

"Okay, Dmitri. You'll have it in a couple of days or we'll haul ours over to you until it comes. I'll personally talk to Steinway, I'd be surprised if they wouldn't go out of their way to make sure you get it immediately. Sorry about Gmund, Dmitri. He was a friend?"

Dmitri nodded again.

Giorgio started to speak again, hesitated, then finally spoke. "Do you hear from Linda?"

Dmitri shook his head quickly as though to get past the issue quickly.

"Sorry. I thought she'd surely write. I'm sorry, that was none of my business. Hey, look, I'm not going to do any more prying. You're my performer and I'm your agent – that's the way I hope it stays. Hey, you know, I think you need a telephone. I'll get it taken care of if you agree. I think all you have to do is sign some papers at the telephone company offices. I'll pay the first six months – I suspect I'm gonna be the one calling you the most."

Dmitri agreed to consider getting a phone, but not yet.

Dmitri began to join the rest of the world again when his father and mother came to fetch him to go visit Pavel's new daughter, Clara, named for the beautiful aunt in Kiev. Clara was a week old, and she was still waking often through the night to exhaust her parents, who proclaimed themselves almost too old to have a child at last. Clara cried after they arrived, and Pavel's wife Sylvia wanted to share her crying with someone else.

"Here, Papa, you try," she said.

Papa Esterhaats took her, but she cried still harder. He passed her on. "Marina, you try."

Clara's grandmother had no greater success. "You need a piano here, Pavel. Then Dmitri could soothe her."

"With Bartók maybe?"

Sylvia almost jumped to protect Dmitri from teasing. "I bet you don't even need a piano, Dmitri. Here." She took Clara from Mama Esterhaats and handed her to Dmitri.

Dmitri thought he'd never seen so small a person, and he knew he'd never held one. He took Clara with greater care than he'd ever used to handle Linda's violin. She was barely bigger than his hand, when he put one hand behind her head and the other behind her body, his hands overlapped.

"Clara," he said and Clara stopped crying to look at this strange face smiling at her.

Everyone else laughed but Dmitri took no notice of them. He held Clara for the rest of the evening, he held her until she fell asleep, and then he continued to hold her until Sylvia led him to the bedroom to put her in her crib. They stood there watching her for several minutes and then Sylvia stretched up onto her toes to kiss Dmitri's cheek.

"Clara's already performed her first miracle, she got Dmitri Esterhaats to visit our apartment for the first time. I guess I know where we can find a babysitter someday soon."

Every few months thereafter, Dmitri became babysitter to Clara Esterhaats.

Dmitri's first performance in New York after returning to play was in Carnegie Hall. Linda had always dreamed of getting to Carnegie Hall and of performing for the King and now the Queen of England. Dmitri never fully understood either wish. Now he hoped she'd made it to Carnegie Hall before he had. He thought he might ask Giorgio, but then he decided not to. For one thing, Giorgio had rightly, tactfully declared he would never again pry and Dmitri was glad of that. But even more important than that, he feared the possibility of discovering Linda hadn't yet made it.

When the Carnegie Hall program had to be scheduled, Dmitri's mind was still incapable of more than a few minutes concentration. He decided he'd have to play the most strenuous music in his repertoire if it was to hold his attention. He chose major pieces by Bartók, Debussy, Prokofiev, and Ives. And then, almost as an afterthought to balance the program, he added Scarlatti. When time to rehearse his program came a couple of months later, he was struck at the oddity of the mix, and he wondered how he'd chosen it and whether anyone would come.

The day before his performance, he went to see Giorgio.

"Dmitri, Christ, I'm glad to see you! Look, you've got to get a phone. I've been pulling my hair, I wondered whether you remember Carnegie Hall. I was going to go over to your place this afternoon and camp out if I had to until I found you. I'm a nervous wreck. Don't get me wrong, it's good I should be the nervous wreck and not you, I like your cool style, you don't flap, but boy, am I glad to see you. I sent you a card almost every day for the past two weeks, you never answered. Next week, I'm getting that phone put in. Why didn't you at least answer one of my cards?"

"I didn't see any cards."

"You didn't see them? Something's wrong with the mailman for your building, we have to get that checked."

Dmitri thought for a moment. "I haven't been reading the mail. It's in a box at the door."

"You don't read your mail. That's why . . ." he stopped himself. "Okay. That's okay. There's no law says you have to read your mail. But I'm getting you a telephone, Dmitri, don't tell me, 'Not now, later,' this time either. Next week, I promise. Now, back to tomorrow night. You're all set?"

"Yes."

"I'll come for you with the limo. Say seven o'clock?"

"I can just walk. It's not far."

"No, I'll come get you. I want you looking perfect, no sweat from walking, no chance of getting wet in the rain, no accidents along the way, I'll be there seven o'clock."

Dmitri realized Giorgio wanted to collect him in the limo to make sure he got there. At that thought, he smiled slightly and, evidently seeing him, Giorgio beamed. Giorgio's Italian instincts overcame his carefully constructed style, and he moved from grasping Dmitri's arms to giving him a great hug. Because Dmitri was nearly a foot taller, the hug had a slightly impersonal character, but Dmitri patted Giorgio's back as he would've done his brother's or his father's.

"Hey, kid, you're gonna make it. You're gonna be one of the greatest. You can take my word for it, I've seen a lot of them, I've even worked with a lot of them. I've never had a better bet. You know I was reluctant to take you on, those rumors, but I was wrong, completely wrong. I shoulda jumped. From tomorrow night it's all yours, Dmitri."

Dmitri remembered Ben Schein's constant compliments to Sofia. "Thank you," he said, "but it isn't necessary."

Giorgio gave him a quizzical look, then suddenly smiled. "Okay. No more. But I'm gonna be there, you'll maybe see me in the front row. That's the only other compliment you'll get from me. Knock their socks off, kid."

Dmitri had evidently become old and mature enough to be a kid. He'd forgot why he came to see Giorgio, so he departed to walk and play a bit before being ready by seven o'clock tomorrow evening.

The greatest compliment Dmitri got for his performance was from Jelly Ujfalussy. When he returned to his apartment afterwards, he found a note taped to his door: "I had to sit at the back – no pass. I missed seeing your wonderful hands. I am happy you are returned. Jelly." Dmitri smiled for Jelly. No one was able to reach him, he had no phone, he wasn't looking at his mail, yet she could reach him almost instantly. Moreover, she'd somehow got past the building's night doorman, who was curmudgeonly and strict. Dmitri remembered her saying she was lucky to be so beautiful she could always get in. His opinion of the night doorman's humanity rose at the thought he still had the hormones to be affected by Jelly.

When he got up on Sunday, Dmitri tried playing some of the new things he was working on, but Linda intruded in his mind and seemingly down into his fingers. He went to the harpsichord and played Scarlatti, who'd had no place in their repertoire, but even Scarlatti's music reminded him of his running the keys to test the tune of his pianos at all the stops on their tours, an action that oddly provoked admiring comment from Linda almost every time he did it, especially admiring when he picked out which keys to tune from a single high-speed run. "You can't make sense of a bill for two cups of *café au lait*, Dmitri," she once said, "but you can remember the sounds of 88 keys heard at a fraction of a second each and then call out by name which ones are out of tune." At Carnegie Hall the evening before, he'd managed to get through his program without the distraction of such memories, but the force of will to do so must have drained him of any further capacity for now. At midday he finally surrendered, he got up and set off up Fifth Avenue, walking sometimes briskly, sometimes idly past the museums and in and out of the park. At the top of Central Park he turned west to Amsterdam and walked on to Fort Tryon Park. It was late October, his favorite month for walking, and this day was especially good. Walking uphill he might've liked it better a bit cooler, but he would accept the compromise of having every day like this. Even that trivial thought sparked memories of Linda Ney, of his telling her he'd play *continuo* for her Brahms for the rest of his life as a compromise to block the reality about to engulf him.

He turned back south, down Amsterdam to Columbia University, through the campus to Broadway and south again. He was hungry and thought to stop for something to eat. He needed a deli, he'd seen dozens it seemed, but just this moment he saw none. Then he remembered Jelly Ujfalussy's note. He would go to Anton Staebli's Seventh Avenue bar. If Anton was there, his guffaws would override Dmitri's maudlin thoughts.

Although she was the shortest person in the group and must've had difficulty seeing over the others, Jelly was the first to see him come in.

"Dmitri!" she yelled. "Welcome." And she backed her words with a welcoming hug.

"It was great," she said, "not enough Bartók, but great."

There was such rejoicing in the group that Dmitri felt embarrassed to be imposing such a burden on them. It took him a long time to convey the message he was hungry, and then food was brought out to feed him several times over. There was enough energy, zeal, overlapping conversation, and pleasure in renewal to drive all else from Dmitri's mind and he found himself happy in this company of musicians and fellow travelers who talked more about musicians than about music. But eventually, people asked questions about the past five years and Dmitri found himself recalling things he didn't wish even to recall much less discuss.

"You haven't changed, Dmitri," Anton said, "the living master of reticence."

"No," Dmitri said.

"Who can beat you at it?"

Dmitri didn't answer. No one else spoke for a moment.

Very quietly, Jelly said, "You give Anton reason to think he is right, Dmitri."

Anton smiled and gently put his hand on Dmitri's shoulder. "That's okay, Dmitri."

When Anton and the others were occupied with conversation noisy enough to give her privacy, Jelly said, "I saw you with Linda Ney. I must have been wrong. I apologize."

Dmitri was too distracted by mention of Linda to recall the earlier conversation, he didn't know what Jelly meant.

"Linda must be nice for anyone she allows to be near enough to see it."

"She was," Dmitri said with hesitation.

"I do not know how you played without making mistakes, you only looked at her."

Now Dmitri could not stop the flood of visions of Linda standing before him in all her spectacular gowns, playing her violin, usually facing away from him but occasionally turning with a swoop of her bow to let him see her face, eyes closed, her neck taut to hold her violin, shoulders almost always bare, as Jelly's always were, before driving her bow back up and turning her face fully back to the audience. While these visions gamboled in his mind, he didn't choose to speak.

"Sorry," Jelly said. "She should have loved you too."

Anton suddenly became alert and his face turned serious. "I'll buy an extra round. How many?"

Jelly counted herself in. She'd been too young to drink the last time Dmitri had seen her.

"Jelly only drinks on the free rounds," Anton said. "She says she doesn't want to drink every round."

Dmitri recognized a tone of criticism rare from Anton. "I'll buy a round for Jelly," he said.

"No," she said. "That is not why. I do not want to drink on every round because I do not want to get a belly like yours, Anton." She reached over to poke his belly, then turned back to address Dmitri. "I have money. I work now, as simultaneous interpreter."

His face betrayed his wondering what that work was.

"I can translate from English, German, Russian, Polish, French, Czech, or, if it is an emergency, Romanian, Italian, or Greek into any other. I can even do Latin and Old Church Slavonic, but no one needs those. A little bit Japanese and Arabic. Or I can do all at once if you speak slowly. But they do not like to use me because I have impossible accents in all languages except Hungarian. And no one needs to interpret into Hungarian because Hungarians already know everything."

"Forgive my accusation, Jelly," Anton laughed. "I'm only a Swiss German, I don't know everything."

"I accept your apology – *if* you tell me when there is another free round."

Anton laughed.

"That is not a laugh," Jelly said, "that is a guffaw."

Alas, no one could understand the word she used because no one could decode her accent. Finally Anton figured it out when she became irritated on the fourth request to repeat it.

"Guffaw! I guffaw. Jelly, you're a genius if only your accent didn't hide the fact. I do guffaw, to laugh is not enough; to guffaw, that is here the need." He guffawed to prove it.

"The great guffawer," Jelly said.

Again no one understood her word.

"You are all terrible. You want to get me fired as simultaneous interpreter."

Someone knocked at Dmitri's door. It must be the housekeeper or a maintenance man, Dmitri thought. He started not to answer but then he realized they'd merely come back to bother him again. He opened the door.

Jelly Ujfalussy stood before him. "You did not answer my card and you did not come to tea. Anyone with the least manners would do one of those. Why, Dmitri?"

Again she'd got past the doorman. Dmitri was impressed. "I'm sorry, I didn't see a card. Did you put it on the door?"

"No, you foolish person, I sent it by mail."

"Oh," Dmitri said, looking behind the open door. "Maybe it's in here."

Jelly leaned forward to peer around the door to see the large box with letters covering its bottom to a depth of an inch or two.

"What is that?"

"That is the mail," Dmitri said, annoyed at himself for mimicking her stilted avoidance of contractions. "When I go on tour they put it there. Now I put it all there."

"You have not read it?"

"No."

"You did not even notice my name on my card?"

That seemed like an odd question, of course he didn't. "No, I did not."

"You need help."

Dmitri smiled at her. "Help? Can you hire someone to read your mail?"

"And someone else to answer it. Is that what you want? By the way, that is a new phrase I learned, by the way, would you invite me in?"

"Come in."

Soon Jelly offered help with the mail. She began to go through the envelopes reading off the names of senders. Her card was one of the first. She opened the envelope and handed the note card to Dmitri. He was surprised at her handwriting, her script was an elegant cross between Gothic and Roman scripts, as though she used a brush or quill, her writing was wonderfully clear even while it was beautiful, there was no problem of odd accent in it. She'd invited him for tea that afternoon.

"I'm sorry," Dmitri said. "We could have tea here."

"Too late, sorry."

She continued her reading and Dmitri interrupted her to take one of the letters. It was from Colette Meursault. He opened the letter and read it:

> Monsieur Esterhaats,
>   I have heard you play last night. I think Debussy would
> have been pleased could he have heard you play his
> *Preludes* so well. I am very proud of you. Perhaps you
> would call on me sometime in the next two weeks while I
> am visiting New York again after so many years?
>
>   *Votre,*
>   Colette Meursault.

Too long had passed, she would now be gone. He shook his head.

"Is it bad," Jelly asked in an unusually gentle voice.

Dmitri handed her the letter.

Jelly read it almost instantly and looked up to ask something.

"She was my best teacher," Dmitri said to keep her from having to ask, "I haven't seen her in nearly twenty years."

"See, you should open your mail. Now it is too late. You have missed more than my tea, Dmitri."

He stopped her from reading out more names from the envelopes. "I will do it later," he said without firm intention.

"Only if you promise to do at least ten tonight and ten more every night this week. Okay?"

Dmitri shrugged.

"No, you will promise. Say, Jelly dearest, I will do as you say. Say it."

"I will do it, Jelly dearest."

"Then we can have tea after all."

"No," Dmitri said, "it's too late now."

Jelly giggled.

Dmitri walked her to her own apartment and then walked aimlessly for a while before returning home. He pulled the box of letters over to his piano bench and picked up a few. The task seemed absurd, there were more letters in the box than he'd ever got in all his life before, more came in every day at an alarming rate, there was nothing he could do about them but ignore them. But Jelly had inveigled him to read the damned things. The first one he picked up had no return address, but it didn't need one, he recognized Linda's hand.

> That was really your greatest moment, Dmitri solo. I think
> it was fair that you got to Carnegie Hall first. Love, Linda.

It was unfair that that should be the first letter, he still had nine to go. Dmitri straightened his back and resolved to go on. The next few letters were irrelevant, he could throw them out, then there were several from Giorgio, the ones Giorgio had mentioned sending, he could throw them out. There were magazines and other things that he threw out. There was a note from Pavel suggesting he come to dinner, hoping he was in town and could reply, but saying they would all understand if he was too busy to come or to answer the note – they were always covering for him in anticipation of his default. Dmitri sat for a couple of hours, making a pile beside the box, leaving only Linda's note on the bench beside him. He accidentally knocked the note off, then reached down to pick it up. Linda, he thought. She'd actually gone to his concert. It would only be fair for me to go to one of her performances, he thought. But as soon as he thought it, he knew he wouldn't do it.

To stop his musings, he took out another magazine and saw part of the bottom of the box. He also saw another envelope with Linda's graceful hand. He didn't want to open it but he couldn't leave it unopened. He tried to pry the flap open without tearing it, but that was impossible, with her typically attentive care, Linda had sealed it too thoroughly. In the end he tore it open.

> Dear Dmitri,
> It is only fair that I pay for the bow. I'm sorry to confess
> I looked through your pockets to find the receipt, but I
> needed to know how much I owe you. I should be able to

pay it all soon, maybe in two years. I will send checks whenever I get good fees. This one you can thank to the Academy of Music in Philadelphia, where they say we are much loved after our back to back concertos with Ormandy. I hope you are well and playing beautiful music, from Bach to Bartók, maybe even including Brahms. Be sure to pay attention to Giorgio's advice. I look forward to being in your audience soon.

Love,
Linda.

Dmitri picked up the check and looked at Linda's signature on it. It had much of her own beauty, he supposed it was a blend of German and French school girl styles, but it was also secure and deliberate, as she often seemed to be. Dmitri looked at it until he was overwhelmed with visions of Linda. No matter what was fair, he couldn't cash the check, the bow was a gift, she didn't owe him for it. He took the check into the kitchen and set it on fire from the stove. He held it as it burned, watching her signature go first, then the money and the date, and, through some misunderstanding of the flame, his own name last. Forgetting the flame would be hot, he held on until it reached his thumb and finger. Then he suddenly dropped the corner of the check on the floor, where it continued to burn until there was only ash. He tried to remember what Linda told him to do with a burn from their tea kettle in an English bed and breakfast. He thought she'd said to use vinegar. He had no vinegar, but he had some soured wine. If it doesn't work, he thought, I've probably lost my middle C thumb for a while. He poured the wine over his burns and, once again being distracted by his thoughts, he continued pouring until the bottle was empty.

"Christ," he said. Then, realizing he'd picked up that expression from Giorgio, he said again, "Christ." Then he laughed at his cursing the fact he'd cursed. Jelly would like that, he thought. "Jelly," he said. "Christ." A thought of Jelly, whom he hardly knew and for whom he had no romantic leanings, had actually displaced Linda from his mind for a brief moment. And here he was repeating "Christ" at short intervals the way Jelly repeated her newly learned words and phrases at short intervals until they were hers. Maybe he would survive.

Giorgio, he thought, that's why he was asking about the mail. Linda asked him whether I said anything about her letter. Now that is really unfair,

Linda. He looked back at Linda's letter: "Be sure to pay attention to Giorgio's advice." They were talking about him, Linda was trying to manage him even at a distance. Dmitri became angry at the thought – not so much at either Linda or Giorgio, only at the thought that anyone thought he needed to be managed. It was as if he was angry at himself for having seemed in need of managing even by those who abandoned him. He brooded for several days on that thought, it came to him incessantly, no matter what he did to trump it with other thoughts. His anger rose and fell with the brooding, he wasn't really sure they were trying to manage him, but even the possibility ruined his music for him. In the end he decided it was intolerable to live with the suspicion they were managing his life.

Dmitri went to Giorgio.

"I think Linda Ney and I should have different agents."

Giorgio was taken aback but he recovered and dropped his usually complaining or enthusiastic tone. "I understand, Dmitri. I'll help Linda find someone else."

"No, no, I don't mean that. I wouldn't do that."

"Come on, it's you or both of you, that's the choices."

"That's not my choice. She was with you before we met."

"I know, Dmitri, but I'm not dropping you. That's final."

"It isn't final if I don't agree. I don't want to be performing now anyway. I can wait till the contract runs out."

"Do you even know when the contract runs out?"

That was too much for Dmitri, Giorgio was now treating him the way Linda teased him, saying he didn't know what went on in his expenses or the planning for his engagements. "I don't care when it runs out. I'm out, damn it."

Giorgio dropped his softer plaintive tone and became hard and determined. "Dmitri, look, I can't drop you. Look, I swore . . . I have to stick with you, I understand you, you've gotta have somebody who can work with you, who knows how to, someone . . ."

"You swore?"

"Dmitri. Come on. Let's give it a few days and talk some more. I'm not letting you go."

"If Linda leaves you, I'll know what you swore," Dmitri threatened. "Then you'll have neither."

"Christ, you guys, why didn't you get married? Christ, you slept overnight in Philadelphia lots of times, that makes you common law married – one night is enough in dopey Pennsylvania. I should've reported you to the Philadelphia authorities so you'd be married now. Dmitri. Hey, look, I'll take you to lunch, come on. I'm your agent, let's just keep it that way, an agent is a fiduciary, someone who acts in the client's interests, that's all I want to do for you, Dmitri, I swear. If I'm doing it wrong, tell me and I'll straighten it out."

Jelly Ujfalussy stood at Dmitri's door, yet again getting there without being cleared with him by the doorman. Although he was still irritable while trying to reconcile himself to sharing Giorgio with Linda, Dmitri smiled at Jelly's effrontery.

"I need a place to stay," she said. "Do you have room."

Dmitri grimaced. "I only have one bed, and no couch."

"Is your bed big enough for two?"

It was and Jelly came in with a small bag. "It's only for two nights," she said after leaving her bag in his bedroom.

Dmitri was beyond speech.

"Is there anything to eat? And a beer?"

"There's cheese. I think there's wine."

Jelly went into the kitchen to check. "Dmitri! Look at this refrigerator!" He came to look. "What's wrong?"

"There is nothing in it. Are you starving yourself?"

"There're lots of things in there."

"Pickles. That makes a good meal. Capers, that would be for the next night. Sour cream. Mustard. Butter. And cheese for a snack."

"I haven't been shopping this week."

"Have you been out this week? No, you have not. You are going out right now with me."

She quickly did an inventory of the cabinets. "These spices, Dmitri, that is all you eat? Pepper and dill? The dill is for the sour cream, but what do you put them on, Dmitri?"

While passing through the long sitting room, Jelly pointed at Dmitri's harpsichords. "You have three harpsichords. You have not one egg but you have three harpsichords. Can you explain me that?"

"They're different, they're all tuned differently, they're for playing different pieces."

"You will have to show me and explain me the theory. If you are going to have three harpsichords, you should have at least some eggs. We will get some for you."

They went shopping. Then Jelly made dinner, the best dinner he'd had in a long time, incomparably the best ever in his apartment. He tried to help by slicing onions, but she slapped his hand and took over to slice them faster than he could run up the keys of his grand. She was a miracle of speed in the kitchen, never measuring, never weighing, but confident of every move she made. For two days she sped up his life and energized him even while she wore him out.

The morning after her second night, she woke up to find him already out of bed. "Come back here, Dmitri," she called, more in the tone of an order than of an invitation.

Dmitri came back.

"This will have to be the last time for now," she said. "But I will come back someday." She pulled him into bed.

Afterwards she said, "If you will play Bartók, I will make breakfast, breakfast that will be enough for the whole day, Hungarian breakfast."

"That's with paprika?"

"You wash your tongue, Dmitri Esterhazy. If you are so rude, I will not make you eggs paprikas. Unless maybe you play double Bartók."

As he played and she cooked, he wondered when she would come back.

"Why two days?" he asked as they ate reddened eggs.

"My roommate has a lover, she wants a fiance, he is visiting. It is her apartment, that is deal I have for staying there."

"How often does he come?"

"May I come back next weekend?"

Dmitri shrugged.

"Try, Dmitri, just try to follow principle to say half at least as much as you think."

Dmitri immediately wondered, Would life with Linda have continued if he'd said more of what he thought?

"See what I mean," Jelly said. "I know you are thinking, I see this line here" – she reached over the table to draw her finger along his forehead – "fighting against this line" – she reached over with her other hand to draw another line and her two hands got entangled as they drew their separate lines. "But I don't see these lines" – she forced her finger between his lips and drew it from one corner of his mouth to the other – "doing anything. Why is that, Dmitri?"

Dmitri had no choice but to smile.

"Dmitri! To smile is not to speak. Say something or I will scream!"

"I hope you come back next weekend."

"I will accept that. It is not saying much. Every doorman and usher in Manhattan would say me that much. But I will accept it and not scream. Later maybe I scream. Not now."

When she was ready to leave, Dmitri went with her to carry her bag. In her strapless gown and shawl she shivered all the way. As she entered her own building, her combination of chattering teeth and accent made it almost impossible to understand her parting words: "Remember your new principle: say half as much as you think. You do not have to follow it with taxi drivers or people on the street. But next weekend. Remember."

The next weekend, Dmitri bought Jelly a coat. She wanted an elegant coat for formal evening wear to go with all her gowns or, he thought, to go with her image of the elegantly beautiful woman who could expect favors from every doorman and usher in town. But she was reluctant to let him buy it for her.

"You let me give you tickets to my concerts."

"That is different, Dmitri Esterhazy, and if you do not understand the difference I do not understand you. The tickets do not cost you anything, they do not cost anybody anything, I do not remember ever seeing the hall sold out for your concerts, my tickets are for wasted seats. It is better for everybody if I am there because then it looks more sold out."

"It's not so different. To buy this coat I'll only use wasted money. I have more money than I'll ever spend. It's better to use it to put a coat on you than to let it be used by a bank for nothing."

"That is not a very strong argument, Dmitri, but I will let if suffice. But if it suffices now, it cannot suffice the next time."

She'd got in three suffices in one go, that must be a new word, Dmitri thought.

"Say at least half of what you think."

"You are beautiful in that coat."

"That is all?"

He misunderstood, thinking she was asking for a greater compliment. "You are *stunning* in that coat. And that is true."

"You are deliberately misinterpreting me, but I will accept that. It will suffice."

Linda told nothing of her life, Jelly told everything. Linda's retelling and memories brought her near collapse, Jelly recalled all as though it were ordinary matter of fact, as though it were emotionally one with the day of the week, yesterday's weather, or the current price of cabbage. Jelly was sent to Zurich at age eleven to live with an aunt to get her out of the way of the war. The aunt soon died and Jelly was passed on to a friend of the aunt's in Geneva. When the war in France ended, she made her way to a harbor and found a berth on a boat to New York. She learned as much English as she could on the boat and talked her way through immigration. She'd talked her way through so many things she assumed that was the only device, there were never correct reasons for officials' doing anything, there were only persuasions and flirtations. Even when it would be easier to be straightforward, Jelly's instinct seemed to be to take the longer road of outsmarting and manipulating people. She built up expectations and then when she got what she wanted she dropped the gullibly expectant without further thought.

"The world is run by men," Jelly said, "but Jelly Ujfalussy has the world by the balls."

Jelly's family were caught up in the war, her parents and her brother, all cousins, aunts, and uncles, were dead, perhaps everyone she'd ever known in Hungary was dead. "The world is a lot dumber than it was before war," she said.

Jelly came often. She even joined Dmitri on a trip to perform in Chicago, Los Angeles, San Francisco, and Seattle, a four orchestra tour, tricked upon him by Giorgio, his thoughtful fiduciary working for Dmitri's interests. Jelly enlivened the trip so much he began to enjoy touring again. In another year her roommate's romance became torrid and Jelly halfway moved in with Dmitri. He might never have asked her to, but he enjoyed her company and he made her welcome. They went through can after can of paprika, hot and sweet.

When Jelly came twice in one week, Dmitri said, "Mary's lover is already back?"

"No, I'm back."

After she fell asleep that night, Dmitri mused over the oddity of his position.

I don't care about anything and therefore I get it all, he thought. I don't want to perform much, so they pay me more; I don't want orchestras, so they want me; I don't really want Jelly, so she is mine.

For most of his life he'd ached for such things, but now he no longer ached. He once wept for Liszt, later he was bored by Liszt, now Liszt was okay but not satisfying. Pavel once half teased and half admired him for his great capacity for delayed gratification while Pavel, as though he were finally a real American, wanted things here and now. The admiration was misplaced, delayed gratification was no gratification, it was ashes on the tongue.

After a few days Dmitri's normal pessimism returned and the world seemed more reasonable. He even began to want Jelly. The change was well timed, because now she fully moved in with him, bringing all her clothes and her vast collection of dictionaries, everything she owned in the world.

Jelly took over the management of Dmitri's daily life. She did shopping while he walked along with her, she went through the mail everyday so that his box would not fill up again and so that any bills might get paid, she put him on a regular schedule for eating, she exhausted him enough to get him to sleep well. She seemed the most unlikely of people for him to live with and yet it worked so well he was content to let it continue without end.

While going through the mail one day, she said, in the strangely gentle tone she occasionally found for him when she was trying to protect him, "This is from Linda Ney, Dmitri."

Immediately Dmitri recognized the lovely hand. Again the envelope had no return address. "How did you know?" he asked. "You didn't open it and there's no return address."

"I do not know how I knew. I knew."

Dmitri opened the letter. It included another check with the note:

> Dmitri darling,
>   Please, you have to cash my checks. I cannot control my finances if I don't know what is happening. If you are reading this, then you must have got the check. It isn't fair for you not to accept it, Dmitri, please.
>
> Linda

Dmitri darling, she called him, and then she wrote the most formal of her occasional notes with checks, he thought. Dmitri darling was her device to steel herself, gritting her teeth, resolved to do what she had to do. He read the note several times, each time it became colder in his hand, but no matter how cold it or Linda might become, he couldn't cash her check. She gave him no address to write to tell her he would not accept the check, but he didn't need to tell her, she knew, she was merely refusing to agree. He wondered how to handle it to make his action final. He could ask Giorgio – no, he could not ask Giorgio, he'd done his best to break the connection through Giorgio to Linda, he wouldn't reconnect now. He could try to find out . . .

He suddenly noticed Jelly standing completely still beside him where she'd handed him the letter. She looked very unhappy.

"Here," he said, and he let her read the note.

He told her the story of the bow.

"Why does she think you will not accept it?"

"I didn't lend her money, I bought her a gift. She knows that. She doesn't owe me anything. I couldn't accept it."

"Then tell her."

"I did."

"Tell her again now. Send her check back to her."

"There's no return address."

"Dmitri! How can you be so stupid? I thought you were Hungarian. I will find address. Tomorrow you will write to her."

Jelly found the address, Dmitri wrote a short note and enclosed the check with it. His chief difficulty was to begin, to find a form of address for the Linda no longer his. In the end, he settled for Dear Linda because Dear sounded empty and noncommittal, it could be used for a complete stranger.

"I have something for you next time you're near enough to come by," Giorgio said over the telephone.

Dmitri was going for a walk while Jelly studied her dictionaries, so he went immediately to Giorgio.

"The record finally came. It got held up in production, there were lots of problems. I thought you'd want one. I have as many as you want."

Dmitri did want the record, only one, although he didn't know why he wanted it because he was almost certain he didn't want to listen to it.

"Thank you," he said quietly.

"I also got another one for you. You said there was a record of one of Sofia Milano's concerts. Well, I got somebody to track it down. It's been out of the catalogs for a long time, but he found it used. It's in pretty good shape, I don't think it was ever played much. It's a two record set on 78s."

Because this was a greater surprise and because it came from a time in his life that bothered him less directly, Dmitri reacted with real pleasure, saying, "Oh, thank you," as though he meant it.

"Do you have a record player, Dmitri?"

"No."

"I'll have my man bring one around sometime tomorrow morning.

Remember, this one is 33 1/3, these are 78. You have to use the right needles or you can wreck them. Get my man to show you how to do it when he comes."

On the box of Sofia's recordings there was a beautiful picture of her from before the time when Dmitri knew her, but it was clearly his Sofia at her most wonderful, enjoying Verdi or Puccini with her mouth open in full voice, her eyes gleaming, her chest swollen. Dmitri was relieved to see there was no picture, only modern art, on his and Linda's album.

"When they wanted a photo for the cover, you were already split," Giorgio said. "You were looking terrible and Linda looked scared when I asked her if she wanted to do it." Giorgio caught himself, he was supposed to be an agent, not a personal confidante. "Sorry, Dmitri. Hey, I listened to all of them. You're wonderful with Milano, and the violin and keyboard duos are a smash. I don't know how many people are likely to want just that pairing." He laughed, "But it doesn't have any competition, I can tell you."

Dmitri didn't want compliments, but he was beginning to tolerate them from Giorgio.

The next morning when the record player came, Jelly wanted to hear something from the records. Dmitri randomly chose Puccini, Tosca's *aria*, "*Vissi d'arte*," I lived for art. It was a thoughtless choice, because his Italian from those days was still intact and the song immediately reminded him of Linda Ney's slow, implicit declaration that she couldn't have both lives, him and the violin, and that she must take the violin. Tosca lived for art even while she lived for love, she had the gift of complexity Linda needed. The beauty of Sofia's voice was brought back to him, not directly by the record, which sounded awful, but indirectly by provoking his memory. Sometimes when she'd sung Tosca, Sofia's voice rocked his chest, it vibrated down into his arms and fingers as he played. In the memory of that beauty, Dmitri wanted to listen to no more of the recording. And he wanted none of his duo with Linda in any case.

"We do not have to hear more," Jelly said in her gentlest, most protective voice.

Why do people want to protect me? Dmitri wondered. His mother, that was understandable, she was his mother, and Horace Gmund when he was only a child. But Mrs. Weiss, and now Linda conniving with Giorgio to take special care of him after leaving him, and even Jelly, the most detached person he knew. He wanted to be irritated with Jelly, but he couldn't, he only smiled forlornly at her while shaking his head.

She stood from the floor and he looked at her. Her evening gown was splitting beneath her left shoulder.

"We're going to get you a new dress," Dmitri said. "Maybe we'll get you something simpler to wear when you don't need to get past doormen."

"I cannot have more than three dresses. My suitcase will not accept more."

Detached Jelly, he thought. "For every one we get, you can throw one away. Or we could get you a larger suitcase."

"I cannot carry a larger suitcase unless I throw away some dictionaries. I cannot throw away dictionaries."

When he was not performing for several months, Dmitri played harpsichord for himself. He liked its greater precision. And perhaps he liked the newness of its challenge for him when he needed newness more than ever for distraction. During that period, his preferred instrument contradicted his preferred music. The harpsichord was more precise, more accurately fitted to his ear than the piano, which was well-tempered into vagueness, imprecision, and generality. With its greater precision the harpsichord was at once capable of finer expression and of less expression. It was, like Dmitri, carefully constrained into a special task and not capable of anything broader.

But Jelly didn't like the tone of the harpsichords, she couldn't study dictionaries while they played. She wouldn't impose on Dmitri, but he knew she'd much prefer Bartók and other dissonance. Some days she took her dictionaries with her to the park and came back in high energy to make lunch or dinner or to drag Dmitri out for a picnic with her. Once she came back to find him playing Scarlatti on a new harpsichord. Dmitri didn't notice the door opening and closing, so deft was she at slipping through the world unnoticed when necessary. He played for a long while, perhaps an hour, before he sensed some presence in the room. At the end of his piece he turned to look and found Jelly two steps behind him. He rotated his stool and reached out to pull her to him.

She sat on his lap. "I will like it some day. It is too good not to like it."

It hadn't occurred to Dmitri to think something good but not to like it. He'd always judged bad what he didn't like. He gave Jelly a confused laugh.

"You think I will not like it? You think I am inflexible?"

"You will like it. I'm sure you will."

"Why do you laugh?"

"I always think what I don't like is bad. But Hungarian logic is better. You can know something is good even though you don't like it."

"What is good that you do not like?"

Dmitri fell into his standard pensive mood of silence.

"Say half what you think," Jelly said.

"Brahms." That was not quite half, but it was enough.

Jelly and Dmitri took a vacation in New England and Quebec. He took her to all the cities and towns in which he'd performed and impressed her with his memory of streets and places.

"I walked a lot," he said.

Jelly's energy and brightness in the face of trivial obstacles seemed to Dmitri a greater gift than any gift of memory he might have. She took obstacles as a challenge, as he took new, hard music. She got them into hotels that were said to be full, although for that she had attractions he couldn't match no matter how much will he brought to bear. She could walk as fast as he could, she could walk as long, from dawn to midnight, she had even more stamina than Linda. She made daily life as contented as he imagined it possible to be. There were no meteoric highs, but there were no lows either. She heard there was a White Mountain, "We will climb," she said. She was told the Atlantic off Maine was terribly cold, "We will swim," she said, and she taught Dmitri to swim. She saw sailboats, "We will sail," she said, and they found someone to take them out and she learned the ropes while Dmitri failed at almost every move while she giggled so hard their gruff, down Maine captain incongruously giggled too. She pushed Dmitri into bed in moments when he thought they were on their way out to drive to the next town or to go to dinner or breakfast, she woke him in the middle of the night and then, despite her efforts, still got up early to set out again. Dmitri lost ten pounds while eating like a hog, *Du Schwein*, he thought.

"Say half . . .," Jelly said.

"*Du*," he said with an uninterpretable smile.

"You cheat. I know. But I accept that. That is what lovers call each other in German. But we are not German."

"No, we may be many things, but we are not German."

Jelly giggled. "I could be German."

They stayed away for all of August and into September, they had no plans, no destinations, only the next town, and they were not bothered by the mail or the telephone. Dmitri was not to perform again until October, and he enjoyed this longest break from his piano. It wouldn't be so bad if it lasted forever, he thought. He wasn't sure what he felt for Jelly. She was different, and his feelings were different. But, he thought, it was enough. He shook his head, wondering whether she'd give up her suitcase life.

"Okay, Dmitri," Jelly said.

"I was wondering what it would take to get you to own more clothes."

"I do not need more clothes."

"Jelly! You climbed a mountain in an evening gown. You went sailing wearing one of my shirts and a bikini. That shirt was so big it acted like a sail, you nearly got blown off the boat every time the wind changed. You don't even have a bathrobe, you have to use one of my shirts for that."

"I have no place to put more clothes."

"In the closet. That closet is huge."

Jelly would not continue the conversation.

Maybe, Dmitri thought, if she thought the apartment was hers, she'd put more clothes in the closet. He grinned at her. "Say half what you think, Jelly."

"I say more than I think. If you say one word I say twenty. I have said enough."

In Boston he'd bought her new shoes and new underwear, but then she threw away her old things. In Quebec City, Dmitri bought her a bathrobe and he talked her into a pair of pants, a blouse, and a breezy dress for these hot days. These could not displace other things. "They belong to you, Dmitri, You put them in your suitcase."

It was a beginning.

When they returned to New York, Jelly hung her clothes from Dmitri's suitcase on his side of the closet. Dmitri shook his head. He would make the apartment hers and then she might be willing to take over her share of the closet.

Jelly was delighted again to be in position to cook, so they'd driven straight through without stopping for dinner. Now it was late, but she made dinner while Dmitri returned the car to Giorgio.

"When you come back, you will do your mail."

"Jelly," he said in a threatening tone. "I will not do the mail tonight. I might not even do it tomorrow."

When he returned, she pushed him into bed.

"You should have done your mail," she said.

"Dinner will get cold," he answered, half from hunger, half from exhaustion.

"It will be better cold. You will taste the paprika better."

They made love and lay together for a while, letting the dinner get colder. Soon the phone rang. Jelly jumped but Dmitri didn't stir.

"You have to answer it."

"No, I don't. If it's important, they'll call back."

"Maybe it is your mama."

Dmitri surrendered. His mother would never call so late, she had to go to a neighbor's phone, and she wouldn't intrude on anyone at that hour. But he wanted to put poor Jelly at ease, she who was at once master of the world and slave to its demands.

It was Pavel.

"Mitya, I've been calling for several weeks. You were not on tour, Mr. Gaspari didn't know where to find you or when you'd be back. Mama is ill."

"I will go to her first thing tomorrow, Pavel."

Pavel did not speak.

Dmitri's exhaustion and hunger were gone in that silence. "Is it bad?"

"It's hard to say."

Dmitri feared it was hard to say not because Pavel didn't know but because he couldn't bring himself to say what he knew. "I will go, Pavel."

He hung up and told Jelly he was going to Brooklyn.

"But dinner first."

"No. I have to go."

In two minutes he was gone.

7

Marina Haimovich Esterhaats

Dmitri took a taxi to Brooklyn. His father met him at the door and gave him a hug. He spoke Russian as he often did when his wife wasn't in the room to prod him to use English, which she found much easier than he did. "Mitya, you are here." he said. "Mama is awake. Go to her."

Dmitri went into his parents' room. His mother was lying on the bed. "What is it, Mama?"

"I don't feel well, Dmitri. I had a little operation while you were gone. I'm still tired. It takes time. Maybe if you play for me."

He helped her walk into the living room to lie on the couch near his piano. Halfway there, her face drained white and Dmitri lifted her in his arms to carry her and lay her on the couch. She'd lost much of her weight, she was lighter than Jelly Ujfalussy, who barely existed apart from her wonderful Hungarian mind.

"What should I play?" He was blushing red at not seeing her sooner, at not yet wanting to ask what was wrong.

"Play what you like best in your concerts."

As a child in Kiev and Amsterdam he could remember her asking for Chopin. He sat at the piano and thought over the scores for a few minutes, and then he played a series of Chopin *polonaises*. When he turned to look back at her after a while, the pain had left his mother's face and she smiled at him. He played for her through the night, because she couldn't sleep. His father came in at some point to cover her, and then very early in the morning Dmitri made her a bowl of soup. When she had trouble sitting up and holding a spoon to eat her soup, Dmitri winced.

"Mama, where is it?"

She put her hand to her abdomen as he lifted the spoon to let her sip. Soon she slept and his father rose. Dmitri went to the kitchen and asked him what was the problem.

"When you were gone she felt bad. She went to the doctor. She had an operation."

"How long will it last, Papa?"

In whatever language, his father used fewer words than Dmitri. "Not long."

Dmitri went out to rent a hospital bed to put in the living room and he called Giorgio to cancel his performances for the next few weeks. As he came back to his parents' apartment, he remembered he should also call Jelly. He would have to wait until evening when the neighbor with a phone returned. When the bed arrived, Dmitri lifted his mother onto it.

"Dmitri, it isn't necessary," she said. "I use it today and you tell them to take it back tomorrow."

"That's a possibility, Mama. We'll see." His tone was one he'd invented to answer Linda when she was finding greater difficulty in the world than was there, when he knew what would be done and knew it would be easier done than said.

She asked him to tell her about the cities where he'd played. He started with American cities. He told her of Chicago, St. Louis, New Orleans, San Francisco, Milwaukee, she loved the sounds of the names. He told her about buildings and places in the cities, and after a couple of hours of delighting her with them he realized the places he was describing were the places he'd been with Linda. He didn't specifically remember cities from his own tours, where he hadn't shared walks with Linda, his performances might just as well have been in nameless places, in halls set among anonymous buildings and people. He told her of lovely cathedral towns in France, of churches in Italy. Those days when life had been most beautiful with Linda he made most beautiful for his mother.

Dmitri talked almost continuously for three days until his mother said, "It's so beautiful. When you were a little boy, you talked to me like that. In Kiev. But you don't remember that."

"I remember the kitchen where we talked and I remember Aunt Clara."

"That kitchen. Once you stood in the door almost all day, talking."

"You were making the cake and food for my birthday, my fourth, I think." He'd stood in the doorway to the kitchen, his arm out to support him as he leaned against the doorframe, his legs sometimes crossed as his father crossed his as he stood. He'd felt as though he was growing up, he was an adult of sorts, talking of serious things with his mother, discussing with her, resolving issues, recalling significant things, sustaining discourse at the highest level, as his mother must have done at the meetings she went to with his father. In his childhood, he'd never again felt so adult and serious minded, at least not that he could remember, perhaps he'd never even as an adult felt that adult and serious minded.

"How do you remember that, Dmitri? That was it, your fourth birthday. You remember so much. You probably even remember the cake I made."

Of course he remembered the cake, it was the same one she'd made for his thirtieth birthday just before he met Linda. "It was my favorite cake."

She laughed. "You remember too much, Dmitri."

Dmitri also thought that he remembered too much. But that was not what she meant.

Friday the doctor came and, after sitting for a while with Dmitri's mother, he joined Dmitri in the kitchen.

"Do you know what's wrong, Mr. Esterhaats?"

"Cancer," Dmitri said. As soon as he said it, he wondered where he got the idea.

The doctor looked annoyed and, for a brief moment, Dmitri thought he'd been too pessimistic in his assessment. "They told you?"

Dmitri felt himself blush. "No," he said. "I just thought . . . What is it?"

"Your brother and father wanted me to tell you, they thought . . . I don't know what they thought. Hell, it doesn't matter what they thought. You're right, Mr. Esterhaats, it's cancer, intestinal cancer, it's very far along, it's everywhere. I'm very sorry. It's the curse of central European Jews."

The doctor explained it would only be a matter of weeks. Dmitri's mother was steadily losing weight. The doctor would be coming back to arrange for intravenous feeding and he would teach Dmitri to administer anesthetic shots. If someone wasn't there all the time, they'd have to get a nurse.

"Does she need a nurse if I'm here?"

"From what I can tell, that would be better than a nurse. One more thing, your father and brother think it would be best if we didn't tell Mrs. Esterhaats what it is."

"You think she doesn't know?"

"No one has told her."

"She knows. She may not know exactly what it is, but she knows what it means."

"I wouldn't be too sure."

Dmitri didn't bother to contradict him.

His mother began talking less. After a short while, she would say, "Play for me, you must keep in practice."

Dmitri stopped saying, "What should I play, Mama," because she always answered, "Play what you like." At first he played only Chopin, but he knew she would grow bored with it, as she'd always done. He tried to think of other composers whose work he thought she liked. Liszt she'd grown to love because she associated Liszt with him, but most of Liszt was too noisy. Mozart she loved from his first year or two at the piano with his aunt in Kiev and from the years in Amsterdam, but Mozart was too sweet for the occasion, Dmitri couldn't have sustained Mozart. He played some of Beethoven's middle sonatas and then after a few days he knew: He played Bach, *The Well-Tempered Klavier*. It honored the occasion with restraint and respect. There was enough to sustain long hours. He would begin with *Book I* and play in order through to the end of *Book II* and then he would begin again. After he'd been playing Bach for several days it began to happen that, when his mother went to sleep and he stopped playing in order not to disturb her, it was the stopping which disturbed her. His playing enabled her to sleep.

His mother interrupted Dmitri's playing between two pieces. "Tell me about some place, Dmitri."

He went over to her bed and sat beside her. He told of Autun, of the tiny cathedral where he and Linda performed free of charge after their wrists had healed.

"There were sculptures you would like, Mama. One was a fat little man squatting down holding two bags, one off to each side. He had his mouth open to cry out. Standing on his head was a tall woman. The priest said the man was supposed to be greed, he was holding bags of money. The woman standing on his head was supposed to be charity. After we played in that cathedral for five of six hours, the priest who hosted us showed us all the sculptures and took us into the museum where the originals of many of them were, where you could see them better. When he explained what that one was, Linda said, 'It's a good thing we played for free, isn't it?'"

"Linda? Was Linda your violinist?"

"No, Mama. I was Linda's pianist."

"Only her pianist?"

"Mama, Mama. How can I say it? One thing: you would have liked her."

"If you liked her so much, I would have."

"Now Mama, how do you know I liked her so much?"

She smiled. "When you came to dinner then, you smiled while you played the piano. You were in a hurry to leave, I knew you must have somewhere to go, but you smiled. Before that, after that, you never smiled while you played and you were not in such a hurry, sometimes you even stayed overnight. Sometimes you played funny music, you even played jazz, I never heard you play jazz any other time. The neighbors wondered who'd visited us, they wouldn't believe you played that music. She brought jazz to your life."

"No, I played it here because she wouldn't let me play it any other time. You might say she brought jazz to my life, but not jazz music. Anyway, just how do you know her name?"

"Dmitri, there were reviews. You know I have many reviews. It's impossible to have a life as secret as you want it."

Dmitri began to take down her hair to braid it as he'd often done as a child. She winced when he began to comb.

"Oh, I'm sorry," he said, "I'll try not to pull it again."

"No, it's okay, it feels good, Dmitri, it's such pleasant pain, I don't mind."

He worked her hair in silence. Although he could do it very fast, almost instantly, he did it slowly to sustain the moment, combing gently and long before he turned to braiding. The mix of black and silver hair gave the effect of a braid within the braid, her hair in a compound fugue, a model for some future Bach.

"What happened with Linda Ney, Dmitri?"

"You know it was hard for us, Mama, for you and Papa, and Pavel, and me, we had to leave Russia. But it was harder for Linda's family. Not for money, I think – I don't really know, but I think they were well off until they had to leave Germany under the Nazis. Then they didn't go far enough and the Nazis came to them again like Aunt Clara. Linda's life was very painful. She thinks she can't give up any of what she has left for anything other than to play her violin, she wants to play with orchestras, not with a pianist. Maybe she thinks she owes it to her brother, who was a violinist, Linda thinks he was a great one. He taught her violin but he died under the Nazis."

"Oh. How sad."

"It was a hard time to be alive, nearly impossible to live well." He recalled Linda's parting word to him, Live well, and only now realized how grand that wish could be, there could hardly be a grander wish from Linda.

"Is she good, Dmitri?"

"She's wonderful."

"I mean with the violin."

Dmitri laughed. "I know what you meant. That's all I meant to answer too. You can't trick any more out of me."

"She's a beautiful woman, Dmitri."

"Mama, how do you know that?"

"I saw her picture."

"Where did you see her picture?"

"She's a great violinist, you said it, didn't you? A great violinist has records. A great pianist should have records too."

"What records does Linda have?"

"I can't remember the composer, the one you played with her, I have reviews, you played the whole orchestra. On the record she has an orchestra."

"Locatelli?"

"Locatelli, Dmitri, Locatelli."

"The whole orchestra is called *tutti*, Mama, that means 'all' in Italian, like *tutti fruitti* ice cream. I played *tutti* so Linda could solo with music that showed how good she was. Sometimes she called me . . ." He fell silent.

"Yes?"

"She called me her Dmitri *tutti*. Maybe I was silly enough to think she meant I was all her world."

They were both silent for a while until he finished the braid, when his mother said, "But it didn't work."

Dmitri was not sure of her inflection, whether she was stating a sad truth or asking a question. If it was a question, his silence was an answer.

"Play for me, Dmitri."

The following day, after Dmitri fed her a cup of soup, she stroked his face. "I'm glad you told me about Linda Ney. I always wanted to ask you."

"Why didn't you?"

She shook her head. "Dmitri, you make it sound easy. You never made it easy."

"Poor Mama. I must've been insufferable."

"Not always. Just between six and thirty-six. And sometimes the other years."

"Dmitri, when you were born, I don't know when, maybe you were a week old, or maybe two. I picked you up and I looked at you and I knew you were special. If I brought you in the world, I owed you more than I could give. I wanted to do so much for you. I tried. But it was such hard times. I didn't have enough time."

"Mama, almost everything I remember is with you. You did more than anyone should."

"I left you six days with your Aunt Clara and then I had you every evening and every Sunday. And in the morning when you got up before anyone else and I got up to be with you. I was afraid you couldn't survive, you trusted everything and you loved music. One would be bad, but both, that was terrible for you. After we left Russia and your Aunt Clara, you went to school. It was very hard for you, and I couldn't really help. And then you were too old to want me to do anything for you, you were fifteen, there was nothing I could do. But I wanted to, Dmitri, you always seemed outside the world."

"If you're going to talk nonsense, Mama, I'll have to play the piano. Shostakovich or Prokofiev, something really loud, something really Russian, something that would turn Pavel green."

"Shostakovich. He's nice."

Dmitri laughed, the description was incongruous. "Stalin didn't think so."

"Do you know the songs from Jewish folk poetry?"

"Yes. I once played most of them in concert, the ones for soprano solo, for a great Russian soprano. She could almost knock me off the bench with her voice. Do you know the words?"

"Some. I will try to sing."

Dmitri played, adjusting his speed now and then or backtracking to give her time to recall the words. He remembered her singing when he was a child; he couldn't remember ever hearing her sing again after they came to Brooklyn. He wondered whether she'd quit because she wanted only to speak her new language and her songs were all in Russian and Yiddish. Now her voice was weak, but she held the tune and gave a beautifully committed account of the difficult songs, especially "A Girl's Song" and "Happiness." For once, Dmitri wished he had a recording.

"My ear is good but my voice is bad," she laughed at the end. "Did you understand the Russian, Dmitri?"

"Where did you learn that, Mama? Not in Russia, I don't think Shostakovich wrote it until much later."

"I think I knew some of the songs, maybe with different music, but I forget what I remember. I learned them all at the Russian community house. We have a Jewish section and a Menshevik section. I'm in both. Papa's only a Menshevik. Poor Papa, he wants to quit the Menshevik section, he says it is now the section for the past. But he had to be in some section and there is no section for the present, Papa says there is no Russian present."

Dmitri was playing Bach and his mother was sleeping when he heard talking outside in the entryway. He couldn't remember what time it was, he'd lost track completely, but, without turning to the window, he sensed it was not yet dark outside. Pavel, he thought. But there was another voice, a woman's voice. Sylvia, he thought. Perhaps he should wake his mother to let them visit with her for a few minutes. At the end of his Bach fugue, he paused rather than start another piece. His mother stirred and he went to her.

"Mama." He stroked her face and handed her a glass of water. "Would you like to see Pavel and Sylvia?"

She closed her eyes and nodded her head yes.

Dmitri understood. He gave her a shot to ease her pain, then sat with her for another few minutes to let her recover. He cranked up the bed, straightened her hair, and wiped her face and forehead. Then he gave her a bit of apple juice.

"Dmitri," she said.

"Yes, Mama?"

She lifted her hand and he leaned over so that she could reach his face. "I'm so much trouble for you."

"Mama, you owe me more trouble than you could . . .," Dmitri started, but then he could find no way to finish.

"I'm ready," she said. "I hope they brought Clara. I want to see her again."

Dmitri went to the kitchen to fetch Pavel and his family. Clara came in and stood quietly beside the bed for a minute while her grandmother held her hand. He came in to pick Clara up so that her grandmother could see her from her high hospital bed. After a brief moment, he turned to leave Mama Esterhaats with Pavel and Sylvia for a while. Clara pulled away to get down from his arms. She went over to the piano and looked back at Dmitri. She'd been there for family gatherings a couple of times when he played and she'd sat with him. Now she put her hand up on the keyboard, very gently so that she made no sound. Finally she turned to leave the room with Dmitri.

"Grandpa wouldn't let us in while you were playing. I couldn't hear very good."

"Grandma was asleep then, the piano helps her sleep."

"Did you wake her up when you stopped?"

"Yes."

"She's going to die."

"I'm afraid so."

"I don't know anybody who died. Do you?"

"There are people I knew who're dead. But I didn't know them when they died. Your great Aunt Clara, I knew her when I was your age, then I never saw her again before she died."

"Was that Bach?"

Dmitri picked her up and put her on his lap. "Yes, you have a good ear."

"Papa said it was Bach."

"I guess your papa must know all my composers. He had to listen to them for many years."

"That would be nice."

"Maybe not always."

"I would like it always."

"If you guys had a piano, I'd play when I visit you. Or maybe someday you'll visit me. I'm not a great cook like your mother, but you could come over for cheese and things, I do those very well. I have a grand piano, it's huge and it's beautiful, if it didn't do anything you'd still want to look at it, it has such a fine gloss you can see yourself in it. You might like to try playing it."

"Would you let me?"

"Would I *let* you? I would insist on it."

Grandpa Esterhaats returned with ice cream for Clara. She showed no enthusiasm for it and Dmitri suspected she ate it more to please her grandfather with her apparent pleasure than to please herself. Don't be too much an Esterhaats, he thought, a little bit might be okay, but not too much. While she ate, sitting on the telephone book, sitting on all Manhattan, Dmitri stared at her. She was beautiful with her long black hair, like her great Aunt Clara's and her grandma's, but she and her hair looked freer than they and theirs ever were.

"Tell me something about Linda Ney, Dmitri."

"What sort of thing would you like to hear, Mama?"

"Is she funny?"

Dmitri wanted to tell the story of their fight and bath in Dijon, but that seemed inappropriate. "Sometimes she was. In England once someone hissed us at the end. I almost never cared about the audience but Linda always did. I thought she'd be upset, I was just getting up from the piano and couldn't see her face. I hurried a bit to be able to lead her offstage. But she looked around to find that person and she pointed at him with her bow and she hissed back. I loved her for that, I wanted to give her a big hug right there on the stage. Everybody laughed and then they started giving us such a loud ovation we had to play two or three encores. Giorgio says audiences usually follow the lead of the first person to boo, or applaud, or stand, or whatever, so before Linda hissed that guy, the audience were probably all about to agree with him. But the English are so fair and sporting they had to side with us after Linda showed the character to hiss back. For the last encore she insisted we do 'God Save the King' – it was King George then. I said no, she said yes, so we did it. That forced everyone to stand and sing for us, even the hisser. I think Linda grinned through the whole song."

His mother took Dmitri's hand. "You wrote cards from so many places and you sent letters with money and you never wrote her name. Why is that?"

"Sometimes I'm funny too, Mama. I can't explain that." In truth, he couldn't explain it, not even to himself. It had taken Jelly's determined program to make him sometimes say up to half what he thought.

"You wrote cards from Bologna. Papa laughed at one, it was the window of a delicatessen, it had baloney in the window. What's Bologna like?"

"It seems like half the shops are food, especially bologna and other sausages. If you went to all the cities I've ever seen and you had to pick out which one was named Bologna, you'd certainly get it right."

"Is Paris really so nice, Dmitri?"

"Paris is . . ." Visions flooded Dmitri's mind. "Yes, Mama. Paris is beautiful, wonderful, rich, I don't know, there aren't any adjectives good enough, maybe in French the adjectives are good enough. Of course, it helps to have a guide who speaks French along with you. With the right guide it's my favorite city in the world."

"Linda speaks French?"

"Mama, you're being too sly. Linda lived in Paris for several years. They were very hard years. When we were in Holland and Italy, I did the talking. She couldn't stand not knowing what was going on in the discussions, so she learned a lot of Italian and Dutch very fast. I think she speaks Italian better than I do now. In France, Belgium, and Switzerland, she did the talking. I hardly learned any French. I guess that's because I could listen to her speak French for hours, it wouldn't matter if I didn't understand a word of what she said. She said that was always my problem, I listened for the beauty and missed the meaning."

His mother bit her lip as her face drained white and she glanced toward the needle.

Dmitri gave her the injection.

"Thank you, Dmitri," she said, when color returned to her face. "I don't know why it does that. I ignore it for a while and it doesn't even bother me, and then . . ."

Dmitri stroked her forehead, drying it with his hand. In his most expansive discussion of her condition, his father had said she was too stoic and not stoic enough and that was her problem. She was too stoic, so that she waited far too long to see a doctor to stop the growing pain. And she was not stoic enough to ignore her pain altogether.

"Play for me."

"Do you remember your Aunt Clara, Dmitri?"

"Of course I do. She was almost as beautiful as you."

"She was more beautiful than me, you know it, Mitya. She was younger than me."

"She was wonderful at the piano. I think we spent the whole day on the piano bench. She taught me Mozart by playing it and letting me play after her. I kept wondering what the pedals were for. She said they didn't matter and I couldn't reach them anyway. Once I said if they didn't really matter, they wouldn't be there. She said I had justice on my side. She let me play Mozart while she did the pedals. It made a huge difference, a wonderful difference. It was hard for her to stretch her feet under me to do it, so she got a chair that was lower and let me sit on her lap so she could do the pedals. Some days I sat on her lap all day, it must've been horribly uncomfortable for her. She said it couldn't go on like that, she was going to have a baby and that baby would push me off her lap. She was making blocks to put on an extra pair of shoes so I could try the pedals myself." He shook his head and his tone changed. "But we left before they were ready. I didn't know we were going to leave. I didn't know that was why she came to say goodbye that morning when we got up so early. She was very strange, I didn't want to hug her, she kept saying I should remember I was her son too. She looked unhappy but she was acting very happy, she was laughing all the time."

"I'm sorry, Dmitri. We couldn't tell anyone. We couldn't tell you and Pavel because we were afraid someone would trick you into saying something. Clara was the only person we told, we wanted her to know where to find us when she came later. It was wrong what we did but it was necessary. It was too dangerous for you. Someone warned Papa men were asking about him, others in the group were taken away, we had to leave everything and go, we couldn't wait. It was dangerous to take suitcases or travel together, that made it look like we were emigrating. I took you, and Papa took Pavel. Papa wanted Pavel to go with me to protect me because he was a lot older. But I wanted to take you to protect you. We were fine. There were wonderful people at every city to help us, they took us to sleep in barns and gave us food and then they put us on the right trains with tickets for the next place. Or they put us in boxcars. Or they took us in wagons to secret places to cross borders, there were so many borders. Then we had to walk and sleep in the woods. They never asked us anything. They never answered anything. It took almost a month."

Dmitri remembered that trip as wonderful, as the final magic of his childhood before the world turned on him. It was perverse, they were fleeing, in fear for their lives, and he remembered it as a time of happiness beyond measure, perhaps one had to miss the meaning to get the beauty.

"We must've talked twelve hours a day on that trip."

"Fifteen, at least. And you did most of the talking, Mitya. Somebody was always hissing you to be quiet when we were walking through the woods. Do you know, Dmitri, I wasn't afraid. I was happy that whole trip."

Dmitri smiled and picked up her comb to comb her hair.

"It didn't seem bad to leave Kiev. We never fit there. Your father was Russian and I was Jewish, we didn't speak Ukrainian right. Ukrainians thought your father was one of the czar's men, someone to control them. But he was a socialist. Then socialists came to power and they thought we were reactionaries. We couldn't survive in Kiev. I guess we never fit anywhere. We've always been foreigners." She laughed, "We were *filthy* foreigners when we got to Amsterdam. They took our clothes and gave us new things and they never gave the old things back."

Dmitri had been shedding his pasts from the beginning, it seemed.

To ease his mother's sleep Dmitri would play twelve, sixteen, eighteen, toward the end even twenty hours a day, breaking for a nap morning and evening while his father sat with her and talked to her. Dmitri would also stop playing to sit beside her, but less and less as the *crescendo* of her pain exhausted her more and more. At the beginning of the fourth week he noticed her hands shaking, as Linda's often had, especially before performances. Dmitri took his mother's hands in his and they grew calm. He couldn't remember ever having seen her nervous, his own physical equanimity was hers.

"I don't know why they do that," she said. "I'm not nervous, but my hands are. They must be afraid."

Dmitri didn't answer. It would be hours before he would speak again. He held her hands a while longer and then returned to his piano to play

Bach, his hands nervously forcing the tempo for more than an hour before Bach patiently brought them under control.

His mother stopped eating soup, her intake was reduced to intravenous dextrose, and she began to sleep almost around the clock so long as Dmitri could play Bach, waking for an hour or so at a time in the morning and afternoon, and sometimes in the evening when Pavel came. The pain survived the heaviest permitted doses of morphine, and when it woke her she would struggle to smile and converse.

"Bach is so beautiful," she said. "Are you improvising? Or is that the way he wrote it?"

"This time it was his way, Mama. Sometimes I improvise . . ." He stopped himself before explaining why he needed to improvise, he couldn't say that even in this greatest of all his performances he required novelty to sustain interest. "I think of ways you might like it better."

"Dmitri," he thought she said. He went to her. He stroked her face. She turned to smile at him, but her smile couldn't resist her pain. She bit her lips and closed her eyes to cry as her face turned white. However stoic she was it could not be enough now. It was a long time before her next shot. It would've been cruel to wait. Dmitri injected the morphine. As was the case for the past couple of days, her arm didn't react to the prick of her skin with the needle. In a couple of minutes her face regained some of its color.

"What can I do for you, Mama?"

"You always gave me life. You still give me life." In a minute she added, "Play for me, Dmitri." Her voice was barely audible, but Dmitri had heard the request so many times he could now have understood it if it were made in silence.

Dmitri played while thinking, as though he were talking to her, Mama, you can let go if you want to, you don't have to continue for me.

Soon he could hear her breathing become louder as she fell asleep. He improvised to form a fugue Bach had neglected among the possible combinations of the themes of the preludes of *The Well-Tempered Klavier*. While he played, his mother died, and when he knew she'd died, he continued to play lest his silence be an affront to the peace which had finally come to her. He continued to play, not to finish the sequence of pieces, but in order not to stop, he wanted to linger. When at dawn he heard his father stirring awake in the other room, he stopped abruptly, and with that his father knew and, although he couldn't know that at the time, he ruined that brief, interrupted *toccata* for himself for many years to come. Dmitri barely had time to go over to kiss his mother's forehead before his father came in. Dmitri went to the kitchen to leave them alone in that moment. After a while, the doctor came, and Dmitri left the room again to fail at napping. When he returned to his mother's bed, he found her dressed in her only pretty dress, her shoulders covered with a Georgian shawl. The loose fit of her dress showed how frail she was and suggested her wasting away. Dmitri took his mother's combs and her brush from the bedside table and he undid her long braid. He combed out her hair and then brushed it until he realized that close to him it was wet and was not clinging to the brush. He wiped his face to no avail, his eyes wouldn't stop, they'd taken it upon themselves to mourn and he couldn't control them. He hadn't cried since the first time he sat at Horace Gmund's grand piano and there was nothing more to affect his life enough to make him weep again. It was too late for a profound marriage as he might have enjoyed with Linda, had she been able to enjoy it with him. He had no children. There was nothing but himself to lose and that would be to lose nothing.

He put his mother's beautiful hair, with its black and silver strands weaving in and out as though it were still braided, on top of her head, pinning it in place with her combs, as she would've done for a full dress occasion. "I look like a Jewish bride," she once said when he helped her do that.

Pavel came with food, but no one ate, and Dmitri went to the bathroom to wash his face and shave. His mother had asked not to be buried, to be cremated, so there would be no marker, no memorial. "The land is for the living," Dmitri's father quoted her.

The funeral brought together their several friends and his father's one relative of his own generation, a cousin who'd come by a different route to live in Brooklyn. Dmitri's mother had no surviving relatives from her generation – all had died in the war or the holocaust. Beautiful Aunt Clara, her husband, and her two small sons had gone to Amsterdam shortly after Dmitri's family left for America, and there, hideously, after having come so far, they'd been caught up by the Nazis. Dmitri and Pavel and Pavel's daughter Clara were her gifts to the world beyond her time.

Young Clara stood and sat with Dmitri, holding his hand throughout the service, as though she were the inheritor of his mother's caring spirit. At the end of the service, he lifted her onto his arm and carried her with him out of the temple. Back at the apartment afterwards, Clara sat at the piano and looked at it, trying keys, then catching herself as though it were wrong to make noise. Dmitri sat beside her to run a scale up from middle C. Then he took her hand and led her through the notes. She smiled at him. She seemed inordinately tiny beside him. He played Mozart, then

Debussy. She remembered a piece he'd played for her a year or so earlier when they'd all had dinner here.

"Would you play the one about the lost penny?"

He smiled at her. "You remember that? That must've been over a year ago. Beethoven, 'Rage over a lost penny.'" He wondered whether she remembered it because of its title or because of its music. He, too, had loved the piece as a child at Aunt Clara's piano, and he was unsure whether it was the silly title or the music that drew it to him at that age.

On hearing the title again now, Clara suddenly shook her head.

Dmitri pushed the bench back from the piano and lifted Clara onto his lap facing the keyboard. He rubbed the top of her tiny head with his chin. "It's okay, Clara. Your grandmother loved that song. She'd want me to play it now, you can be sure." As he heard his voice connecting these generations, he was astounded that he still had the power of speech.

The day after the funeral, Dmitri's father went to stay with his cousin for a few days and Dmitri took a taxi to return to his apartment in Manhattan. As the taxi approached the Manhattan Bridge, Dmitri suddenly said, "No, go to the Brooklyn Bridge."

"You shoulda told me sooner. Going there now, that's ass backwards."

"I know."

"It's okay with me, Buddy. You're paying the tab."

At the Brooklyn Bridge, Dmitri asked the cabby to stop. He paid and got out.

"Hey, look, Buddy, no suicide stuff. Life's not worth dying for."

Dmitri shook his head. "No, no suicide stuff. Life's not worth dying for."

It had been many years since he'd walked across the bridge. Now he stopped again at midpoint to gaze through the webbing, to hear anew his first broken bit of Liszt. It was only October, but tonight it was too cold for the clothes he'd worn to Brooklyn several weeks earlier. It had rained until late afternoon and the bridge and railings were wet, the wooden walkway was slippery. The webbing glistened from the drops of water still slowly working their way down to the bottoms of the cables. Dmitri liked the cold breeze that went through his thin jacket and shirt, that blew through his hair, now long overdue for a haircut. The sun had set but the clouds were still backlighted in pink. He stood there until the sky turned dark and Manhattan turned bright. Although he'd done almost nothing but play the piano for several weeks, still, just now he wished he had a grand out here. He was light-headed from exhaustion, but he could have played Liszt until he collapsed over the keys. He leaned against a railing and felt his leg turn wet through his trousers, but he stayed there. He looked down to test whether he could see drops of water from the bridge hitting the East River, but the angle was wrong. A barge moving slowly down river came into view beneath him. He envied the barge, he would've liked to be floating in black nothing, drifting gently.

Long after the barge was gone and the sky was dark, he finally turned to walk toward Manhattan, toward his apartment. Not home, just his apartment. He no longer had a home.

When Dmitri reached his apartment, he planned to go straight to bed. But he couldn't immediately sleep, he was, as Linda often said after their evening concerts, too tired for sleep. He paced the floor and soon bored himself with the limited path. He sat at each of his instruments and checked its tune. He got up and walked, ending in the kitchen where he got a glass of water. On the refrigerator he noticed a note: "I waited six days. You are sorry, Dmitri Esterhazy. You are not so beautiful you can get in whenever you want to, Jelly."

In a contradictory reaction Dmitri halfway smiled while he blushed at the thought of Jelly. He'd remembered to call her many times and he'd tried to do it on the evening of the sixth day, half a day too late, and for several days thereafter from a neighbor's phone. Then he mostly forgot all about her, about all the world, about anything not immediately connected with his mother.

Jelly left no address on her note, her former roommate was married and gone from New York, Dmitri didn't know how to reach Jelly unless he was willing to go to one of Anton's bars. He wasn't willing to do that.

Dmitri showered and still he was not ready to sleep. He went to his closet for a fresh shirt. There hung the bathrobe, pants, and blouse he bought for Jelly, the clothes she said were his because they wouldn't fit in her suitcase. Her own things, all of her things, down to the last dictionary, were gone.

Dmitri thought about Jelly. He was embarrassed at leaving her without calling. But, without much hard thinking, he noticed he didn't miss her. That was perverse. He valued her for her wonderfully energetic mood, and just now he didn't want energy around him, prodding him, mobilizing him. For at least a year, she'd come and gone from his life on a random schedule that was all her own, then she'd gone with him on every tour, and finally she'd virtually moved in to stay with him. He enjoyed all parts of that odd life, he even enjoyed the randomness of Jelly's comings and goings, it took no planning from him, it required merely that he respond to prodding, prodding in an implausible combination of effrontery and gentleness, occasionally laced with lethal Hungarian wit. He wasn't sure, but he thought he'd been on the verge of asking her to marry him. It might not have been a mistake, it might've worked very well, he might've been happy with her forever. He certainly would've enjoyed having her on tours with him. More than that, he didn't know. All he really knew was he didn't need her. And he knew this because he hadn't needed her enough even to think about her during the past weeks with his mother. Maybe he was too self contained now. Or maybe he was empty. Maybe those were the same thing.

He went to his piano and played Bach until he fell asleep.

After a few days, Giorgio came to see Dmitri. Giorgio knew from Pavel what had finally happened. Giorgio was graceful in his kindness to Dmitri and Dmitri thought for once it was okay for him to be a confidant. In Paris he instinctively knew Linda would have to play a memorial for Jerusalem Neimann. Now he had to play a memorial for Marina Haimovich Esterhaats, or *Esterhaatsa* it should be, unless she was to be memorialized as a woman of the new world. Other than playing that memorial, there was nothing else that mattered to Dmitri. He asked Giorgio how soon it could be done.

"Scheduling something new, you know, Dmitri, that can take very long unless it's just at a corner church or something. It's not like the old days when we were booking you into fill-ins and small-time stuff, these halls are booked for a year or two, even longer. I don't know how long it'd take. But, you know, well, you're already booked into Carnegie Hall end of December, it's your second time there, you don't want to . . . well we could make that the memorial. But it's up to you, Dmitri, you've gotta think when you want to do it. Only, if you're not playing Carnegie, I've gotta tell them now."

Dmitri would suspect only later that this was a sly and tactful move to keep him in the schedule, just as he'd probably been instinctively sly and tactful in leading Linda into her memorial for Jerusalem to get her performing again, to bring her back to life. Dmitri asked Giorgio to have the program changed, to list the memorial, and to include a note to say there would be no encores, he would not again make the mistake he'd made with Linda's memorial for Jerusalem. Immediately off the top of his head he scheduled Mozart, Chopin, Liszt, Debussy, and his mother's favorite numbers from Bartók's *Mikrokosmos*, all music he'd loved as a child, music she loved the more because he did, plus one thing he'd discovered only later. But at that moment he couldn't bring himself to schedule Bach, couldn't think of playing

Bach for anyone less intimately deserving than his mother. Apart from leaving out Bach, he'd never had a more obvious program to select, he had no doubts, no second guesses, so clear in his mind was his mother, with all her loves and tastes and tolerances.

After the memorial concert, Dmitri's father moved into the home of his cousin. Dmitri went back to Brooklyn to supervise the moving of his piano from the old apartment to a local school. They were going to put a brass plaque with his name on it; he asked that they not do that but the music teacher pleaded with him. "We need to give the kids incentive, they have to love music, and an . . . well, an exotic name – that would help a lot, Mr. Esterhaats. I could tell them you learned Bach and Bartók on that piano." Dmitri relented in the end, he shared the purpose but doubted the technique, but he had no special expertise to contradict the teacher's expectations of the magic of the exotic name, perhaps it would work better for the kids than it had worked for him in his life with the piano. Dmitri helped his father with the last bit of his packing and he put his own few things into a small suitcase to take with him, things he'd left there for the odd occasion when he stayed overnight, things he'd really left there to give his mother the sense he hadn't yet left her home, her care, her life. When all was done he sat at the piano to play until the movers came.

It had been hard to get the piano into the apartment, now it seemed even harder to get it out. When the movers finally had it on the sidewalk outside, the piano displayed numerous new scratches. Oh well, it's going to a school, Dmitri thought, they'll treat it even worse. During all the years after he left home, his mother periodically brought in a piano tuner to keep the piano ready for Dmitri whenever he happened to come home. He often told her it wasn't necessary, he could tune it whenever necessary, but still she had it tuned. He thought she didn't want to risk losing occasion to have him play, to have him linger, and she knew him well enough to suspect that a mere five minutes for tuning the piano might be the crucial obstacle to his staying.

Before the movers loaded the piano on their truck, he stood before it and played one of the *Goldberg Variations*. He started to walk away after finishing and then he laughed. Dmitri turned back to the keyboard and stood at the left end, as the old Pole had done at the moment when he was trying to play Liszt. Dmitri crashed both hands down hard to play the inadvertent chord the old Pole had played to stop his Liszt. "I do not hear Liszt," he said. He was startled at his own noise, that he remembered the chord exactly despite the passage of decades, he was startled that he'd originally heard the ten distinct notes even while immersed in his Liszt. The old Pole had struck as Dmitri was running up the keyboard in a wonderful flight into romantic freedom that was utterly shattered by the chord. He supposed that the old Pole had not intended to strike any particular pattern of the keys, he had only wanted to slam as many as he could with his ten fingers, and that, as a pianist, he'd kept his fingers distinct as though he were picking out particular keys. Today Dmitri liked the chord, it was powerful and resonant, even in this auditorium in the open with its infinitely dissipated acoustic, it belonged in the piano four-hands literature, he would have liked to play it for the old Pole, perhaps by working it into a particularly noisy bit of Liszt. He struck the Polish chord three times in quick succession, making peace with a tiny part of his past, letting the sounds hum their way to silence through the sympathetic throbbing of the strings of the piano.

Finally, Dmitri watched his once beloved piano, the object he'd loved most in all his life, go slowly down the street and around the corner. His parents had become accustomed to the sound of his Steinway upright grand from Horace Gmund. They'd become able to sleep, talk, read, or listen to the radio as though Beethoven, Liszt, or Mozart didn't fill their ears, it disturbed them only when Pavel was ill and when Dmitri pounded it like a kettle drum for Prokofiev and others.

All those years of training had given the piano power to soothe his mother in her final days as nothing else could've done. As the piano disappeared now, it occurred to Dmitri it had really become his mother's piano, no longer his. He should have kept it for her. In giving it away, he was yet again shedding his past.

Clara Esterhaats

There were no grand influences left in the life of Dmitri Esterhaats. All influence was from the past, the present was only daily routines and concerts, his own and others. For better or for worse, he was now fully formed, even if it was not so fully. Some of the influences from the past were now desiccated, the life dried from them, leaving only their residues of technique and taste. Other influences were more vibrant, they could jump before him in an instant when he struck a chord or recalled a moment. But even these had begun to lose their feel, increasingly they jumped before him only in form, not content. They had ghostlike power to take over his mind, to seize him unawares, but their power didn't last, they couldn't control him. When he really wanted to, he could drift in black nothing like the barge on the East River, he could be detached and free.

Despite its visual leavings, Dmitri told himself the hard parts of the past were really gone. He'd mastered his own life, he'd come to tolerate himself despite his failings. He didn't have natural gifts for such mastery, as Jelly seemed to have and as he seemed to have for the piano, but he'd used Linda's devices of hard work and long thought to free himself, to cut himself away from the past. There was less of him as a result, but it was better not to have so much, not to be so much.

He occasionally had moments of doubt, moments when his past seemed orchestral, as though it were a vast whole, some part rising into view this minute, some other part the next minute, especially his mother and Linda Ney, but also Jelly Ujfalussy, Sally in Alabama, Sofia Milano, Horace Gmund, Aunt Clara in Kiev, *Mademoiselle* Meursault, Pavel, even Colonel and Mrs. Weiss, with occasional brief notes for a few others. Like the themes in his favorite music, they usually rose with dissonance tempered with beauty. As he could remember whole scores from his youth through the years with Colonel Weiss, so he could also remember whole scenes of his life from then, with all the words and facial expressions and all the sensations of their time. His greatest achievement now was to purge the sensations from his present, to keep them under control as nothing more than memories, like notes and markings on a page without sound, to reduce his past to its score.

Jelly Ujfalussy, one of the least fractious, least dissonant of his influences, stood at Dmitri's door. He was chagrined – not chagrined to be seeing her but to be seeing her only after so long a time without explanation.

"I'm sorry . . ." he started.

"I know you are sorry, Dmitri Esterhazy. You are very sorry. You lack something as a human being. You are a wonderful pianist, you have lovely hands, I will always want to hear you play. But you are deficient, that is a word I found for you. You are uneasy in your skin, I do not object to that. You are also rude, I do object to that. I stayed here six days after you left. I will never stay here again."

"I was . . ." Dmitri wasn't sure what he was, he didn't continue immediately, it seemed to him his chief deficiency was his insufficient fondness for Jelly, he should've loved her.

"I will hope to see you at concerts and at the bar. I will still enjoy talking with you."

"I shouldn't have done that to you, Jelly."

"It is no matter. People have left me all my life. I learn to forget them. I had to live. I will still live. I came to tell you something, I do not come to complain. Please do not stay away from the bar. Anton and the others are very sad. If it is your wish, I will stay away so you can come."

"No, Jelly, don't do that, don't stay away. I'll come. Not just now. But soon."

"Thank you, Dmitri Esterhazy."

She turned as if to go, then turned back. Dmitri had the sense she was giving him some kind of second chance.

"I have thought when I come here you will explain me why you did me what you did. But you do not explain."

"I'm sorry. My mother was . . ."

"I know, Dmitri. I went to the Carnegie Hall. I asked for my pass, there was no pass. They cannot make a mistake with a name Ujfalussy, I knew you did not arrange it. I had to stand, there were no seats, not even the old usher Joe could get me a seat. There was no more standing room tickets, but he let me stand. I do not object to that, that was okay, I understood you might not think of me to get me a pass. The old usher gave me a program. That is what

I objected, Dmitri. I saw it was a memorial for your mother. I learn it that way, Dmitri. Can you understand? I am sorry for you, Dmitri, that your mother died. I want to cry for you, I do not even cry when I learn my mother is dead. But for you, Dmitri, I know. But it was terrible when I learn it that way. I wanted to leave. I tell you I did not stay for you, I am thinking you are a terrible, hateful man, I stayed for your mother and the usher. I do not say it was the most cruel thing anyone has done me, I will not tell the most cruel things. But it was cruel, Dmitri, it was very cruel."

Dmitri's mother said he seemed outside the world. Now he felt outside the world. Not so much uneasy in his skin as Jelly said, but out of concern, so out of concern he could be cruel without noticing it, without being motivated to do anything about it. Very little mattered very much. The most satisfying thing he did was play his harpsichords or his piano from morning until late evening.

To atone in small part for his cruelty, Dmitri instructed Giorgio to make sure there was always a pass to all his New York performances for Jelly in a front row seat, just past the middle where she could see his face as he played. Thereafter there were few greater pleasures to him over the years than to see Jelly sitting there with her earnest expression and her spectacular beauty as he walked out to begin a concert, stopping front and center to bow, as though to her. For New York, because Jelly was there, he always thought the audience mattered. He often walked with her afterwards to one of their bars, sometimes finding Anton Staebli or some of the others, sometimes finding no one. Occasionally he would be recognized by someone who, having first looked at Jelly, only then noticed him as they walked the street or sat in the bar. They would greet him, while glancing repeatedly at Jelly.

Jelly challenged Dmitri's silly grin while he was being greeted by an apparent admirer who'd been to his concert.

"That guy was much more interested in you than in me," Dmitri said. "I think he has twice as much respect for me now because he thinks I'm clever enough to land you. And after seeing you his wife was beginning to get interested in me too, she must think I've got something."

"He would lose all his respect for Dmitri Esterhazy if he knew the truth. You were not clever enough. Not half clever enough, Dmitri. And his wife should have better sense."

One of Dmitri's greatest joys was to play for Anton's *lieder* performances in New York now and then.

"*Und dann und wann ein weisser Elefant,*" Anton laughed. And now and then, a white elephant.

The joke was doubly on Anton. It was a line from a poem of Rilke recently set to difficult music that strained Anton's abilities. "I think it's time for this white elephant to retire."

Dmitri was startled. "No, why?"

"My vocal chords are too old to take on stuff like this. Doing the chorus at the Met is enough now, although they do too damned much Verdi. I can't do solo recitals anymore, I can't compete. You've got Horowitz, I've got Fischer-Dieskau. Only, Horowitz is older than you. Fischer-Dieskau is younger than I am, Dmitri, *younger.*"

Dmitri knew there were signs of decline, but he didn't like facing them.

"Hey, Dmitri, don't worry about it! You don't have to retire. Singers retire, their instrument wears out. Pianists never retire, they go on to the bitter end, their instrument can always be repaired or replaced. I know your kind, Dmitri, you don't drink much, you're as thin as you ever were, you'll be performing when you're 95."

Dmitri instantly visualized five decades sliding before him, traveling, performing, occasionally coming to the bar, continuing everything to age 95, a longer time still to go than he'd lived so far. Few visions of his future could've been less appealing, he'd rather repeat his past, that would bring more novelty. "Christ," he said.

Dmitri performed as Giorgio scheduled. He pressed for fewer engagements, Giorgio pressed for more. Giorgio couldn't resist high fees, and Dmitri's refusals to perform drove his fees so high Giorgio scheduled him more. Only Jelly could figure that one out, Dmitri thought. He found little joy in traveling alone, his chief joy was in playing, and traveling often reduced the time he had to play. He especially hated international traveling alone, going to places he'd want to explore if he were with Linda or Jelly, who would've made walking more than walking. Instead of exploring his cities, he let them spread themselves in neglect outside his hotels or rehearsal rooms, while he spent as much time playing as he could, often playing music not on his scheduled programs to help him sustain spontaneity in the performances.

What time he spent away from his hotel, rehearsal, and performance rooms, he spent in museums and music libraries looking at autograph manuscripts of the works of his composers. In London at the British Museum he found Bach's own copies of some of the *Well-Tempered Clavier,*

Book II. The pages were beautiful, he'd've liked to put them on his walls above his pianos and harpsichords, just to see them was to hear wonderful sounds. Looking at them also recalled his mother and her agony as he played. In the manuscript of the dramatically quick *Prelude in D minor*, Dmitri was brought to a stop where his mother had awakened with a moan and distracted him from his playing when he went to her to give her a shot. She apologized for interrupting. He hadn't seen the score of this piece in decades, perhaps not since Amsterdam. Now he counted down to the 25th bar, where the forward urge of the music was overwhelming, where his mother interrupted and he stopped. The music was a torrent surging under Bach's control until it crashed in his mind in that bar.

Dmitri studied the pages and Bach's glorious notes, with bars crossed out, with extra lines jammed in at the bottom of a page to finish a rippling fast passage where Bach's very script conveyed the rush of the music. To see the music like this, not finally and perfectly printed, was to see it alive and spontaneous, as though improvised from beginning to end, as though it were racing ahead even of Bach in his need to reduce it to a page. Dmitri heard the rising and falling of the sounds, the urgency to be followed soon by peace and gentleness, he even felt the fingering of the notes, but he couldn't hear beyond the crash, he couldn't hear into the peace and gentleness, he could only hear as much of it as he'd played one late night in Brooklyn.

At the end of the afternoon, after Dmitri'd heard the first 25 bars of the prelude a hundred times, the librarian gently took the manuscript from him. "I'm sorry, Mr. Esterhaats," she said. "You can come again if you wish." For many years he'd used that prelude and its fugue as a short encore. Now he no longer used it. After seeing Bach's version of it, he would've had to play it differently.

Even worse than traveling, Dmitri hated the state dinners of the music world, hosted by conductors, impresarios, sometimes even by mayors, as in Kiev, Moscow, and Leningrad, where they were reluctant to let him speak Russian, where they wanted to treat him as a native son and a foreigner all at once, where Dmitri began to introduce himself by saying, "I'm from Kiev," in English. To enliven those dinners, he needed Jelly with her effrontery or Linda with her occasional out-of-character insults. Jelly would've been especially good in Japan and Russia, he could see Jelly asking his Japanese host why she was the only woman in the room, had the Japanese given up on their wives? Linda might've done her best in England and Scandinavia, he could envision her yawning openly at a Swedish dinner. Dmitri lacked the kind of public strength of character demonstrated by all his women. His strength was to withdraw, which maybe was no strength at all.

But far the worst of traveling was being away from his niece, Clara. After planning a move to the Westchester suburbs for several years, Pavel and his family suddenly moved to the Upper East Side a year after Mama Esterhaats died.

"It's closer to Papa," Pavel said.

But Dmitri had reason to suspect Pavel felt obligated to watch out for Dmitri, to take care of him now that their mother could not. A few days before her death, he heard Pavel promise their mother he would look after Dmitri. He hadn't wanted to overhear and regretted it. Yet it wasn't Pavel whose attentions affected Dmitri. It was his daughter, Clara. In a few odd moments after returning from Europe, Dmitri had begun to teach her the piano and she'd taken lessons since then.

"It would seem wrong not to have a piano going in the background," Pavel said.

Now she was near enough to walk to Dmitri's apartment after school and on free days. She spent two afternoons a week and most Saturdays at Dmitri's grand when he was in town. For her tenth birthday, Dmitri had Giorgio get a baby grand to replace her console piano. He first proposed getting a grand to Pavel.

"Dmitri, a concert grand is seven feet four inches long."

"It is?"

"Our living room isn't big enough for that. Do you really think she needs more than a console?"

"Yes, she's too good for a console."

Pavel seemed impressed with the judgment of his daughter. "Okay, if you really want to do it, maybe you could get her a baby grand. That would fit better."

Later, Dmitri realized Pavel knew the length of a concert grand only because he must have checked into getting one.

The following year, Dmitri got a second grand for his own apartment, so he and Clara could play duets. Clara loved Dmitri's room full of pianos and harpsichords so much she asked him to hold her eleventh birthday party there. The party came two days after the second grand. One of Clara's friends, upon entering, said to her in disbelief, "Your uncle lives in a museum."

Sad to say, Dmitri thought, there's truth in that. The truth was especially sad for one to whom the past was odious and best kept in the past, not on display.

"Do you know what, Clara?" Dmitri asked one afternoon during a lesson. "You are the first American in the Esterhaats family."

"You and Papa are Americans."

"No, we are Russians – and I think we'll never forget it. You're different."

"I don't want to be different from you and Papa."

"Maybe you're not much different, only younger and freer."

"You're free."

Dmitri had meant Clara was free of external burdens. He didn't know what she meant. But if she meant he was free of internal compulsions, she was almost right.

"Yes, I guess so," he said. "Mozart four hands. *K381*."

"Okay."

"Which part do you want."

She giggled. "I'll sit on the left so I can be the heavy. You take the high road and I'll take the low road – but you'd better not get there before me."

Dmitri's face betrayed him.

"You know, *the song*," she said with teenage emphasis, "'and I'll get to Scotland *afore ye*.'"

"I don't know that."

Clara turned into Sally before his eyes – the only American woman he'd known before Clara – in truth the only American he'd known at all. To confirm his vision of Sally, Clara's eyes widened as she proclaimed in disbelief, "Everyone knows that song, Uncle Dmitri, you *have* to know it."

He hadn't had to know it before, but now he did, and he was meant to learn it before they turned to Mozart. Clara then played the heavy among the four hands and Dmitri wanted to let his part drop out to listen to her. She'd joined his earlier Clara as the greatest of Mozart pianists, listening to her now was almost like hearing Sofia Milano sing for the first time, like hearing Linda Ney sing beside him in *Notre Dame*. He could say nothing without wrecking the magic of the moment, but he still felt the less for keeping silence. He could see only the top of her head, swaying with its glorious long hair as she played with her intense absorption in the music she made. He wanted to kiss her head and merely listen, but he continued to take the high road.

Later Dmitri said, "You know, Clara, someday soon you have to make a choice. How much do you want to be a pianist? If you want it really badly and you're determined to do it well, you need lessons almost every day."

"You don't think I'm very good."

"I wouldn't say something like that to anyone who wasn't very, very good – it would be silly for someone who wasn't really good to work on the piano every day. I'm saying it because you can be as good as you want to. Your decision is how good to be. You don't need to make a decision now. Think about it for a few months. Or longer. If you want more lessons, I'll give you a lot more."

He could say all of that not only because he knew she had the natural ability to be very good but also because he knew she was struggling with her parents over how much time she could give to piano.

"How did you decide?"

"The way I did it was ignorant. I never asked anybody for good advice, I don't know why. Maybe it's not Russian, Russians have to invent everything for themselves. You're a lot smarter, Clara, you're an American who uses the telephone and finds out everything, you take advantage of experts to save your having to work out everything alone. If you want to be a pianist, you'll go to Juilliard or some place good. I never did that, I don't know why. In fact, one thing, if you're going to develop, you'll have to have other teachers. In a couple of years you'll have to tell me the truth, tell me, Sorry, Uncle Dmitri, I've learned all Dmitri Esterhaats has to teach, I have to go on to other teachers. Dmitri Esterhaats will have to find someone less talented to teach."

"I'm too much trouble for you."

"No, Clara, that is *not* true." He looked at her looking at her feet. "Are your parents worried about that?"

She looked stubbornly intent on silence. Maybe she was an American, but still she was an Esterhaats.

"Clara, you are what I live for those days you come here. I'd teach you forever, I'd be the saddest person in New York the day you went to another teacher."

"No, I would be."

Dmitri knew whatever her sadness, it would be tempered with excitement at the prospect of new beginnings. But he didn't contradict her.

Clara became pensive. She walked around the room looking at the harpsichords. After a while she started opening closets and drawers, and she found Dmitri's two albums, the two-record set with Sofia Milano and the one-record album with Linda Ney. Her eyes grew big. She held the record for a long time without speaking. Finally she said, very quietly, "She's a bad lady."

"Why?"

"She was mean to you."

"Hey, come here. Do you want me to tell you about her?"

"No, I don't like her."

"I bet if you knew her you would. You'd love to play with her, Ravel's *Tzigane* or Debussy's *Violin Sonata*."

"*Tzigane* is just to show off."

"That's true. But you've got to have it if you're going to show it off. Linda Ney's got it, she's a great violinist. It's very hard to be a great violinist."

"Not that hard."

"What do you mean, Clara?"

"She could be a great violinist and treat you a lot better."

He put his fingers through her hair, turning her head to face him, leaning forward to put his forehead within inches of hers as they sat side by side on one of the harpsichord benches facing out into the room. "How do you suppose anybody knows how she treated me? I'm famous the world over for never telling anybody anything. Nothing. Zero. *Niente*. Zilch. I'm a lot more famous for secrecy than for playing the piano. This very morning, street sweepers in Peking were asking just how many secrets I could possibly have. Russian spies are standing outside this building right now trying to find out what I know, they assume if it's secret it must be important. A woman you've never met – she has an incredible name, Jelly Ujfalussy – Jelly used to insist I should say half what I thought. I can tell you that was very hard, I never succeeded, I never will succeed. My mother wasn't even sure about me, she found out Linda Ney's name from newspaper reviews of our performances. From newspaper reviews! That's terrible. I didn't know I was *that* secretive. With all those secrets that only I know, and even I've forgotten a lot of them, your father and your Grandpa Esterhaats can't know very much. Everybody tried to figure things out. They probably did a good job of figuring, but when you start with numbers like zero they don't add up to much, and if they think Linda Ney's a bad lady, they got it all wrong."

"Well, I don't know. They think being a pianist is a rotten life. They say you've had a hard life."

"That's what they think?" He wondered, How odd, it wasn't rotten being a pianist, why would they think that? "Maybe they're not entirely wrong. It's not rotten. But maybe it was hard for a long time, until recently. But your father had a hard life too, until recently." He laughed. "But we're Russians. That's what it means to be Russian. A Russian who didn't have a hard life would commit suicide in despair. Remember, that's where you're different. Just that one little detail can make all the difference in the world."

Clara frowned.

"Young lady, we're going to play a duet. Mozart! My two hands vote for Mozart. Then you tell me if that's a rotten life. What do you vote?" They'd had time to learn only one duet piece with the second grand.

"Mozart. And then Bartók for encore."

"You know that?"

"What do you think, you dope, I only play here? I have my own piano too, you know, and I still have piano at school."

"Well, when I was your age, I never heard of Bartók. Then when I did, I played him all the time. When I found out he was living in the Bronx I went walking near his apartment, hoping maybe I'd see him."

Her eyes widened. "He's been dead a long time."

"Mozart even longer."

"But you didn't hope to meet Mozart."

They went to the pianos. Despite the odd acoustic, Dmitri had them set up side by side so he could readily glance sideways at Clara as she played, could watch the intensity in her face, the concentration that kept her from noticing anything but her piano. She looked very much like the Aunt Clara of his Kiev memory, and their odd juxtaposition, Dmitri older and Clara younger, was startling and beautiful to him.

After their encore, Dmitri said, "Someday we're going to do that at Carnegie Hall, Clara, I bet you."

"It wouldn't be a rotten life?"

"It's not a *rotten* life. Sometimes it's a hard life. A lot of the time maybe. Maybe almost all the time."

Clara laughed. "That argument won't work. Mama and Papa don't want me to have a *hard* life."

Soon she asked whether they could listen to his records.

"Hmmm," he said. "My player's not very good."

"That doesn't matter."

He could think of no more false excuses. "How about one *aria* from the Sofia Milano album?"

Clara looked at him very carefully, then took his hand.

"You've never opened the one with Brahms and Bartók," she said. She looked intently at him, as though waiting for an answer. "You've never heard it, have you?"

"No."

"If I had a recording, I couldn't wait to hear it. I tried to record once with Papa's tape recorder. It didn't work right, it sounded terrible." She went to get the records. "I could just borrow them, Uncle Dmitri. I would take good care of them, and I would bring them back."

Dmitri put his hands on her shoulders and held her before him lest the moment pass too soon. "Okay. Promise you'll tell me where you think the pianist goes wrong."

"I might tell you what I think of the violinist too. I'm not going to like her."

"I'll ask Giorgio to get good equipment here some Saturday so you can make a tape recording if you like."

She almost jumped. "And we can do four-hands!"

"No," he smiled at this slyest of the Esterhaats line. "I think your two hands will be just enough, Clara."

"I know a young girl who wants to play piano, but her parents think it would be a rotten life. What should I say to her?"

"Do you think you have a rotten life, Dmitri?" Jelly said.

"It's not *rotten*, I wouldn't say that. Sometimes hard maybe."

"I tell you what I think, okay?"

"Sure. Okay."

"Are you really sure? You may regret."

"I'm really sure."

"If you are dentist, you spend lot of time being dentist or you are bad dentist. Dentist like anything else. If you spend more time at anything, you should be better at it. Is that right?"

"Sounds right to me."

"Okay. Now. If you spend more time being a person, you should be a better person. Same as dentist. Yes?"

"Okay."

"You, Dmitri, you are unlucky. To be a pianist takes all your time, you do not have enough to be a person also."

"I might accept that," Dmitri said in a paraphrase of one of Jelly's standard responses.

"I do not say you should be a worse pianist and a better person. I just say there is difficulty. I say maybe you choose the right thing. But I have prejudice, I want very much to hear good piano. If you only play Schubert and never Bartók, then I would say you should work harder to be a person."

Dmitri grinned at her and started to say something.

Jelly giggled. "Do not try to be a dentist. You would ruin all my teeth."

Dmitri forgot what he'd started to say.

"I am lucky, Dmitri. I do only one thing. I spend all my time being a person. Maybe I spend some time listening to piano, but maybe that helps me be a better person too. When I do not want to live with you anymore, I am glad you are better as pianist. If you are such a good pianist you are not such a good person, but you make me happy when you play. That is not worth nothing, Dmitri. Remember it."

"And I'm lucky to know such a good person."

"You wash your mouth, Dmitri. You will buy us a bottle of champagne and wash it very well."

Giorgio spoke very tentatively, as though he feared to say what he planned to say. He walked around the office, he toyed with papers on his desk, he looked out the window and down at the floor, he seldom let his eyes catch Dmitri's.

"Hey, Dmitri, I'm not sure whether I should even say anything. But they asked me to, I'm your agent, I have to ask, that's my job. What it is, there's gonna be a fundraiser for Lincoln Center, they want to do a series of performances by great chamber groups. They have lots of quartets and other groups, octets, trios, you know. But, well, what they want, what they need, hell, I'll just come out and say it, they want to get Ney-Esterhaats back together for one of the shows." Giorgio looked at once relieved and alarmed at having got the words out. "Look, hey, I told them they shouldn't count on it. I suggested they might get you to do piano quintets, Shostakovich maybe, with one of the quartets you've played with. They say, No, they want real groups that have names as groups, groups with life histories. Christ, life histories. If you wanta say No, I understand, I'll tell them No. You might think it gets in the way of other things you want to do. But it's two years from now so you can take a while to think it over."

Giorgio's nervousness was misplaced, Dmitri thought, Dmitri wasn't much affected by the request, it was as if he hardly cared. Ney-Esterhaats had a life history, but the life was now gone.

"You have spoken to Linda," Dmitri said, in a challenging tone. It was not a question, Dmitri knew Giorgio always checked out every other angle before talking to him.

"She's . . . how to say it, I don't know. She's willing to consider it. That's it, you know how she can be, I don't know, a bit uncertain. But only if you're really willing, she says."

"What's the difference between really willing and just willing?"

"Dmitri, I couldn't possibly say. Half the time I don't understand either of you. And I sure as hell don't understand both of you. Don't put me on the spot in Linda's place."

"That was long ago, Giorgio, ten or twelve years."

"Thirteen almost exactly."

"So in two years it would be fifteen." Linda would've teased him for getting the arithmetic right.

"I know, Dmitri, thirteen years, Christ almighty. Coulda been a hell of a thirteen years. The Lincoln Center people want to bill you as a fifteenth anniversary reunion."

"I will think about it," Dmitri said.

"While you're thinking, remember, there's a lotta money in it. I think I can really stick it to them, especially if you agree not to perform or record anywhere else together before their concert. Ney-Esterhaats was one of the longest running violin-piano duos around, most of them just get together now and then. You guys were a real duo, you had class, like Ginette and Jean-Paul Neveu, there haven't been many in that league. Anyway, I can promise it would be your biggest fee ever."

"You told Linda that?"

"Yes, I . . ."

"She needs money?"

"Dmitri, everybody needs money. The only people who don't need money are the kind of people who put up the spare change to sponsor this thing."

Dmitri knew his wasn't a fair question, either for Linda or for Giorgio. He regretted asking it. Why was he being so mean-spirited toward someone he no longer cared about, someone he hadn't seen in thirteen years? Maybe she really wanted to do it, maybe she wanted to play their music again, maybe she even wanted to play with him again, they played together as though they read each other's thoughts, as though they were really one with each other and their music, despite their wanting different music. That was something she might think was worth recreating for a moment.

"I'm sorry, I didn't mean that," Dmitri said, contritely. "It's up to Linda. If she wants to do it, I don't care. No, I don't mean it that way, it's true but it might sound wrong. You can tell her I'm really willing to do it if she wants to." He paused, he didn't believe it would ever happen, Linda would balk.

Nevertheless he wanted to get all the issues out of the way now just in case so they wouldn't come up again. "She'll need to work out a plan for rehearsal, she can't stand leaving that up to anybody else. Sometime I'll give you a list of pieces I'd want us to work on, she can give you her list. Or if she wants to we can get together and talk about it."

Giorgio looked grim, as if Dmitri were being too severe.

"It's okay, Giorgio. That's how we worked when we started before. From the very first day. It sounds formal and rigid, maybe it was a bit formal and rigid. But it didn't bother me."

Again Dmitri thought she would not do it.

Dmitri also thought it unreasonable of the world to make Linda Ney's well being depend on him when she'd chosen otherwise. She must be making at least as much money as he was. But she'd always spent more. Still, he couldn't stand in her way by not joining her now any more than he could stand in her way by not parting from her earlier. He walked home mulling over the tribulations of trying to work with her and discounted them by what he thought was the low chance she'd finally be willing to work with him. She would have to think it would be intense and difficult, it would force them together for at least several weeks if Linda was to rehearse properly.

"I'm not a natural and I don't have your memory, Dmitri, I have to think and work to get it right, I have to play it at least ten times the week of the performance. And I can't work on duos if you won't work with me."

If they were to play well together they would also have to become attuned to each other as they once were, they had to be half merged, half autonomous.

"You follow me wherever I go, you follow so fast it seems like you're leading me. I love that. It always works, Dmitri."

It would not be possible for them to be half merged again without dramatic changes. Or perhaps now that Dmitri no longer wanted Linda . . . But that was not worth thinking about.

Dmitri went to the piano with no clear intention what to play. He'd been playing Scarlatti on a harpsichord before going to Giorgio, working on tempos and variations. His mind fixed on something just as fast for the piano, and he found himself showing off in an encore for an absent audience to his thoughts by playing Schumann's *Toccata* for the first time in ages. When he finished, it seemed natural to turn to Brahms.

Christ, he thought, I no longer want Linda but I think of her and I want Brahms. Jelly's right, I must be too stupid to be Hungarian.

"So you and Linda Ney are going to get back together for the Lincoln Center fest?" Anton said.

"Yes. For one performance. Two years from now." Dmitri shrugged for Anton.

"You are going to play with Linda?" Jelly said. "Should I come and sleep with you too, for old time sake?"

Dmitri was so taken aback he had no idea how to answer.

Jelly grasped his nose as though to pull it off and then stuck her finger into his belly. "Do not even think about it, Dmitri Esterhazy," she said loudly while shaking her head violently at him, "do not even think about it. And if you do think about it, do not say anything you think, not even half what you think, not one word." Then, with instantaneous calm, she added, "But you can buy me a beer."

"Will it be hard, Dmitri?" Anton asked gently.

"Who knows, Anton. I don't. It might be hard for Linda. It shouldn't be hard for me, I don't seem to care very much anymore."

"That is the Bauhaus principle of growing old gracefully, Dmitri: Eventually less really is more. I oughta know, I'm a lot older than you. Follow that principle and you'll live to a grisly old age." He put his half-finished glass of beer on the table and laughed as he turned to leave. "See: More," he gestured at the glass of beer. "*Auf Wiedersehen, Kinder.*"

"Okay, then I will buy *you* a beer," Jelly said.

"No, I will buy one for you, Jelly. My pocket is heavy with money that's going to waste." Dmitri got the beer.

"I am living with Charles," Jelly said.

"The flute?"

She giggled. "He is my first American."

"Maybe he has a bit of Hungarian blood."

"No, it is certain not. He is dumb, it is impossible he is Hungarian. He does not understand about music, why it works. He only knows how to make it. When I am funny he thinks I am serious. When I am serious he thinks I am funny."

"That isn't always so easy with you, I think you like to confuse people."

"Maybe you have some truth. I will allow that. Still, he does not understand music."

"He's supposed to be very good."

"He is. He plays for Bernstein. He sometimes has solos with the orchestra."

Immediately Dmitri thought of Linda Ney standing solo before the Philadelphia Orchestra. It was beautiful beyond description, Ormandy the visual master at his best with the most beautiful of soloists standing near him in a purplish pink gown, the only splash of color on a grand black and white tableau. Bernstein was sloppier, more dramatically romantic, much less suitable for Linda in his sprawl.

"I do not tell you you have to say what you think, Dmitri Esterhazy. But it is a little rude to think that much without saying *anything*. Do you not think it also?"

"Sorry, Jelly. I was thinking about solos with orchestras. Charles is lucky to have his built into the job. He can work with the same people all the time and still do solos."

"You were not thinking about Charles."

Clara demonstrated the success of her practice at home while Dmitri was away by playing Prokofiev's seventh *Piano Sonata.* Dmitri watched and listened in astonishment. He didn't even know she'd been working on it. She played with such concentration on her hands and the keys that she didn't notice his presence, his often startled facial expressions as she played through passages he thought would bring disaster.

"That is wonderful, Clara, I want to hear it again."

"I promised I wouldn't be late for dinner."

"Not today," Dmitri laughed. "Next time will be soon enough. That is the greatest thing you ever did."

"I know."

"You can be sure I didn't do that when I was your age."

"Why not?"

"Well, it wasn't written yet for one thing." In a rare move, he laughed at his own comment. "If it had been I think I'd've been embarrassed by it. Hey! I nearly forgot. Someone asked me if I'd be a teacher at a summer camp next summer."

"You'd be away all summer?" Clara asked as she looked down at the ground.

"Wait, Miss Esterhaats, please, no interruptions until I finish. It's in the mountains in New England. It's a beautiful place, it's about two months. It's music all the time, the students do solos and chamber works, they're great musicians. So what do you suppose I said?"

Clara evidently didn't wish to answer.

"I said I might be able to do it – "

Clara's eyes closed.

" – but only if my own favorite student could come."

Clara jumped. She grabbed him and whirled around him, laughing, then hugged him before whirling some more. She could display her enthusiasms as he never could, Dmitri thought, maybe she could even experience them as he never could. That is a cold thought, he thought.

"You have to audition for it. The regular audition time is after New Year's Day, but they would let you audition earlier if you're ready."

"Could I do Prokofiev?"

"You certainly could."

"Would you help me?"

Dmitri shook his head at her and laughed.

She frowned at his laugh, he wasn't being serious enough. "It needs a lot of work, I know, I've heard you play it."

"When I was even younger than you are," Dmitri said, "I played the piano with Clara Yellin. You know of her, she would've been your great aunt, you have her name. What you might not know, we don't even have pictures, is she was one of the most beautiful women in the world and she was a great pianist. Only, almost no one knew that. I think that was very sad. The whole world lost. And maybe if the world had known she was a great pianist, she'd still be alive. I knew it and I think your grandmother Esterhaats knew it, maybe no one else, not even her husband. You are as beautiful as that other Clara and you are a great pianist. And this time the world is going to know it. The *whole* world is going to know it."

"Not yet," Clara said as she sat back down before the nearer piano.

Dmitri almost laughed. Her confident, determined tone reminded him of Linda Ney at her best. He picked Clara up to swirl her up and away from the piano bench, a move he might not make again, now that she'd suddenly begun to grow taller. "Maybe you're right, maybe not yet, but if you get any better, Clara, I'll have to report you to Giorgio Gaspari. He'll put you to work. He's put me to work tonight, and we've got to get you home for dinner so I can get there on time."

"Can I go?"

"Well, let's see, tomorrow's Saturday, no school. That should be okay. But you still have piano lessons tomorrow and you know your teacher is very strict about being on time."

"You are not strict about an-y-thing, Dmitri." She said it syllable by syllable, as though to emphasize each in turn, could make each rise specially from the whole.

"Cruel Clara. I think we'd better call Mama and ask her what she thinks about your going to a concert that might not get you home till nearly midnight, especially if you go carousing with the artist's camp followers afterwards."

Clara in her slyness asked Dmitri to call, Clara's mother could deny Dmitri nothing, and Clara went. When Dmitri came on stage to play, he was delighted to see Clara Esterhaats and Jelly Ujfalussy, easily the two most beautiful women in Manhattan, one barely a teenager, the other in her confident thirties, sitting side by side in likely ignorance of who they were. Before taking his seat at the piano, Dmitri walked past the piano to slightly past center stage and bowed to them, giving each a private wink, causing Clara to turn to Jelly and giggle with her hand over her mouth, causing Jelly in all her seemingly stern maturity to giggle in turn at the strangely familiar face next to her, no doubt more familiar from its resemblance to Dmitri's face than to Clara's infant face when once Jelly helped to babysit her.

It seemed necessary to tell them who they were for fear they'd find out some other way and think him a terrible man for being so secretive. As though to justify his coming to center stage, Dmitri said, "This concert is in honor of two of the most wonderful women in New York, Clara Esterhaats and Jelly Ujfalussy." He reached out his arms toward them. "I am honored to have them in the audience. Fortunately for them, they both like Bartók."

Clara telephoned Dmitri to tell him she couldn't come in the afternoon to her lesson. He let the phone ring several times – "eleven, at least," Clara said with a giggle, "I thought I was going to have to hang up and go on to school." Dmitri finally answered only because he became confused about what day it must be, if it was a school day, Clara wouldn't be calling, but only American Clara had the understanding and the resolve to let it ring until he answered.

Clara had to go on a school outing to a museum in Brooklyn. "What will you do without me there after school to bug you, Dmitri?"

That was not a question he could readily answer. What he would do was merely what happened as the day passed. He, too, wondered how he might spend the time instead, he'd looked forward to her playing, his own was no substitute.

"I'll be okay, Clara," he said.

"Should I skip the museum?" She sounded concerned for him, he must've said the wrong thing or used the wrong tone.

Dmitri laughed. "Certainly not. You'll just have to spend extra time on Saturday making up for lost lessons."

Dmitri pondered through the morning. He ran up the keys of his pianos and some of his harpsichords, but he played nothing. Now that his return engagement with Linda for Lincoln Center was fixed and drawing near, he decided the time had come to listen to her play. He didn't wish to go public to do that, to go to a concert. He might stumble into a bad event if he was recognized – being recognized had nearly ruined others' concerts for him – or if Linda happened to see him. Besides, he wanted to hear her, not to see her, it was her playing, not her, he wanted. He objected to records, but there was no other compromise available. He had their record, but he didn't want to listen to his own recording with her, he wanted only her. Maybe this was the day to find the record his mother mentioned to him long ago, Linda's solo in Locatelli's *L'Arte del Violino*. He'd long avoided finding the record, then he'd almost forgotten about it.

Dmitri went for a walk, visiting several record shops, in some of which he found no Locatelli but only a record of Linda soloing in Tchaikovsky's *Swan Lake* with George Szell conducting. Degas dancers wearing tutus were the cover, there was no picture of Linda. In one shop he found her doing Vivaldi's *Four Seasons* with an Italian chamber orchestra. That was more fitting. Again, the jacket cover had no picture of Linda and her violin, it was a painting of the red priest himself, as though painted by van Gogh. Dmitri read the jacket blurb. It said this was the most often recorded piece of music in the catalog. Even though Dmitri'd never heard any of the other recordings, probably never would hear any, he still lost interest now in this one, it was a jewel debased by its commonness. After walking from one shop to another for most of the day, on the point of giving up, with a mixture of disappointment and relief, Dmitri finally found what he sought in a small baroque music shop.

There on the cover, standing off to the right, was Linda in another purplish gown, like the one she'd worn in Philadelphia with Ormandy, only less pink, more assertively adult and alone. Her bearing was confident, not fragile, her arms and shoulders bare, raven hair framing her face, violin extended from her chin, bow in the air as though she were conducting Dmitri in his brief *tutti* passage before she would join in with her solo or as though she were fencing off the world. Although it must have been soon after their separation, this was Linda matured past her Philadelphia symphony performance, past all her years with Dmitri. She was not otherworldly or saintly as in her memorial concert for her brother, but she was still unreachable. The record had Locatelli's eleventh concerto for violin and orchestra on one side and the twelfth concerto on the other, both from *L'Arte del Violino*.

"Locatelli – that requires some fiendish fiddling," the clerk said. "I doubt anyone'll ever master it."

"Linda Ney has it mastered."

"It's a good record? I've never listened to it."

"I haven't either."

The clerk gave him the native New Yorkers' stare of disbelief that anyone so utterly stupid could possibly be standing before them. "So how do you know?"

"I've heard her play it."

"In concert?"

"Yes."

"Ney? Jesus, I missed it? When was it?"

"It was in New Orleans the first time, maybe sixteen or seventeen years ago."

"And you think you can remember it from then?"

It was a fair question, but Dmitri shrugged rather than tell the truth: He could remember it as well as he could remember anything, he could hear and see Linda doing it this very minute, her sound and sight were driving almost everything else from his mind, he could even hear her mistakes and her irritations at herself during rehearsals, he hardly needed this record to hear her play.

Dmitri handed the clerk a twenty dollar bill.

"Nothing smaller?"

"Maybe. I don't know." Dmitri pulled bills from various pockets until he found enough one dollar bills.

"Buddy, look, don't do that sort of thing."

"What?"

"Pull all your money out for anyone to see. This is New York, you know. I love it, but it's still New York."

Dmitri shrugged and put his left over bills back in various pockets.

"Okay, here's your change. Thanks for the tip on Ney. I'll get one out and play it."

"I think this was the last one in the bin."

"Christ. I think it's already out of the catalog, there's not a lot of demand for Locatelli, you know. Well, enjoy it. If you're right about Ney, you've got a collector's item you'll enjoy for years. In any case, you were lucky to get to a Ney concert, even if it was all that many years ago. Be sure you don't scratch the record. If it's as good as you say, you might find you want to listen to it every day or so, so you might want to tape it and save the record – that's what I do. You need a new tape? I've got some good ones here on sale."

Dmitri shook his head, then he wondered what the sales clerk made of the gesture, which must've seemed like a rejection of good advice.

After getting Giorgio's record player out of the closet and setting it up on the floor, plugging it in, and turning it on, Dmitri slouched back on the only comfortable chair in his apartment, holding Linda's album, looking at its cover. In his mind there was a quiet war, visions of Linda storming the redoubt of indifference, sometimes winning to hold the ground briefly, sometimes losing and fading from thought.

A few years earlier, the sight of the record jacket would've intruded to override everything, he'd have thought about her for days. Not he, but time would finally have given him respite. Odd, he thought, why can she intrude at all now? He wished Clara hadn't missed her lesson today. He hissed at Linda staring up at him and he heard her hiss back as though he were an impudent heckler in her vast audience. Christ. Giorgio, I have no other word but yours. But his visions of Linda were mostly only visions, he felt very little, the past intruded its facts and sounds and visions but little or none of its emotions. The present was dull, almost blank. Time had exorcised Linda not only from his daily life but from all his life. He thought that wasn't good – no, he was *sure* it wasn't good. But it was what was, and in some ways he liked it. He wanted to be able to tell Jelly he now understood her logic, it was not only possible not to like what was good, it was possible to like what wasn't good.

After a long while, Dmitri broke the seal of the album and removed the record. He had no facility with the task, he tore the inner jacket trying to get the record out without scratching it. As he understood from Giorgio's man, the most important things were not to scratch the record and not to get his fingerprints on it. He who was so dexterous at the piano now handled the record so clumsily he nearly dropped it at every move. To protect it from himself, he put it on the player. Then he sat back down, looking at the record player, wondering when he'd get around to putting the needle down to play.

Once he played the record he knew he'd have difficulty playing it again, it would be unlike Linda to play with such mechanical sameness.

Dmitri had brought the record back to his apartment at the height of the afternoon rush hour, when the sun was glaring through his rank of western windows overlooking the park, and he hadn't turned on any lights. Now it was dark, there was only background glow from the street lights and lights out in the park and occasional flashes from the traffic below, he could see only the general shapes of things, not the details. He could no longer really see Linda on the cover lying on the floor beside him, he could no longer see the pink of her gown, he could only see that someone stood there, someone without benefit of color. Her bow, extended horizontally as though to provide a platform for Locatelli's name, blended into a blur with the name and the title, *L'Arte del Violino.* The most dramatic shape in the room, the only distinct shape was the record player with its speaker-lid open before him on the floor. It was at the end of a pale shaft of light, as though it were spotlighted for its performance, as though it could somehow substitute for Linda Ney as the featured soloist.

I guess the time has come, Dmitri thought. He lowered the needle onto the eleventh concerto.

Immediately, Dmitri found the opening *tutti* passage insufferable, he wanted to go to his piano to drown it out. But the sound and its anticipations transfixed him, he hadn't heard the music in many years, it lifted him to float in black nothing, to drift in sound where there was nothing else. Although he hated the orchestra's sound, still he knew it was right, he might even say it was good, it did a better job of setting Linda apart than his piano did, elevating her as her strains rose out of the orchestra's, out of the other violins, so unlike a *staccato* rippling piano in their graceful progressions. Despite the poor sound of the player and the record, Dmitri knew Linda's playing was as good as he'd ever heard it, the muted sounds of her violin through the poor resolution of the equipment washed over him, bringing visions that contested with each other to hold his attention, stimulating his ear to add what the record couldn't convey. He listened throughout with anticipation of what he knew was to come, of Linda scaling the heights and then descending again, of her racing through sequences, of bursts of sound and *glissandos*, of bowings so fast and hard they shook her to her toes, and him too. He was wrenched by every fulfillment of his anticipations, as though reacting with disbelief it could be as beautiful as he knew it was. And throughout he saw her doing it as she'd done it many times at his side, he saw her in a succession of all her gowns, he saw her bowing hard, swaying, almost bouncing, he saw her beauty beyond imagination, beyond grasping or holding.

The intensity of listening under these conditions was harder than playing *tutti* for Linda, it exhausted him, he was stiff from his neck to his ankles at the end, his fingers were nearly frozen into fists, his elbows and knees were locked in place, his eyes burned from staring too intently at nothing while his inner visions swept the field, his lungs seemed near bursting, as though he'd held his breath for the duration of the music. Dmitri recalled a concert he and Linda played in Bergamo, Locatelli's birthplace, where over two evenings and an afternoon they played all twelve of the concertos of *L'Arte del Violino*. Linda was exhausted by the demands of keeping all twelve alert and ready in her head, the demands of rehearsing all of them too many times in one short week. Her bow lost several strings Saturday evening and Dmitri redid it. "My violin will probably go now." To calm her, Dmitri restrung it for her before the Sunday sessions. On Monday morning, when they walked down off the top of the hill, where they were staying off the main *piazza*, Linda couldn't walk back up. She yielded to her exhaustion and gave up plans for rehearsal that day. They sat in a church for many hours, Linda often leaning her head on Dmitri's shoulder. Dmitri felt now as Linda must've felt that day. He was too worn down by the tensions of her performance to relax, too exhausted to walk, too drained even to sustain coherent thought. He needed a quiet cathedral in which to rest.

An hour or two or more passed.

Dmitri decided not to play Locatelli's twelfth concerto, he was not up to so much work again just now. He also thought he might never listen to the record again once he'd heard it, and he didn't wish to foreclose hearing Linda again in the future if their concert failed to happen. Dmitri sat for a long while to try to relax. He stretched out his hand, the hand Linda called his treble clef, with its fingers splayed. There were no rings, only fingers, Dmitri wondered how a pianist could work with rings, would he have worn a ring if he'd married Linda? The hand reached into the beam of bluish street light falling on the record player. The shadow of his hand on the record player was unsteady. It wasn't shaking, as the shadow of Linda's hand before a performance or his mother's hand near the end would've shaken. Dmitri wondered for a moment whether his steadiness was a matter of steely nerves or of catatonia in this moment. Catatonia was his universal device to escape difficult moments, moments of pain or frustration or denial. But his hand was not as steady as the shadow of the solid hand of Dmitri Esterhaats should be. Dmitri tried to hold his hand in place until he could master it, until its shadow steadied on Linda's record, still turning on the record player. After a long while he noticed his shoulder ached. In his effort to gain control of his hand, it had only grown less steady. Dmitri withdrew his hand from the light.

A month or so later, after the summer in Vermont had been set, in a regression to a younger, playful mood, Clara inspected Dmitri's cabinets again.

"You have a new record. It's Linda Ney doing Locatelli." She held the record in silence for a moment. "And you've played it, Dmitri."

"That was probably her favorite music for a while, maybe it still is."

Clara said nothing more. She set the record on a harpsichord and went idling around the room for a minute before going to the kitchen. In a few minutes she brought out a tray of cheeses, crackers, and breads and a *paté* that she must have brought from home. She invited Dmitri to have lunch.

"What's Locatelli like?" Clara asked.

"He's baroque, late baroque. He was a virtuoso violinist so he wrote pieces he could play to dazzle people. He's very demanding. Anyone who does it well is spectacular. Some violinists think it's just show-off. I think it's beautiful, it's strenuous and kinetic, hard driving and powerful, a lot like Shostakovich in his strongest stuff."

"Linda Ney likes show-off music."

Dmitri did not wish to quarrel with Clara's grudge against Linda. To do so was to quarrel with her parents and, as Linda would have said, it would be unfair to pass that burden to Clara.

Clara spread *paté* on a piece of melba toast and handed it to Dmitri. Dmitri took a bite, lost control of the crumbling part in his hand, and stuffed all of it into his mouth.

"Could I hear the record, Dmitri?"

Dmitri's tongue was encased in paste for the moment and he was slow to respond. Finally, he swallowed enough to speak. "Sure. The player's in that cabinet, you probably saw it on your searches."

He stood to go make tea.

"I can play it here?" Clara called after him.

Only with her question did Dmitri realize the transformation that now let him face hearing Linda with equanimity. "Sure," he called back. "We could wait till the tea is ready."

When he brought in the tea, she had everything ready to go.

"Which one are you going to play?"

"Number eleven comes first," she said.

Dmitri grinned. "Orderly Clara."

"You think I'm too orderly? Then . . ."

"No, no, no, I'm just teasing."

"You can't tease what isn't there."

"Hey, Clara, come on, play the one you want."

"I want to play number twelve. Unless you insist on number eleven, we'll hear number twelve."

Dmitri had been orderly, beginning with number eleven, he'd teased Clara only because he was charmed that she was like him in this minor respect. But she was tougher than he was, she refused to be orderly once she recognized her urge, he suspected she would be on the alert for orderliness for weeks to come.

Dmitri watched Clara's face throughout the piece. She betrayed astonishment at every turn, she almost danced with her body as she sat, she grew tense through every run, and she burst with pleasure at every culmination. And when the piece ended, she looked instantly disappointed that it did not continue, although, with her orderly, structural sense, she must have thought it was right to end it there.

Dmitri decided to say nothing. After a minute or so, Clara spoke. "She's good." Clara looked angry and disappointed. "She's fantastic. . . .You were right."

"I was right?"

Clara blushed and would not answer.

For the afternoon, Clara wanted to play dazzling pieces, Schumann's and Liszt's most diabolical pieces. Dmitri feared she was competing with Linda, as though she'd been personally challenged.

"It's getting late," Dmitri said some time after six. "You should either call your parents or let me walk you home."

"I don't need to be walked home. Do you want me to go?"

"No. Never."

"Would you call Mama, Dmitri?"

"Isn't that cheating a bit?"

"Everything's cheating."

Dmitri stood and rubbed his hand along her hair to the back of her head, which turned up for her to look at him. "Okay, I'll call her," he said.

"But it'll just be more cheese if we eat here."

"Did you and Linda Ney eat in restaurants?"

"Often."

"Could we eat in a restaurant?"

"It's Saturday night, it might be hard to get into a good one." In truth, Dmitri was not very resourceful for such tasks and in any case he hardly knew restaurants. His best device was to think what Jelly would do, Jelly was resourceful beyond anyone else he knew. Immediately he thought of one of her standard choices. "There is one on Madison that a musician runs, he says he doesn't know whether he loses more money as a chef or as a cellist. He sometimes lets us eat at a table in the kitchen when he's full. Should I call him?"

"If you call Mama after."

At nine-thirty they went to *Ai Sette Celli* for dinner and sat in the kitchen. By then, Clara was very hungry despite snacking on cheese. "This late we could probably get into any restaurant," she said.

Dmitri feared she was right, but it hadn't occurred to him to think so earlier.

"*Ai Sette Celli.* Is that seven cellos?" Clara wondered as she looked at the cover of the menu.

"Yes. Jelly says it's a pun on seventh heaven, which is *sette cielli*, but which sounds almost the same."

"I thought you knew Italian. Is Jelly right?"

"Yes, I guess so, my Italian is just speaking from . . ." he seemed reluctant to say it.

"The opera singer."

"Yes, Sofia Milano. In English you say you're in seventh heaven, in Italian you're carried to the seven heavens, that's *ai sette cieli*."

"How long has it been since you saw her?"

"Linda?"

"Yes."

"She used to do that, ask a question that was a continuation of an earlier discussion as if the earlier discussion had been going on right then instead of hours earlier." He especially remembered the explosive instance in Dijon.

"How long?" Clara insisted. Dmitri had once teased her that she should be a professional interrogator.

"That's very easy, Clara. How old are you?"

"Almost thirteen, you know that."

"Yes, I know that. That means it's been just over thirteen years since I last saw Linda. You came along just in time to replace her in my life."

Clara looked stumped for a minute. "That's a nice thing to say. I think it must even be too nice, because it can't be true, I think that might make it a rude thing to say. I couldn't really replace her. Besides, I'm never going to be as good."

"It's a bit early to say that. You already have a much bigger repertoire than she did when I met her in her late twenties. Locatelli and Bach were her very best. You can't compare them to your average."

"I don't have anything like Locatelli. Mendelsohn?"

"Your Mozart and Bach are also magnificent. And you're gaining on Prokofiev, Schubert, Debussy, lots of them. I didn't do that, I did them one at a time, each one was a new love, I consumed one and then looked for another. You feed them all together and someday soon they'll all grow up together."

"Bach violin is harder than Bach piano."

Dmitri couldn't answer that, he held the same opinion.

"Did you ever hear her play Locatelli?" Clara asked.

"Many times, many times. I played *tutti*. For every time we played one, we rehearsed it fifteen or twenty times minimum. The first time was in New Orleans. The last time was in Bergamo, Locatelli's home in northern Italy. Linda played all twelve of them there on two evenings and one afternoon, those were long recitals by today's standards, it was exhausting because we were rehearsing Locatelli all day long for days on end. Linda said we played Locatelli between fifty and sixty hours in one week. She collapsed for several days after that. Linda was wonderful at that music."

"She still is."

Dmitri smiled. "Yes."

"How much better was it live than on the record?"

That was a loaded question. She was already intimidated by the record. "It was better. The sound, of course, was a lot better. But you can tell from the record how good the performance was. There would be no surprises in hearing it live, no further discoveries. You already know how good she is."

Clara looked pensive. "I guess I will have to hear Linda Ney to know."

"You can just call her Linda, she'd like that."

"I don't care what she'd like."

He had to know it was true, he shouldn't have forced her to say so. "Here comes the cellist chef – that's hard to say."

Clara was not ready to laugh or smile. "For you maybe."

"Hello, Dmitri."

"Alfred, this is my niece, Clara Esterhaats."

Alfred's eyes grew and he broke into an enormous smile. "*The* Clara Esterhaats?! We are hearing wonderful things about you, everybody wants to hear you. How old are you?"

"Almost thirteen."

"After your first paid performance, if you come back here for dinner, the dinner's on me. I'd say champagne too, but I'm sure champagne would be illegal, I can't serve you champagne until you're eighteen."

Clara almost laughed.

"Hey, I'm forgetting why I came over. Jelly's out front. She wants to join you. Is that okay?"

"Jelly?" Clara asked. Her face was radiant. She had met Jelly only once, when the two sat together at the 92nd Street Y concert that Dmitri dedicated to them. Afterwards, they all went to a sedate restaurant rather than the usual bar and talked until Clara fell asleep immediately after laughing very hard at one of Jelly's twisted lines.

"Yes," Dmitri said, answering both at once.

Alfred went off to fetch Jelly.

"How many people does he do that for every night?"

Immediately, Dmitri knew her point. "Alfred is the musician's greatest booster, he encourages everyone, especially young beginners. But still, he had to know about you, and how could he know if someone wasn't praising you?"

Jelly came with her companion, Ricardo, one of the original seven cellos of the restaurant. He'd since succeeded too well as a cellist to be at the restaurant many nights. Now he deposited Jelly at their table and he went to work to make them a special treat.

"You have grown, you are bigger than I am," Jelly said.

"Everybody is bigger than you," Clara said.

"Yes, but I can be bigger at trouble. You do not wish to cross me."

Clara laughed. For Jelly she laughed.

"Hey, you stop that. I must be taken serious. What serious discussion do you have before I come."

"We were talking about Linda Ney," Clara said, "nothing serious."

"Not serious maybe, but dangerous. This man does not like it to talk about Linda Ney."

"Do you know her?"

"Yes. I do not like her."

"I don't either," Clara said.

"You know her?"

"No."

"That is okay. You do not need to know her to dislike her. And this man," she turned to Dmitri, "what do you think?"

"I thought she was wonderful."

"Do not be impressed," Jelly said to Clara. "Every man in Manhattan thinks I am wonderful when I want him to do something for me. I am foolish, I ask for tickets and tables in the kitchen, I should ask for jewels and clothes and limousines. But they are more foolish, they get nothing but the pleasure of giving me something. I am not impressed by men who think a woman is wonderful."

The two worked over Linda Ney for an hour or more while largely ignoring the only person around who knew very much about her. Dmitri often drifted into idle thoughts that were broken by the laughter of the two women, leaving him to enjoy their laughing in doleful ignorance of what was funny, it was an abstraction from humor, it was beautiful, not funny, to watch them.

Dmitri rejoined the conversation when Alfred and Ricardo came to talk with them as the chores of the kitchen lost urgency.

"You should be giving recitals, Clara," Ricardo said. "Your uncle should do something about that."

Clara turned to Dmitri. "Should I?"

Jelly became very quiet. She watched Dmitri.

"There will be time," he said. He'd promised her parents he would protect her from being overwhelmed, he would keep her life private until she finished school. He would not block opportunities for her but he would not make them either. Now one dinner at the seven cellos might undo all their intentions.

"I speak any language when I know a few words," Jelly said. "That is enough. It works. Even Japanese and Arabic I speak. But recitals I do not give in any language except Hungarian and French and German. I practice a few years more and then maybe English. I want to start at Carnegie Hall. Until then, I only make jokes."

Dmitri could not have handled that so gently and well. He smiled and winked at Jelly. To cover for his blunder, Ricardo took Clara on a tour of the seven heavens.

At the end of the evening, as they left the restaurant, Clara asked Jelly, "How did Dmitri find this restaurant?"

"I find it, I bring him here. Everything he knows about New York today, he knows from me. Ask him. He is honest, he will tell. If he does not, I kick him."

"It's almost true," Dmitri said. "But someone else told me about something."

"Who told you what?" Jelly challenged.

"I'm sorry, I forget who it was and what it was."

"Dmitri always forgets things, the things he forgets most are the things he never knew," Jelly said. "Oh! and *I* forget! I forget Ricardo. I must go back to get him. You, Clara, you can trust this man except his judgment of women. When you give recitals in a few years, I will come. Now go."

One of the two women he loved most in the world was telling the other one that his judgment of women could not be trusted. Dmitri smiled for both of them and took Clara's arm to walk her home.

"Tomorrow is Sunday," Clara said. "Could I come early, Dmitri? I have a lot to work on."

Odyssey Deneuve

At the sumer music camp in Vermont, the most interesting person for Dmitri other than Clara was Odyssey Deneuve, composer in residence, who taught counterpoint and structure in chamber works. She was herself a subject in counterpoint and structure, she was lanky and seemingly tall, though she was not tall. She looked soft and gentle but she was tough and often acerbic and pushy. She was elegantly dressed when she was dropped off by a limousine but as soon as she'd got her cabin she changed into bum's clothing, and thereafter she made the students look bourgeois. Although they'd never met before and he'd never played her music, she collared Dmitri immediately to ask if he would help her with a composition, she needed someone to play the ensemble part while she worked on the piano solo. "I've only got the ensemble in reduction," she said.

Dmitri was in a flaky, teasing mood, and this bright, flinty woman somehow reminded him of Jelly Ujfalussy. He could not resist teasing her with a bit of Jelly's Hungarian logic, that, after all, one could not reduce what did not already exist. But Deneuve was faster at reading his thoughts than he was at speaking them.

"I know," she said. She tapped her forehead. "Up here, it's almost whole, it's from here that it's reduced."

Dmitri smiled tolerantly.

"And if you believe that, Esterhaats," she said, "you're full of shit."

To work on her piece, they had to arrange to move two pianos together. His rehearsal room was bigger than her composing room, so the camp moved a second piano into Dmitri's cabin. That was a good thing, anyway, he thought, because it would let Clara join him for working together as they always did. But it had the odd effect of making him feel more nearly at home with his museum collection of pianos and harpsichords rather than isolated off in Vermont.

"What's in the ensemble?" Dmitri asked.

"You mean the instruments? I haven't decided yet, that's why I only have the reduction, call it a sketch if you prefer to be technically anal, or is that anally technical? I want to see who's best in the camp, whatever works, I'll put in. It'll be my Vermont piano quintet or octet or whatever. Vermont, *Opus 37*, and piano – those three things I'm certain about, the rest is potluck. I'm able to get started only because I've got you as a fall back for the piano."

"Your piece should be for the students."

"I agree, that's what I mean it to be. You're just a fall back, there are some pianists among the students, there's a girl, Clara Esterhaats, I assume anyone with that name is a relative of yours. Christ almighty, I never heard of another Esterhaats, are you guys turning into a plague?"

"How does someone get the name Odyssey Deneuve?"

"Dmitri Esterhaats can ask that question? Huh. Esterhaats must be Hungarian by way of Holland, but Dmitri, that's not Hungarian, and you don't quite have an accent. You must be a mess. I'm a lot simpler. My original name was Janet Odyssey Jones. I don't know why Odyssey – maybe that's what my mother had to give up when she had me, so it's part of my name as an accusation. But the whole ensemble, Janet Odyssey Jones, that was not so good. I thought of J. Odyssey Jones, but that made me sound like a WASP lawyer in Wall Street – I might marry one but I wouldn't want to be one. But that gave me an idea, I looked for someone to marry with a better last name. Deneuve was great, I thought he must be the guy. So I dropped Janet Jones and there I was: Odyssey Deneuve, holy Hannah. Even my friends were fooled. Until they see me, some people think I might be related to Catherine Deneuve, that's a nice thought, but I need a little work on the accent. Naturally, Deneuve was a shit, so I dropped him too and kept only the good part, the label – hell, I could have had that without ever marrying the jerk. The next time, I married a person instead of a name, and that's worked a lot better. It helps that he's a successful financial wizard who manages a huge mutual fund. The people who invest in that fund do okay, but Roger gets rich. That means I can afford to smash really expensive things when I need to, crystal penguins, gold plated bananas, the fucking works."

Dmitri wished he'd seen her smash a crystal penguin or a gold plated banana.

Odyssey visited Dmitri almost every evening after dinner and they struggled with bits of her music, which she seemed to prefer to write a few bars at a time. After two weeks of that, Dmitri strung the bits together from his memory and played the lot. Odyssey started with him but then stopped playing and just listened.

"That's magic," she said when he finished.

"Yeah, I don't understand why it works, but it drives to some kind of goal, like Shostakovich but with a lot more variety, more complexity in the development."

"That's magic too, but I was talking about something else. You did that all from memory, you don't have any of my notes. And I never told you anything about the order, we were just working on a piece at a time. I'm not even sure I had any order set. But the way you did it, that's the order it needs. Maybe it took a Russian to see that."

"That was just the ensemble reduction. I want to do the piano part."

"Demanding fucker, aren't you? Give me time."

In addition to playing through bits of her music, they sat and talked, sometimes for hours, with Odyssey doing most of the talking. Dmitri enjoyed almost every minute of her. But he was still Dmitri and occasionally his mind wandered and lost touch with what she was saying. Soon she would stand before him, lean over to kiss his unkempt head, and then swat him. "You can dream without me," she said once as she left. "Dmitri's in his heaven, all's quiet with Odyssey's world." "It must be interesting stuff you have in there, fella." "Fuck me, I outlasted my welcome again." "Key-rhist, this man, what if I were talking about something important instead of just my life? You'd think we were married twenty years." "Why don't you say it out loud, Esterhaats, then we could at least keep up the semblance of conversation." He heard all of those remarks because she had the sense to swat him before speaking them.

It was Thursday afternoon, when Odyssey seemed always to visit him, but Dmitri had been surprised by a crushing headache that he hadn't taken seriously until it overpowered him. He shouldn't have skipped lunch, he should've closed the blinds earlier, he should've got up to walk around more often. He'd noticed signs of the headache a few times from late morning until now, but he'd always been distracted back to what he was doing at the piano or what his students were doing with it in the early afternoon. He hoped Odyssey wouldn't come. He was standing in the middle of his room, with the blinds now closed, slowly swaying as he walked in a circle, letting his mind drift, detaching himself from the throbbing in his head, from the raging display in his eyes. Now and then, when the effort to escape failed, he put his hands up to cover his face. There was racket in the distance, clanging and banging, which he tried to put at even greater distance, he halfway floated free but he couldn't break completely, noises tugged at him to bring him back to ground. When Odyssey came in unannounced, Dmitri sensed she was there, but he was struggling to stay out of touch. Why had she come in without knocking, he wondered, and then he thought of the clanging and banging, part of it must have been Odyssey at his door, but to try to think, to attempt to manage the world, brought only pain.

"Migraine?" Odyssey asked very quietly. She turned Dmitri slightly and then gently forced him to sit so that she could rub the back of his neck. "If it works out right, maybe you get one terrific day after it's over. Almost makes up for the pain. I've got stuff to stop it if it isn't really underway yet, but it looks like it's too late for that now. Anyway, that stuff just makes you feel crummy for a couple of days, it's a vasoconstrictor, it closes your blood vessels, shuts everything down, it'd dull your hearing, numb your fingers, probably shrink your prick for the day. Not good for a pianist. When I'm composing, I think it's better to let the migraine go and enjoy it for what it's worth."

She turned his head and pressed her thumbs firmly against the tops of his cheek bones under his eyes. Sharp pain radiated from his cheeks through his head but the nauseous pain of his headache diminished as though his nerves could only transmit one kind of signal at a time.

"The woods back that way are very dark, you might want to take a walk there, in mid afternoon the sun goes behind the hill and you're in the comfortable shade, no glare at all, reminds me of Dante's *selvaggio oscuro*. That's were I go."

"You've had migraine here?" His head screamed at him for daring to speak.

"Every Wednesday so far. I'm not sure what's with Wednesdays. As long as it's reliable, though, I can plan for students on Monday, Tuesday, and Friday, migraine on Wednesday, and composition on Thursday. Wednesday sucks, but on balance it's a good schedule."

Dmitri was not quick witted at the moment, but he now understood why Odyssey usually came to his cabin later in the day on Thursdays, it was to ask him to help her by playing some part as she worked on her compositions. He knew what day it was from her afternoon visits just as he knew Sunday from her full day visits. He'd known her less than a month and already he thought of her as a calendar. Thinking through even that much had his head cramping and pounding again while his closed eyes alternated between explosive lights and throbbing blackness. There was nothing he could do, if he lay down now he would start vomiting, he could not stay seated, he would have to stand and walk.

Odyssey gently coaxed him back to his feet and walked with him hand in hand toward the woods. She stayed with him a long while until the shadow of the hill overtook them. He then walked alone, sometimes stopping to sit on a fallen tree but then walking some more, in no direction, without attention to where he was. At summer's late dusk he lay for a moment with his head between his arms. Lying down brought up the memory of a dreadful headache soon after his family had moved to Amsterdam, he had lain then, pounding his head on the floor. His mother had come yelling for Pavel to help her. Pavel sat on him and pinned his flailing arms, his mother wedged a pillow under his head and then held his head firmly in place, he did not know how long they stayed like that, he only remembered getting up early the next morning and going to the kitchen where his mother came to him almost immediately in her nightgown and robe. She put her hands to his face, turning it up to look at her, then she pulled him tightly to her and held him for a long while before making him a feast for breakfast. "You need a piano, Mitya," she said.

Now in Vermont, he was torn between pain and nausea, walking reduced the nausea, lying reduced the pain, nothing could reduce both at once. For the moment Dmitri suffered nausea, he was floating on an active sea that tipped and rolled him, churning him, driving the nausea into his head and out to his extremities. In his dizziness he found it hard to rouse himself to stand again, he lost connection with his body and floated free, above the waves that rocked him, he floated farther and farther until he lost connection with everything.

Many hours later Dmitri was awakened by the sound of a bird. He sat up from where he lay and looked at the clear sky, fuller of stars than any sky he remembered seeing since he and his mother traveled from Kiev to Amsterdam. He was very hungry and, as he took note of that peculiar fact, he realized his headache must be past, and with that realization, as though by theoretical deduction, he relaxed his shoulders. He stood and looked around, but he had no bearings. Finally, he glimpsed the sliver of the moon through the trees on the top of a hill. The moon was either east or west, the hill that it limned must be west, and as he walked what he thought must be south the moon sank in the sky to confirm his choice. He walked the woods the way he walked New York as a child, paying no heed to where he was, attending only to where he was going, following an abstract rather than a particular route.

In his cabin, Dmitri found dinner wrapped in foil. He thought of Clara and then supposed it must have been Odyssey. He ate and then he wanted to play piano, he wanted Odyssey's piano solo part from her Vermont ensemble or the solo sonata she was working on. But it seemed unreasonable to bang his piano while everyone slept, his cabin was set far out from the main house where the students were, but not so far from the other resident teachers's and artists' cabins, and it was not a lovely Mozart that he wanted to play but a hard-driving, pounding, sometimes screaming Odyssey Deneuve.

It was growing light outside, so Dmitri went to the lake. Odyssey had tried to teach him canoeing. He thought it funny that he could be so incompetent with so simple a thing. From mid-lake he caught sight of Clara on the dock and he struggled to bring the canoe in to her. She laughed when he nearly turned back around just before the dock.

"You must be okay, Dmitri," she said.

He must be okay – Odyssey must have told her. "You conclude that on the evidence of my canoeing?"

They canoed for a while, out and then back into the sunrise. Although Dmitri sat in the stern, Clara steered them to parallel the dock without any noise as the boat made contact. They went to breakfast. Odyssey was there, she'd never before been seen at breakfast, there was doubt around the camp that she could function before noon.

"Thanks for dinner," Dmitri said.

"That was Clara's idea."

He smiled his embarrassment and hugged Clara gently.

"I think I can play anything today," he said. "Would you let me try whatever you have ready, Odyssey?"

"I want to hear that!" Clara said.

"Do you know it?"

"I've seen some of it. I can't even read it. I used to think Richard Strauss was complicated."

"Other times, other conventions," Odyssey said. "It's easy when you get used to it. Easy to read, anyway. Not so easy to play always, though. I can't even play what I write for piano. I have the sonata for you – right in that envelope."

At midmorning Odyssey came by to ask how her piano sonata had gone and Dmitri said he thought he was getting it under control, apart from some things he couldn't interpret from her writing.

"Show me now?" she asked. "No one's on my schedule until two o'clock. I'll tell them to send us two box lunches to your cabin."

"They do that?" Dmitri wondered.

"If you want to work through lunch instead of coming in. Hey, don't tell me, Esterhaats – you've been here a month and you didn't know that?"

Dmitri shrugged. He'd been skipping lunch instead of coming in. He would even have been missing many dinners if Clara did not fetch him when he failed to notice the gong.

"How the fuck do you stay alive all these years?"

Dmitri started to note that he had a lot of help from the Odysseys and Claras of his life, but he thought that might be a bad answer.

"Your headache yesterday – did you skip lunch?"

Dmitri nodded.

"Christ, Esterhaats, Jesus H. Christ. You're so fucking busy or idle or whatever that you can't even bother to try not to have a migraine? And you're so little connected to people here you don't even know you can get a box lunch delivered to you. I knew that already the first day I was here. And the people here think I'm weirdly disconnected, some of them claim they've almost never seen me. Esterhaats, I just don't know about you, you know."

Dmitri walked with Odyssey back to the main house to order the box lunches and then they wandered back to his cabin via the lake.

"Clara reads you a lot better than she reads my music," Odyssey said.

Dmitri did not intrude but let her speak.

"She was afraid for you last night when you didn't come back. I said we could get the camp to go looking for you. She insisted we not do that, she didn't want to take control of your life, she thought that would be worse than your sleeping in the woods. She has a complicated view – she's afraid you can't cope but she's convinced you will when it comes down to it. Sort of a bumbling master. I think there's a contradiction somewhere in there, but it still sounds right. Christ."

She paused but Dmitri stayed silent.

"Clara said I shouldn't say anything . . ."

"Ai." His slight protest was tantamount to a scream.

"Sorry, just checking the boundaries here, I wanted to know how far I could go without stepping in shit."

"It's everywhere, you can't miss it," he laughed.

"Will you still play my stuff?"

Odyssey made changes as he played and they achieved joint satisfaction on the third pass. "That's how that works," she would say and she would ask him to do it again, only heavier or lighter or faster or slower. When, on a tenth replay of several bars, he let his base and treble hands float free of each other, Odyssey jumped and shook her two fists hard to the separate tempos.

"That's it, that's it, that's it! Keep it like that here and here," she said as she turned the page. Her pages were a jerrybuilt disaster waiting to wreck someone's performance, with pieces taped on for additions, with pages that folded down or left or right in a confusing disorder, it was pop-up music, and now she knocked the whole mess to the floor as she tried to find the later passage.

Dmitri laughed and picked up what was now a pile. He immediately had it sorted on the piano and he turned forward to the passage she wanted.

"That's it – how did you know?" Odyssey asked.

The question seemed ridiculous, obviously he knew. But he didn't know why he knew and he couldn't answer her. He shrugged. "There's order to the music even when . . ." he gestured at the messy assemblage of sheets instead of finding the relevant words.

". . . even when it's a mother-fucking mess, huh?"

"I wouldn't have put it that way."

"No, Esterhaats, I'm sure you wouldn't. I guess that's why I had to – somebody around here has to get it right."

It seemed to him that the changes made the piece harder.

"What you changed – was that because I got through it too easily?" he teased.

"You didn't think the changes made it better?"

He had to admit he thought they did.

"Can we do it again after dinner?" she asked.

That was an odd 'we', Dmitri thought. We would do it again when he played it. While thinking of that, he failed to answer her.

"Or some other time – whenever you want to, Esterhaats. It's just that I've never heard it before, it's too hard for me."

Dmitri was mystified. "Too hard? You played all the hardest parts for me."

"That was a trick. I can do any six bars but sometimes I can't string together the whole thing. It gets tied in knots. My husband says it's all coherent, just the way I am. I think that means totally incoherent. Maybe that's what he's saying in his sly way. I'm idiotic."

"So does that mean it takes an idiot to play your music?"

She spread her arms beatifically to frame him before her. "I don't know. All I know is you can do it. After dinner? Tomorrow? Sun . . ."

"After dinner."

They both spent the rest of the afternoon with students and then came back to his cabin after dinner. The many hours break from the piece let it settle in Dmitri's mind and fingers, and now he played it with ease and flow, spinning the little bits of string together, checking the score only once or twice at the breaks. As he ended, Odyssey clenched her fists in the air, grabbed him and pulled him from the bench, and hugged and kissed him before whirling him around the room with a strength that surprised him.

"You know what I need?" she asked. "I need someone to give it its premiere. I can't do it. Would you do it, Esterhaats? Do you like the piece enough?"

"I would love to do it. Thank you for asking me. I'm at Avery Fisher Hall in October. Maybe then. Later I could do it in Los Angeles and Chicago, I can't remember where else I have dates, maybe Toronto or Philadelphia."

Odyssey clenched her fists and raised them above her head. Then she grabbed his head and kissed him. "And you know what else I need, Esterhaats?"

He did not.

"I'm testing the boundaries again, forgive me for being so pushy. Somehow, I think you must be used to that, hell, maybe you like pushy women." She put her hand to his face.

Dmitri smiled at her, perhaps he did like pushy women, he'd even loved a couple of them.

"Anyway, I've got to push a bit to get what I want. I need someone to record the piece. I've got a deal with a company, I just have to choose the people to play my stuff. Would you record it? There would have to be something else to go on the other side. I would have to write that."

It seemed like a trivial, natural request. Of course, he thought. But then he remembered it hadn't ever been "of course" to record before, it had seemed a mortal conflict with Linda and Giorgio, it had seemed unthinkable to him. Why was it "of course" just now? He felt oddly embarrassed for Linda, as though he'd deceived her or cheated her.

"Maybe I could write a piano duo for you and Clara. Would you record it?"

Dmitri had lost track of what was "it," but whatever it was, evidently he would do it for Odyssey. "Yes."

Again her fists went up. "Wait right here," she said, and quickly left his cabin. In a few minutes she returned with a bottle of champagne and two glasses. Dmitri still stood where he'd been when she left his cabin. "I didn't mean you had to wait right *here*," Odyssey said.

Dmitri had been thinking through a passage of the sonata, he'd forgotten her instructions, he had no idea what she meant now. He felt uneasy at the thought of drinking so soon after a headache, but he couldn't easily deny Odyssey just now. She removed the foil and the wire from the cork and tried to twist the cork. It was too tight. She put it on the floor and tried holding the bottle down with her feet while she tugged. Then she asked Dmitri to hold the bottle while she pulled. He tried to hold the bottle upright, but she was shorter than he and she had to turn it toward her to grip and pull the cork.

"Damned cork," she said, "it will turn or I will."

Dmitri was unsure what her threat meant. "I guess I will have to see that before I understand it."

Odyssey rolled a loop with her eyes, laughed very hard, and began to lose her grip. But then she grimaced and pulled one more time while almost twisting the bottle out of Dmitri's grip. The cork shot out into her midriff, "Fuck me," she said, and then she and Dmitri struggled to right the bottle as it spilled and blew champagne over hapless Odyssey. Despite their laughter and bumbling, they managed to salvage nearly half the bottle.

"That's my half," Dmitri said with a gesture at her shirt and pants. He was relieved that there'd not be much for him to drink.

"At least I kept it from getting on the piano," Odyssey said as she leaned slightly forward and shook her shirt. "This is one time it's a good thing I'm so flat-chested, who would've thought that would ever be good?" Dmitri got her a towel and offered her a dry shirt, but she kept her own. "I never got drenched in champagne before, I want to make it last a while." It lasted until well past midnight, when Odyssey left.

Saturday afternoon, Odyssey told him that a student quartet had canceled its recital for the evening and the camp needed someone else to perform. "I said you might do it. Did I go too far this time? You know I'm no good at boundaries. I'll apologize and say no if you wish. I really mean that – just say. It's only written in chalk on the performance board. Life should be as easy as that, just take an eraser with you and make corrections as you go. What a fucker that would be."

"You're not going to make any more changes in the sonata before tonight?"

"I'll try not to. But I do have one idea," she grinned.

"It doesn't matter, I'll just play it from memory anyway. I only have to remember which version," he teased.

"That's the misery of the composer – she's always at the mercy of the fucking performer. I usually end up hating performers, I'll try not to hate you, but here's fair warning."

Clara was the first person in the recital room after dinner. She took the front center seat, from where she could watch Dmitri's hands. But she had never sat so close to him during a formal performance and she watched his face more than his hands.

"You were singing the whole time, but you didn't make a sound," Clara said. "You were in a different world, it was as if we weren't even there." Later she added, "I'll never be able to play that piece like that."

"Never? Never – that's a funny notion. All it seems to mean for you is that it might take you a week. I took longer than that to play any Debussy halfway intelligently."

"Would you help me try Miss Deneuve's sonata?"

"Sign up for some time with Miss Deneuve Monday morning to get her to teach you the conventions so you can read it. Then sign up for time with me Monday afternoon. I bet you can do it that day already. If necessary we can work overtime after dinner."

"You're with Miss Deneuve after dinner."

"She and I can work some other time."

"Not to work. You're just together. She's very nice."

Clara's smile was radiant and he sensed that Clara was playing matchmaker. She had inherited her grandmother's role in Dmitri's life, she was striving to take care of him when he was not competent to take care of himself. Dmitri wanted to pick her up, to hug her, and to tell her that *his* life was not her duty, her only big duty was *her* life. But he didn't know how to say that gently enough, he did not know how to stop her in her forlorn quest, he could only stop her in the particular effort of this moment. "Miss Deneuve is married," he said as gently as he could while seeming nonchalant.

"*Miss* Deneuve?"

"That doesn't mean anything. Great performers are always just Miss. Her husband's name is not even Deneuve. When you're seventy-five and surrounded by grand children while you're performing at the White House, the President will call you Miss whatever, probably Esterhaats I'd guess."

Clara looked distressed, she would not look at Dmitri but only stared at her feet, his effort at humor missed its mark.

"Hey, Clara, that's not why we're here."

"I thought . . . I'm sorry. You seem to like her."

"I do. I like her a lot. After you, I like her better than anyone else here."

"I don't mean . . . I don't know what I mean. That's why I never come . . ."

In an instant Dmitri understood something that had made him wonder for most of four weeks, why Clara no longer came to him after dinner to practice or to show him what she could do. He'd assumed she'd found friends and was spending her evenings with them. Although he'd missed her many times during those weeks, although he'd partly come to regret coming to Vermont where he saw so little of her, he'd been reluctant to invite her to join him for fear of intruding on her. They were mutually solicitous and mutual losers for their efforts. The President would surely call her Miss Esterhaats, she could never escape the curse of being an Esterhaats.

"Walk around the lake under the stars?" Dmitri asked.

Although it was not cold, it was a bit cool in the Vermont early night, and when they reached the footbridge over the creek that fed the farther end of the so-called lake, Clara was shivering. Dmitri hugged her close to warm her. At first she resisted but soon she put her arm around him and walked with him. She clearly did not wish to talk and Dmitri let her have silence. She must have worked out a complex set of expectations for him and now she had to purge them from her thoughts, she had to restore in her mind the world in which she had few expectations for him. It might take time to undo the work of four weeks.

Monday Clara did not sign up with Miss Deneuve.

"You don't want to try that music?" Dmitri asked when she came to him in the afternoon.

"I don't know . . . not just now. Would you be annoyed?"

Dmitri laughed almost inaudibly. "No, Clara, I wouldn't be annoyed." She was less Esterhaats than he was, she at least had the sense to state her worry. "It's great music, it's not less great because she's married, but there's a lot of music to master, you don't have to take on Miss Deneuve right now. But she can still become your friend."

"I thought she already was, I liked her, I thought she liked me, I told her a lot about you. I shouldn't have."

Dmitri put his arm around her. "You were right about one thing: Miss Deneuve does like you. But I know something even more important than that: she thinks you're good enough that she wants to write a piano duo for us."

Clara visibly stood straighter as her eyes widened. "She does? She's going to?"

"Well, you can't ever be certain, she still has to have good musical ideas for piano duo, that's a combination she's never written for. But piano is her favorite traditional instrument, the one she plays best. We can't be sure she'll get it done anytime soon, I don't really know how she works, but that's what she said she's going to do. She says she likes the sound of Esterhaats and Esterhaats."

"Then I should learn to read her, huh?"

"Will you sign up tomorrow?"

"Okay, if that's what you want, Dmitri."

She still held a slight grudge, Dmitri thought, she wanted him to be responsible for her submitting to Odyssey's instruction. In the darkness he could smile privately as he nodded his head yes, that was what he wanted.

Monday evening, Dmitri asked Clara to come back to his cabin if she was free after dinner. He went to ask Odyssey to come as well, but then he thought it would be better not to invite her, because then she might not come. If he merely left her alone, she would choose to come on her own. And so she did.

They played the two pianos in various combinations, ending in the most natural arrangement with Odyssey conducting and Dmitri and Clara playing.

"We need three pianos," Clara said.

"There's not a lot of music for three pianos," Dmitri answered. "A few reductions of orchestral parts for duo piano concertos, maybe."

"That's such a crazy combination not even I would write for it," Odyssey confessed. "Or maybe I would if you had a twin sister."

Clara laughed. "If I had a twin sister? That would change everything. I can't even imagine it."

She had the stolid Russian genes of the Esterhaats clan that block imagination. Or maybe it was the Hungarian genes that insist, as a matter of powerful Hungarian logic, that one cannot imagine oneself as other than what one is – that would be a contradiction in Hungarian. Dmitri smiled his sympathy for poor Clara.

"Christ, I can," Odyssey said. "The two of you would be insufferable, that much beauty in one place. You know what I can't figure out, though?"

"What?"

"You look just like Esterhaats here, but you're beautiful – what is going on? It's like a painter who paints a perfect picture of something only that the picture makes it beautiful instead of ordinary. Forgive me, Esterhaats, I don't mean you're so ordinary, maybe you know what I mean – anyway, I hope you do, I think I don't. Fuck me, I should just shut up."

Clara laughed and moved over to take Odyssey's hand. Odyssey shrank back, almost tripping over the piano bench. Dmitri's eyes widened at that odd vision.

"Sometimes I wish *I* could just shut up," Clara said, "I'd be a lot better off, but I can't stop it, I just talk, I'm nosy and imbecilic. Maybe I could learn from you and say out loud that I should just shut up, I wonder if I have the courage to do that or whether I would be too embarrassed."

Now Odyssey moved over to put her arm around Clara's shoulders, which, despite her young age, were already higher than Odyssey's. Dmitri was stymied – Odyssey flinched from contact one minute and then gracefully offered it the next. She was a grand contradiction.

Odyssey proposed that they take an outing Sunday and drive around the state.

"I don't have a car," Dmitri said.

"And I don't drive," Odyssey laughed. "I'm maybe the only person my age who grew up in Connecticut who doesn't drive. I had to work at it, too, I can tell you."

"Maybe we could just go for a hike."

"We'll go for a drive."

"How?"

"Leave that to me. You take care of getting box lunches for us. Or maybe you could talk your niece into going along and she'd take care of the box lunches, she's probably more reliable."

Odyssey's intentions were so preposterous that Dmitri decided to assume she could do it. He did not even have to ask Clara about the box lunches, she assumed that task immediately when she agreed to go along. Clara was also to fetch Odyssey after breakfast to make sure she was ready to go by nine o'clock. She got the box lunches and handed them to Dmitri as she turned to go wake Odyssey. Dmitri followed her without thinking.

"No, Dmitri, she asked me to do this alone. She might not want you to see her room."

Dmitri sat on a bench near the lake, where he wondered what was the point of their efforts. As he sat, a large black limousine turned toward the main house. "Odyssey," he said. He picked up the large bag of their three box lunches and went over to the chauffeur.

"You have come for Odyssey Deneuve?"

"Yes sir."

Dmitri put the lunches in the car and went back to the kitchen to ask for a fourth.

"Who is it for?" the woman asked.

"The chauffeur."

"The chauffeur? We don't usually . . . well, I guess a chauffeur has to eat too." She prepared another lunch.

Clara said, "Dmitri! You thought of that!" She seemed too clearly to be surprised, an outright accusation of incompetence and thoughtlessness would not have half so insulting.

"Esterhaats," Odyssey said, "who would've guessed?"

Dmitri shook his head.

"Come on, Esterhaats, say it. You think we think you're an incompetent shit, don't you?"

Clara laughed, Odyssey laughed, Dmitri even thought he heard the chauffeur laugh.

Some time after noon, they parked at a covered bridge that Odyssey seemed to know. She handed the fourth lunch to the chauffeur. "We'll be back in a couple of hours, Jordan. You have Mr. Esterhaats to thank for this." Behind them was a phalanx of restaurants.

Jordan grinned, "Thanks, Mr. Est . . ."

Odyssey was about to correct him when Dmitri intervened. "That's okay, I couldn't pronounce it either if it weren't my own name. I'm not sure I get it right even as it is."

They crossed the bridge and walked for half an hour or more along a narrow path that followed the creek uphill toward its source. They reached a point at which the creek bent back in almost a hairpin curve and there, on a gentle slope, they sat to eat lunch.

"This is my favorite spot," Odyssey said. "We have a house right over there, you can't see it, it's in the trees, but from the house you can see this spot. This is one place a violin is better than a piano."

"Trumpet seems more fitting."

"I don't like trumpet. Anyway, it's wrong for this spot, you need a peaceful sound here. Just watch how peaceful it is," she said as she lay back and went to sleep immediately.

Clara had brought a towel to use as a picnic cloth, now she propped it into a tent to shade Odyssey's face. Clara was far too young to be so solicitous of the comforts of others. Dmitri feared she'd learned that from taking over too much responsibility for his care, probably as delegated by her mother at first, but now acting independently from her own motor. It was an unfair burden.

Dmitri drew Clara off to the farther edge of the clearing where they could talk while still keeping an eye on Odyssey. Clara had sudden sources of energy, she spoke almost the whole time, she told Dmitri of the other students, of the pieces she was working on, of the difficulty of keeping her C# over middle C in tune, and through everything she said there seemed to come hints of her missing her time with him and his pianos.

"Do you have free time ever in the morning?" Dmitri asked. "I never see students then and Odyssey's still asleep then. We could work on some duo stuff then – if you can." He remembered Odyssey's schedule, with migraines on Wednesday and apparent exhaustion on Tuesday. "And Tuesday and Wednesday evenings are usually good too."

"I'm supposed to practice in the mornings."

"Maybe you could do some of that in the late afternoon and evening."

"I'll try. Do you really need me to come then?"

It was a struggle to suppress his urge to smile, but Dmitri successfully pursed his lips and nodded. "I don't want to get in your way, but it would be awfully nice to do some duos."

"Maybe we could all three get together Monday and Friday evenings," Odyssey said, startling Clara as she put her hand on Clara's shoulder. "That was the most fun I've had in a long time."

"More fun than ridiculing Dmitri in the car?"

"Ridiculing Esterhaats seems to be too easy. You know what Jordan probably did with your box lunch? He probably gave it away or put it in the trash so he could get a hamburger, fries, and milkshake. So there you were very thoughtful, Esterhaats, and it didn't do a damned bit of good, it just got in the way. Ain't life a crock? And you know the worst? I envy Jordan his lunch, except that I prefer to have oysters before my hamburger and fries."

Two months in Vermont matured Clara by several years it seemed. Over the course of the next year, she subtly changed her role with Dmitri. She not only looked after him in minor ways, seeing to it that he had food and that he kept his schedule when he had one, but now she began to try to understand him, to analyze him, to tell him what she thought. After one of his concerts, she met Anton and Jelly, who insisted Dmitri bring her to their deli the next day, Sunday. Clara and Anton sat on tall bar stools at their stand-up table and sang ludicrous songs from Anton's massive *repertoire* of illicit lyrics. The one Clara liked best was about the Amsterdam Dutch, the Rotterdam Dutch and, especially, the Goddamn Dutch.

"I like it because Esterhaats is Dutch but I'm not."

At the end of a long afternoon, Anton said, "Why don't you give up the piano and join me in revelry and song, Clara, it's a lot more fun. Pianists have no fun – just look at your uncle, a sour old man, more to be pitied than partied."

Dmitri and Clara walked slowly back to the east side.

"Your friends are all women, Dmitri, have you noticed?"

"There's Anton."

"Yes, maybe Anton. But he's the only man you could even think to mention. And even him, I don't know, I'm not so sure. No, in fact I am sure. You enjoy talking with Anton, I know. But if he moved away or stopped coming to that bar, you'd be fine, your life wouldn't really change. I would be sadder than you would. Jelly and Odyssey are more important to you, and you haven't even known Odyssey very long and you don't see her very much. Have you seen her any time other than when you premiered her sonata?"

"Once before that, when she had to come into Manhattan for something."

"When you see Jelly or Odyssey you smile, Dmitri. It's a deep smile, I can't describe it. Everybody must notice it. You smile like that for Mama, too. Not for anybody else, not for the students in Vermont or the other resident teachers."

Clara didn't mention herself, the most important person in Dmitri's life, the one who provoked most of his deep smiles.

"Odyssey says you write her letters, she says she doesn't think you ever wrote letters before, it's as if you were inventing the form, yours are different, they're like talking, there's almost even a dialogue as though you're thinking what she answers and going on from there, you jump off the page at her, you take over her day when she gets even a short one, when she's composing she never knows whether to open your letters or save them. She says your relationship is close and intense unlike anything else she knows, but it's abstract, it's more like composition than like performance, she thinks it might go on forever even if you didn't ever see each other.

"Jelly says she always thought she'd eventually go to Paris because it's the art capital of the world," she continued. "But now she says New York has become the art capital, it's taken everything away from Europe, it even took the Europeans, there's hardly an American in New York. But you know,

Dmitri, if she went to Paris, you'd stop going to the bar, even after performances. You'd probably stop eating in restaurants, unless maybe I forced you to.
Your life without Jelly would be reduced, it would be like all those piano
reductions of the orchestra part you play so I can practice piano concertos. A
hundred instruments and players reduced to one keyboard and one person.
You couldn't live without Jelly and Odyssey. Everyone thinks you're doing
Jelly a great favor to arrange tickets to your concerts for her, but it's you who
benefit most from her coming to the concerts, because then she joins you
afterward for a couple of hours or more. You may prefer duos and solos for
playing, but you need ensembles for living the way you do, ensembles of
women, lots of women, different women, women who can outsmart you face
to face and keep you from blending into your piano."

Dmitri took Clara's observation to heart and he began to wonder why
his friends and favorite people were almost all women – something he'd never
wondered before. For one thing, they were much more likable than men, he
thought, they were warmer, more open, even Linda and Odyssey were more
open than most of the men he met. They understood and knew things he
didn't know, things that startled and delighted him, things that anyone
should want to know. And their presence made him feel good. There was no
man like Jelly, and none that he knew like Linda, Odyssey, or Clara, who was
too young to be a woman but too savvy to be a child for him. Nor did he
know men like *Mademoiselle* Meursault, Sofia Milano, Sally in Alabama, his
mother, or his Aunt Clara. It seemed impossible that there were such men.
He liked these women for the wonderful things that made them different in
his view. But perhaps that was Clara's point, perhaps she would not disagree
with his reasons for liking all these women, she merely meant to say he was
somehow overlooking other kinds of people, men. The more Dmitri thought
through her query, the less he thought he understood his answers. How odd,
he thought, he was stumped by a teenager.

After hearing Clara speak of his writing to Odyssey, Dmitri was
reluctant to write for a while. He wasn't sure why he was uneasy, maybe it
was just his old secretiveness, maybe he was uncomfortable with having anyone but Odyssey know those letters. But then he thought that, from what
she'd said, Clara evidently hadn't seen any of the letters and knew only of
their existence and not their content, she knew adjectives and adverbs about
them, not verbs or nouns from them. And then he got a card from Odyssey.

It said only, "Dmitri, try this," gave six bars of music, and then closed, "Love, O." That card, impertinent and modest, bossy and warm, formal and informal at once, conjured Odyssey before him, there was as much dialogue from it as from any of his letters, he was sure. Thereafter he got a card every day or two with another six bars, and after every card he wrote her. The music of the cards was obviously not in order and Dmitri worked on various orders to try to string the bars together into a whole. The final card in the series announced that Odyssey would be in Manhattan on the following Tuesday and that she would come by to see him if he was there.

"Forgive me for looking so bad, Esterhaats," Odyssey said when she arrived on Tuesday afternoon, "my hair is a mess, I can't make it behave, I look like Einstein at twice my age and half his brain."

"You look terrific," Dmitri truthfully said.

"Oh, fuck you very much, Esterhaats," she answered, with charming inflection.

Dmitri was caught in confusion as he struggled to separate her intonation from the literal meaning of her words, his mind tended to force meaning from the music of her voice rather than from the words. He was too slow figuring it out to permit him to laugh once he understood it. "Einstein was beautiful, anyway," he said.

"So is a cockatoo, but who wants to look like a cockatoo? But I didn't come into this ridiculous city to settle that issue," Odyssey said, "I want to hear you play my cards."

Dmitri smiled. He did not think Odyssey was deceitful, but he was sure she came into the city for some other reason and that she then took advantage of the trip to visit him. He had invited her to come many times, had suggested he visit her many times, but they had only seen each other when something else brought them together, if they were ever to see each other very much, it would be in Vermont at the music camp, but he didn't know whether they would be invited back or whether she would go if invited. Perhaps, in her rationalization of this day, she had elevated her visit to him to her principle motivation for coming to Manhattan today. Her greatest demand in the world was for control, control of her name, control of her music, and, foremost, control of her time, and she exercised her control from the cockpit of a bulldozer, plowing the world out of her way, scheduling even her migraines. As he thought about her and her devices for control, her substitute for mastery of her world, he wanted to hug her. But Odyssey could not be hugged, she could only hug. In declining one of Dmitri's invitations, she'd said, "I'm not the guest type, I'm more the host type, pushing everyone around with food and drink – the evil side of generosity. But now I don't even do that anymore. I'm no longer so evil, so generous."

He played Odyssey's cards in the best order he'd found.

She laughed out of control at the end, going around the room, doubling her fists and shaking them with laughter, she went to his other piano and struck a chord, then played one of the cards. Soon she asked him to play them in a new order.

"That works too," he said at the end.

"It works *too*? You don't think it's a better order?"

Dmitri spread his fingers in the air as though to refuse comment.

Odyssey laughed again, very hard and very loudly. "I think it might work in every order," she said. "Would you try it in every order, Esterhaats?"

There were twelve cards. He was reminded again of the inventor of chess. He could not determine how many orders there were, but knew the number was outrageously large.

"I can't do it," Odyssey said, "I can't take it beyond about six bars at a time, I need you to take it further to see how many ways it works."

"There isn't time to do it now."

"Oh, I'm sorry, you have something else to do."

"No, not today. But today wouldn't be enough time. There are a lot of orders, I don't know how many. Roger could probably tell you how many orders there are. Ask him."

At midnight, Odyssey called. "You were right, you didn't have enough time. Roger says there are almost five hundred million orders for my cards," she said. "That makes a hell of a mountain out of twelve tiny molehills. If you played one order every day, it would take you over a million years to finish all the possibilities. John Cage would love it."

Dmitri visualized himself trying the task. "After a few years, I'd get the orders all mixed up, I'd never know whether I'd done them all."

A few days later, in an idle moment, Dmitri tried Odyssey's cards in a random order that did not work. He debated with himself for a while whether to write her, then decided he should call her. But as he went for the phone, it rang. It was Clara ostensibly calling just to talk but really calling to remind him that he was to begin rehearsals with Linda Ney the next morning. She wondered whether he would like her to walk with him to the studio, she was going shopping near there anyway, she would like the company. "I have to shop for the new school year. I could even come to the rehearsal sometime, maybe to take you out for lunch."

Clara seemed to think she must be caretaker of his life with women, now she wished to protect him against the ogre Linda. His relationships had gone from exploratory with Sofia, to comfortable with Sally, to profound with Linda, to fun with Jelly, and finally to abstract with Odyssey. That seemed to mimic the path of his life, perhaps it was the most natural path, but there was clearly nothing further in that direction. The moments of his life with women were like Odyssey's cards, they were individually good, even beautiful, but when strung together in the wrong order they worked badly. Perhaps another order would have been magnificent.

Clara, Clara, Clara, Dmitri thought, you are too young to be taking on this burden. Giorgio would be calling him tomorrow morning in any case. He smiled as she said he would for Jelly and Odyssey. "Lunch break is not so easy," he said. "There's no telling when it will happen. We're just taking lunch with us so we can work through."

"I'll bring yours. Mama has some wonderful things. I want you to have a nice lunch."

Yes, Dmitri thought, she wanted to think he would have at least as nice a lunch as Linda, she wanted to think Linda could not think him poorly equipped to live in her world. "Only if you're really sure you want to walk then."

"I'm *really* sure," she said with crystal clear diction. "Unlike some people, I know what I want when I want it."

Maybe that's why you usually get it, he thought.

Linda Ney

L inda and Dmitri were both remarkably clumsy about seeing each other again, they could not gracefully say hello or hug one another, they almost shook hands before they both thought better of it, they struggled over avoiding and not avoiding eye contact, they surreptitiously checked each other's appearance. The contrast with the farewell hug Clara had given him just outside the building and the glacial manner of Linda's hello was comic. These two stiff, hostile people had only three weeks to prepare their concert, which would include one piece by Odyssey Deneuve that would be very strenuous for both of them but especially for Linda. Choosing to make that piece, in its premier performance, one of his two contributions to the program seemed sadistic to Dmitri in retrospect. He wondered what odds a bookie would give for the failure of the Lincoln Center celebration. Dmitri suppressed a laugh at that thought and then wished he hadn't suppressed it.

He stood before the piano and ran up the keys. "B flat over C is off," he said. He'd meant to leave his wrenches at home, there could be no need for them here, but, in one of those bumbling failures that had often brought him perverse success, he'd failed to take the wrenches out of his pocket. In a minute, he had the key in tune. Now, to be sure or to be idle, he did not know which, he ran up the keys and back down, with a flowing rush of several steps forward and a few backward. An idle listener might have wondered whether that was a previously unknown work that Debussy had intended as a show piece.

"C," Linda said, and Dmitri struck C several times as she adjusted her strings.

"Are we prepared?" Dmitri meant his question as a tease.

Linda took it as an impatient challenge. "I'll let you know," she said. In another minute, she turned to ask, "What do we do first?"

"Anything from Bach to Bartók."

"That was not an answer."

"Locatelli."

"I haven't played that in a while. Anyway, we should practice with our program, don't you think." That final phrase was one Linda could use interchangeably with, "you'd better think."

"Maybe we should do something not on the program so we can wreck it without worrying about it."

They played Beethoven, Brahms, and Debussy, and they wrecked them all. Linda was angry but she avoided complaining about Dmitri. He played little pieces by Beethoven while Linda went through the sheet music in her bag. At "Rage over a lost penny" she began to hum and smile.

"That piece started Clara on the way to the piano," Dmitri said.

"Is she good?"

"Very good."

"Why doesn't she play?"

"Her parents want her to get through school at least half normal."

"A lot of good that might do her. That's what my parents did for me. Tell her she might grow up to be like Linda Ney."

Dmitri did not say that Clara would weep at the thought. He remembered their first encounter, when both were succumbing to hunger but neither was willing to be first to capitulate, and he proposed they have lunch.

"I didn't bring anything," Linda said. "Maybe we could go out somewhere fast."

"We can share mine."

"What do you have?"

Dmitri had no idea what Clara had packed for him, but to cover for his ignorance, he smiled at Linda and opened the bag to spread elegant things before her in their first gracious gesture of the day.

"Who did this?" Linda asked, a bit shyly. She knew Dmitri didn't do it but she might wonder who there was in his life to do such a thing.

"Clara and her mother."

"How old is Clara?"

"She was born just when we separated."

Linda seemed reticent to begin conversation thereafter. She even had difficulty proposing what they should play. That would have made the afternoon very nearly impossible, except that now Dmitri was less bothered by misconnection than he once was. He could play for himself if necessary. Although he hadn't played it in more than fifteen years, Dmitri began the *tutti* introduction for Locatelli's twelfth concerto from *L'Arte del Violino*. Playing it now was Dmitri Esterhaats at his most idle, it was a whim, perhaps even a destructive whim, like his crossing streets without looking for traffic, it set up a wide range of possibilities, some of them bad. He played the piece far more to challenge his memory than to hear it or to get them to play it together, he merely wondered whether his earlier memory had failed, this was not only something he had not played in a long while, it was something of a kind that he hadn't played, Locatelli was not otherwise in his *repertoire*, Locatelli dated only from his years with Linda. There was therefore no closely relevant body of music on which his memory could build to reconstruct the piece, he could play it if at all only on brute memory of the piece itself. True, he had heard it once with Clara and he had heard the eleventh once by himself recently in anticipation of playing again with Linda. But with no more than that to go on, he was not sure his deteriorating memory could handle the piece now.

In playing it, he concentrated hard and immersed himself in it, and he made it as concentrated as he was.

"Dmitri," Linda commanded.

Although playing the piece was an idle move by Dmitri, once he'd begun, he found no natural stopping point and he ignored Linda's reprimand, or perhaps he did not so much ignore it as fail to register it, his thoughts were elsewhere, they were tied up in his fingers and his keyboard, in Locatelli's sonorities, Linda's voice and Linda were no part of his moment, he was floating away from the tedium of this strenuous day, floating on the odd medium of a Locatelli reduction that seemed still to live in his fingers even though he could not remember it well enough to think ahead to its difficulties.

"Oh . . . okay," Linda said. She took up her violin and in a moment she entered on schedule.

By the end of the afternoon they were playing reasonably well, by the end of the week they were even playing together, and by halfway through their second week they were playing as Ney-Esterhaats once had played in their best days in Europe. That Wednesday afternoon, after nine hard days of rehearsal, Linda laughed. We will make it, Dmitri thought. Thereafter they were in sync and he could lead her anywhere, unless she led him there first, except that no one could have led her through Odyssey Deneuve's sonata.

Now they had every meal together, and after dinners they walked Manhattan until nearly midnight.

"I haven't walked in New York except to get somewhere in a long time," Linda said.

"It's best when you have nowhere to go," Dmitri said.

"You still look good, Dmitri."

Dmitri smiled.

"You're not going to say I'm still okay?"

"Okay? You're still . . . maybe I won't say it. But it's true. You're still beautiful, you'll be beautiful when you're eighty."

"Hey, not so fast." She let them walk in silence for a block or so before she spoke again. "I saw Jelly Ujfalussy, maybe it was a few months ago, maybe a year, she went out of her way to say how beautiful Clara is. Jelly wanted me to be bothered."

"Were you bothered?"

Linda laughed.

"Someday, if you give yourself a chance, you might find out you have a lot in common with Jelly."

"Name one thing."

"Well, when you put it like that, I'm not sure."

"Jelly is a tart, she has no purpose in life but to please men, it's all a performance," Linda said as she led them into the evening's restaurant.

"*Sounds* like us."

"Maybe. Maybe you're right. We're all just idiots for hire. But there's still a difference – sex, Dmitri, sex, sex, sex." Linda had raised her voice and silence fell over the room. "If all the women in the hall sat on our right and all the men sat on the left, so the women could listen to you and the men could listen to me, then we'd be a lot more like Jelly."

They had set their program as they had done when they were scheduling their first few concerts many years before, each proposing two pieces and then working out an order in which to play them, all done through Giorgio's man. Dmitri's proposals then were generally idle, he could as well have proposed a huge collection of things from which any choices were acceptable, but Linda set the rules and he followed them. This time his proposal that they do Odyssey Deneuve's new violin and keyboard sonata was not idle, it seemed half the reason for going through with their concert, if they didn't do it now, he'd have to find a violinist to do it with him on another occasion soon. But that would be a less impressive premiere for Odyssey than the Lincoln Center festival, and Dmitri now thought of his and Linda's reunion as Odyssey's event. But when they got around to attempting Odyssey's sonata during their first week of rehearsal, Linda complained at the choice.

"I don't like her. Her stuff is very hard. It's not clear there's any reason to make it so hard, it's just hard for the sake of being hard. You seem to do it very easily, you have a weird gift for it or you work very hard. But just because it's hard doesn't make it good."

Dmitri should have anticipated the possibility of Linda's objection, but now he was caught by it. "It's very good. She wrote it for us."

"She wrote it for us?"

"How is Odyssey so different from Locatelli? They both write to the limit of what instruments and performers can do. They make it hard because that's the way to do things that can't otherwise be done and haven't ever been done before."

Linda was evidently not listening. "She wrote it for us? We'd be giving the premiere performance?"

"Yes. If we do it soon enough."

"We can try it a bit. But I can't make any guarantees we can do it for the concert."

Linda could never make any guarantees – although she never reneged on doing what she said she might. In any case, the sonata would be in the printed programs and posters.

Once their playing was going well, Linda began to drop quiet comments into the pauses of their rehearsals and their meals, comments without context other than the context of twenty years, in which they did not seem to Dmitri to fit naturally.

"Dmitri, do you know that I've even played Bartók by choice for my own solos?"

Dmitri smiled.

"I've increased my *repertoire*. You more than doubled it for me, you made me do new things. I now like doing new things. That's very peculiar, I should probably resent you for that. Some days I don't believe myself, I get up not wanting to play Bach or Schubert, but wanting to find something new to try. Maybe eventually I'll even like doing Odyssey Deneuve." She shook her bow at him, "But don't count on it."

"Have you been back to France, Dmitri?"

"Once, for a short tour, mostly Paris."

"I go almost every year now. After my parents died, I even thought of moving back there."

"Ohhh, I'm sorry. What happened?"

"They were just very old, they were nearly forty when I was born."

Dmitri wanted both to continue this conversation indefinitely and to end it immediately. Linda was saying more in a casual moment than she'd said in five years of their living together. He reacted as though he were jealous of his present self on behalf of his earlier, less fully informed self. It seemed unreasonable that the Dmitri of today should learn so casually about her life when the Dmitri of fifteen years earlier would dearly have liked to know details of her life but was never privileged to learn them.

Linda laughed, she evidently thought it was merely arithmetic that was perplexing him. "Mama was eighty-five and Papa was eighty-seven. Sometimes I thought they hated each other and now I'm sure they always did, that makes sense of lots of things I remember already from Berlin and Paris. I wouldn't continue the way they did, they were stubborn, they wouldn't go public and admit their mistake, they just stuck it out, they were together more than sixty years. That seemed far too long for so much hatred, I thought it was certain to break down twenty or thirty years ago, even still five years ago. But then, despite all the hatred, it turned out he couldn't live without her. He was still in very good health when she died and he thought he'd finally have a few good years after she was gone from his life. But it didn't work that way, he couldn't stand being alone, he didn't really mourn for Mama, he just couldn't stand living without her, he died only a few months after she did. I think it came as a big surprise to him that he needed her after resenting her presence for all those years. Poor Papa, he died startled."

"Do you know, the day before we first started, Giorgio said he was responsible for us because we'd never have paired ourselves. I think I turned red in the face. To say you pair yourselves in German, *sich paaren*, is to use gutter language to say you fuck each other. When Giorgio said that, I suddenly suspected that's what I wanted to do, just go to bed with you. If anybody had asked me in a normal conversation, I'd've said that was inconceivable, because I thought it was, I'd never like you that way, you were not my type. You were the earnest, striving immigrant type, growing up poor and struggling to make it in the world. I was never poor, I was sure I would make it in the world, I was cosmopolitan, all I needed was not to be in a Nazi world. But I had to work like hell with music and you just did it, you weren't striving at all, if no one wanted to pay to listen to you, you just played for yourself. I couldn't do that, I had either to practice something or play for an audience. But then Giorgio said what I really wanted in that accidental way . . . you and he didn't even know he'd said it, I couldn't laugh or make a joke, I couldn't say anything. I was just stuck with my weird thoughts. You may not have noticed, but I didn't say another word at that meeting. It was true what he said, we'd never have paired ourselves, either in English or in German, without him. But right that minute I should have told Giorgio to leave us alone so we could do it in German."

Dmitri was too slow in revising his understanding of Linda to answer immediately. This moment might fit with her audacity in proposing they both sleep in the bed in New Orleans or with her sudden pleasure in their sprained wrists that they could indulge in Paris for several weeks. But on those occasions, she wanted him. Today, there was evidently no reason for her audacity, it was merely for the hell of it, Linda at her audacious best. And how odd her view of him was, he'd never worried about making it in the world, he didn't even care whether he did, he only cared about music, and once about Linda. And he'd worked hard for his music, he'd done hardly anything but work for it until after he and Linda had split.

Some time later, after they'd played a movement of Bach, Linda added, "That was part of the reason I was so nervous before our performance the next night. I was afraid if it didn't go well, we'd never get another chance to pair ourselves."

"I went back to that hotel in Dijon where we fought," Linda said. "It's now surrounded by the city and there's no farm with it anymore. I asked if they'd eaten the rooster. They said they'd eaten *all* the farm animals. I said that was okay, I only wanted to know about the rotten rooster. She thought they probably had it with mustard and wine, but she couldn't remember for sure. Old cocks are tough and chewy, so they need to be baked with lots of slather, and her favorite slather is mustard, she said. Now only dogs and cats run through the halls when you try to make love and there's no kikiriki to ridicule you when you're slithering in slime. But they still use those stupid rubber sheets. You get soaking wet just sleeping on the bed."

They had worked very late, it was now turning dark in the late summer evening.

"Let's quit," Linda said. "We could go for a walk, have a long dinner somewhere, and forget about music and Lincoln Center." She called to make a reservation and they walked for half an hour. She did not like risking a restaurant without a reservation.

As they sat at their table drinking wine, Linda said, "We should have quit hours ago and just gone for a walk. Like old times."

Dmitri smiled and shook his head at once in an involuntary gesture that revealed he was charmed by disbelief in what he'd just heard from her. Going for a walk in the middle of the day was not like old times except while they were unable to practice because of their sprained wrists or occasionally on the day after a hard concert when Linda was too tired to rehearse. They'd never broken from rehearsal before a concert for anything so frivolous as a walk.

"You don't think so, Dmitri? You think we should just work all the time?"

Dmitri smiled and shook his head again, he'd exhausted his stock of gestures for such moments.

"How was Sofia Milano?" Linda asked.

"Sofia Milano," Dmitri repeated while trying to figure out the point of the question. "How was Sofia Milano?"

"Yes, she was your first, wasn't she?"

"Yes. I hadn't ever toured with anyone before her."

"Dmitri! You . . . Dmitri. I don't believe you! But apparently you're really true."

"Your life was so hard, Dmitri, you never had enough pleasures to learn how to enjoy them. Music was the only pleasure you learned to enjoy. I couldn't do anything about that."

She'd done everything about that, except stay with him.

"You told me Debussy was hard. I thought you were crazy. But he really was hard for you, wasn't he?"

Dmitri hesitated to answer. "Yes. I thought he was hard."

"Colette Meursault? Was that her name?"

"Yes. *Mademoiselle* Meursault taught me Debussy."

"So you could play at Elaine Wolf's?"

"Yes." Dmitri was perplexed that she could know that.

"My parents knew Elaine Wolf very well, only later. She was very generous to us. She bought me a violin when we first came to New York early in the war."

"She didn't know Colette Meursault was my teacher."

Linda suddenly turned her head to look at him as though to show her doubt. "She told me about it when I told her I was going to be playing with a pianist named Esterhaats. Every time she mentioned you, she said, 'My Esterhaats.' She told me the whole story. 'This is someone different, Linda, you watch out with My Esterhaats.' I wasn't sure whether she was warning me about what you might do to me or warning me not to do anything to her Esterhaats." Linda laughed. "I still don't know which it was. Probably both. She made me very scared of you."

"When I suggested we could both sleep in the bed in our New Orleans hotel, do you know what you said, Dmitri?"

Dmitri, who could remember hundreds of musical works down to the last note and tempo, who could remember fiction in ridiculous detail, who could often quote back to people whole conversations from long ago, had no idea what he'd said in that wonderful moment in New Orleans, the gift of the moment had fogged the details in his memory, which was little more than a sense of beauty and magic. Almost his full memory of the moment was of thinking, I've thought of this for ages and now this is the moment. And his continuing to think, This is the moment, lay over the entire night until he fell asleep after dawn, as though the moment could not itself break through the startling realization that this was it.

"I thought you might say we should get married, that would've made sense, it flowed naturally from the moment, if you were writing that scene, that's what you'd have to write. You know: I propose we screw, you propose we marry. What else could you say? I was wondering, would I keep my name or change it to Esterhaats – Esterhaats is wonderful, it's almost a joke, is it Dutch?, is it Hungarian?, or just some strange magic. I'd grown to love it, it seemed like my name by then, Ney-Esterhaats, I even wished it were my name just for the sake of the name. But I didn't have to decide about my name, you didn't say anything about marriage or even about us. What you said was that it wasn't a very comfortable couch, the god-forsaken couch in our hotel room. You slept on that couch the night before, that miserable thing, it was a very uncomfortable shape and its cushions were worn out. I was giving myself to you in the greatest moment of my life, it had taken me months to get myself to do it, it was the most spectacular thing I'd ever done, the most spectacular thing I'd ever even thought of doing, I've still never topped it, and then I really did it, I just opened my mouth and did it as though it came naturally, I was completely astonished, Locatelli was a miracle worker, that was finally the moment, there in a dumpy hotel in New Orleans."

The greatest moment of her life, Dmitri thought. It was plausibly the greatest moment of his life as well, except that it had very nearly escaped his memory. While thinking that now, the moment passed for him to respond to what Linda said.

"I wanted to sing *Exsultate, Jubilate*," Linda continued, "I wanted to screw instantly and go on screwing all night, and then get up the next morning and get married, and then turn our tour into a honeymoon for forty years, who would give a damn about making money so long as we could cover the expenses of loving each other in cities all over the place. And what did you do, Dmitri? You talked about that goddamned couch as though my great proposal were just a mechanical decision about comfort, if only they'd had a comfortable couch, we wouldn't have had to sleep together, we could've maintained our dignity." Linda lifted her hands in a prayer of helplessness and unbelief, then put them to her head. "Dmitri, Dmitri, Dmitri."

"Elaine Wolf told me about Horace Gmund's shop where you worked," Linda said. "Did you notice that the sheet music Giorgio got for our rehearsals was from his shop?"

Dmitri blushed slightly. "Yes."

"Mrs. Wolf said Gmund was in turmoil trying to find a way to keep you employed when he didn't really have work for you and when he was barely keeping out of bankruptcy anyway. She made a deal that she would pay your wages as long as you worked there and then she even bought lots of music just to have you deliver it to her."

Dmitri cringed and stared down at his keyboard.

In a moment he felt Linda's arm across his shoulders. "Mrs. Wolf wondered whether your working there finally saved Gmund from going broke."

Dmitri's hands opened slowly as though to release something, and then they ran up the keys in a liquid Debussy roll as though he were checking the tune, either of the piano or of his fingers. Why had Linda never said anything about all this before, he wondered.

"What should we play, Dmitri?"

He recalled Colette Meursault asking him to play Bach for her as she departed from Mrs. Wolf's party. "Bach," he said. With Bach he could float free of the moment, he could fold himself into the music, he could regain himself.

"I still have my Kittel bow, the one you gave me."

Dmitri knew which one, he had noticed it immediately when she first took it out their first morning of rehearsal, he had even noticed that its brass fitting at the end had just been polished. It had also been polished by the shop where he'd bought it, the salesman had taken it away and then brought it back wrapped for giving to Linda. Then, when she removed it from its wrapping, Dmitri saw the bright, freshly polished brass gleaming at him. For their first practice now, the Kittel had also just been restrung, as though to make sure their rehearsals went as well as possible.

"It has been a wonderful performer." Linda had been about to lift it to play, but now she paused. "Jerusalem used a Kittel. Sometimes he let me use it when I finally moved up to a full size fiddle. I thought that was the only true bow for fiddling. He had it with him the day they arrested him. They smashed his violin case, they had no idea what they were doing, an Amati and a Kittel, smashed in the name of superior culture."

"Now what?" Linda asked.

"Now what?"

"Dmitri, why is it you're always so slow witted?"

"When am I slow witted?"

"When I was trying to get you to propose that we stay in one room in our hotels in order to save money, you never understood, once you just suggested we stop eating – that would save money, at least as long as we lived, I suppose. I thought, Now this is clearly not a stupid man, why is he being so stupid? I thought that a lot. Finally the desk clerk in that Chicago hotel was our second Giorgio, he paired us when we would never have paired ourselves."

"You never understood about Germany, did you?"

Dmitri was unsure of the direction of the question and he did not immediately respond.

"Remember? When Jean-Robert asked us whether we wanted to go to Germany to make more money, he said there were a couple of places that would subsidize us. That's why we fought in Dijon."

"We fought in Dijon," Dmitri said, "only because we were so bad at talking to each other that we fought before we understood what was at issue. Once we understood, we no longer needed to fight, and we went off to Paris."

"Are you saying you didn't think it was a trivial thing to decide to go to Germany?"

Dmitri did not wish to argue, he shrugged his shoulders.

"You didn't care about Germany because you didn't have anyone who was murdered by them, Dmitri."

Although he was impressed by Linda's equanimity in this moment, her apparent lack of anger, Dmitri's face must have betrayed great annoyance.

"Who did you have?"

Dmitri checked the tune of his piano from top to bottom instead of bottom to top. It was in tune that direction as well, there was at least that much logic to the universe.

"I'm sorry, Dmitri, please forgive me. I didn't know. Who was it? Please tell me."

"We know too little, don't we." In truth, Dmitri was surprised that she did not know, he would have assumed that she did, that in their five years together he would surely have told her of Aunt Clara.

"Who was it," Linda persisted.

"My first piano teacher was my mother's younger sister, Clara, in Kiev. She and her husband could not go to Amsterdam when we did because she was about to have a baby. They went several years later and then they were going to come to America. They missed their chance, things happened too fast. The last time I saw her I was about seven."

"I'm terribly sorry, Dmitri."

"You can't be sorry for someone who died thirty years ago."

"No, Dmitri, I'm sorry for you, for us, that I didn't know you more than I did."

"I thought we would get married in Paris with our sprained wrists," Linda said. "But it didn't happen. We just went on with the tour. For a long time, I kept thinking that was what we'd do, we'd marry in a French civil ceremony that's so bureaucratic and official it makes the thing seem silly, but after a long time the whole idea finally faded from my mind, and soon after that you asked me. That's when I was the stupid one, I had gone through too much reliving of my life in Paris and Jerusalem's death, I was too grudging to get back into our previous mood then. I will never understand that, why were we so obtuse, Dmitri? When I think of it I feel dumb. And I feel embarrassed."

A little later she added, as though it were an afterthought separated from the original thought by an hour of music and random chatter, "Maybe it wouldn't have worked anyway. If so much misunderstanding got in the way of getting married, maybe it would have wrecked any marriage we could've had."

"When you gave me this bow," Linda said as she held her bow out toward Dmitri, "I said I would only try it, I wouldn't keep it, just a few bars. Bach, of course, that was my mistake, I couldn't just play a few bars of Bach. I'd only try it, I wouldn't keep it. That's just what I said to Giorgio when he proposed I form a duo with you. I said I would only try it, just a few performances, but not for very long." She laughed and then bounced her bow *pizzicato* across the strings of her violin. "I still have the bow."

"Hold my hands," Linda said as they stood offstage waiting to enter for their Lincoln Center reunion. When he took her hands in his, she leaned against him and relaxed. "You don't know how many times I've needed you the past fifteen years," she said.

How many concerts had she given? he wondered. Fifty a year maybe, that would be times fifteen, that would be . . . damn, that would be a lot. "Hundreds," he said.

Linda startled slightly. "What?"

"Hundreds of times you needed me to quiet your hands before your concerts."

Linda looked at him as though he were daft. "Dmitri," she said with a shake of her head. Oddly, Dmitri thought, her hands suddenly became firm and no longer nervous.

The stage manager signaled for them to walk out. Linda kissed Dmitri quickly, grabbed her violin and bow, and strode to center stage. She was no longer nervous, not even later when they played Deneuve's nearly impossible sonata.

To celebrate the premiere performance of her piece, Odyssey reserved a private room for drinks and dinner at the Pierre. She led Jelly, Linda, Clara, and Dmitri down and around the bottom of Central Park and then up to the Pierre, where they spent the late afternoon and evening. Dmitri walked with Jelly most of the way, Clara walked with Linda, and Odyssey walked twice as fast and twice as far as anyone else as she went back and forth between the two pairs. She was bouncing with delight and energy, Dmitri heard not a single shit or fuck from her the whole way, she was like Clara, he thought, the slightest success made her happy and at ease with her world, made her think she could do whatever she wanted, made her believe the world was compliant. They were both childish, but that made them better adults.

"Jack had to go to a meeting right after the performance, they've got to decide what they're going to do when the market opens again Monday morning, they think it's going to be volatile. If he gets through, he'll join us later. For some reason he thinks saving the western world's economy is more important than this party. Men are jerks – don't take it personally, Dmitri, I only mean it as a generalization."

In that group there were more pasts than anyone should have to experience all at once. Dmitri could not keep his visions stable, they switched from the women before him this moment to the women of his many pasts. He was the only common tie among these people and yet he felt least connected to the group, the parts formed a novel whole in which his role was more to listen than to speak, and he listened until something sparked other thoughts and he drifted off for a while to return only when asked to by one of the women or when his other thoughts ran out. Perhaps the others could be more of the group of the moment because they had fewer pasts here, each mainly had a past only with Dmitri. Perhaps the present would not be as rich without pasts, but it would be more manageable, more comfortable, more pleasant, as it seemed to be for these women with each other. Without their pasts, he and Linda might have a much better present, even he and Jelly. Dmitri closed his eyes in contemplation of a present without his pasts and then he smiled at his own illogic, his self-indulgent silliness.

"Dmitri," Jelly interrupted from the distant past, "you are supposed to say at least half what you think."

"Half what I think, Jelly?" He shook his head. "That would embarrass you, it would embarrass everybody here, it might even embarrass me."

Linda spoke quietly, "It wouldn't embarrass any of *us*, Dmitri, only you."

Linda and Dmitri had difficult schedules that got in the way of their performing together again for a couple of years until Linda finally arranged with Giorgio to give them long breaks together with a possible concert at the end. She asked Dmitri to join her for lunch to invite him to perform with her. "If it works well, we could try another tour, one season maybe."

"That's a big commitment," Dmitri said, "we'd have a lot of music to refresh."

"I know it would be a big commitment. In all kinds of ways. After so long without commitments, maybe that would be good. I would like to play Bartók with you again."

Dmitri forgot that comment when he proposed they do Carter, which was far more troubling for Linda. He would happily have changed his choice for her, but she would never suggest he do so. After two weeks of rehearsing, she still was frustrated by it and Dmitri proposed they switch to Bartók or even Schubert.

"It's printed, Dmitri. There are programs and posters, they all say Carter. I never change a program."

He could not say she'd once changed one, the memorial concert for Jerusalem.

"Besides," she said, "there's only a week left now and that wouldn't be time for Bartók."

"It should be enough for Schubert."

She ignored his suggestion.

On Monday, they began a twelve hour day at eight. As the day went on, Dmitri slowly lost his voice. When she missed something he was saying in the afternoon, Linda suddenly realized Dmitri was in trouble. "What's wrong?" she asked with alarm.

"Sore throat," he said.

"It's flu."

Dmitri grinned at her instant inference of the worst from the least evidence. "That's what my doorman thinks," Dmitri said, his teasing lilt muffled by his sore throat.

"The doorman is your medical authority?"

"I don't ever need a doctor. But I don't think it's flu. It was just too cold in my apartment last night."

"Russian folk medicine? If it's flu, our concert is dead."

"I've never missed a concert in my life except when we hurt our wrists on the crooked floor in Dijon."

"That's the past, Dmitri, what about Saturday night?"

Dmitri realized he'd erred in leading her to fret. He wanted some way to put her at ease. "The worst that would happen is that my niece could do the piano parts, she's wonderful, she'd be better than me. If I can't do it, Clara could do it with you," Dmitri idly whispered, still teasing, as though to soothe her pessimistic nerves.

Linda almost exploded with exasperation. "How could Clara possibly do it?"

Now Dmitri bridled in defense of his beloved Clara. "Her best friend from the summers in Vermont is a violinist. She does piano-fiddle duets with her all the time. She has a huge *repertoire*, she likes what I like and her violinist friend likes what you like – the perfect combination. She's great on the Carter. Clara's very good, she follows the violinist so well no one could tell who was leading."

"Then how do you know?"

Dmitri was stumped.

"She probably wouldn't do it anyway. I have the feeling she doesn't like me."

"I'll call her. Try it with her tomorrow if she's willing."

"How would that work?"

"She would have to get my half of the fee." With that remark, Dmitri decided that he did have the flu and he would miss the concert.

"I guess I don't have any choice, do I?"

She did have a choice, she could have chosen to take the risk and count on Dmitri. But that was too great a risk for Linda and therefore she wanted to delete him from the program, which meant she could not afterwards decide it had gone well enough to justify their taking another tour. Her effort to make a commitment would fall before her compulsive fretting about making sure the concert went well. Dmitri called Clara and arranged to get her to rehearse the next day with Linda. Clara was obviously ready, but she asked Dmitri to explain the situation to her mother.

"Dmitri," Sylvia Esterhaats said, "if you say she won't get dragged into that world full time, if you say you'll protect her, I'll believe you and I won't object. Can you really say that?"

"I will arrange to get Giorgio to take her on as her agent and I'll make him swear he won't let her do too much for a few years still. He will do anything I want. He hasn't taken on anyone new in many years, he says he has enough to keep him busy until he retires, but he'll have to make an exception for Clara. She's almost seventeen already, she is ready to start if it's kept gentle for a while."

In the end, Sylvia agreed to let Clara perform. Dmitri realized there could be no change of heart now, Clara would take his place or the concert would be canceled. He would have to have the flu no matter how he felt. Linda might have been capable of replacing Clara with him after a day or two, but he was not capable of wrecking Clara's chance now that she'd become committed to it. As he now thought of that, he noted only two emotions in response: happiness for his wonderful Clara and relief for himself. Odd, he thought, I would have said there was nothing I wanted more than another tour with Linda. Later he would think that he had reacted too much to the momentary burden of dealing with Linda's petty compulsion about the slight risk of failure, that he had not stepped outside the immediate moment to consider how wonderful life with her was on the whole, but it was his petty compulsion to deal with moments rather than wholes – and in that, he laughed, he was not so different from Linda. He needed the audacity to see Linda whole rather than merely by the moment. Loving her during their five years together gave him that audacity then, being in love was the greatest audacity. But he no longer loved her, the love had faded, and although it might come back quickly if they took another tour, it was not available to push him into a tour.

Dmitri had no flu. He sat through the Ney-Esterhaats concert in perfect health, his sore throat gone. In a perverse sense, although he and Linda had canceled appearances for four weeks while they recovered from their Dijon injuries, he'd still never missed a concert to illness. At that thought, he laughed during the ovation after the first number and Clara, her ears tuned to his laugh, turned to smile at him, to laugh, and to bow specifically for him. Dmitri did his best to lead the applause and Ney-Esterhaats had to do four encores, sorely testing their limited joint repertoire of less than a week.

When they were celebrating after the concert, Clara went to the ladies room, and Linda said, "You pretended to have the flu just for Clara."

"If I'd thought of it, I might have."

"I think you did."

"Did Clara fail you?"

Linda was silent for a long while. "No, Dmitri. She didn't fail anyone. She is wonderful. She was extremely polite and diffident, as though afraid of me or in awe or something. But she has no reason for that, she deserved to be there."

Dmitri was invited to give a series of four to six concerts in France. He'd been saying No to almost everything. But, without thinking why, he said yes to France, especially to Paris. He preferred four, they preferred six, but they left it open for him to give a final number later. He immediately thought he would play half French music and split the other half between contemporary American and other music. And then he forgot about it for several months until he received a telegram asking for his programs. He dropped the telegram in the box of mail beside his door and went back to playing with Clara.

"Dmitri," she said, "that's a telegram."

"Yes."

"You have to read it."

"I *have* to read it?"

"I will read it." She fetched it and read it to him. It was from Paris in less than perfect English: MUST HAVE PROGRAMMS FOR SIX CONCERTS IMEDIATE. MUST PRINT. PLEASE. BONFLEUR.

"Okay," Dmitri said.

Clara looked at him. "Immediate," she said. He must have looked forlorn or bored at the prospect. "I will help you do it."

"Okay, how about tomorrow afternoon."

"Now."

She went to his box of mail and fished out three earlier telegrams, all unopened, from Bonfleur. "Dmitri, how do you ever manage to give your concerts?"

"Giorgio handles all that stuff."

"Why isn't he handling this one?"

"I don't know. Oh, the cultural *attaché* at the French embassy asked me to do it, it's an official exchange, Jelly arranged for us to meet. Maybe I forgot to tell Giorgio."

"I'm going to call Giorgio right now, you get something to write on, and then we'll work out your programs." She held out one of the telegrams. "Here he says if you do not reply imediate, he will have to schedule all six."

"I think I meant only to do four."

"Now you'll do six." Her tone was parental, judgmental, and Dmitri smiled in response, because that was a tone that he thought he'd never used with her.

He and Clara spent two days putting the programs together. He wanted her to come with him and he offered to pay her way and said he would arrange for her to do duos with him, but she said it was impossible.

"Impossible?"

"Impossible. Remember? I agreed to do another concert with Linda. Linda wants us to rehearse full time for two weeks – just when you're in France."

Linda was always complicating Paris for him.

"Linda would rehearse Bach or Mozart for two weeks," Dmitri said.

"We're doing Mozart."

M. Bonfleur met Dmitri after his first concert in Paris. He was gracious at a level that transcended the mores of New York civilization. "My aunt said you are wonderful, I should get you to play. She was right, *Monsieur*. You are more French than the French pianists."

"Your aunt? Bonfleur?"

"*Non, non. Mademoiselle* Colette Meursault. You might know of her, she was a pianist, she has not played for many years."

"She has not?"

"She has arthritis, she cannot play now."

"I know *Mademoiselle* Meursault, she taught me to play Debussy. The Debussy I played tonight, she taught me that. Could I see her?"

"I will call her in the morning. May I call you at your hotel to confirm, *Monsieur* Esterhaats? If she can see you, I will arrange for a car to take you. But please *Monsieur* do not be affronted if she cannot see you. She sees almost no one."

Dmitri bought two dozen tulips for *Mademoiselle* Meursault.

"How did you know, *Monsieur* Esterhaats? Tulips are my favorite flower."

Dmitri was clumsy, he might have said the elegance of the tulips befitted her, instead he told her the trivial truth even while he thought better of it. "Someone once told me French women especially like tulips." The someone was Linda, Linda had sometimes dismissively dissected French culture and mores. "Roses in America, tulips in France," she said.

"If not camellias, eh, *Monsieur* Esterhaats? So I have been – how do you say? – I have been typed."

Dmitri reached out his hands to lift hers. He remembered her hands as the most beautiful he'd ever seen, they'd been more graceful than he remembered his Aunt Clara's, they could have been Rodin's model, but now they were crippled almost beyond function, they were knotted and cramped, they looked like pain. Still they were beautiful, Rodin should have done them like that as well. He bowed to kiss her right hand. A maid brought in tea and cakes and took away the tulips.

"I wish I could hear you play, *Monsieur* Esterhaats. It is too hard for me to go by car. I am not a master of pain. You are, I think. You played one day with a terrible headache but you said nothing. When you are older, you may think that is your greatest talent."

It was true, he had played with an awful headache, now that he knew what a migraine was he thought it was certainly a migraine, but he would not have remembered without her recollection. Now he wondered how she knew. The curtains beyond the piano were normally closed, but that morning they were pulled aside and Dmitri played while facing the glare of the full morning sun and, before the morning was over, he had a raging headache. After his time with her that day, he walked for hours, avoiding traffic and its noise when possible, avoiding the sun, which hurt, walking slowly, idly, without direction.   Whenever the sun caught his eyes at the east-west streets and on a few occasions when it reflected into his eyes from the windows on the avenues, his head pounded and focused its pain in his eyes, and at the end of the Brooklyn Bridge, when the sun had long since set behind him and therefore headlights glared, he vomited until he could vomit no more. He had walked Manhattan through many such headaches, but he thought this was the worst. It was from this one that he slowly began to discover that glare could be a disaster for him, as it often was in his dreadful Alabama years, beginning with his first day at Colonel Weiss's base, when he rode in an open truck in the bright sun from the train to the base.

When Dmitri reached home very late after his spoiled lesson with *Mademoiselle* Meursault, his mother was the first to see him and she knew at once. She stayed his father from scolding Dmitri for being so late and put Dmitri to bed. It was the following day, in the euphoria after a migraine that has run its course, that he had his greatest breakthrough in playing Debussy, that day he could do no wrong at the keyboard and nothing took effort. At the time, he hadn't understood the magic of that day. The euphoria was a better variant of his usual habit of floating outside the world with his music, in the euphoria he floated but still he was half-connected to the world, he had power over it but it had no power over him. He now might have agreed with Odyssey and have traded a headache every second day for the euphoria of the other days or, at the least, he'd happily have scheduled a migraine every Wednesday and new music every Thursday.

Some of Dmitri's migraines were memorable, the first one he remembered from Amsterdam, the one after a lesson with *Mademoiselle* Meursault, the first one on arrival in Alabama, one with Linda in Manhattan, one in Vermont with Odyssey. He did not know whether they were memorable because of their severity or because of their circumstances. The one with Linda was the only one in his life that he did not finish, her codeine killed it before it put him to sleep. Linda, he thought, we left everything unfinished. Funny, he thought, the one with Linda was the only one he was sure was not followed by euphoria the next day. Or perhaps the euphoria was merely trumped by his joy in having Linda move in with him.

Dmitri usually cared nothing for his audiences, yet here was the one person in France he would love to have in his audience, and she could not get there. "You have a piano," Dmitri said, "I could play here." For almost no one else then living would he have offered.

"Have you never heard Debussy on a badly tuned piano, *Monsieur* Esterhaats? It is a horrible thing, any civilized government would make it a crime. It is much better just to drink your tea."

"I have tuned pianos all over France or I would never have played Debussy here. I have wrenches in my pocket."

"There are tuning forks somewhere – but you would not need them, would you?"

Dmitri tuned the piano and then he played. When he noticed *Mademoiselle* Meursault struggling to stand from her sofa, he went to help her up. She wished to walk over to the piano and to sit beside him on the bench as she had done in New York. With his help, she reached the bench.

"I apologize, my dear Esterhaats, but could you tighten my back brace so I may sit straight on the bench. Pull the laces tight."

In Dmitri's memory of her from before the war in New York, *Mademoiselle* Meursault sat magnificently straight on a bench, she did it as though she were at ease, as though it took no special effort. He'd suspected even then that it was a matter of cultural commitment and of character more than a matter of technique for playing the piano, although it added to the visual beauty of her playing. Clearly, her urge to sit straight now went beyond the demands of technique.

He played for a long time, playing pieces she mentioned. He did not notice how long, but afterwards, when he recalled the pieces he played, he realized it was the French half of all his six concerts here plus much of the rest of Debussy and Ravel solo piano. It must have been close to five hours. It ended when Dmitri noticed *Mademoiselle* Meursault's pained face. He lifted her and carried her back to her couch.

In a few minutes, someone came in and gave *Mademoiselle* Meursault her pills. It was a second maid, Dmitri supposed, she looked different from the earlier one.

"I'm sorry, I played too long," Dmitri said.

"No, don't be sorry, my dear Esterhaats. Debussy was a better pain killer than these," she said. "That was the nicest day I've had in a long time. *Mademoiselle* is going to bring out some cheese and wine." She smiled slyly, "But I'm not supposed to drink wine, so she'll bring champagne. You will not object?"

Dmitri broke up the bread into bite-size pieces and put various cheeses on several for *Mademoiselle* Meursault. She apologized that she would drink her champagne from a mug, and Dmitri asked if he could have one too. She would not allow it. "A mug cannot be clean enough for champagne, my Esterhaats. This one wants to be drunk cleanly."

Repeatedly he found himself studying the label of the champagne or the textures of the cheeses in order to let her struggle with her food and drink in privacy. From his perverse tendency to speak his thoughts as though they were part of the conversation, he idly read the date of the champagne. "1957."

"Yes, that was a very good year. For champagne and, I think, for Dmitri Esterhaats. I read very much about you that year."

It was not so good a year that he would have wanted to repeat it. But perhaps there were no years that good.

"You know, my dear Esterhaats," she said, "when Elaine Wolf said you were the best young Debussy interpreter in America she meant to be comparing you to me and she meant me to understand that. She liked to insult people. But you know, my Esterhaats, she failed, I was not insulted at all. I smiled at her when she said it, I even agreed with her, and she was the one who felt insulted, perhaps she thought her effort had been betrayed. And she did not even know where you got your Debussy! Such a betrayal. I had such great success with you that I almost decided to become a teacher. But then I thought, no, it would be a mistake. The success was yours, not mine, I would have been a failure as a teacher of most pianists."

Dmitri shook his head, he would not allow her to say such things without objection, but he lacked her easy grace and he did not gainsay her words. *Mademoiselle* Meursault reached out to place her knotted hand on his knee. Dmitri took her hand and held it for a long while.

"The maid is standing in the doorway," Dmitri said after a long silence. "I think she may want something."

"She is not a maid, she is a nurse, she must not be allowed to hear you call her a maid. She comes at the end of the afternoon. She wants to give me my hot salt bath before it is time for her to go." She signaled the nurse, who turned and left the doorway.

"May I help you walk?"

"No, my dear Esterhaats. She will bring the chair. You should let her take care of me now, I must let her and the doctor do their jobs or they will feel useless." She laughed. "It is I who am supposed to feel useless."

She offered her cheeks to his kisses. Then she put her knotted hands on his cheeks and smiled for him. "Thank you for my private concert, my dear Esterhaats. I have waited years for such a concert. I have such fond memories of your first concert for me."

Dmitri was painfully reluctant to leave. He knew that, when he did, *Mademoiselle* Meursault would enter the past of his Aunt Clara and his mother, where, although he would not forget about her, he would leave her alone and not bring up her memory, she would not be forgotten but also not often recalled. He did not wish to let her go there just yet, she was the last tie to his life when he still had the possibility of a life, she was nearly the last remaining person who seemed wholly forgiving to him. He sat too long beside her and now the wheelchair arrived. He kissed her hand a last time and stood to leave. He intended to be like Linda, he intended not to look back, he even thought to discipline his resolve as he walked in mourning to the door, but, as he closed the door, he caught sight of *Mademoiselle* Meursault rolling away from his life.

On one of his walks through Paris, Dmitri came across the lovely church where he and Linda had performed the memorial concert for Jerusalem Neimann. The main door was latched closed. On a whim, he went to the side door through which they'd entered for their performance. It was open and Dmitri went in and found a harpsichord on the dais. He sat and played Bach for a long while. During one piece, while he was too intent on the music to notice anything else, a priest grabbed his arm to stop him.

"You must not do this. Just who do you think you are?"

Perhaps because it was French, Dmitri listened too specifically to the actual words and he was startled by their insinuation. When he was challenged, his language became more articulate, as though he really knew French fluently but were normally reticent to speak it. He had once demolished provincial bureaucrats who blocked Linda's purposes, and one of them said, "You are from Paris." In his driving anger of that moment, he did not laugh as he did when he recalled the moment later. Now, to his blockheaded priest, he replied, "I *know* who I am, I do not *think* it."

"Well, it isn't good enough. You will leave immediately. What is your name?"

"I am Dmitri Esterhaats."

"I am a pianist, I know of Dmitri Esterhaats, you are not Dmitri Esterhaats, he would not be playing here."

French logic at high tide. Dmitri dared to disagree. "I played one of my greatest concerts here, with Linda Ney, the wonderful violinist. We played a memorial for Linda's brother, Jerusalem Neimann, whom the Nazis murdered." Why was he telling this man? The great, silent Esterhaats was telling his life's story to this incorrigibly dull, rude man.

"You are a *charlatan*."

Dmitri smiled. "Perhaps." He turned back to his keyboard to play an improvised *Marseillaise*, he and Linda had often performed it as an encore when Linda thought the audience was insufficiently responsive to their concerts, but the priest would not let him finish it now.

"In a church, *Monsieur*, the *Marseillaise*. Dmitri Esterhaats would not play the *Marseillaise*."

"I played it often when I was touring several years in France. The audiences always gave us a standing ovation when we played it."

"You are a *charlatan*. Who would schedule a memorial service for a Jerusalem Neimann in a Catholic church?"

"At that time, this church was a cultural institution, apparently it is no longer a cultural institution, but back then it had concerts, we were scheduled to play a concert, we turned it into a memorial, it was our last performance in France."

The priest looked stumped. "If you are not a *charlatan*, why was Neimann murdered?"

"I don't know."

The priest returned to triumph. "You toured with his sister and you do not know?"

"Miss Ney did not know." In truth, Dmitri had no idea whether she knew. "Perhaps those who murdered him did not know. After he was murdered, Miss Ney's family escaped from Paris to New York."

The priest stood for a moment without speaking as though he were struggling with a decision. Finally, he seemed to decide and he crossed himself. "You may play, but you must leave before six." He turned to go and turned back, "Please," he gestured at the harpsichord. "But no *Marseillaise*."

Shortly before six, Dmitri stood to leave and he was met at the door by the priest. "Will you come again tomorrow, *Monsieur* Esterhaats? Please."

"I'll try."

"You may come through this door. I hope you will be here at four. Please."

Dmitri had planned to walk on the other side of the Seine tomorrow, perhaps along the *Champs Elysées*, but he came back to the harpsichord as invited. At four the priest came in with an elderly man, whom he introduced as *Monsieur* Fischer. Fischer changed to English, which he spoke elegantly and with only a slight accent. "Let us sit down there, Mister Esterhaats."

The priest left and Dmitri sat with Fischer, who took a folder of papers from his briefcase. "Jerusalem Neimann," he said, "was doubly unfortunate. He was a German Jew and therefore eligible for deportation, not eligible for French protection. But worse than that, he happened that day to be in the home of another German Jewish family long sought and at last successfully found. The Germans claimed they were politically active and that they were using their baroque ensemble as a cover for their meetings. In one respect perhaps Neimann was fortunate. In fighting to protest his capture and the capture of his friends, he was fatally beaten, or so the Neimanns heard from another German Jewish family living nearby. That witness thought Neimann wanted to die. He had often said he would never let the Germans take him alive because his death would release the Neimanns from concern for him so they might flee from France. They went to Geneva and then to New York. They settled here," he offered Dmitri a sheet on which, among other things, there was an address in the Bronx not far from where Bartók lived, the Bartók whom Linda found so difficult to play. "You must know Miss Ney from this address."

It was odd that Dmitri learned of Linda's earlier address only now. He wondered whether she'd still lived there when they began to play together before she moved into his miserable apartment in the Bowery. He did not know how to react to such knowledge now. There were even the names of Linda's parents, Oskar and Sarah, whom he'd never met. He believed he'd never heard her father's name before.

"As you know, her parents were music teachers."

"How do you know all this?" Dmitri asked.

"We try to find records on all the Jews who were jailed or killed or deported. We do not want them to be forgotten. We also keep records of all memorials to them. We have no record of your memorial. Could you tell me about it?"

He slowly worked out the date and told the program.

"You remember the program, Mr. Esterhaats?"

"Yes."

"You are sure you are right?"

Dmitri could not understand that question. He could not double check his own memory to test it – what more could he say than he'd said? "That's what I remember."

"That was nearly two decades ago."

Putting it that way made it sound too distant, decades and centuries sounded ominous though they were merely so many years in series. "Linda kept our programs. Maybe she still has it. I'm sure she would be happy to send it to you if she could find it. The printed program was wrong because we changed it for the memorial. We took out the modern music, Bartók or Debussy maybe, and put in more Bach."

"Ah, I see," Fischer said. He pulled out a copy of the program for the performance. The insert on the memorial and the changes was missing. "Father Arlesian found this. He even found a poster. It is wrong too."

Dmitri took the program. He remembered it as more substantial. It was merely a single stiff sheet of paper folded in the middle and poorly mimeographed. It even had his name misspelled. It included pieces by Bartók and Prokofiev that they hadn't played. As he looked at the program, Dmitri became slightly perplexed that Fischer had it already. "Why do you ask me questions to which you already know the answers?"

Fischer reached to stroke Dmitri's arm and leaned intimately close to him as an East European might do. Unlike New Yorkers, Dmitri did not flinch from such physical closeness, that much of his Russian background had survived many decades in New York. "Forgive me, Mister Esterhaats. I do not distrust you. I distrust the evidence of the world. Some of it is terrible, more terrible than a human can imagine. I cannot believe the evidence I find but still I try to get it right. You have helped me get it right, you have given better evidence than printed posters and programs. That is all we can do for Jerusalem Neimann, get it right what happened and get his memorial right. You and Miss Ney have done more than I can do. I try to do what I can."

"Thank you. I'm sure Miss Ney would be grateful."

They looked at each other in silence for a moment as Fischer leaned back again.

"That is all?" Dmitri asked.

"I know a little more. Linda Neimann went to an English language school already as a little girl in Berlin, her parents probably wanted her to be ready to leave Europe without a lot of pain. Jerusalem Neimann taught music in her English language school here in the *rue de Vaugirard*. Most of the teachers were native English speakers until the war drove them away. The school closed when its Jewish teachers and pupils began to disappear and its French headmaster was arrested for opposition to the Nazis. That was about a month before Neimann was killed. I taught astronomy in another school that closed at the same time." He shook his head. "At that time, astronomy. Already then I could not believe the evidence I saw all around us."

"I didn't know Jerusalem Neimann," Dmitri said, "I don't know what kind of person he was. Can you tell me that?"

"I cannot tell you much. These papers don't tell things like that. I met him in Berlin, before we all came to Paris. I didn't know him, he was younger than I. But I met him. He played violin in a small ensemble in a strange cabaret that had political satire and classical music, usually baroque, I think. That's where I met him. He was about twenty. I think I saw his sister, she was young, maybe ten or twelve, she stood beside him and clung to him throughout an entire evening, even while he performed. I wish I knew more. All I can really say of what he was like is that he was very tender with his sister and she seemed to idolize him – or maybe she was just shy in that noisy room full of adults and smoke. I don't know anything bad about him, but I probably wouldn't say it if I did. We who survived should idolize all of them."

Fischer arranged to deliver to Dmitri's hotel a large envelope of what information he had on the Neimanns, and Dmitri walked back to the building that had brought Linda to ruin during their last days in Paris together. It was now a law office. He entered and was stopped by the receptionist. He tried to explain without saying too much.

"The war was long ago, *Monsieur*, we know nothing about the building then. We have been here only twelve years."

"May I see some of the building?"

"No, *Monsieur*. These are law offices, some of them are busy, they cannot be interrupted. You may write a request to the manager. Perhaps he will let you visit later."

"I must return to the United States Monday. I could not do it later."

"*Monsieur*, it is a matter that is out of my hands."

Dmitri smiled at her as he conceded his defeat, "No, it is in your hands, but it is out of mine." He spread his hands palms up before her. He recalled Jelly's definition of the French bureaucrat: The bureaucrat has no power, the bureaucrat has only the power to deny any reasonable request. With his palms still turned up, Dmitri said, "You have the power to deny any reasonable request."

"Are you American? Your accent is not American, it is almost French."

Dmitri took out his passport to show her. She opened it to read, "New York," in an accent that beautified even as it mangled the peculiarly un-French words. "A great city, I want to visit New York. Kiev, you were born in Kiev?"

"Yes."

"Are you a lawyer?"

"No, a pianist."

"The hands," she said. She returned his passport. "Why do you wish to see this building? There are hundreds that are better."

"Many years ago I loved someone very much. She cried when she saw this building – see? over there, across the street, she stood near that tree and cried. Her brother died here." The receptionist was like the priest, Father Arlesian, Dmitri could speak to her freely and tell her things he'd never told anyone. Even to say to this anonymous woman that he once loved Linda very much made him wish Linda were here beside him now, made him sense her even in her absence.

"I will do the talking, *Monsieur* Esterhaats," the receptionist said as she put her finger up as though to seal his lips, "remember, it is in my hands. But you must make no further reasonable requests."

She asked a colleague to answer the phone and to watch the door and then she took Dmitri into what must have been the formal sitting room of the mansion. "This is our meeting room. Sometimes we only meet here to drink coffee."

Dmitri could imagine a meeting with Jerusalem Neimann present, the meeting that led to his arrest. This bright, airy room, with its pastel colors and graceful furnishings seemed too elegant and restful even for Paris, it was autonomous, it floated free of the local world, it was without conflict or pain. If he'd been asked to define civility, Dmitri could have done no better than to attempt it while standing in this room. The rest of the building was of interest primarily in that it was massive, with many rooms on five floors. Life in this building must have been gracious and pacific, it seemed incongruous that the Gestapo had once invaded it, that violence had torn a family from it, that Jerusalem Neimann had been fatally beaten here.

"What was here before the law office?" Dmitri asked.

"For many years it was a music school, I think."

It made eminently good sense that it should have become a music school, the grand conference room must then have been the recital room, a grand piano would have stood at one end. As they came back downstairs, Dmitri asked if he could return to the ground floor meeting room, where he stood in silence for a long while. He imagined himself sitting at the piano and Jerusalem Neimann and Linda Ney standing before it with their violins.

He and Linda were about thirty, Jerusalem a decade older. Linda and Jerusalem often exchanged glances as they played. They were playing Bach, spinning their disparate sounds into a glorious whole, a thread through time, a fugue of their lives. Jerusalem chose their pieces and Dmitri and Linda played whatever he said was next. Dmitri paid no attention to the audience, perhaps they were only the family of the house.

Although it seemed glorious, full, and stately, the vision could not have lasted more than a minute. When he sensed that the receptionist was fidgeting behind him, Dmitri turned to leave.

"There must have been a piano here then," the receptionist said. "There is none now, or I would let you play so that you could say you have gone to Paris to play."

Dmitri smiled. "Oh, I have come to play in Paris. I'll play again tomorrow night."

"Do you play Russian music?"

"No, not tomorrow night. It will be Debussy, Ravel, Ives, and Bartók. I am part of a cultural exchange, I represent American culture." Dmitri almost laughed as he said it, it was incongruous, and yet in its incongruity it was somehow right, he did represent American culture.

The receptionist shared his smile. "And the American way to do that is to appropriate the best of other cultures."

Dmitri would have liked to think she meant him, but he knew she meant Debussy and Ravel. "Would you like a ticket?" he asked.

"Is it possible? I could not go without my husband."

Dmitri used her telephone to call Bonfleur to arrange two tickets for her. "Do you like that music?" he asked.

"Debussy and Ravel I love, I don't know Ives, but Bartók I hate."

Dmitri smiled. "Then I will play a Bartók encore and give you a second chance to like him. Unless the audience doesn't like my concert, then I can't do an encore, it will be out of my hands." Again he turned up his palms for her. "So if you are convinced about Bartók, you should hiss immediately at the end and the audience will probably join you in driving me from the stage. Just remember, you have to start hissing before anyone else starts cheering or clapping. The first loud reaction carries the whole audience."

She shook her head with a suppressed smile.

"It's true," Dmitri insisted. "In one concert, someone hissed during the first piece I played. Almost no one clapped at the end of the piece, and at the end of the concert they actually booed. At the break, the manager asked me if I wanted to end it there but I wouldn't quit. That concert was no different otherwise from dozens that have required a half hour or more of encores, in fact, some of those were much worse performances. But they booed me off the stage and I've never been invited back there. I'd like to find the guy who hissed and ask him what he thought was wrong. It was great."

"And you want me to give you a great time tomorrow night? But my husband will be there, *Monsieur* Esterhaats, I will have to be well behaved."

As he was about to leave, she thought to ask where the concert was.

"At the *Opéra*, at 8:30."

"At the *Opéra*? Ah, yes, I understand," she said, as she almost bowed to him, "an exchange of *high* culture."

"Your tickets will be at the box office. For *Madam* Payot." He thought of them as for *Mademoiselle* Meursault, to whom he'd asked Bonfleur to dedicate the concert.

The day after the concert, Dmitri walked past other addresses in the Fischer file on Jerusalem Neimann. He visited Linda's school in the *rue Vaugirard* and he found the small hotel that he and Linda had visited – according to Fischer's notes it was Linda's family's home in Paris, as he'd supposed while visiting it with her. He did not enter the building but only walked around the area for a long while, discovering that the neighborhood streets were full of inexpensive hotels not far from the Eiffel Tower, hotels that seemed to have grown seedier since he and Linda were there – or perhaps he'd grown less seedy. He finally ended his tour when it struck him odd that he was more interested in where Linda had lived in Paris than in where his family had lived in Amsterdam.

He sat in one of their *cafés* and had tea, as though he were a caricature of his Russian past, and he rummaged through the envelope of papers Fischer had prepared for him. He decided to send the packet to Linda when he returned, it was not so much that he wanted to know no more of her past, but that he thought it wrong for him to seek out what she'd never told him. He wrote a note to Linda on a nearly blank page and then, after sealing the envelope, he rubbed his eyes and wiped his face with his hands. There in the mirror beside him he was startled to see Edith Piaf, who was singing while polishing glasses behind the bar. He wondered whether she was the same Edith Piaf he'd once seen with Linda, the one whom Linda had joined in song until she glared at Linda and shut her up. It was time for Dmitri to shut her up, too, to stop her from talking to him from the distant past, to stop being a part of every reminder, of every mood. Perhaps it was just a problem with Paris, which he could only see through Linda's vision, but he seemed not to have the resolve to tell even the residual Linda in his head to leave him alone, to let go.

As soon as Dmitri returned from Paris, he was to go to dinner with Clara. She called to remind him. "Dress very well, it's a nice restaurant." Clara seemed strange over the phone, distant, perhaps nervous. He'd never known her nervous before. She couldn't be nervous for herself, it must be for him, she must have what she feared was bad news for him. As he contemplated that, he began to distance himself from the evening, to observe it rather than live it, to let it run its course without participation from him.

At dinner Clara was uncharacteristically irritable.

"This is very nice," Dmitri said, "I've never been here before."

"Dmitri, you've never been anywhere before."

He grinned. "I was just in Paris, Lyons, Cherbourg, Marseilles, and Toulouse, so I'd disagree but I'm sure you'd make me wrong." He was startled at that moment to recall Linda's saying, "Correct you? I'm going to *destroy* you," for his wrong views of Schubert twenty years ago. That was an odd association from too long ago. Why should I think of Linda? he wondered. This is Clara.

"No Dmitri. You've been everywhere on tour, but you've hardly been anywhere in fact. When we travel to play duets, we walk for hours. We'd do the same anywhere, we even do it in New York. It doesn't matter where you are, that's all you really want. You pick restaurants at random when you're out but mostly you suggest we eat in our hotel. Well, that's going to change. I'll plan the trips in future. And I'll certainly choose our restaurants."

"I like that, I'd be happy for you to choose, you're very good at it. Does that mean we'll have more trips?"

Clara blushed. "Of course, I . . . I'll always want to do piano duets and four hands with you, Dmitri . . . I . . ."

"Hey, hey, Clara. I was just teasing."

Dmitri sensed that Linda was pervading the evening. She and Clara had played a Mozart concert while he was in France. It was partly Linda who sat at the table with him now. And with that thought, Dmitri knew why Clara was nervous. He realized she was not merely irritable, she was mad at him for what she had to tell him, she didn't want it to be true, and she held him responsible for the bad news.

"See that man coming?" Dmitri said. "I think it's time for you to choose our wine. Or will you choose champagne?"

"Which would you prefer, Dmitri?"

"I thought you said you'd do our choosing in future."

"It's just . . . well," she raised her hands in great irritation as though to hurl something at him. "The future's come so fast."Clara needed training for the future. She stumbled for a couple of minutes before capitulating to the easy choice: "I think we'll have champagne."

"Yes m'am." the *sommelier* said as he turned the list to the pages of champagne.

Dmitri could not let hapless Clara suffer any longer, he asked whether they had the champagne *Mademoiselle* Meursault had served.

The *sommelier's* eyes widened, and then he nodded a slight bow and said, "Very well."

Of course, Dmitri thought, Colette Meursault probably served the best.

"Is there a year?" the *sommelier* asked.

"1957, if you have it, *s'il vous plai*t." He wondered what he'd say if they didn't have it.

"Of course."

Clara looked mystified. This was not her Dmitri. "How did you do that?"

"That's my favorite champagne, especially the 1957," he teased. "That was a very good year for champagne."

Clara shook her head. She seemed to doubt either him or herself. After the champagne, she said, "Dmitri, I have to be serious for a minute."

Dmitri laughed. "Okay, be serious."

"Dmitri, please. You too."

He struggled to become serious. It was not a mood he could bring on easily while facing beautiful Clara, even if she was grimly irritated with him.

"I want to talk about Linda."

Now Dmitri was serious, the smile left his eyes, his face turned still. He started to say he knew, it was okay, it really wasn't bad, but he let Clara tell him her news of Linda.

"Dmitri, I'm sorry, I don't know why I should be here right now, but I agreed to."

With a love of five years and forlorn afterthoughts of nearly twenty more, Dmitri understood. "It's okay," he said. "She was always a bit afraid to face an audience. You might think she'd expect me to be an especially hard audience just now, although in truth I've always been her best audience."

"Dmitri, what I'm trying to say, it's not that, it's . . . Dmitri, I don't know how to say it." She held her hands up, her angular fingers seemed to be ferociously gripping something imaginary, perhaps it was his throat, Dmitri thought. "Dmitri," she said very loudly, "stop looking at me for a minute, you always look straight in my eyes, you hardly even blink, how can I say anything?"

"I'm sorry, Clara, I'll just look at your hands or my champagne or something."

She said nothing.

Dmitri tried his quietest tones as though he were coaxing her through a difficult passage in Prokofiev. "You can just say it, Clara, don't worry about how to say it, it couldn't take more than four or five words." He wanted to say he could even say it for her, but he had the sense not to.

"Okay." She closed her eyes for a minute and then opened them to look at him. "Linda is getting married."

See, only four words, he wanted to say. "Yes, I know."

"You know? Who told you?"

He didn't have a proper answer. "You did."

"Yes, of course I did, but that was just now . . . I thought you were saying you already knew, I don't know what . . . When did you know?"

"I don't know exactly. But this whole evening you're more Linda than Clara. You're irritated with me the way she sometimes was, you're even nervous, you could only have learned that from Linda. It seemed you must be bearing bad news for her that she was afraid to bear. They shoot messengers who bring bad news. She must be using you to tell me the way you get me to ask your mother to bend the rules for you, Linda knows I won't shoot you no matter what her message. So if she has something that dangerous to tell, what else could it be? But it's not so bad, Clara. She should've got married by now. Twenty years ago I would have married her. But that didn't happen." He shrugged.

"Dmitri, you would have married her four or five years ago, I remember finding the album you did with her, it was just in a stack of records in your cabinet, you hadn't listened to it, I didn't know anything about her but I knew you would've married her then. Mama and Papa never met her but her name makes them sad, it kills dinner conversation if I say I'm playing with her. They can't say anything nice so they don't say anything. Mama adores you, she thinks you're an angel. Papa too, only he thinks you're a bit incompetent for an angel. They've gone to all my concerts before but they had excuses not to go to my concerts with Linda. They think you would still marry Linda – I don't know what they would do then, they would have to meet her and be nice to her."

"Maybe I would have married her four or five years ago. Maybe I would even have married her when we played together for Lincoln Center."

"Maybe even last year."

"I don't think so, but okay, maybe even last year, I don't really know."

"Would you marry her now?"

"Someone else is going to marry her now."

"I know that, Dmitri. Remember? I just told you. But what I'm asking is *would* you?"

"I'm not very good at figuring out what I'd do *if*. I usually stick to what to do *when*."

In a silence while they ate, Dmitri recalled thinking to tell the Linda in his head to go away, to let go her hold on him. Now, it seemed, she might, there was evident finality in her getting married. He was not entirely pleased at that thought but he was relieved.

"I think she's making a mistake," Clara said. "She's doing it to make life comfortable, not to make it great."

"Have you met him?"

"No."

"So how do you come to think she's making a mistake?"

"I know you. And I've heard her talk about you. She sounds almost like Mama, except that she knows a lot more about you. She's even taught me things you never taught me."

"What?" Dmitri felt slightly insulted.

"Things she said you did. I asked her, if that was so, why didn't you teach me? She said you might not teach some things because you didn't even know you did them. You dot quarter notes sometimes to let the base and treble drift apart and then you bring them back together as though they were separate strands of a fugue. Linda thinks you might've got that from jazz but she also thinks you might've just discovered it yourself. I never even heard you play jazz, Dmitri. Separating the base and treble makes good sense with Debussy, Linda thinks, but you even do it with some Bartók. You did that when you were just sitting at the piano and playing. You would do the same piece several times and eventually you'd turn it into a base-treble fugue. I've never seen you do that – maybe because you're never just playing when I'm around. I'm the one who's playing and you're helping me. And you never taught me to check the tune of a piano. Linda says you did that hundreds of times while you were together and you did it incredibly fast and with dozens of patterns. You probably never did it with me because you always keep your pianos in tune, there's no need to check when I'm there. She says both those things are things you never were taught, you just happened to do them to avoid endless repetition. She thinks maybe you were never taught anything, you just did it all."

"There she's definitely wrong. I worked with teachers for years to learn everything – methods, styles, everything."

"Linda says you never had a real teacher."

"I had lots of teachers. In fact, I just saw one of the best of them all in Paris, Colette Meursault."

"She was one of the best of them all, of all the teachers you had? Dmitri, listen to what you're saying, Colette Meursault was a pianist, a performer, a *minor* performer, she was not a teacher. And you saw her for only a few weeks, Linda said. Colette Meursault never had a real student."

He smiled radiantly. "She had one. She taught Dmitri Esterhaats to understand Debussy. *That* was a major achievement."

"Linda is right. Even with your facts, it's clear that Linda is right to say you were not really connected, you weren't well taught, you just did it all in some weird way. If Colette Meursault was one of the very best teachers you ever had, you never had good ones."

Dmitri was perplexed. "How does Linda know all that? How does she know anything about Colette Meursault?"

"Not from you, Dmitri, you know that very well. She had to find out other ways."

That was odd, he'd just spent his last few days in Paris finding out about Linda in other ways.

"Nothing to say?" Clara said. "Damn. How did I know that?"

The mood of the evening had been building too consistently for him to be surprised by her tone now, but still he was surprised at the whole evening. For years she'd despised Linda and now that she'd changed her views of Linda, it seemed she had to revise her views of Dmitri. Clara was genuinely angry with him, she had never before been angry with him, he was astonished and fascinated to see her this way. She was angry with him for letting Linda get away, for reducing his life to what it was. Perhaps part of her anger was even for what he'd done to Linda, reducing her life to less than it should be, leading her to marry for a comfortable rather than a great life.

"One last thing about Linda, Dmitri. Why do you think she wanted to do Lincoln Center with you?"

He shrugged. "It was a lot of money. I don't know."

Clara's face went through contortions that brought tears welling in her eyes. That was the influence of the alcohol, Dmitri thought. She put the palms of her hands against her eyes and said nothing for a minute or two. Finally, she wiped her eyes, wiped her hands on her napkin, and shook her head slightly as she spoke. "Don't you think it was possible Linda thought you might get back together, Dmitri?"

He was confused. "We did."

"Not to perform, Dmitri." She reached out to seize his wrist in her strong grip. "To live. To live, Dmitri, to live. Maybe the offer from Lincoln Center was just an opportunity. Maybe Linda was finally ready."

Dmitri began to reason through that history, he put things together that fit what he'd just heard, it was coherent and plausible, it was even interesting to sense the revisions going on in his mind, as though things were being rearranged and corrected, as Odyssey constantly rearranged and corrected her music even as he played it for her, clusters of notes were shaken and compacted and then moved to other places and the whole piece was altered. Linda had revised her views of her parents' hatred of each other and had then reinterpreted their past actions to fit her new view. Dmitri too could reconstruct the past to fit a new interpretation.

He gazed at himself from a distance and took account of what he'd done since Lincoln Center. A lot of teaching, including summers in Vermont, and several concerts with Clara felt warm in his memory, but there was little else. He hadn't even really thought much about Linda, though he'd worked with Clara to prepare her for her second duo with Linda and thought about her then, and he'd stumbled across her past in Paris and had thought about her very intensely for a week or so then. Perhaps something as trivial as her worry that he had the flu had changed their lives. And before that, perhaps his slow-wittedness at Lincoln Center had changed their lives, his failure to seek Linda out for dinner, or playing for fun, or being her continuo as she rehearsed for orchestral performances, those were a grand wasted opportunity. Clara had tears for his missed opportunity, but he had none, he had hardly any feeling for it, it was merely gone.

As they toyed over dessert and the last of their champagne, Clara returned obliquely to Linda. "You've never had a child, Dmitri. You'd love a child, I know."

"Yes, I think I would. But that didn't happen."

"Poor Dmitri."

"Hey, wait a minute. There's no poor Dmitri. I don't regret one tiny bit that I never had a child."

"I don't believe that."

"It's true."

"How could it be? Dmitri. How could it be true? That's idiotic."

"It's not idiotic. If I'd had a child, I probably wouldn't have spent so much time with you. Even if I'd only had a wife – there's just not that much time. Clearly it would be impossible to regret something that would've prevented my working with you all these years, I wouldn't even be who I am right now if that were changed, to regret not having a child would be to regret even being here, as though I wished somebody else were here instead. Who could do that? – that's impossible."

"Not impossible, Dmitri. Illogical maybe. But not impossible." In fact, she seemed to regret what he'd done, though her life would have been radically changed if he hadn't done what she regretted.

Dmitri recalled a younger Clara, their first time in Vermont, where she said she could not imagine life as a twin, it would have changed too much. And now she wanted him not only to imagine but to regret not having an even more radically different life. How had she learned illogical regret in the meantime?

"Illogical is as good as impossible, Clara," Dmitri said. He said it gently, as though he were instructing her in how to ripple through a phrase of Debussy.

Clara tossed back the last of her champagne and then demonstratively clunked down her empty glass. She was tipsy but still resolute as she looked hard and straight at him. "For you, Dmitri, damn it all, that might even be true."

11

Dmitri Esterhaats

Clara left a message with his doorman for Dmitri to meet her and Linda at the Carnegie Deli, across from Carnegie Hall. Clara was like Jelly, she instinctively knew how to make sure he got the message, she managed her world as though by natural talent. But she went too far, she gave him explicit instructions on how to find the Carnegie Deli, he'd walked past it hundreds of times on his childhood and later walks through Manhattan, he'd even eaten there with Anton Staebli many years earlier and once with Ben Schein when Schein carefully dodged helping Dmitri as an agent soon after Dmitri and Sofia Milano had split. When he performed at Carnegie Hall or went to others' performances there, he sometimes noticed that the deli had longer lines than the Hall. Clara had long ago taken on a role as parent to him in certain matters, now she was generalizing the role, making it less parental but more extensive and even intrusive, although Dmitri still found it pleasing and funny, he could not suppress a smile when he realized she was doing it, and as he read her instructions of how to find the Carnegie Deli, he smiled, although, in truth, he smiled almost every time he thought of Clara or saw her or read one of her notes of instruction to him.

Linda, ever punctual but for their final concert in Paris, was already at a table when Dmitri arrived at the deli. She stood to let him kiss her cheeks in the extraordinarily formal French style, so formal it was a parody of intimacy. Her cheeks even flattened and lost their lovely curve as she turned her face away from him once to the left, once to the right for his kisses.

"You picked the place," she said.

Dmitri was unsure whether she meant it as a query, a challenge, or a statement of a mere matter of fact. She was a natural violinist, a master of refined nuances of tone and meaning, nuances that often passed Dmitri's pianist's ears, so attuned to the precision of tones that lacked all ambiguity. "No, maybe Clara. She told me to meet here."

"That's good."

"You don't like it here?"

"This is a gossip's place. It's almost as bad as that bar farther up where musicians and their camp followers hang out. I guess it's getting better now, there are so many people here because it's famous for its food." She looked around. "A lot of heavy people. Do you suppose they got that way because they eat the gigantic servings here? or they come here because, being so big, they need the gigantic servings?"

Dmitri assumed he was not meant to answer that, he sensed that Linda was in a raspy mood, and anything he said might go wrong anyway. He started to go behind her to sit beside her at the table, but she turned to him and gave him a quizzical look.

"What is it?" he asked.

"Why don't you sit across from me instead of beside me, then I can see you."

Dmitri balked for a moment, then he did as ordered through her grudging effort to invite, to be graceful, her "Why don't you?," her perennial substitute for "Do." She was trying to control him, as she always did when she was not in control of her own life, telling him where to sit, how to look at her. He wanted to say so, but he didn't want to irritate her, she probably needed warmth, not accusations. He should not be second guessing his every word, he should not be trying to read her as though his life of the moment hung from her sensibilities, he should forget about her mood and just talk. But he began to think of how he would say it if he did say it, and then, as though that were merely an extension of figuring out the best way, as he sat down across from her, he said it. "You try to manage me when you can't manage yourself."

"I know," she said. "I'm sorry."

Now he wanted to say, Good lord, but it might really irritate her to imply that he thought she didn't have the capacity for self criticism.

"I used to do that only to you," she said. "Now I'm more generous, I do it to anyone handy. Do you suppose that means I've grown? Besides, I read somewhere that men who can manage men manage men who can only manage things. Maybe it works for women too, maybe not in my lifetime but in some future lifetime, Clara's maybe."

"It probably works for women too. But it won't do you much good to manage men who can't even manage things."

"You'd think I'd know that by now," she said in her tone of universal pessimism.

"What's out of control?"

"Me – you just said it."

"How are you out of control?" He wanted to add that she was one of the most in-control people he knew. Then, as though such effrontery were a new style, because he thought it, he said it, "You're the most in-control person around."

"Dmitri, use your brain, why do you think anyone is really in control? Just because they're afraid of going out of control, you don't have that problem, maybe you wouldn't understand it."

"Maybe I would. Try to knock it into my thick head and see. How are you out of control just now?"

"I don't know what to do. I know what I want to do. But it seems dishonest to want to do it, because I didn't want to do it before."

"That makes it a lot clearer."

"Careful, Dmitri." Her face turned grim, she closed her eyes. "Damn," she said. "Goddamn it."

He left the moment to her.

"Okay. Maybe I should say before Clara gets here, she wanted us to tell you together, but I'm the one who should do it. Listen, Dmitri, and please don't interrupt."

"Okay."

"That was an interruption. Here's what . . . No. You know what you wanted more than anything, or that's what you said, you said you wanted more than anything for us to stay on tour forever. We could solo with orchestras when that worked out but otherwise just tour, we could maybe live some of the time in Paris, some in New York. And you know what I wanted more than anything. I didn't want to tour or perform in a duo, I wanted orchestras and records. Do you remember that?"

He could never forget it, but to say so now would be an interruption.

"Dmitri, I'm sorry. I don't know how to say any of this, I'm just so sorry. You were right. The duo is right for me too. It is still the best thing I have ever done."

Dmitri had too many reactions to gain control of any of them, he had too little mastery of the moment to know whether to feel elated or distressed, both urges, for elation and distress, must come from somewhere in the past, the prospect of Linda's wanting to be in a duo was too late in coming to affect urges of the present.

"When we were together, there were two reasons for wanting to play with orchestras and to make records. One of those was that was what I thought I wanted, to be the solo violinist with all those people performing behind me. The other was that I thought that would get us more money. Money isn't a problem anymore. Jack has more than we can spend."

Dmitri smiled at her. Her 'we' had changed its content in that account as it had in her life.

"No, Dmitri. I'm not there yet. Don't smile. I don't know what to say. I want to form a duo with Clara. I know it isn't fair." She reached across the table to put her hand on his. "I know that, believe me. But understand me, please, Dmitri. I couldn't do it any other way. There's Jack, I can't . . ."

Because she could not find further words, he felt free to interrupt. The moment was too complicated for anything but a quip, something he could say without thinking or connecting words to himself. "You could call it Ney-Esterhaats II."

"Clara says it would have to be Ney-Esterhaats 1 1/2."

He'd been topped before he quipped by someone who was not even there. He could see and hear Clara saying it, she filled his head with her presence, she was laughing, but she wasn't laughing with him, she wasn't grabbing him to swirl him around or to hug him, he was not there, she was laughing without him. Finally, Dmitri's feelings were organized. The two women had obviously already worked it out. Now they wanted, or Linda wanted, not to get help in working it out but to get his okay on what she would do anyway. Dmitri felt profound sadness and he wondered whether he'd be sad if Clara had told him of the plans instead. Perhaps not, he thought. But it would have been cheating for Linda to let Clara handle Dmitri in this moment, and Linda had acted with her occasional audacity to take the moment herself.

"I'm sorry, Dmitri."

"Don't be sorry. The past is past."

"The past is never past."

"Clara will be wonderful for you."

"I know. I'm almost jealous of her. When I think what my life was like at her age. She's ten years ahead. We were still struggling at thirty. Remember? When we played the memorial for Ginette Neveu in Paris, we were almost Ginette's age and we were on the edge of bankruptcy. Ginette's dying saved us, it gave us a big audience for the first time, they came for her, not for us, but that still made our Paris agent take us seriously, her dying let us struggle on long enough to get a career. Clara will never be filler for provincial music series that can't attract bigger names, for five years we were just filler. Clara's already played Carnegie Hall, she's booked with the

Philadelphia symphony – that was our beginning."

Dmitri let pass that playing with the Philadelphia symphony was in fact their end.

"She's booked with Boston, Seattle, San Francisco . . . and Giorgio just got Chicago to sign her." At last she smiled just slightly, she even hinted at laughter.

The mood had changed completely, she'd got past her burden of telling him, and now Linda would soon be at her best. Dmitri smiled with her or at her or for her, or perhaps all three. For the first time since seeing her sitting distracted at this table, he was glad to be looking at her, to be with her, even if perhaps he was only along for the momentary ride.

Linda smiled back at him, a bit quizzically. "If they weren't scheduled so far ahead," she said, "Bernstein would probably put her on with New York tomorrow. She started the way he did, filling in at Carnegie Hall for someone who was ill. Only Clara fits more naturally than Bernstein or than you and I, she was better dressed."

"Better dressed?" He was startled at the perversity of the thought, he wondered what it could mean – Clara was better dressed than Dmitri would have been had he played? The remark seemed out of context, lunatic, as though Linda had slipped from one conversation into another as she'd sometimes slipped from one piece into another while playing, as though a particular chord or *pizzicato* were a doorway that connected two pieces, as though her mind were passing through and taking the moment along, taking it from him if he was not quick enough to join her in the passage.

"On such short notice," Linda answered, "Bernstein didn't have a tuxedo and black tie, just a business suit, he looked ridiculous. I think it was even brown tweed or something equally absurd. Clara certainly didn't look ridiculous. I think she was the most beautiful person I've ever seen on stage. Her accidental debut at Carnegie Hall. "

Visions of Linda and Clara flashed through Dmitri's mind. He couldn't judge which was more beautiful. Linda had the advantage of standing free and clear with her violin and, as though to underscore her own point that Clara was far ahead of them in her career, the advantage of age.

"She's done so much better," Linda concluded, elliptically, wistfully.

"That's just Tolstoy."

"What? *That's* Dmitri Esterhaats: That's just Tolstoy," she repeated with an air of contempt. "I've read almost all of Tolstoy. Where does he say anything relevant to her success?"

"He says history is not made by Napoleons. Napoleons are made by history. We came out of our time, Clara comes out of hers."

"You are a fatalist," Dmitri.

"Giorgio thinks I'm an optimist, I always assume everything will work out fine."

"Maybe, but you're also a fatalist, you figure it doesn't matter what you do, it will just happen."

"That's why it will all work out fine."

"Dmitri," she shook her head and smiled, "Dmitri, Dmitri."

"Clara does that a lot, you two should get along very well."

It looked as though she might be biting her tongue to suppress another Dmitri, Dmitri, Dmitri.

"So money is no problem any more?" he asked.

She shook her head.

"Odyssey Deneuve is married to a rich stock manager," he said. "She says that means when she blows up she can smash a gold plated banana – that gives a special satisfaction."

"God, she needs to do something after writing that music."

He laughed. "That sonata was a bit arduous for you?"

"I had to *glissando* almost clear off the stage and then turn somersaults to get back, stand on my head, and pluck my G-string before retuning half a tone down for all those plosives. And that was just the opening phrase. How many composers have to tell you how to dress to play their music?"

"I didn't notice the G-string," Dmitri said, "I must've been too involved with my piano. Too bad."

"I shouldn't say it, but that's the story of your life, Dmitri. Anyway, Odyssey's instructions weren't completely clear. All her notation said was 'Pluck your magic twanger.' It didn't even say how many times. What the hell is that?"

"What was what?" Clara Esterhaats said, as she walked up to their table.

Dmitri reached out to lead her over to his side of the table where he could hug her and make sure she sat beside him. Clara slyly slipped past him to keep him sitting across from Linda. He caught the attention of a waiter, saying, "Three flutes and a bottle of champagne please. We have to toast the world's greatest duo, Ney-Esterhaats *II*." He wanted immediately to put Clara at ease if she was nervous about telling him about the duo and to give Linda credit for her taking up the burden of telling him.

"French or American?" the waiter asked.

"French," Linda said.

Clara sat. "Thank you, Dmitri. I run a little late and everything's done, you don't even need me."

"You miss the point. We both need you. We compete for your time."

Clara's face turned radiant. "Call me anywhere anytime you want to do piano duos or four hands."

Dmitri lifted his finger to admonish her. "Since when? I couldn't even get you to go to Paris to do duos with me."

"You have to work a little on timing, some people are better organized and faster with their invitations. But we're going to do it. We just have to let Giorgio in on the plans, okay? I'm even going to try to talk you into recording some with me." She shrank back and lifted her hands as though to protect against the impending onslaught.

"Good luck," Linda said in a pessimistic tone.

"You were talking about Odyssey when I came in. Are you working on something new for her?"

"Never, never, never," Linda said.

"That's Odyssey's new concerto for violin and circus organ."

"It's never, Dmitri, never."

"Oh, too bad," Clara said, "she loved how you did her sonata at Lincoln Center. She said she would write for you guys at any time."

"She gave us the gold plated banana for that one. I keep half the shards and Dmitri keeps the other half, then every fifteen years we'll get together and see if they still fit into a whole banana. I'm not so sure I'm not losing my shards as the years go by. Another decade or so and we'll find out."

"You guys *need* champagne," Clara said as it arrived.

"The last time we drank champagne together," Dmitri said to Clara, "you got drunk. Maybe this time you can handle it better."

"This time we're splitting it three ways instead of two." In fact, after her first glass, Linda would switch to beer and leave the champagne to the two of them.

Dmitri wondered whether there was any music for duo piano and violin. Odyssey might write one for them. "Where will you play?" he asked.

Linda took charge of the answers. "Giorgio thinks he can get us a dozen dates next year and more than that the following year. All in North American concert series."

"That's a manageably short tour."

"No tour. We just fly in the day before and back the day after."

That plan lacked appeal, it was depressing even to think about it, that was what Dmitri commonly did for his solo appearances, it took most of the point out of traveling to perform. If he were a group, he would want to travel as he and Linda did. Or perhaps their traveling together was good only because they were together then.

"This will be the greatest year for both of us," Linda said. "We both solo with Solti and record with him."

"That is wonderful," Dmitri said, hugging Clara and beaming at her. "We don't have enough champagne."

"Linda's a bit afraid of Solti," Clara said.

Linda inhaled sharply and then caught herself before speaking. "Not afraid, I'm not afraid, that's not it. Solti's just too taut for me. He pushes everything beyond its limits. He's like you, Dmitri, he sees the world through Bartók's eyes, his Mozart on the piano is okay, but his conducting is cruel, if he were a composer he'd write with an ice pick. When he conducts, he strangles people because they can't play quietly enough and then he strangles them again because they can't play loudly enough, they're strangled no matter what they do. He fits Chicago, he's big, cold, extreme, and abrasive."

Dmitri had played for Solti and loved him most of all his conductors. Solti did scare Linda, he thought, maybe even he, Dmitri, had scared Linda, for five years maybe he made her life too taut, pushed her beyond comfortable limits, wore her down with his cruel Bartók eyes, staring and dissonant.

"Where did you hear Solti do Mozart on the piano?"

"Dmitri, Dmitri, Dmitri," Linda said.

"There are records, Dmitri," Clara confided in a mock whisper.

"What will you do with Solti?" Dmitri asked Clara.

"Bartók," she giggled, "cruel Bartók. Are my eyes right for the part?"

"And I will do Brahms – as conceived by Bartók, no doubt."

"So you will just fly in, do your solos, and fly out."

"You know better than that, Dmitri, with orchestras there have to be rehearsals. I hate the thought of rehearsing with Solti more than the thought of playing with him."

She had spent most of five years rehearsing with Dmitri Esterhaats. That was evidently enough.

Jelly Ujfalussy and Anton Staebli were being shown to a table when they spotted Dmitri. "May we join you?" Anton asked. He was personally too open to everyone even to think an additional person could be an intrusion.

"Sure, but we only have one more place," Dmitri said. "Maybe we could move."

"No more tables," the waiter said, "except one back there for two people."

"I can sit at the end," Jelly offered.

"No, we can't add another chair, there'd be no room to walk," the waiter said with a dismissive tone as he waved his hand to indicate the narrow straits of the aisle.

"Is the manager here, Al or Seymour?" Jelly asked.

"You can't throw a scene with these guys . . ." Linda began with annoyance, but Dmitri raised his hand to command her silence.

"You do not know Jelly. Jelly never throws a scene but she *always* gets what she wants."

"You know that is false, Dmitri, not *always*," Jelly said.

Dmitri knew she meant him, but he said, "There is probably not a male animal in Manhattan who can say no to her and stick with it."

Seymour came and in two minutes Jelly was sitting at the end of the table. "I am thin so I will not be in the way."

"If you're not able to finish your plate, we'll give you a doggie bag," Seymour said.

"I can finish it for her," Anton offered. Anton was the only person Dmitri knew who actually wanted to eat as much as they served here.

"No, no, she needs it," Seymour answered, grasping his own flab and shaking it to indicate Jelly's sad lack.

Sometimes reticent, sometimes audacious Linda smiled as Jelly took her seat in the aisle. "Pretty good," she said.

For the next two hours, Seymour and his staff had to rebuff repeated requests to put chairs at the ends of other tables. Jelly alone sat in the aisle. That was the metaphorical story of her life in Manhattan, tripped over by everyone, visually standing out from every crowd, treated as a special exception by every male in her vicinity, yet left alone on her odd pedestal where only favors could reach her, not people.

It seemed very important to Dmitri to get everyone to understand his view of why records would not finally kill public performance but produce an audience for it. It was important to him because it was his confession to

Linda that he'd changed his view of recording as she'd changed her view of the duo. The chief difference was that his change of view was abstract, it was about the effect of recording on the world, not about its value to him. He was still opposed to recording for himself, he hadn't pushed Odyssey to finish a second piece that he could record with her Vermont sonata, although he wanted to record her in order to gain her an audience. It was thinking about her and her lack of an audience in live performance that led him to change his views.

But no one was listening to him now. He reached out his hand to tap the middle of the table and then left it there as though to hold onto the focal point.

Linda reached out her hand and slipped her index finger under Dmitri's hand, lifting it well above the table. "Dmitri has the most graceful hands I know," she said.

"They are Hungarian," Jelly said. "He was lucky the genes worked out that way."

Dmitri struggled to regain the discussion. "Back to the point," he said.

"Who's interested in the point?" Anton asked.

"I am, and if all of you understand it you will be too."

"That is okay, Dmitri," Jelly said. She turned to the others. "His brain is only one-fourth Hungarian. That helps but, as you can see, it is not enough."

Linda began to giggle, Jelly giggled, Clara giggled, and then Linda mixed in her guffaw as though to invite Anton to join the joke on pompous Dmitri. The array of the three women's faces about Dmitri was spectacular, he could only smile, almost laughing, as he stared at them around the circle over and over. Clara stopped giggling long enough to kiss his cheek, as though to declare her sympathy with him, her loyalty to him, and then she started giggling again.

Thereafter, no one could gain central attention and the conversations broke up into smaller groups. Jelly and Linda drifted into French and then even into Hungarian, a private world of their own, a world that utterly excluded the others. Dmitri tried to recall any knowledge he should've had that Linda spoke Hungarian, but he could not, he suspected she spoke Polish, she had relatives from Poland, perhaps she also had relatives from Hungary. As long as he lived there would evidently be new discoveries about Linda's past. Often, in their Hungarian patter now, Linda and Jelly giggled together and occasionally, as they giggled, Linda turned to look at Dmitri and began to mix her guffaw into her giggle. For more than twenty years these two women had been hostile to each other although they'd hardly known one another, they'd been distant and wary at Odyssey's dinner party at the Pierre after the Lincoln Center premiere. Linda had always complained of Anton's bars and delis where performers talked with non-performers, yet now she preferred conversing with the only non-performer in the group. Or perhaps she'd come to think Jelly's was merely a different performance. Dmitri recalled the conversation between Jelly and Clara at the restaurant *Ai sette celli*, when the two women spent much of the evening tearing Linda down, expressing their dislike for her, and rejecting his claims that she could be wonderful. Yet Clara had fallen for Linda almost immediately after first meeting her over their instruments although that was a time of Linda's compulsive fretting about rehearsal, a time when Dmitri found her least congenial. And Jelly was now finding Linda to be the nearest thing to a kindred spirit she'd found in their community, with their lunatic mastery of languages and their common cause in ridiculing Dmitri. Funny, he thought, Linda's hold on me is finally broken and they now love her.

"I saw Odyssey Deneuve," Jelly said.

Her accent mangled the name so badly it took a while for Linda to say, "Oh, Odyssey, yes. I haven't seen her since Lincoln Center. Where did you see here."

"I saw her . . . No, this time I will not say, I always say everything. It would embarrass her if Dmitri knew."

"So just tell *us*, Dmitri can try not to listen," Anton said. He was fond of musical gossip.

"I saw her in the negligee section at Saks. She is the only woman in civilization who shops for negligees in overalls. She had one that was red, one that was black, and at least one that was almost invisible."

"What did you have, Jelly?" Anton wondered.

"You will certainly never know," Jelly answered. Then she turned to Dmitri, "Would you be discreet, Dmitri?"

"Dmitri?" Linda said. "Dmitri will be perfectly discreet. No one is ever going to get *anything* out of him."

"Actually, it's easy for him," Clara said, "he is totally reliable, because he just forgets everything anyway." She kissed Dmitri's cheek.

Clara was wrong. He had not listened attentively enough even to know what it was he should be discreet about, therefore he could not forget but he could also not fail to be discreet. He chose not to tell Clara of her error. Or perhaps Clara was right, perhaps he had heard but had already forgotten.

There was silence for perhaps thirty seconds. Jelly did not allow silences. "I am reading Sartre," she said.

Anton slammed his glass down. "Sartre? So that's where you're getting that stuff. Why are you reading Sartre?"

"He is very different. You can read his books in several languages at once and see that he means several things at once. That helps a lot. Other writers should be as smart. He is almost Hungarian." Jelly plucked Anton's glasses from his face and held them nonchalantly off to the side as though to mimic Sartre of the Left Bank.

"It must be Sartre – I can't see a damned thing," Anton said.

"What is Being?" Jelly asked.

Anton was quicker to answer than anyone else. "I wouldn't touch that with a pole."

Jelly startled, then instantly giggled, "But with a Czech or a Hungarian maybe?"

For Jelly, language was visual, she saw what she said or heard, and ambiguities worked wonders in her visions, sometimes in several languages at once. Dmitri regretted that he did not have all her languages to catch all her visions.

"For that one, I'll buy your round of beer," Anton said. It was a cheap round, with only Linda, Jelly and Anton.

"We do not have Being," Jelly explained. "To be is to have a character. Not to have a character is not to be. But we trivialize having a character into having a style, into performing rather than being. That is not Being, that is closer to nothingness."

"That makes sense, I like that," Linda said. "I was reading Sartre when we were in France, but I never did it seriously enough. But you are right, Jelly, that's my problem, I only have style. If I were doing it all over, I'd know how to do it a lot better, I would've made life a lot better." She grinned for Dmitri, "I might even have said Yes when we came back from Paris. . . ."

Dmitri could hardly believe Linda was so casually saying such things, especially in this crowd.

She continued. "I spent half my life planning how to live it and I guess I'll spend the second half regretting how I lived it. Dopey, isn't it? A lot of nothingness. Sartre would pity me. Or maybe he would mock me."

"Why would you regret?" Dmitri asked.

"Dmitri, you haven't changed, you're still incredible. And I still don't believe you."

"He's mostly ridiculous," Clara said, putting her hand to his cheek, "but for some reason he thinks it works for him."

"If you want to read Sartre again," Jelly said to Linda, "I am translating some of him into Hungarian. That is the best version yet. You will not really understand him unless you read him in Hungarian. French, German, and English are inadequate for him, in them existence is too thin. Existence is much better in Hungarian, it is thicker, it has more spice. Even Sartre would understand himself better in Hungarian."

"I guess I can't read him then," Anton said with relief. "He certainly makes no sense in English."

"That is unfair," Jelly said. "Nothing makes sense in English. English is too hard. I still do not get it right."

Dmitri smiled at her.

"You are a stinker, Dmitri. English is hard. There is too much to learn. In Hungarian we do not have he and she, I have to learn that here."

"*That* is a lot to learn late in life, I admit," Anton said.

"Now we begin to understand why there aren't more Hungarians," Dmitri said.

"You wash your mouth, Dmitri. Your mind, *he* is filthy. You understand nothing."

Clara came to Jelly's defense. "I am partly Hungarian."

"I know. With a name Esterhazy, it is hard not to be part Hungarian. That makes you smarter."

"It makes her her," Dmitri said.

"The funny thing, Clara, what I do not understand," Jelly said, "is you are only half as Hungarian as Dmitri, but you are twice as smart."

"You should go to the box office about half an hour ahead of the curtain for tickets," Linda said to Jelly. "If you're late, they may sell them. There will be two, so you can bring a friend. Whenever we're in New York, they'll be there for you – I can have our agent send you a schedule if you like."

Dmitri smiled, put his thumb up, and winked his congratulations to Linda. She evidently did not understand but only grinned her silliest look of absence. No matter, Dmitri thought, she had finally made it, she would have Jelly Ujfalussy in her audiences. And Ney-Esterhaats *II* had already been scheduled before Esterhaats *I* was told. Now, as he saw Clara and Linda standing side by side, preparing to leave the deli, Dmitri thought the two beautiful women from two generations would be a spectacular duo, their intensity would be explosive. They would be like Linda's Schubert, their tranquil beauty erupting into hard-driving energy to overpower their audiences with music. Dmitri liked the idea, he virtually took credit for it in his mind, because he'd been the cause of their first joint performance at the time of his first cancellation other than for his sprained wrist. He was their Giorgio, pairing them when they would never have paired themselves. He wondered for a moment whether he liked the idea of Ney-Esterhaats *II* more for its own sake or more for the sake of blocking Ney-Esterhaats *I*, which was a part of the distant past where it now should finally rest. His life was instantly easier for not having to work with or around the old duo, but it might just as instantly become less full if Clara had no more time for piano duos.

Outside, the three women conferred about time for a dinner the following Sunday. "I'll get reservations," Linda said, "and pick you up, Jelly first."

Linda pointed to a large black car, a limousine perhaps – Dmitri wasn't sure what defined a limousine – and said to Jelly, "Look for this car, eight o'clock." Linda then climbed into the car and disappeared toward New Jersey. Jelly and Anton wandered up Seventh Avenue to their bar.

"Hey," Clara said. "Going my way? Wanna walk?"

"Even if I weren't going your way."

"I know. Forgive me. I didn't know what to do, I . . ."

"Clara, you don't have to apologize, I'm glad, it's the kind of thing I wanted for you. There's only one possible objection to your duo – you two will be so beautiful that people will be distracted from the music. You may have to play from behind the curtain."

Clara took his arm and they walked toward Fifth Avenue. After a long silence until the Seventh Avenue traffic noise was well behind them, she spoke. "I decided to do what you'd have insisted I do if I'd asked you. I'm sorry, that may be too many ifs or something. You were away for a couple of days when we had to decide on a booking Giorgio offered. Linda said she'd been thinking about it ever since our first time. It hadn't occurred to me. She said you probably weren't really too sick to play that time, you just wanted to get out of playing with her. I realized that was obviously going to be more than a booking decision. But that was how it worked, the booking came first and it required a decision."

Linda actually saw the event as his having withdrawn, she saw her own constraints as constraints of the world that applied as fully to him as to her, if his performance was at risk, he had no choice but to step aside for a replacement. Dmitri tried to tease her and then to help her handle the slight uncertainty only to cause her to eliminate the uncertainty by eliminating him. And she concluded that he wanted to withdraw, that he wasn't prepared to face the uncertainty of the moment or perhaps he wasn't prepared to face her. He felt his face smiling and turning red with embarrassment all at once. Odd, he had no reason for embarrassment, he was only embarrassed because she thought he had reason to be, his involuntary reactions were being driven by her view of him.

In a moment, Clara spoke again, but her voice was less confident, "Giorgio also wants me to talk you into joining me to make a record."

"Do you want us to make a record, Clara?" He wondered whether Giorgio was using her to get him to record or whether he really wanted both of them.

"I want to have children and, if something happens to me, I want my babies to be able to hear what their mother could do – even if what they hear won't be perfectly right. One of the things I do best is duos with you."

That was an answer Linda might have liked to be able to give, but she never could. If she'd had that answer, he would have relented for her. "Have you worked out the program?"

She poked him for teasing her orderliness. "I have some ideas. Do you have ideas?"

"Odyssey Deneuve has a new sonata for two pianos that she says she did for us. She wants us to perform it. Remember? She promised to do such a piece our first summer in Vermont. Maybe she'd let us record it."

Clara, as a young teenager that first summer in Vermont, had been charmed to learn that Odyssey thought her good enough to compose a piece for her. "She really did it." She smiled. "That would take a lot of practice, she's not easy."

'She's not easy' sounded like a generalization for the women he had known. "Do you have time for practice?"

"Start tomorrow?"

"Okay." He smiled his comfort in this lovely moment.

"My place or yours?" she asked.

"Mine has two pianos."

"Then your place it is. The old museum."

Soon Clara stopped to look in the Tiffany windows. "Giorgio said this would be very hard."

"That was the past. The past is gone."

Clara turned to look at him. "The past is gone?! What past? Your past?"

"All past."

She clasped his head between her strong pianist's hands and shook him. "It's not gone, Dmitri, it's there, here, I can almost feel it straining in there."

"What little past isn't gone is struggling to be gone, that's all the strain you feel."

"You know, Dmitri, you've told me almost none of that past, just a little bit about Aunt Clara and a bit about Papa. Linda's told me more about you than you have, but she only knew you for five years and I've only know her for a little while, " she raised her voice as though there were not a hundred people within earshot and she gripped his imaginary throat before her and shook it. "Dmitri, Dmitri, Jelly's told me more, and I've seldom talked with her, maybe once or twice a year since I met her at your 92nd Street Y concert, remember? Papa's told me what he could but he doesn't know that much either. Grandpa's told me a bit, but he hardly knows anything. Your own family, they know hardly anything except what they saw and they saw less of you than any family ever saw of a kid, there were days when Grandpa didn't see you because you left before he got up and came back after he went to bed, other days he only saw you for a minute or two when you went into the kitchen to cut a piece of bread to take with you for the day. And when you were home, you only played the piano and you hardly ever talked. That's the past your family knows, it's not a real past, it's an absence of any past. Did you ever think, Dmitri, Linda might have loved you more if she'd only known who you were – IF SHE'D ONLY KNOWN WHO YOU WERE, DMITRI, HOW YOU CAME TO BE?"

It was a hard question, not one he wished to think through.

"If somebody tried to write your past, they couldn't do it, Dmitri, they couldn't find anything there. You haven't even allowed recordings," she waved her arm off to the side as though to sweep away everything and accidentally swatted a young woman who was leaving Tiffany's. "You're finally willing to record because – and tell me this isn't the whole truth, Dmitri – you're finally willing because it will help Odyssey Deneuve. There's nothing left of *you*, this is it," she gesticulated with her hands before her as though to behold the bit of space he occupied. "You don't tell me about your past, but I know it's not gone, Dmitri. Sometimes I think it's all there is in you. Why don't you tell me more of it?"

"I don't know. . . . If I tell it, I feel it again. I don't know . . . I don't want . . ." That was lame and he left it unfinished.

"Was it all so bad?"

"Bad? No . . . No. It wasn't bad, it was good, almost all of it was good."

"So why don't you want to feel it again?"

"I don't know . . . Most of it, till I was at least thirty-five, until at least the time you were born, those years were just struggling to become and be. That's not much to tell about."

"And after that?"

"Well, that was . . . I don't know. I guess by then I *was*. So there was no more struggling, so nothing to tell anyway."

"Dmitri."

"Yes."

"You won't get away with that."

"Maybe not. But I wasn't really trying to get away with anything."

"You weren't?"

"What was I getting away with?"

"First there was nothing to tell because you were struggling and then there was nothing to tell about it any longer because you'd stopped having to struggle. Jelly said she's a trivial version of Sartre, she's reduced Being to having a personality. You try to reduce it to having a style of distant . . ." she shrugged and let her arms fall for lack of a word.

"Distant what?"

"I . . . oh, I don't . . . oh hell – distant vacuity or something."

Dmitri whistled. "Vacuity. Strong. I achieve being through vacuity, that would be through nothingness, wouldn't it? Jelly would like that."

"Sartre would be confounded – but Jelly would like it. She would too. She's crazy." She put her arm through his and dragged him around the corner to look at the other windows. "I had to scream at you, but at least I got something, I guess. First the struggle, then the non-struggle. Do you know this is the first time you've ever even said such a thing, this piddling remark is a breakthrough?"

"That's funny."

"FUNNY? THAT'S BLOODY GODDAMNED WELL PECULIAR!" she shouted at two hundred pedestrians.

"How do you do that, Clara? You're more American than I am and you're more Russian, too. What's left of me?"

"Hey Dmitri, THAT WAS GOOD, that was really good, look what you can do. But it wasn't the answer to the problem of struggling and then not struggling. Give me an answer."

For Dmitri, this had become a performance he could watch from a distance though he was in it. He floated free and watched. "First I had to struggle to learn the music I wanted to learn. Then I had to struggle to get to play it anywhere, and I don't mean concerts or recitals, I mean just finding a piano I could use. That's it . . . it was hateful, there was nobody to give advice, my mother couldn't, Horace Gmund gave a little – he was the first person I ever met who actually knew something about the world I wanted, and most of what he knew was from reading papers, he was not really in the world, he was just a servant to it so he knew a little about it. There was no uncle, no Manhattan School of Music or Juilliard, I just went looking for things, and you wouldn't believe how ignorant I was, how little I knew of what to do. I didn't even know to try to get into Juilliard or some place. I spent several years in the army playing for the private dinners of a training base commandant who had more sheet music than I've seen since then. He had more than Horace Gmund. It was . . . I nearly got sent to Anzio beach just for saying I thought Stravinsky's piano music was not as good as his orchestral stuff and not in the league of Bartók and Prokofiev. I was in competition with other guys to be the house pianist, and the losers went to war. One of the ones I beat drowned at Anzio, another gave up the piano after he came back from the war. That Colonel never heard Stravinsky piano until I played it for him, he knew music only by reputation, and on that he could decide who went to war. Then Linda and I covered expenses for a beautiful life and she thought we were a failure. Finally, one day, a few months after Linda and I split, I began to get more offers than I wanted to play. When I turned some of them down, they started doubling their offers and my fees went up. I've never struggled again. That probably happened because of Linda, who virtually forced our agent – that was already Giorgio – to get us billed with Ormandy at the Philadelphia symphony."

Dmitri paused for a moment while what he said caught his own attention, he hadn't thought of it before, he probably owed his easy comfort to Linda. Perverse, he thought. Even more perverse, he'd discovered the fact by saying it.

"Then I got a bargain price on a huge apartment in a luxury building about a hundred yards from the center of the universe with a kitchen, bathroom, and bedroom to handle the mechanics of staying alive and a grand room for music with masonry walls and floors to protect neighbors from my noise, I can play Prokofiev at three a.m., what more could you want? After that I've never needed another thing. All I really needed was you."

"And now I'm going to play with Linda."

"Clara! That is exactly what you *should* do. I *want* you to do it. Don't say that ever again."

"Okay, I won't say it ever again. *If* you keep talking."

"Besides, Clara, look at you, you have turned out so well that people think I must be a great teacher when all that really mattered is that you have talent. But they give me the credit and now I'm a teacher at Juilliard, teaching kids who're far better than I was at their ages. So people will give me credit for them too. I can't lose."

"Dmitri, the difference between any of them and you at their ages is that they have teachers and you didn't."

"We're going backwards in this conversation."

"Okay, let's go forward. I said, '*If* you keep talking.' So now it's your move."

"What else do you want to hear?"

"You're doing that deliberately, Dmitri."

"What?"

"I want you to keep talking, damn it, not right this minute, but forever. I want you to remember things and talk to me about them, talk to Jelly about them, Anton, anybody, even a taxi driver, get in a taxi and make the bastard work for his money, tell him to take you to Jones Beach or Montauk, talk to him the whole trip out and back, that would give you practice, you need practice, Dmitri, it's just like mastering Bartók, you've never tried to do it but you can master Being, just practice it, practice it, practice it. Make Jelly proud. It'll never get you to Carnegie Hall but it'll make you a lot better companion at the Carnegie Deli. And maybe it'll get you the next Linda who comes along – if you're lucky enough to have a next. If you don't do that, you'll seem like Nixon. Nobody knows what he thinks or feels about anything. Maybe he doesn't feel anything, maybe inside his skin he's just a shriveled, mean little residue. You can't be that, Dmitri."

Clara turned away from Tiffany's and headed across 57th Street, then stopped halfway across to turn and thrust her finger at him before what seemed like half the world, several of whom bumped into him when he abruptly stopped. "AND IF YOU DON'T DO IT, DMITRI, IF YOU DON'T TALK ABOUT YOU, I'LL SCREAM," she screamed, "I'll break our record over your head," she smashed one on his head in the air, "I'll break them over your head by the dozen," she smashed more and more, "I'll break other people's records over your head, and I'll scream with every record. What I want, Dmitri, is I WANT YOUR PAST TO BEGIN FROM RIGHT NOW, TODAY. AND I WANT IT TO GO ON FOR THE REST OF YOUR LIFE."

"I thought you hadn't spent much time with Jelly Ujfalussy. You learned Hungarian logic awfully fast for someone with only a one-eighth Hungarian brain."

"You can joke, that's okay. But don't think you get off, Dmitri." She smiled and shook her head and then suddenly she turned and frowned at him. "You're always terrible with arithmetic, you can never figure out a tip, not even on ten dollars, damn it, if it's real you can't do it, you screw up ordinary life, you can't get its number right, BUT JUST TO MAKE A JOKE YOU CAN DO THE GENETIC FRACTIONS ON MY BRAIN IN THE MIDDLE OF 57TH STREET IN RUSH-HOUR TRAFFIC, GOD DAMN YOU."

Dmitri started to say it was easy, Jelly had said her brain was half as Hungarian as his and Jelly'd already done the fractions on that, but the light changed and they were trapped in the middle between New York cabs screeching past in both directions at once. Dmitri wondered why his women were all so fond of leading them into danger together. And he wondered whether he'd survive this moment ever to have a past. He might have said these things to Clara, but the traffic noise was too loud, there seemed to be more horns than cars, there was screeching, yelling, and honking in every possible order, there was noise beyond noise, cacophony and dissonance enough to satisfy cruel Solti with his hundred percent Hungarian brain. To block it all, Dmitri drifted further into thought, he could deduce and infer and associate to escape his life of the moment, he could speculate and maybe even reminisce, all in a silence of his own making.

Clara challenged him to make sense of himself. He would have to try, at the very least he'd have to try while she was in his presence, she would not let go, she was tenacious and merciless, American and Russian. But it would not be easy for him to meet her demand, he had got through much of life on little more than stoic resolve. At least from the time soon after he arrived in Amsterdam, he'd steeled himself against daily life and floated in his world of the piano, where he could be detached, free, oblivious of annoyances and pains, and when he couldn't play he walked, hearing the piano, working out transcriptions and fugues. He had played and walked through frustration, through hunger, anger, humiliation, migraine, through everything that got in the way, he'd played through Linda's rejection of life with him, through his mother's dying, through his private grief afterwards, even, in later years, through banal emptiness. He'd played ten, twelve, fifteen hours in a day, there were days, months, maybe years when his entire life beyond merely surviving was playing, his life was like his apartment with its three tiny functional rooms and its grand hall for music, he lived necessity in miniature and music in gross. His mother said he was miraculously never sick, but if he'd been sick no one might have noticed because he might simply have played through and in fact no one had noticed anything except the occasional migraine.

To reconstruct his past for Clara, he'd finally now have to live through the burdens he'd blocked with the power of his piano, to experience things he'd rightly chosen at the time not to experience. Or maybe he couldn't make up for lost experiences, maybe he hadn't merely floated above them, he had blocked them so well that many of them hadn't happened, they were not in him, there were not even traces of them, he was neither very American nor very Russian, he was nearly nothing, no one. The piano had become his past, it had engulfed everything else he might have been, it was all that he was.

He was like Linda and Jelly, they were all self-creations, Linda with her violin and her craving to perform with an orchestra at her back rather than living in a duo, Jelly with her *idiot savant's* mastery of languages, including several that no one should have to speak. Or maybe they were self-suppressions, killing everything except the violin, languages, and the piano. All three of them had wit that was logical and sly rather than personal, they were all too civilized because their pasts were too uncivil. Anton said they were all migrants from other worlds and therefore discon-nected, but Anton wasn't disconnected, his wit was personal and, unlike the others, he fondly remembered and often told of his prior world. Jelly told her past without inflection as a series of random events uncolored by emotion, as though they were a series of bureaucratic hassles rather than life itself, and, as she once said to Dmitri, she did not ever tell the worst parts. Twenty years ago, Linda told nothing, now she told some things, but not much. Dmitri did not fondly remember and he seldom told, what some might call memories came more nearly as discoveries to him, discoveries he did not wish to make. But Clara was his life and if he was to live in the future he would have to live through the past for her. He turned to look at her, but he met the full glare of the western sun and squinted his eyes and flinched away without seeing her.

For the moment, he'd rather put off the past and work out the fugue that governed the passing flow of taxis and buses or the solo part that might lift him above the cacophony of his world. Standing on nothing more than a yellow stripe to protect him from the violent traffic, he was floating free, losing touch with the moment, which was no moment to savor anyway. Clara's hand gripping his arm above the elbow kept him partly moored, but only physically. Dmitri could hear and see a fugue of themes that were ill-defined, like the lanes of traffic, sometimes merging and crossing, changing identities, sometimes separating, a fugue with disconti-nuities and sudden transformations as though Bach were written by

Odyssey Deneuve. If he could connect no better than this to the present, the past would have to be put off at least until tomorrow morning when Clara came for rehearsal. That would still be too soon for the past.

Wings Press was founded in 1975 by Joanie Whitebird and Joseph F. Lomax, both deceased, as "an informal association of artists and cultural mythologists dedicated to the preservation of the literature of the nation of Texas." The publisher/editor since 1995, Bryce Milligan is honored to carry on and expand that mission to include the finest in American writing, without commercial considerations clouding the choice to publish or not to publish. Technically a "for profit" press, Wings receives only occasional underwriting from individuals and institutions who wish to support our vision. For this we are very grateful.

Wings Press attempts to produce multicultural books, chapbooks, CDs, DVDs and broadsides that, we hope, enlighten the human spirit and enliven the mind. Everyone ever associated with Wings has been or is a writer, and we know well that writing is a transformational art form capable of changing the world, primarily by allowing us to glimpse something of each other's souls. Good writing is innovative, insightful, and interesting. But most of all it is honest.

Likewise, Wings Press is committed to treating the planet itself as a partner. Thus the press uses as much recycled material as possible, from the paper on which the books are printed to the boxes in which they are shipped.

Associate editor Robert Bonazzi is also an old hand in the small press world. Bonazzi was the editor / publisher of Latitudes Press (1966-2000). Bonazzi and Milligan share a commitment to independent publishing and have collaborated on numerous projects over the past 25 years. As Robert Dana wrote in *Against the Grain*, "Small press publishing is personal publishing. In essence, it's a matter of personal vision, personal taste and courage, and personal friendships." Welcome to our world.

C

This first edition of *Dmitri Esterhaats*, by
Russell Hardin, has been printed on 70
pound non-acidic paper containing fifty
percent recycled fiber. Titles have been set
using Cochin type; the text in Caslon. The
first 10 signature sets to be pulled from the
press have been numbered and signed by
the author. This volume was edited by
Robert Bonazzi. All Wings Press books
are designed by Bryce Milligan.

On-line catalogue and ordering:
www.wingspress.com
All Wings Press titles are distributed to the trade by
Independent Publishers Group
www.ipgbook.com